ARKHAM HORROR

It is the height of the Roaring Twenties – a fresh enthusiasm for the arts, science, and exploration of the past have opened doors to a wider world, and beyond...

And yet, a dark shadow grows over the town of Arkham. Alien entities known as Ancient Ones lurk in the emptiness beyond space and time, writhing at the thresholds between worlds.

Occult rituals must be stopped and their creatures destroyed before they can drag our world into their ruined domain.

Only a handful of brave souls with inquisitive minds and the will to act stand against the horrors threatening to tear this world apart.

Will they prevail?

ARKHAM HORROR™

LAIR *of the* CRYSTAL FANG

S A Sidor

ACONYTE

First published by Aconyte Books in 2022

ISBN 978 1 83908 188 0

Ebook ISBN 978 1 83908 189 7

Cover art by Daniel Strange

Distributed in North America by Simon & Schuster Inc, New York, USA

Printed in the United States of America

9 8 7 6 5 4 3 2 1

ACONYTE BOOKS

An imprint of Asmodee Entertainment Ltd

Mercury House, Shipstones Business Centre

North Gate, Nottingham NG7 7FN, UK

aconytebooks.com // twitter.com/aconytebooks

SPRING, 1928

1
The Slabs

It Kills Without Mercy!
Police Discover Another Strangler Victim!
Evil Lurks Under Arkham!
More Blood Down the Big Drain!

Stanley Budzinski read the fresh headlines as he passed the newsstands on his way to work. Arriving at the jobsite, he chose a shovel for his day of digging. Rain trickled off his wool cap. The streets gleamed, gutters gurgling with runoff from the morning showers. The city had decided to start its controversial "Big Drain" renovation project in the Merchant District, at a hub where the sewer system and storm drains knotted together like a plate of spaghetti. Business owners weren't happy with the extra trucks clogging traffic. The road in front of the site was closed, one side of the street torn up, a giant crater gaping in the earth where before there had been a vacant lot between shops. Everything was a muddy mess. And it was only the beginning.

Stanley descended a ramp into the hole where that old weedy lot used to be.

He walked on planks through pools of suspicious brown water collecting outside the Main Street tunnel. Who knew what noxious flotsam and jetsam bobbed below the surface? He stepped over a low sandbag barrier, entering the open pipe mouth. The tunnels were tall enough in this part of the system that he could stay upright. Sludge spattered his boots. Each step made an obscene sucking noise like a plunger. Dreadful odors saturated the pipes. His job was dirty, brutal, and unforgiving. Stanley knew the score and accepted it because he needed the paycheck.

This new lurking menace that the *Advertiser* kept shouting about was another matter.

He felt those newspaper headlines being slowly chiseled into his brain each day. And he refused to pay two cents to read any more nonsense about killers prowling in the pipes. That didn't mean his companions on the job didn't gobble up the lurid articles like pieces of candy.

"Maybe the reporters are just making it up?" he'd said to them while they devoured their sandwiches. "Anything to sell a few more copies, right? Who believes the garbage they print?"

His fellow workers believed, that's who. Lots of other people too. Neighbors, relatives...

Even his sweet wife, Lena, who toiled all day at the commercial laundry.

It seemed that everyone was choosing to live in fear these days.

Not Stanley. Not yet. Although he was nervous that he might be joining them soon, because the atmosphere in the sewers wasn't good anymore. Not like before. In the old days. He couldn't really explain it either, only that lately, whenever he was alone in the pipes going about his business, he'd get a queasy feeling, like he *wasn't* alone... like someone else was there.

Watching.

But he always pushed the feeling away, ignoring it. How was he supposed to get his work done if he was always looking over his shoulder?

The transport teams were still in the early stages of laying tracks to move men and equipment in, rubble and dirt out. For now, the only way to access the system was on foot. Stanley followed a string of electric bulbs festooned against the arching brick wall. Licorice black snaky wires supplied the juice that gave them their power, bringing light to the subterranean gloom. Looking ahead was dizzying, as if you'd tripped and fallen down a bottomless well. Sound echoes in tunnels. They're usually loud places; drills and jackhammers chewing away. But this morning, aside from his own footsteps, the pipe was silent. Eerily so.

He realized he hadn't seen a single worker yet. Where was everyone?

Probably deeper inside, he thought, where the excavation was happening. Stanley increased his pace, convincing himself it was the humid air making him sweat so much.

The papers claimed the killer lived in the pipes. Or, at least, the creep was using the system to move around the city undetected, and to dispose of a growing number of dead bodies.

Three confirmed victims to date.

Same method of murder. Similar patterns left behind. Each of the deceased was found floating in, or around, the sewers. One woman. Two men. All the victims had their necks wrung.

Once they were knocked out, the strangler made an incision in their throats. The fiend bled them to death. Some said the murderer must be a disgruntled doctor. The cuts might've come from a scalpel because they were precise and well placed. The killer understood how to throttle victims without killing them, so that their blood was still pumping. No one knew the reason for stealing the blood, except the murderer. That only made the crimes worse.

Because where facts failed, rumors grew. Multiplying like mushrooms in the seepy dark.

The newspapers didn't help, coming up with their "monster of the sewers."

News stories stirred the pot. People cooked up private theories about the mysterious bloodsucker. It was a mad scientist who needed fresh blood for experiments. Or there was a giant South American bat that stowed away on a ship and escaped from the docks. The bat flew into the underground pipes to roost and feed. Cannibals, goblins, demons, evil spirits, witches...

Hogwash.

Stanley shook his head. He felt a stab of a pain in his neck. That came from hard labor, not spooky campfire tales. As if there weren't enough real ways to die down here, they had to make things up for people to dread. Curse this loose talk of demons! The strangler, they said, was beastly strong. Inhuman. Leaving people with their skulls twisted the wrong way around...

Stanley recalled an afternoon not too long ago, when a crew discovered a pale corpse floating in the muck. He hadn't seen it himself. But the work was shut down. There'd be no pay for the rest of the day. The cops marched in like invaders. The sewers were *his* turf. Not theirs. He didn't welcome trespassers. Real or imaginary. He'd heard the police were alarmed by the "unusual" condition of the remains. The men in blue went so far as to take down all the sewer workers' names. They made a list. They even questioned a few crewmen who'd been to jail a time or two for violent offenses. Hinting the killer might be a lowly digger, someone like him.

Stanley fumed at that. "I'm no criminal," he'd told Lena that night. "I earn my bread."

He'd pounded his fist on the table.

Lena had touched his arm gently. "It's wrong of them to make you feel guilty."

"Every type of foulness ends up in the sewers," he said. "You can't imagine."

Thinking back, Stanley felt his anger rising again. He stomped harder into the sewer ooze. Day after day, he and his cohorts made sure every awful, hideous thing that went into the pipes got whisked away. Out of the city, to the river. And beyond. They kept Arkham clean. Over the years, he thought he'd pretty much seen it all. But there was one thing he'd never seen.

He'd never seen a monster.

"Hiya, Big Stan," a voice said suddenly.

Stanley felt himself jump inside. He planted his strong legs and waited, looking ahead.

It came from farther down in the tunnel. The bricks glistened with slime. Higher up, crusted swirls clung to the walls like rancid cake frosting. Stanley froze in his tracks, his train of thoughts derailed. Hairs prickled on his arms. He wished he'd brought a safety lamp and didn't have to rely on the naked bulbs illuminating the tube. Shadows. There was room for too many shadows. Stanley squinted, ready with his shovel to strike any attacker who might rush at him.

Then he sighed in relief.

It was only Paddy O'Hara. The light from Paddy's safety lamp revealed the man's puffy cheeks stretched in a jack-o-lantern smile. Paddy, happy to see him. Good Ole Paddy.

Paddy O'Hara was Stanley's shift boss. A demanding fella at times, but friendly enough. Stanley had worked for worse tyrants. Paddy wasn't too bad.

"Morning, Paddy. Are we the only two fools who bothered showing up today?"

"What? No. I sent the others for more rails." Paddy sounded distracted. His head tilted as if he were listening for something. Voices? Paddy's bloodshot eyes pinched with concentration.

Stanley waited for instructions.

Eventually Paddy said, "I hope you brought your big muscles today, boyo. We've run into an unexpected delay. Major obstacle. We need to bust it out before the others get back with them rails." Paddy chewed the stem of an unlit briar pipe he'd brought all the way from Galway. He didn't light up this deep in the tunnels. Not unless he wanted to risk an explosion. Firedamp and stinkdamp were dangerous gases that could build up, forming flammable pockets. If the methane and hydrogen sulfide didn't ignite and blow you to smithereens, they'd knock you out and smother you. A pair of real boogeymen who didn't need embellishment from the papers!

A stripe of gray mud marked Paddy's jaw. He looked tired, Stanley thought.

"What sort of obstacle?" he asked the shift boss.

Paddy removed his pipe. He pointed the gnawed bit at Stanley.

"Just you wait and see. It's a head-scratcher, this one. A real head-scratcher." His eyes showed a frantic glimmer.

"Let me guess. Something not marked in the plans?" Stanley said.

Paddy feigned a look of shock. "In the plans?" He guffawed. "Remind me now, what are those? There are more unmarked tunnels down here than marked ones. I swear we'd be better off wandering in the depths, not knowing what to expect. Whoever drew these maps was having a hearty laugh at our expense. A devious joker they were." Paddy sucked airily on his pipe.

Weeks ago, the Arkham city council had finally agreed to the mayor's Big Drain proposal: a renovation of the deteriorating waterworks running beneath the whole town. From the start, work crews discovered the maps of the old water lines were, to put it mildly, unreliable.

Paddy turned and started walking. Stanley followed him farther into the system.

Above them, the residents of Rivertown were waking up.

A block away, the river flowed between its ancient banks heading toward the ocean. Under the streets, a malodorous stew of hazardous chemicals and human detritus wormed along a well-worn path before emptying into the stream, then joining the Miskatonic, and finally traveling east. In Rivertown, folks said the smell above ground was no better than the sewer. A miasma of fish guts and industrial waste stained the air like a sepia tint. You tasted it in your morning eggs and pancakes, in your coffee cup, or on your partner's lips.

Stanley looked up at the new wood beams bracing the arch of the main tunnel. This support work was the first stage of the renovation project. Foot by foot, they would inspect, repair, and widen the pipes to meet the current demands of a growing New

England city. After the Big Drain was completed, raw sewage would be treated before pouring into the waterways.

Passing from under the safety of the beams, the two men entered a section of unsecured tunnel. Evidence of damage showed everywhere. A web of cracks spread along the tube. One jagged fissure opened into a gap commodious enough to admit a curious child. Chunks of crumbling brickwork, previously located on the ceiling, checkered the floor like steppingstones.

Stanley and Paddy arrived at a "v" split in the tunnel. To their left, a narrow side passage diverged at a forty-five-degree angle.

Paddy ducked into the smaller channel. Cut directly into the bedrock, hewn by hammers and chisels rather than bricked, it was one of many unknown antiquated drains. Many amounted to hardly more than glorified trenches, but they'd lasted… well, no one knew exactly how long they'd been there. This one's shape was oval, like a mouth opening as if to yawn – or to scream.

Stanley and Paddy stooped forward to fit themselves inside the low-ceilinged passage, proceeding in single file. Inside the passage, the flow of water wasn't moving forward. The calf-deep water accumulating at the bottom of the channel suddenly deepened to above the knee. A thin rainbow-colored film coated its surface. Rough, angular rock scraped at the men's shoulders. The air grew thicker; the stink of it was more pronounced. Stanley's throat felt scratchy. His eyes were irritated, stinging and tearing up. He coughed and swallowed a mouthful of bitter spit.

Stinkdamp.

Hydrogen sulfide gas did that to a person.

But he didn't feel dizzy or have a headache. Probably bad air circulation. More bad gases than normal. He'd monitor for signs of gas poisoning. His thinking was still clear. He felt fine.

Then a cold, slippery hand clamped onto the back of Stanley's neck.

And squeezed.

He whipped around, swinging his arms wildly, looking to shove it away.

But there was nobody there.

He rubbed the patch of bare skin below his hairline. Five fingers had fastened themselves like a steely vise above his shirt collar. He felt the echoes of them there still.

Paddy stopped. "Here we go." He hadn't noticed Stanley's panic. "Take a gander at our mystery. This wee channel we're in was packed with rocks. Put here long ago they were. For what purpose... who knows? Every gap was plugged. A crew spent the night digging them out."

"We're working round the clock now?" Stanley ignored the shakes in his hands, hoping to hide any sign of alarm from his boss. But Paddy was too preoccupied to notice anything.

"Now till doomsday... always behind schedule," Paddy said, wiping his sweaty brow.

Stanley's curiosity took over, driving away lingering feelings of fear from being touched by an invisible hand. He wanted to see what Paddy had brought him here for.

What was behind that plug of rocks?

He leaned in, staring over the top of the shorter man. Paddy raised his safety lamp to reveal the obstacle in question, and Stanley was disappointed.

It looked like a cross section of old drain. Nothing especially remarkable except for maybe its odd location. Only a portion of the exposed pipe was visible. The hand-laid stone slabs were expertly fitted together, a specimen of an earlier style of workmanship. It bisected the drain they were standing in, sealing it off, creating a dead end. That explained the bad air flow and the backed-up rainbow pool of waste that had risen nearly to the top of Stanley's thigh-high boots.

"Looks old," Stanley said. "Any idea when it was built?"

"Who knows? It's all gotta come out. The new tunnel is set to go right here."

Stanley was going to need a pick, maybe a digging pry bar to get started. There wasn't much room to swing. He was turning to go back for his tools when Paddy snagged his elbow.

"Feel it first," Paddy said.

"What?"

"The slabs… You gotta feeeeel them."

Paddy's expression contorted. His chin kept trembling. A misfiring nerve twitched at his left eyelid. It was as if he was fighting for control of his own face. Like somebody put fishhooks in him and was pulling his features in different directions all at once.

Stanley didn't like what he was seeing. As if Paddy were changing right before his eyes.

Into somebody else.

A stranger.

Maybe it's the shadows doing it, he thought. Maybe the cramped quarters are to blame. The gases. But that twitchy scrambled look and his odd, sly-sounding request… One thing was for certain: Stanley hated, really, really hated, the way Paddy had grabbed his elbow and hung on tight. Desperate, like a drowning man who'd lost all sense and filled up with panic, ready to drag Stanley to the bottom too.

"What's it you want from me?" Stanley asked. Maybe he didn't understand. It was something simple and he was confused, that was all. He'd give Paddy another chance to explain.

"Touch the slabs," Paddy said. "Have a good feel at them slabbies."

Pearls of sweat popped on Paddy's face. Glassy. Oily. Unclean. He had mud in his teeth.

Stanley didn't know what to do. The stones looked stable. He hesitated, thinking, what could be so odd that Paddy would want him to experience it too? He could think of nothing. When Paddy tugged at him, urgently, insistently, like a spoiled child, he ripped his arm away.

"Get off me, Paddy," he said. "I can see it plain as day. It's only an old pipe."

"An old pipe," Paddy repeated. His skin had gone ashen. His lips were twin purple slugs.

"Say, what's with you?"

Paddy swallowed, nodding as he spoke. "I came down here myself. Before you did. I noticed something. A bit strange it was. Now I'm suggesting that before we bash it to pieces, you give the wall a rub for luck," Paddy seized Stanley's wrist, jerking his arm toward the blockage.

"Let go. Or you'll regret it." Stanley gritted his teeth. He made a fist with his free hand. He'd hurt men with his fists, put them in the hospital. He could do worse if he had to.

Paddy obeyed, letting him go.

He was scrappy, ole Paddy, but he'd be no match for Stanley in a fight. Everyone knew Big Stan's reputation. Toughest man on the job. Look at the size of those hands ... a born bruiser.

Paddy shrank into the curve of the pipe as far away as he could get. But still, he smirked at Stanley like a jolly fellow with a joke he hadn't finished telling. White spittle dotted his slug lips. "See how it feels to you, Stanley. Or are ye afraid?" Paddy's voice stayed low but sharp.

Stanley wasn't about to walk away from a challenge. Not coming from Paddy.

Or any living man.

What did he have to worry about from old stones? He'd touch them and be done with it.

"I don't know why you're so keen, Paddy. But I'll have a go. Stay back."

Keeping his eyes on his boss, Stanley pressed his calloused palm flat against the slabs.

They were warm, like the side of a bread oven after the fire's out at the end of a day; not exactly hot. Pleasant really, like a cozy hearth on a winter's evening. Bitter winds a-howling.

Warm. Like touching another person. That same amount of heat. Matching and familiar.

Blood-warm.

"Can you believe it?" Paddy asked, his eyes rolling like marbles. "Crazy, right?"

Stanley frowned, intrigued. He wasn't worried about Paddy anymore.

He pushed in closer. Using both hands he tested the stones. They all felt about the same: same size, same temperature. "What's back there, do you think?"

"Heck if I know." Paddy tore the briar pipe out of his mouth, grinning ear to ear.

Stanley couldn't figure it out. The slabs gave off a kind of gentle buzzing. He was feeling warmth inside him, too. As if he'd taken a shot of whiskey. Woozy, but good.

"Maybe it's carrying hot water from somewhere?" Stanley said.

"From where to where? The thing runs crosswise! It's not part of the city schematics. Neither sewage, nor rainwater. No steampipes from buildings near this section. Nothing. I've no idea what it is. Maybe King Tut had a lost brother who went to Massachusetts. Buried up to his eyeballs in gold trinkets and gems. Maybe it's the heat of Egypt you're feeling in there. Either way, it's moving out day. Because the Big Drain is coming through! Let's bust in. I want to see!"

"I'll need a pick," Stanley said.

"Here. Take my light. Fetch your tools," Paddy said. Stanley was surprised.

"Come back with me, Paddy. You don't want to wait here alone in the dark."

Part of him wanted Paddy to go with him, but another part wanted to leave him there. He couldn't say exactly why, but he wanted to put distance between himself and his boss.

The urge to dig into the slabs felt suddenly overwhelming. The need. *Break through!*

"It's only a while," he said. Paddy's eyes watering, their whites red. "Go on. 'Fore the others get back."

"You sure?" Stanley asked.

Paddy was scratching the fingernails of one hand into the wall behind him. He probably thought Stanley couldn't see him doing it. But Stanley could see, did see… Paddy digging away with his grubby fingers, grime under his nails like black sliver moons, the raw tips bleeding…

Paddy forced his lamp into Stanley's hand. "Leave me!" he shouted.

Stanley took his safety light and went. He stepped quickly, splashing water high up the sides of the channel. Giddy like a boy.

Stanley only turned once to look back. By then he was climbing out of the narrow drain, at the split where it joined the main tunnel. The air was better; he could breathe again. The irregular walls behind him made wavy shadows. Later, he couldn't be sure what he saw. He told the police that when they questioned him – prodded him was more like it. Asking him the same questions over and over. Tell us again. What did you see down there? What did you see?

"All we want is the truth, Budzinski. Tell us everything you saw."

The truth?

Well, he'd only say what he thought he saw. What more could anyone say?

Stanley insisted that they had to understand that part before he would tell them more.

He couldn't be sure what he saw. Did they accept that?

They said they did.

So, Stanley told them.

"Paddy was all the way inside. Far back there, dancing in the dark. Arms and legs... head too... going every which way, banging into the walls. Jerking up and down like a puppet on a string. Like a mad puppet on a string somebody was throwing around. Only I saw just him alone. Nobody else. It was like he was in there with an invisible man attacking him. And I left him."

2
Pink Candy

"Now, settle down." Charlie Kane spoke to the crowd of reporters gathered outside his office, blocking the steps of Arkham City Hall. "I know you have a lot of questions, so do I. You have deadlines. I understand that. But I'm telling you everything I know. I'm not going to speculate on rumors. The city needs to make a thorough investigation into this situation. I'm on my way to the Big Drain dig site. When I know more, you will too. If you'll excuse me, I have work to do."

Charlie smiled, nodding at the photographers. A steady drizzle fell on politicians and members of the press equally. It was democratic like that. The out-of-towners were here already. He recognized faces from as far away as Providence and Boston. The story was blowing up.

"Mr Mayor?" A Salem reporter raised her hand. "Is your Big Drain project in jeopardy?"

Charlie paused, turning toward his inquisitor. His cheap black suit was getting wet. The lining began to pucker and pinch at his shoulders. But he refused to carry an umbrella. Or worse, have

19

someone carry one for him. He wasn't made of sugar. Charlie cultivated the common touch. He resembled a tavern owner more than one of the slick denizens of the municipal government with their perfect haircuts and expensive tailored outfits. Charlie was a man of the people, or at least he could pass for one, sporting a pair of bushy eyebrows, thick jowls, and a horseshoe of unruly gray hairs frizzing above his ears. Better to hide his eagle eyes that missed nothing.

"Jeopardy? Oh my, no. Arkham needs water sanitation. Our city is overdue for new sewers. If anything, a drain tunnel accident indicates how necessary this change is," Charlie said.

"You admit it was an accident?" Rex Murphy's rain-spotted spectacles shone in the photo flashes like mirrors. The normally upturned ends of his mustache drooped soggily.

"Rex, haven't I always been fair with you at the *Advertiser*? I ask for the same fairness in return. Don't jump to conclusions. Let's gather facts first. The public is best served by the truth."

Charlie might not be young anymore, but he was sturdy, and he knew how to maneuver his way through a throng of journalists. He bulled a path ahead. His assistant had suggested they sneak through a side entrance to avoid confrontation. Charlie insisted they go out the main doors.

"If they smell fear," he said, as they prepared for his speech, "you're as good as dead."

"I'll order the car to be pulled around instead," the assistant said.

"Good plan. I already have." Charlie thumped him not-too-lightly on the back.

When Charlie and his assistant climbed into the mayor's limousine, they found two men seated in the back. Charlie's assistant was startled at the presence of their travel companions, one of whom wore mud-caked overalls that carried the stench of the sewers. The assistant gagged.

"My apologies, sir. I have no idea who these men are." The assistant covered his nose with a handkerchief.

Charlie slammed the door behind them. He rolled down his window, reaching out to wave at the fourth estate who were peering curiously into the car's dim interior as it pulled away.

Turning to his assistant, Charlie said, "Don't worry. I invited them. We need to talk."

The mayor stretched across his underling's lap to shake hands with the working men.

"Mr Kane, it's an honor to meet you," said the closest of the pair who, although dressed for manual labor on a construction site, remained suspiciously clean.

"You must be Hargrove, the engineer," Charlie said.

"Call me Ben," Hargrove answered. "I oversee day-to-day operations on the Big Drain."

"Then this other fine fellow is the person I want to talk to."

"Yes, of course. This is Stanley Budzinski. The police didn't want me to take him away from the scene of the, ah... incident. But when they heard you wanted to see him..."

Charlie looked past the engineer. The eyewitness, Budzinski, hadn't moved an inch. He sat facing the window. Silent as a boulder. Charlie took his hand back. Man must be in shock, he thought. After what happened...

The limo hurtled through the streets, the rain blurring the buildings. Arkham came at them, smeary, distorted, reduced to streaks of earth. Stone, soil, clay. Colors mixing. A sloppy mud pie of a day. The solid world was melting before their eyes.

"Stanley, I don't have a lot of time. So, I'll get to the heart of the matter. When I heard what happened this morning, I was aghast. I decided if I wanted to know the truth, I needed to hear it from one man. You."

Stanley continued gazing out the window at the silver droplets squiggling down the glass. Expelling a sigh, he finally turned to face the mayor, fixing his slate-blue eyes on the politician.

"I told my tale to the cops. I'm done. I never want to talk about it again."

The limo driver swerved to avoid a pair of hooded children chasing a shaggy brown dog.

The assistant gasped. He swiveled around to check for small bodies in the road.

Charlie didn't look. He knew his driver wouldn't mow down dogs or children. The man was a professional. Something like that would be disastrous for the pedestrians *and* the mayor. Charlie's attention was locked on Stanley Budzinski, because Stanley represented another calamity he hoped to avoid. Charlie needed to get a handle on what happened before the press did. He needed Stanley to cooperate. He needed to draw the big man out.

"You work for the city, Stanley. I'm in charge of the city. In a way that means you work for me. I'm not about to pull rank. The truth is I want to help. The people of Arkham depend on us. We're essential. We'll get to the bottom of this." Charlie waited a beat. "Maybe we can help Paddy, too. Lost as he is."

"You can't help Paddy. Nobody can." Stanley sniffed.

"Let's give it a try, Stanley. Might we do that, you and I… together?"

Stanley considered his offer while studying the crooked trails of the raindrops again.

Charlie glanced away.

The limo was crossing the river at Garrison Street. Smack in the middle of the estuary, a leviathan hunched in the molasses current – the Uninvited Isle – looming, rain-whipped, bleak. Snarls of wiry scrub and misshapen trees covered the Leviathan's back; blotches of mossy green mottled their branches, as if an artist had dabbed a paintbrush there without much reason or care.

Just as Charlie was giving up hope, the big sewer worker nodded.

Charlie leaned over and squeezed his forearm. It was like clutching a statue.

"Good. Now, I know the first part of the story. Captain Rollins filled me in on the phone. What I want you to tell me is what happened when you went back into the pipe the *second* time."

"Paddy was gone," Stanley said. "I broke through the stone wall. That's it."

"You're a brave man. Going in after what you'd seen. I wouldn't have had the courage."

"It wasn't courage. I had to dig it out. Something inside my head forced me to go."

Charlie's eyes darted over to his assistant, then quickly back to Stanley.

"It must've been loyalty to your friend," the mayor said. "You were looking for him."

Stanley made a disgusted sound. "I was no friend to Paddy. I let him die."

Charlie didn't want to lose Stanley to a fit of guilt. A guilty man will spend hours turning over the rubble of his failures, searching for absolution. Charlie needed facts. He needed them fast if he wanted to stay ahead of the press and the Big Drain naysayers, not to mention other interests who'd love to see him lose. He had to nip this problem in the bud.

"Tell me about what you found after you knocked out that wall of stones."

"You mean the pink light?" Stanley said.

Nobody had mentioned anything about a pink light. But Charlie went along with it. "Go on, tell me about the pink light."

Stanley lifted his cap, combing dirty fingers through straw hair. He took a deep breath. "When I returned with my pick and bar, Paddy was nowhere. I didn't bother calling for him. I knew I'd hear nothing back. I went to town on the slabs. It didn't take long. I worked up a lather, clearing the broken stones with my hands. Soon enough, I made a hole big enough to crawl through. The stones were warm. The air on the other side was too. I don't know how to describe it exactly. But it was humid. Steamy almost. Electricity making your hairs stand on end like when there's a lightning storm. I had Paddy's safety lamp. Still, there was another light in there with me, dancing around the space. It's like a room back there. A cave, sort of. Or a hub. The ceiling's curved, so it makes a dome. There are passages going off in several directions. Other tunnels. I didn't inspect them. Because the light … the light was in the corner of my eyes at first. Like bright sparks. Beautiful sparks…"

A look of amazement passed over the digger, as if he were seeing it all again.

Then he continued. "Up at the top of the dome … that's where the lights were dancing. Loops of pink sugary light. It wanted me to look at it, this thing I'd found. It was sticking down from the center of the dome. I lifted my lamp and couldn't believe what I saw. As if a giant piece of rock candy were hanging down from the ceiling. Six feet of crystal, big as a man. Heavier, of course, being solid rock. The first thing I thought was, 'How'd this pink candy end up here?' I know it was no candy. It had that look. Those pretty-colored crystals hanging down like a tooth."

"A tooth?" Charlie's smirking assistant interrupted, incredulous.

Stanley was adamant. "Yeah, a tooth. Or what's it a walrus has? A tusk. It was a pink crystal tusk growing from the ceiling. You couldn't see through it, but it was clear enough that it made you think you might be able to, if you tried hard enough. If you sat there staring. But the rock was mostly cloudy. Like old ice. The pink lights went inside. They belonged to it. I couldn't tear my eyes away. I started crying, I'll admit. My cheeks were all wet with tears rolling down."

They were wet again. Stanley apparently didn't care. He brushed his fingers against the interior roof of the limo. From the way he acted, it was the crystal he was seeing and touching.

Charlie watched him, transfixed.

Their ride came to a stop. His assistant nudged him. They had reached the Main Street tunnel to the Big Drain project. Trucks and horse wagons stood idle. Piles of sand, of loose cobbles, were stacked up like burial mounds. Tools stuck out of them. More tools littered the ground, as if they'd been dropped in haste. Warning flares burned in the street. Sawhorses blocked the curious from getting close. Watchful men in slickers loitered, smoking in the rain.

"Let's go," Charlie said to his assistant. "Before the vultures arrive."

Then to Stanley he said, "Thank you for sharing. Now, please take me to this crystal."

3
Murphy Curse

By the time Rex Murphy made it to the Main Street tunnel entrance on the streetcar, the place was already deserted. The mayor and his escorts were nowhere to be found. *They went down,* he thought. *I missed them.* He watched the other reporters scatter like crows in search of corn. After they discovered nothing to feed on, they headed for shelter – on the wing for hot coffee and a sandwich, hoping to wait things out until the mayor emerged. Whenever that might be.

The rain drove nails into the street. He might be too late to catch the mayor, but Rex wasn't about to wait around with the competition only to hear another vague official statement read. He needed to get the story behind the empty clichés and platitudes. Politics was a game of misdirection. While leaders talked publicly, issues got dealt with behind closed doors, sometimes with dirty solutions. Finding out what happened when the public wasn't looking was Rex's job.

As a reporter, it was his duty to be the people's witness.

Something awful had happened this morning down in that pit across the street.

Rex stood under the awning of a tobacco shop, thinking about his next move. The clerk was watching him through the window, as if Rex might be working up the nerve to knock the place over. Rex decided to duck in and make friends. Play your cards right, he told himself. Get the hot tip to break this story. You didn't catch lucky breaks in the news racket. You made them.

Sleigh bells over the door announced his entrance. But it didn't feel like Christmas inside.

Despite the fancy gold lettering decorating the front window, there was something gritty and sad about the place once Rex shut the door. The pinwheel tiles slanted like a funhouse floor and needed a mop. A mouse darted from under a stack of empty cardboard boxes. On the shelves, dust-coated tobacco jars exhibited paper labels too small to read. The counter held row after row of cigars in various shades of tan. One whiff of shop air was all it took to remind Rex of a smoker's abandoned hotel room. The good times had been and gone.

"Hi, there." Rex eyed the case. It was difficult to see inside, like staring into fog.

"Interest you in a fine cigar?" The bald clerk had alarming spots on his scalp.

"No, no." Rex drummed his fingers on the countertop and ended up leaving prints in a tacky layer of grime. He tried rubbing them off with his sleeve but ended up making it worse, smearing a smoky whirlpool on the glass. His hand, the coat, the counter – everything was filthy.

The clerk noticed his efforts and smiled.

"Looking for someplace dry to wait out the rain? Kill a little time?"

This'll be a piece of cake, Rex thought. The guy's friendly. He's no sour pickle.

"That's right," Rex said.

The smile vanished.

"Keep looking, pal. The boss says if you're not buying, you're leaving. That's the rule."

"I would like to make a purchase. Only it's news I want." Rex flattened a damp dollar on the counter. "Your boss doesn't need to know, either." He winked.

The clerk swept up the money. He said, "I am the boss, pal."

"Ah." There went another hard-earned clam, gambled and lost.

"You a reporter?"

"How'd you guess?"

"You look nosy and hungry. Like the rats I see poking around when I dump the trash."

Rex ignored the insult. He'd grown a thick skin. "Rex Murphy. I write for the *Advertiser*. You've got a nice shop here. Maybe I'll mention it in the article I'm writing. Free publicity?"

The clerk-turned-boss seemed unimpressed, but he didn't throw Rex out.

"It never hurts to advertise," Rex added. When he got no reply, he shrugged and headed for the door. Slowly. Before Rex opened it, the tobacconist stopped him with a loud whistle.

"What do you want to know?" the tobacconist said.

Rex bellied up to the cigar case. "A group of men pulled up in that limo parked outside a few minutes ago. I want to know what they did. How they acted. Where they went. If you saw anything happening at the sewer entrance tunnel today, it would help me a great deal."

"I had a front row seat. You're talking about the mayor."

"That's right. Mayor Kane."

"They went down."

"Were there a lot of them?"

"Maybe a dozen. Most of them been here already. Kane got out of the limo with three other men. The whole gang went down into the sewer." The tobacconist chose a cigar, lit it, and began puffing a blue haze around Rex's head. His gluey eyes stayed locked on the reporter's.

Rex stood his ground. There was more coming, he just had to wait for it. People give things up at different speeds. You had to learn patience to be a reporter. But if they were going to talk, it was best not to force them. However, you could try a little encouragement.

He dropped another damp dollar on the counter and watched it disappear into the other man's vest pocket.

The tobacconist said, "A worker went missing. But they found something else down there this morning. It's what got them excited, this other thing they found."

"Was it another dead body? Did the sewer killer strike again?"

The tobacconist shrugged. "I don't know."

Rex sighed. He was sure the "incident" was connected to the killings. The Big Drain was a murder scene. He felt it in his gut. The mayor's assistant was acting too jumpy for an ordinary accident. There had to be more. A part they weren't saying. So, they found something, did they?

"Must be something big," the tobacconist said, leaking smoke through the gaps in his teeth. "They shut down operations. Everybody out. They posted a guard. Put up sawhorses. I had workers in here, talking. That guard you see standing there in the rain was one of them. Eyeing the cigars like you. He said they should dynamite the tunnel. Seal it for good. He wasn't joking either. He complained about waiting around for the mayor. 'What's Kane going to do?' he said."

"Did the guard buy anything?"

The tobacconist pointed to the cheapest cigars in the case, and Rex had an idea.

Rex didn't mind paying for leads. Or doing little favors, if those favors had a good chance of being returned. The disgruntled guard posted at the tunnel entrance was rain-soaked through to his underwear, but he had two brand new fine cigars in his pocket that he could smoke when he got home tonight. And all he had to do was look the other way and let Rex into the tunnel.

"You get caught – I never saw you. You snuck in before I got here. Understand?"

Rex nodded. He pulled on a spare set of boots he found near the entrance. The boots were too big, but they'd suffice. Turning up his overcoat collar to conceal his face in case he ran into anybody who might recognize him, he was hoping to catch the mayor and his people in a compromising situation. Put them on the spot. Cut a deal where they'd give him an exclusive if he promised not to go too hard at them with the typewriter. He'd get to the truth. The mayor would have a fair chance to explain whatever scandal might be crawling up out of the sewers. But Rex didn't want to get arrested, certainly not before he had a story. He doublechecked the camera slung under his arm, keeping it handy. Cameras didn't bring him the best luck. He tended to lose them. Mechanical malfunctions plagued him. Yet, this time might be the charm.

"Are there any more lanterns?" he asked, pinching his nostrils. The malodorous funk was making his eyes water.

The guard shook his head. "They took all of them. Follow those electric lights and listen for voices. Now skedaddle!"

•••

Rex had been walking for what felt like a long time. He kept stopping, kept listening, camera ready. His pulse thumped in his ears. His heart flopped like a fish in his ribcage. Maybe the water did it to him. The sound of water dripping. Water sloshing. Water, water, water.

No voices, though.

The length of tunnel behind him appeared no different from what lay ahead. Yet the space around him felt like it was shrinking. Tighter and tighter, constricting like a snake. He was the field mouse the snake swallowed, being squeezed down, ripple by ripple, into the reptile's gut. He could use that in his article. Rex paused, letting the camera dangle as he retrieved his reporter's notepad. Scribbling words before they vanished from his mind.

"Caught in the belly of the snake. The realization hits. No hope of survival. Is that what the victims felt in their final moments? Did the dilapidated sewers play an active role in their killings? One as suffocating, and as terrifying, as the captor who had brought them there to die. Let us pose this question: Are the sewers of Arkham haunted?" Too wordy. He'd fix it later.

Wishing he had a safety lamp, Rex walked on. An irrational fear overcame him. What if all the lights strung on the wall went out at the same time? What then? He'd be alone in the dark.

Maybe not alone. Maybe the killer was still lurking about. Biding their time. Watching.

A shiver tickled up his spine.

That would be on par with Rex's luck. He tried not to think about it. Whenever the subject came up, he told people he didn't believe in luck, but that wasn't completely true. It was something he said. If he let himself believe in bad luck, a Murphy curse, let's say, he'd have left this job a long time ago. Losing big stories for unexplained reasons – leads, evidence, sources disappearing through no fault of his own – from bad weather to freak occurrences… but, hey, this really wasn't the time or place to start questioning his fate in the world. He'd found himself in the sewers before, figuratively and literally, but at least this time he didn't slide into them unexpectedly. Superstitiousness was a luxury he couldn't afford. Because making a mistake at this stage wouldn't cost him a front page, or a career – it might cost him his life.

He stopped. Cupping his ears with both hands to capture any noises, he closed his eyes.

Bad idea. Lights out. Alone in the dark. The fear kicked in immediately…

Fight to keep the fear down, Rex. Just focus on your surroundings. Listen closely…

There it was.

A murmuring.

Like angry bees in a hive. Maybe it was voices he was hearing. Maybe…

They were coming from up ahead. It was impossible to run through the calf-deep water. He was making quite a ruckus. Ahead in the tunnel he spotted a kind of junction, a second passage cut leftward into the bedrock. Clearly manmade, the narrower channel was where the buzzing was coming from. He forced himself to pause again.

Don't mess up. Make sure you're on the right track. The guard said to go straight. But he also said to follow the voices.

Yes, those were voices. Rex couldn't make out words. But there was a music to it, a rise and fall that gave him the clues he needed to solve where the mayor went. Inside that awfully tight looking, much darker passage, a conversation was happening. He had to follow.

It wasn't just darker. It was black. Lightless. No electric lightbulbs went that way. He had no lamp. Rex didn't smoke so he didn't have any matches. How far could it be? The voices sounded close, sort of.

He could do this. Be bold, Rex. Push on. That big story isn't going to write itself.

Screw up your courage and keep going straight. You can't miss them. They'll get louder and louder if you're doing it right.

It's easy. Like the guard said. One foot in front of the other.

There! He was doing it!

He couldn't go fast even if he wanted to. The footing was slippery. There were things in the water; *underfoot*. He felt them squish. Spongy things. Firmer things yielded then burst apart.

Don't think. Go.

Now there were harder objects too. He tried his best to avoid those when his boots landed on one. Clumps and bulges that seemed fixed to the channel floor. He tried not to think what it all could be. But he knew he didn't want to trip and fall face down. The idea made his gorge rise.

Step, step, step.

The stink was worse in here. His throat felt raw. The skin around his eyes itched as if he'd rubbed his face in a wool sweater. He kept one hand on each wall. It was too tight to stretch his arms out all the way. He worried that he might smack into something with his face. Or bang his forehead. But he was afraid to lose contact with either wall. What if there was another turn and he missed it? That possibility made him clench up and not move for a few breaths. Yet he had to move. Because standing in place seemed about the worst choice of all. Ahead he went, and the noises got louder. They broke apart into words but sounded strangely echoey, even for a tunnel. They buzzed like mouths pressed against a megaphone. Hollow and distorted. And the smell was… utterly beyond unspeakable.

He creeped along.

Was that a glow ahead? Or were his eyes filling in the blanks, showing him things that weren't there? It did look like a glow. Golden and hazy. And the voices were coming from there.

He was sure of that.

"…it is truly amazing. Someone get a lamp over here! Is that writing…? What's it say?"

Voices. A jagged hole in the stone. The light was growing stronger. Flickering images as backlit figures passed through the beams. Rex could see the water around his legs now, a pile of broken stone slabs cast off to one side of the opening, the hole full of lights, voices, people.

Beyond the hole was a chamber. That's where they were, the men with the lamps.

Was that Mayor Kane? Rex couldn't tell. Shining from inside the chamber, a ray of light was hitting him in the face. He held up his hand to filter the brightness and took a step forward.

It was of no use. Just his luck to make it through the worst of the pitch darkness and still not be able to see.

One of the lamps kept blinding him.

Holding his breath, Rex moved toward it.

The oversized rubber boot on his right foot lodged between two discarded slabs hidden underwater. "Oh no," he thought, as his upper half traveled forward and down. He tried bracing against the walls and skinned his palms. The hideous water rushed up at him.

"No, no, no..."

Rex pulled his arms in, closed his eyes, and took a deep breath.

4

Southern Absence

"You are safe," said the voice of Maude Brion's doctor. "Relax and tell me what you see."

Maude couldn't see her new psychologist at the Arkham Sanatorium. She was too busy watching a giant spider eat a man.

"I'm not safe," Maude said. "No one is safe."

Maude sat in a comfortable chair. She wore a hospital gown. A petite woman with a strong jaw and freckles salted across her cheekbones and the bridge of her nose, her brown hair was freshly cut in a springy bob. Her old bob cut had grown out by the time she'd arrived at the sanatorium. Haircuts were free here, and she didn't object when they asked if she wanted one of the younger women who was learning hairdressing to cut hers. The trainee had done a decent job.

Maude's eyes were closed. Yet she knew where she was.

Or was she remembering? Did she make it all up? Was this just a dream she was having?

And what if it were a dream? *Row, row your boat. Gently down the stream. Merrily, merrily, merrily, merrily. Life is but a dream.* Imagining, remembering, dreaming... the differences – never completely clear to her after she visited the rubber station and found the ruins of the temple and those who lived there – were getting muddier, as muddy as the Rio Solimões.

The room was dark and quiet. Dr Carolyn Fern, her psychologist, sat close to her, their knees were almost touching, and she was speaking to Maude in a calm, assuring voice.

But none of that mattered.

Maude knew she was still in the jungle, the steamy Amazon, living in the wild, hoping to shoot enough footage to finish her documentary about the legendary Spider Queen – a mythical figure people talked about along the river. The jungle outpost turned to chaos. Fire. Everything burning. Remote buildings and the forest both ablaze. She'd been lost and now she was found.

But then she traveled to another place, beyond the physical world. It defied logic. The order of events was a jumble. Her head felt like an attic full of things piled on top of each other. Teetering. What was reality? A tissue of lies propping up an artificial world. A fragile world.

That's what she learned on her journey. One of many things…

There existed another dimension, a land of fantastic cities and the Ancient Ones, populated by creatures who might've stepped from the pages of a fantasy book. Magic and wonder. Maude experienced them as fact. She explained this to the nurses and doctors. Maude had the ability to dwell in two places at once: the emerald Brazilian jungle and the Dreamlands.

Maude would tell the medical staff the same story each time they asked her to explain her multilevel sense of reality. "When I'm sleeping, I experience three overlapping planes, if we're also here. If you're not a figment of my imagination." She'd laugh at that point of the conversation, but the medical staff never laughed with her. They wrote messages in her thickening file, and they smiled at her the way adults smile at children deemed too fanciful.

But Dr Fern insisted that right now Maude was seated in her office. They both were.

Which was absurd. She smelled smoke. She heard the screams of the dying.

Maybe she was dreaming? But which reality was the dream? Was one dream woven within another? Which of these states qualified to be called real? Maybe none of them did.

These were the questions at the center of Maude's involuntary confinement to the hospital. She could no longer distinguish dreams from wakefulness, which world was which, which Maude was the real Maude.

When she visited the Dreamlands, time passed more slowly than in the world of her hospital bed, which itself was an odd and artificial existence. Without a clock in her room or a wristwatch, she measured time according to the nursing schedules. Maude was unable to recall how she came to be at the hospital, only that she woke there one gray afternoon, the first of many as it turned out. She could spend months in the Dreamlands while only a single night of sleeping passed at the sanatorium, or so she was told when she relayed her adventures to the morning nurse. Although memories of her travels weren't always guaranteed; she had a sense that most of what happened to her was forgotten along the journey back to her bed.

Sometimes when she dreamed, she didn't enter the Dreamlands at all. She was transported backward in time, revisiting her Amazonian trauma, living through repeated variations of her past, escaping or not escaping from that tragedy which occurred at the web-enshrouded temple shrine. The first doctor who took her case labeled these dreams "recurrent jungle nightmares." Maude called them memories of her southern absence.

The first doctor would often speak in front of her as though she weren't there, especially when she'd been drugged into a half-awake, half-asleep form of semiconsciousness.

"A fixation," Dr Adam Mintz said. "Obsession. See how the patient has filled her mind so completely with these spiders, these bizarre gods, that whether awake or asleep she refuses to let go. Fascinating. The vividness of this woman's fantasies. Quite delusional, too. We'll administer more muscimol next time and see what happens. I'll get a publication out of this. What's she doing with her hand…?"

What Maude was doing was picking a syringe off a steel tray of instruments. What she did next was stab the doctor several times in his upper body.

Dazed, she emerged to his cries and his blood. There was a lot of blood. You couldn't really call it being awake, because he'd poisoned her. The drug concoction, his dream enhancer, made the nightmares multidimensionally worse. The terrors she explored every time she popped up at the Amazonian plantation or in the Dreamlands grew a hundredfold. Maximum panic. Her heart leaping out of her chest. Her brain racing… her thoughts splintering, shattering, spiraling…

After she stabbed him, they locked her in a small room by herself. Belted her to a gurney so she couldn't move. She felt terribly vulnerable. As if a spider had wrapped her in its iron threads, bundling her up, storing her until it got hungry again. A meal in waiting, a body to be slurped up like a bowl of warm soup.

But no spider came into that small room. Instead, her most frequent visitor was Dr Carolyn Fern, Maude's newly assigned psychologist. She was much better than Dr Mintz. First off, the straps attaching Maude to her bed went away. The unit door was still locked, but Dr Fern told her she had no control over that. At the sanatorium the rules were the rules. Second, she didn't treat Maude like an experiment, a subject to be poked, a caged rat who fearfully anticipated the next stinging needle full of chemicals and the unpredictable shocks that followed. No, Dr Fern listened to her. She acted as though she might even believe her. Quite the change.

Only a handful of people alive knew what had happened at the old rubber station. Maude didn't know how to find them again. She asked the nurses to make calls for her, but they told her they couldn't find anyone. Maude was insistent. Ursula Downs is an archaeologist. Her exploring partner is Jake Williams. Andy Van Nortwick writes for the *Arkham Advertiser*. One evening the night nurse informed her that Ms Downs and Mr Williams had left the Miskatonic Museum on a scientific mission to Asia. The *Advertiser* said no one named Andy Van Nortwick worked there.

"I know them," Maude said. "I used to be a movie star. Now I direct films."

"Yes, dear." The night nurse adjusted her blanket. "Don't upset yourself."

"They found me in the Amazon rainforest. I was filming monsters."

"Well, dear, you can talk to Dr Fern about that. You know you had no identification on you when you showed up on our doorstep. We're trying to help you find yourself."

"I'm Maude Brion. I come from Hollywood. I was big in the pictures."

"And I'm Clara Bow," the nurse muttered under her breath. "Goodnight, Maude."

She turned off the light and closed the door, leaving Maude strapped down in the dark.

"I know who I am," she whispered to herself. "I'm Maude Brion."

Slowly, Maude began to trust Dr Fern, until she got to the point where she would allow the doctor to inject her with a sedative that was supposed to make the therapy go more smoothly.

Or so the doctor promised.

Now the two women were alone in a private office with the drapes closed, the lights turned as low as burning candles, and Dr Fern told her she was going to hypnotize her. Maude had seen a hypnotist once performing in a club. He convinced a tuxedoed man that he was a chicken. The man flapped his arms and jerked his head like a barnyard bird, then he tried to lay an egg on the stage, squeezing his eyes with the force of exertion, while the audience laughed hard. Yet Maude still consented to the injection; she willingly stared at the device the doctor held up to help her enter the hypnotic state – a swinging disk hanging on a wire inside a simple wooden frame, and she did start to feel calm and sleepy. She let her eyelids grow heavy and shut.

She breathed deeply, listening to the doctor's soothing voice as it guided her.

One moment, she felt Dr Fern sticking a bandage on her forearm. The next moment, the smothering jungle surrounded her. Frightened birds squawked like mad. Burning trees made a crackling fireplace sound. She needed to go to the river to escape.

Maude had told Dr Fern that some of her dream visions built up gradually, she'd walk down cold steps and enter a kind of forest that wasn't the Amazon rainforest. Different trees, unrecognizable smells. She'd forget about it until she saw it again on the next trip. Other times everything overcame her all at once – an engulfment – like diving into a shimmery swimming pool. Like being swallowed up. She was inside it. Instant Amazon. The smoke, the fire, the screaming, and the giant spider… this time it was happening like that, a quick immersion.

"You are safe, Maude. I am right here with you. Describe what you see to me."

"I see the rubber station. The temple ruins. A huge spider climbing through the treetops."

"Is there anyone in the dream who can help you?"

"Jake and Andy, but they're in more trouble than I am. Ursula can help me, but I can't find her," Maude said. She turned her head, left to right, looking for people invisible to Dr Fern.

Scritch, scritch, scritch… the doctor wrote notes while Maude fled from horror to horror.

Jake, Andy, Ursula – they were real, weren't they? How could she find them now? She couldn't. Not in Arkham or in her dreams of the ill-fated Amazon expedition.

"Now listen, Maude, I'm with you. I will make sure you are protected," Dr Fern said.

Maude laughed. "If you're here with me, then you're the one who needs protecting."

She looked for the psychologist in her dream. But she didn't see her.

"I can't find you," Maude said. "I'm alone. Except for the spider. The Queen is here."

Dr Fern inhaled sharply and let out a startled gasp, as if she'd sat down on a tack.

It wasn't because of what Maude said. Something else had surprised her.

Maude was running through the decayed huts where the rubber executives once slept, where her reels of film were stored. She needed to find the portal before it was too late.

"We're leaving, Maude. Do you understand me?" Dr Fern's voice was tight.

Maude thought the doctor sounded on the brink of panicking. Her words came out in a rush, as if she were fighting to maintain control. Control of what? Maude wondered. Herself?

"What's wrong with you?" Maude lifted her head, but her eyes stayed closed.

"I'm fine. We're going now. You and I together. At the count of three you will wake."

"But I don't want to go. I want to look for the portal to the Dreamlands," Maude said.

"No portals." The doctor's command was firm. "Listen. One, two... three."

Afterward they sat staring at each other, both women covered in sweat and out of breath.

Maude was angry she'd been taken out of her hypnotic state too soon.

"You asked me to trust you," Maude said. "To tell you the truth I know. Painful truths that hurt to tell. Yet you're lying to me. You are not fine. You saw something. Just like I did. And you dragged me out. I wasn't ready to go. I was searching for something. You got scared."

Dr Fern frowned at what Maude had said. She stood up from

her chair and went to her desk. The desk was clean and orderly, files and stacks of psychiatric books squared as if by a ruler. Her legs wobbled. She steadied herself and reached for a pitcher of water on a service cart behind the desk. She filled a glass and drank. Then she refilled it. "Do you want a drink?"

"Make mine a whiskey," Maude joked. "If this occasion doesn't call for whiskey, I don't know what does." Her injection site itched. Maude peeled off the bandage, rebuttoned her sleeve.

After a moment's hesitation, Dr Fern stiffened her back, and without looking at Maude, turned to her desk, unlocked a drawer, and retrieved a dusty bottle of bootleg Canadian liquor. She stared at it, as if she was weighing something. Maude watched her in amazement, mouth hanging open, then she decided to help nudge her doctor toward making the right choice.

Maude said, "I prefer it straight if you don't mind."

Dr Fern cracked open the bottle and added some to her water, then she splashed a small amount of liquor into a second glass.

No more than a swallow's worth. But still… Maude never figured this doctor for a rulebreaker. She seemed as by-the-book as they came. A person who planned their every move.

But you learn things in therapy, even when you're the patient. Maude bobbed in a sea of pleasant drowsiness and nervous expectation. What next? What other secrets did this doctor have locked away?

Dr Fern returned the bottle to the drawer, locked it, and came back to the chairs.

"Under hypnosis, you mentioned the Dreamlands. And a portal. Why didn't you tell me about the portal and this place where it leads before? I can't see it in your notes."

"I'm careful to whom I tell things. Why? Have you heard of it?"

Despite her sedation, Maude felt keenly aware of everything. The world was wiped clean.

"I have." Dr Fern held out the whiskey to her. Color climbed in her cheeks. "I can't believe I'm doing this, but instinct tells me we both need a drink. Besides, I can't see the harm. We've been through something. The bottle was a gift from a friend. I'd forgotten about it until now."

"I wish I had your friends," Maude said, sitting up, taking the glass with both hands. "To friends," she said, toasting.

"To friends."

They clinked glasses.

The doctor continued, "You're on medications. That sedative I administered is still in your system. I don't want you to be knocked out. But a little drop shouldn't hurt."

Maude nodded. "Knocked out doesn't sound all that bad to me. I've done worse."

"What if you dream of the fire and the giant spider?"

"What if I do? I should be used to it. Sometimes I want to fall asleep and never wake up."

A look of grave concern showed from the psychologist.

"Are you saying that you don't wish to continue living?"

"I never said that," Maude answered. "I want to travel in the Dreamlands. My nightmares keep getting in my way. If anything, I want to live more. This world of yours is truly a dull show by comparison. Here's to sweet dreams and bon voyages." Maude gulped down the contraband liquid.

"You make light of your suffering," Dr Fern said. "Yet you admit you aren't well."

"Who among us is well these days? I'll settle for feeling a little less confused."

Dr Fern sipped her drink. A look of puzzlement remained on her face. Maude guessed that the conversation wasn't what was bothering the psychologist. Dr Fern was struggling to come to terms with whatever she'd witnessed during the hypnosis.

"Admit it, doc. You saw my spider, didn't you?" Maude said.

"No. I don't think so." She shook her head. "I mean, no, I didn't."

"You'd know it if you did." Maude wished she had more in her glass. While she was at it, she wished she wasn't medicated or a patient at the sanatorium. "What's your problem then?"

Dr Fern sighed. "The Dreamlands. I hoped this wouldn't happen again."

"You mean you've had patients like me before?" Maude didn't know what to make of that. Being one-of-a-kind meant the doctor didn't harbor preconceptions. But if she had helped someone else in the past… maybe she could help Maude too. To make sense out of the mayhem.

"I can't divulge patient information. That's private. But I will tell you your situation is not unfamiliar to me. I thought I had taken precautions during my hypnotherapy sessions that might prevent my being drawn into a patient's… visionary experience. Apparently, I failed."

"You saw something," Maude persisted. The psychologist nodded.

"Not your giant spiders. I did see you, however. You were underground. Wearing work clothes. In a cave, I think. You had a camera. There were others with you. Two men and a girl."

Maude frowned. "A girl?" She shook her head. "My friends who brought me back from Manaus were two men and a grown woman. And I've never been much of a caver. You sure it was me you saw?

Look, I'm not one to judge, but maybe you had a nightmare."

"I wasn't asleep. I clearly saw you and three others. Two men and a young girl."

"No spiders?"

"None." The look on the doctor's face told Maude there was more to it.

"What's got you scared, doc? Spill the beans, or I'm done with this therapy. Why are you so afraid of the Dreamlands? Of portals? What did you see in *my* nightmare?"

The doctor took a minute to consider.

She's considering whether it's appropriate to share whatever caught her off guard, Maude thought. Is telling me going to improve my condition? Or make me worse?

The doctor decided.

"A giant pink tooth," Dr Fern said.

"A what?"

"A giant pink tooth. Like an animal's fang. That's what I saw. You and your three friends were standing near it inside the cave. It hung from the ceiling. Rough and sparkly. It glowed."

"A giant pink tooth," Maude repeated, as if saying it out loud might help her to picture the thing. No luck.

Maude felt too sleepy now. Yawning, stretching her arms over her head, she felt a small pinch where the syringe had pricked her skin before. The dark office was growing hazy. Her psychologist's silhouette blurred, making her look like one of those saints on church prayer cards.

The doctor was right. It added up. The pills, the shot in the arm, the booze...

Maude's head tilted back, heavy, as if they'd opened her skull and filled it with sand.

Hospitals played with your mind. Like the Dreamlands, time was different here.

She closed her eyes and leaned back into her chair. A smile played at the corner of her mouth. She had to wonder if this session was just another chapter in her long unspooling dream.

5

Cold Light

"A giant pink tooth," Charlie Kane said.

"What?" his assistant replied.

"Well, isn't that what it looks like?" The mayor stepped closer to the unusual formation sprouting from the domed ceiling at the top of the chamber. They were deep in the sewer tunnels; after climbing through the opening Budzinski had made with his pick and pry bar, they entered the once-sealed chamber. It wasn't swampy like the digger said it was when he first broke in. The air was cool, dank. It smelled like wet stone inside, but the odor of sewage overpowered everything eventually. Charlie didn't see any pink lights dancing on the walls. For that much, he was glad.

"Now that you mention it, it sure does resemble a tooth," said Hargrove the engineer.

"Oh, yes, Mr Mayor. Your observation is quite… observant," the mayor's assistant said.

"It's exactly as Budzinski described it," Charlie said. "I can't believe my eyes. I've visited Mammoth Cave and Crystal Cave in Berks County, Pennsylvania. But I've never seen the likes of this. How could a natural formation develop so quickly in this environment? I mean, it simply can't. This room is obviously the result of human construction. Yet this protuberance appears to be the product of millions of years. So, how did it get here so fast?"

"Perhaps our ancestors who built this chamber found it and decided to leave it alone. Maybe they worked around it," Hargrove said. He couldn't keep the doubt out of his voice.

"Perhaps... perhaps..." Charlie remained unconvinced. Some unpindownable quality inherent in the formation spoke to him. It said, "*Intruder.*" Charlie had a hard time imagining diggers making this discovery and just letting it be. No, he didn't see that happening. Humans were greedy. When they found something as eye-catching and rare as this, they took it. Or they destroyed it. Ignoring it would never enter the discussion.

It took a special kind of person to keep a thing secret for long.

Charlie hadn't met anyone qualified yet.

Folks were going to hear about Arkham's peculiar "pink tooth," you bet they would. Keeping them away would be a headache. Soon, they'd need to see it for themselves. A workman missing and now this... oddity. Those dead bodies popping up in the drain system – three of them. The police were coming up empty-handed. First, they said it was gang-related. Connected to bootlegging. Maybe the dead witnessed something they shouldn't have. When that didn't seem to pan out, the detectives switched gears. A mysterious killer on the loose, they said. Evidence was scant. Kooks were coming out of the woodwork. Falsely confessing. Sending anonymous letters. The cops couldn't guarantee anything to Charlie.

But the press was having a field day speculating. It was all too tasty. Once the public had their appetite whetted, they'd become hungry for another taste of the unusual. With a mystery like this, the weirder the better. There appeared to be no shortage of weirdness in the pipes of Arkham.

Charlie stroked his ample chin as he contemplated the issues germinating before him like weeds invading a garden. Act swiftly but prudently, he told himself, like any good gardener, before your judiciously maintained plot is overrun. He had a growing nightmare on his hands, and disaster loomed for his pet Big Drain project if he didn't nip it in the bud.

Whispers would beget rumors would beget gossip would beget scandal and so on... Before you knew it, the situation would spiral out of control. He'd seen it before when the Southside Strangler terrorized the city a few years ago. Leaving corpses on doorsteps with magical sigils painted on their foreheads. They'd caught him, but his legend persisted, a current of fear flowing underneath the surface of things. All it took was a few leaks to bring it back up again. Charlie had to hide his concerns from his associates. It was too early to share.

He needed more facts. Instead, he came upon this... extraordinary object.

Charlie said, "It's a conundrum for sure. Amazing. That color!"

The group of about a dozen men stood pondering the unusual phenomenon jutting down through the dome of a chamber that seemed to be a hub where a series of bygone drains and tunnels of various shapes and sizes met like spokes on a misshapen wheel. Fascinating, what lies under a city, and no one knows. Other smaller crystalline specimens stuck out in clusters nearby.

But it was the man-sized, pink-tinged anomaly which commanded their attention.

They oohed and ahhed but except for the mayor, kept a safe distance back.

Stanley Budzinski withdrew from the group entirely, sitting on a shallow ledge at the perimeter of their lights. Facing away from the object of their fascination, he said nothing. Having more in common with rocks than men, he was soon forgotten.

Charlie approached the "tooth." He squinted at it in the dimness. There, along the cloudy surface of the object, he noticed a faint line of score marks. He touched them, discovering they were rough. Similar scrapes ran underneath, creating a pattern. What at a quick glance might have been mistaken for a flaw, or a bit of damage to crystal, like scratches on a glass, was something else. Being the mayor, Charlie was familiar with monuments, having dedicated several during his term. Some days he even entertained the idea that the citizenry of Arkham might honor him with a statue. Charlie tapped the marks. It was an inscription, a rather long one.

"D, I, O, N, Y, S, I, A..." Charlie read, spelling the first word aloud. Was that a "B" that came next? He couldn't make out the rest. The letters appeared along with a series of symbols. The symbols outnumbered the letters and gave Charlie eerie stirrings in his stomach.

Involuntarily, he recoiled.

It was a message he'd found. Who cuts cryptic codes on crystals in sewers?

Here was the sort of hocus-pocus they'd dealt with in the Southside Strangler case, happening all over again. Egads! He had to be sure of what he was seeing.

"Someone get a lamp over here! Is that writing I see along this side?"

Hargrove rushed forward, raising his safety lamp. The other men lifted their lights higher. Charlie put on his pince-nez glasses, which he normally used only in privacy, yet his vanity was no match for his curiosity right now.

"What's it say?" one of the excavation company lawyers asked.

Charlie couldn't answer because the scrawl he detected along the side of the stone was either too fragmentary or utterly unknown to him. But before he had a chance to say anything at all, there came a watery crash from beyond the domed chamber. Every head turned toward the commotion.

A dark unidentifiable stew disgorged through the opening in the slabs, spraying the slickered men, leaving them dripping wet. They stood stunned, contorting in disgust.

Several among the group were armed. They drew their weapons, hoping for something or someone they might shoot in retaliation. Pointing their revolvers toward the gap, they advanced toward whatever it was that had assaulted them from within the malodorous, tubular gloom.

"To the hole, boys!" a sergeant shouted.

"Is it Paddy?" Hargrove asked. "Have you found Paddy?"

Stanley turned and lifted his chin. The look on his face wasn't one of hopeful expectation but of dread. What color there had been in his stony face drained away.

Guns first, the men clogged the void. Seconds later they dragged a begrimed figure stumbling and coughing over the rubble. It was a man – blinking, gagging, apparently unable to speak. A mask of foul mud clung to his hairy face. Spectacles dangled from one of his ears.

"It's not Paddy! Paddy never wore eyeglasses!" a voice from the group shouted.

"Who is it then?" another asked.

"Who else but the killer?" a third voice said.

The polluted man raised a hand in protest, and something swung out from his shoulder.

"He's got a gun!" said the mayor's assistant.

The thick-necked squad who seized upon the slimy man now wrestled him to the floor of the chamber, twisting his arms behind his back. Handcuffs snapped onto his wrists.

The gun was no gun but a camera, its case cracked open in the fall.

"We've got ourselves the sewer strangler, fellas! Caught him red-handed. Returning to the scene of the crime," one of the cops said. He thumped the shackled man to prove his point.

The man gurgled, sputtering into the pool on the floor.

Charlie walked over to the knot of bodies. The water in the chamber was not so deep that a person might drown, but that didn't mean the culprit on the bottom wasn't offered a chance.

"Get him up," Charlie said.

The pile moved, grew taller. A bit of jostling produced the prisoner, front and center.

The man gagged and coughed. Some of the mud had washed off him.

Charlie held a safety lamp up to the prisoner's face.

"Murphy!" he exclaimed. "What are you doing here?"

Rex Murphy spit out something neither man wanted to identify. He cleared his throat. "Let me explain," Rex said.

"Confess, you mean." From behind, the sergeant held a baton under Rex's chin.

"Back off, Ryan. I want to hear what Murphy has to say." Charlie crossed his arms.

The sergeant stepped away.

"You know this creep, Mr Mayor?" Hargrove asked.

"I do, indeed. Mr Rex Murphy is a reporter for our very own *Arkham Advertiser.*"

"A killer *and* a reporter," Sergeant Ryan said. "It's the ideal cover. Oh, he's a slick one."

"I never killed anybody," Rex said. "You've got me all wrong."

"That's what they all say," offered one of the cops.

"Tell it to our boys at the station house," said another. "See if they care."

"Why else would you be hiding in the sewer, scuttling in the shadows like vermin?" said a security man who'd gotten the worst part of the splashing. "Unless you were guilty." The other men grumbled in agreement.

"My security detail seems to have a hard time believing you, Rex," Charlie said.

Rex said, "I followed you down here–"

"He admits it!" Ryan reddened in outrage at the audacity of the confessed stalker.

"To write a story," Rex said. "I wanted to see why you were headed into the pipe. What you were investigating. Listen, I've got as much a reason to be here as anybody. I represent the people of Arkham. I may not be a detective or a structural engineer. But neither is the mayor."

Ryan waggled his baton until Charlie lowered the end of it with his finger.

"We posted a guard at the entrance." Hargrove asked, "How'd you get past him?"

"I… I…" Rex stumbled, not wanting to give the man up. "I snuck in before he was there. What can I say? I'm the inquisitive type. It's my job to dodge obstacles put in my path."

The cops could not contain their contempt.

"You didn't dodge whatever made him fall into the muck."

"Smells fishy."

"Worse than fishy. Look at the condition of him. I've seen cleaner outhouses…"

"That's enough of that," said Charlie. "Leave a man his dignity, howsoever small."

The men chuckled. A few made a show of holding their noses or waving away a stink.

Rex squared his shoulders. He tossed his head to flip the soiled hair away from his eyes.

"Help me out, Charlie. You know who I am." Rex twisted at the waist, displaying his manacled hands. "Is this how you treat the press? We serve too. The public has a right to know. The news isn't the private property of business owners and City Hall. It belongs to the people."

The gang holding Rex muttered their objections.

The mayor had to admire Rex's nerve. This wasn't his crowd, yet he spoke up for himself, for his ideals. He wouldn't come to any serious harm in the hands of Arkham's finest.

At least, Charlie hoped that was so.

But right now, the mayor didn't need a meddlesome reporter eavesdropping on his conversations or poking into the investigation of this unfortunate sewer business. The "pink tooth" revelation was confounding enough without having Rex Murphy and the *Advertiser*'s readers gawking over his shoulder and second-guessing his every decision. No, he needed the newspaperman out of the way, at least for a few hours. Rex had to learn a hard lesson: class was still in session; the school bell hadn't rung yet. A set of ideals and a few smart words didn't always get you the story you were after, especially if that story might put other people at risk.

Charlie smirked. "As you say, Mr Murphy, I am no detective. My expertise lies elsewhere. I think I'll let the police sort this one out. I'm but a humble servant of the voters."

"C'mon Charlie, don't let them take me in," Murphy pleaded. The realization was hitting home that he wouldn't be talking his way out of this jam.

"You heard the mayor, boys. Get this one to the station for questioning," Ryan said. Charlie tried to tell himself the smile on Sergeant Ryan's face wasn't malevolent.

Amid the swinging safety lamps, as the grinning security detail dragged him away, Rex's gaze fell on the pink tooth. Charlie saw the reporter's eyes bug out as he squirmed for a better view.

"Hey, what is that thing?" Rex jerked his head to see past his escorts. "Is it a rock?"

"None of your concern, Murphy," Charlie said. "Be polite. Call a lawyer."

They crammed Rex into the drainpipe. Charlie heard him scuffling as they hauled him off. The farther they ferried him, the louder he protested. Rex had questions he wanted answered and he shouted them out to whoever would listen. "Did you find Paddy? Was he another victim of the strangler? Where's Paddy?"

Charlie found himself alone with the formation. There was one lamp left on the ground under the tooth. Sighing, he bent over and picked it up. He remembered the way back. The others weren't that far ahead of him. He chuckled. In the hurry to hustle out poor Rex, they'd forgotten him.

He thought he was alone, until he noticed Stanley Budzinski standing in the shadows still as a rock, a rugged slab.

Startled, Charlie said, "Oh, Stanley. You gave me an awful fright." He touched a hand to his thundering chest and lifted the light to see the digger better. The tooth shone like a mirror.

Budzinski didn't answer him. He had tears on his face.

And a steel pick clutched in his massive hands. His knuckles were white as bones.

"Stanley? Are you feeling like yourself, son?"

"I saw the pink lights. Did you see them?" he asked Charlie matter-of-factly. He shuffled forward. The look in his eyes was beseeching.

"No. No, I didn't," Charlie said in a hushed voice, wondering if he was about to die.

"They make beautiful sparks," Stanley said. "But it's a cold light. Cold electricity."

Budzinski turned and walked silently down one of the unexplored tunnels into the perfect darkness. His sloshing footsteps grew quieter and quieter. The mayor trembled. Had he just had a conversation with the strangler? Could it be Budzinski? The man was obviously disturbed. His whole demeanor appeared bizarre and altered from earlier. But was he a killer or in shock?

Charlie backed to the opening in the wall; without taking his eyes off the tunnel where the digger disappeared, he climbed out of the chamber. Debris slid into the water. The mayor had been an athlete back in school. Nimble and fleetfooted. He maintained his balance. Echoing in the distance, above the chatter and sloshing of the policemen, Rex Murphy could still be heard shouting his name. "Charlie! What was that thing? What horrors live in Arkham's sewers?"

That, Charlie thought, was an excellent question.

6
Good Kid

Andy Van Nortwick pushed a broom along the hallway, humming to himself. The broken window in the stairwell landing was letting in a stale breeze. When he finished sweeping, he had to cover the window and clean two more hallways. Afterward, he'd take a break, hoofing it to the other side of Rivertown, to tidy up three more rundown firetrap buildings for the landlord, Mr Papadopoulos.

Mrs Papadopoulos was the real brains of the operation; she ran the show, keeping track of the rent receipts, paying the heat and water bills, and making sure minimum repairs were done to keep the buildings pest-free and barely standing. The lady watched a dollar the way a hawk watches a mouse.

Good-humored Mr P did the footwork: inspecting the premises, checking tenant complaints, and collecting the rent, especially late payments. He used to run a drugstore with a soda fountain, spending the better part of his day scooping ice cream and jerking sodas. Mrs P put the kibosh on that. Papa's Drugs always had too many unsavory customers hanging around for her taste. Andy figured she didn't like how easy it was for Mr P to bet with his bookie. The old guy still gambled up a storm on the ponies, but he had to be discreet. A burly man with sorrowful eyes and thick eyelashes, he was the one who told Andy which jobs needing doing each day.

Andy's mind drifted back to the conversation they'd had this morning.

"Board the window on the third floor at Church Street," Mr P had said. "Those kids were throwing bricks again. I saw a hole. Always up to no good, those kids. Don't they go to school?"

"I don't know, Mr P," Andy said, reading the list of tasks Mr P handed to him.

"You're a good kid, Andy. Those kids should be like you."

Right, Andy thought. They should work their tails off to get a job as a reporter for the city newspaper. Then they should catch a break, follow the lead of a lifetime, and go off chasing their dream to the jungles of Brazil. Oh yeah, and don't forget the part where you lose it all. Where all the evidence you needed to print your career-making story is destroyed.

After that, get fired. Clear out your desks, boys and girls. Make sure the powers that be in Arkham spread rumors about you which guarantee the only job you'll find is sweeping up in the cheapest, shabbiest part of town.

He and Mr P had been standing on the porch of the Ps' Southside saltbox house. Receiving his orders each day, Andy was reminded that Southside was better than Easttown and Rivertown by a mile. Neighborhoods might be not far away and still feel like different worlds.

"Don't forget to open the windows. Get the bad air out," Mr P said.

"Will do, Mr P."

"You're a good kid," he repeated, then opened his palm, feeling for raindrops. "It's gonna be a heavy track today. Good for mudders. Soon we'll have sunny summer days – you, me, and the horses."

Andy knew that opening the windows wouldn't make any difference. Rivertown had its own aroma, and it had nothing to do with the season of the year or which way the wind blew.

Rivertown stank to high heaven.

Blame the sludge that passed for water in the Miskatonic, the factories belching poison from their chimneystacks, and the embedded, rotten, fishy... well, fishiness of the neighborhood.

On Church Street, Andy gathered the dust and broken glass into a pile. He pushed it into a pan and dumped the mess into a bucket where he put the brick he'd found on the stairs. Glass shards sparkled at him from the bottom of the bucket. Outside, rain gurgled in the gutters, dribbled down drainpipes, and pattered on rooftops. But the music of rain wasn't the only sound.

Andy heard a crowd roar like an ocean wave. Shouts and clapping. They weren't too close, maybe at the edge of the Merchant District. Noises traveled from far off, depending on the wind. From between the buildings nearby, he heard shouts and the sound of people running. He wondered what was going on as he carried his bucket to the landing, setting it under the window.

Curious, Andy peered through the hole, where he saw a slice of street.

Must be quite a gathering, he thought, judging by the number of figures crossing the road. Maybe there'd been an accident. Because nobody famous ever visited this part of Arkham – not on purpose, and certainly nobody who'd make regular folks run or cheer in the dismal rain.

Andy craned for a better angle. A utility pole blocked most of the view. He tried pulling up on the window, being careful not to cut himself on the jagged glass still hanging in the frame.

It only budged a few inches.

Carefully wrapping a handkerchief around his knuckles, Andy busted out the remaining pieces, adding them to his bucket. He'd patch the hole later. He stuck his head outside. Cheap pine steps zigzagged up the back of the Papadopoulos row house. They didn't look safe, but he wasn't planning on hanging around and eating his lunch sitting there. He only wanted to see what was happening over on Main Street. He raised his leg and climbed through, putting his weight on the rickety steps. They creaked and shook, knocking against the building, but the staircase held. Out here he had a better vantage point, but not from his current position; that pole was still blocking him. He went up a few steps and checked again. Now he had to contend with lines of wet laundry left hanging in the rain – as good as a drab torn curtain between the buildings – screening off the scene of the action.

A few more steps and he gained the height he needed, but it was still no good as the steps shifted him too far to one side.

He went up to the roof. The tarpaper looked like an oilfield. He didn't dare step on it, worried he might fall through. But he perched on the edge, taking the full brunt of the weather, because something big was happening west on Main and he wanted to see what it was.

He saw more people hurrying out that way. They flowed through the alleys like water finding a route to the river. What was the attraction? Andy tried to picture everything located in that direction. It was shops, mostly. A few vacant lots. He'd been on a walk that way the other day. Why? He couldn't recall. He didn't get over to the Merchant District that often.

Andy snapped his fingers. That was right around the spot where they were ripping up the streets. The new project to repair the city sewers. Now he remembered. He'd taken a trip to Schoffner's General Store to restock his cleaning supplies. Sometimes Davy Schoffner would slip Andy a few extra coins to make a delivery or two on his way back and forth between cleaning houses. The locals had been gathered around the stove playing checkers and griping about how taxpayer money was being thrown away on the project, and speculating it was lining Mayor Kane's pockets. His interest sparked, Andy had gone for a look, and it was chaos he saw.

The Big Drain dig site – that's what those bigwigs at City Hall were calling it.

If something was going on at the sewer, what could it be? The Big Drain was a news story, sure. But it wouldn't draw a crowd even on a nice day. Nobody cared that much about a hole in the street. It wasn't like the strangler story – a killer in the city, no one knowing who the next victim might be. Hold on! The strangler's bodies had all turned up around the pipes. Scuttlebutt said the killer used the drains. A clever subterranean hunter lurked under the streets.

Andy raced down the rickety staircase, moving too fast to worry it might collapse. He came out behind the Papadopoulos property. Not much of a yard, no grass, no garden or shrubbery. Just a muddy plot filled with junk the tenants left outside to rust. A bicycle with no front wheel. A wheelbarrow missing its handles. Cans sunk in the mud.

He looked around with a pang of guilt. He didn't see any

neighbors. Everybody who was paying attention had gone over to investigate the incident on Main Street. Andy had read the headlines. He knew what might be going on. Another murder victim discovered in the sewers.

Was that it? It must be. If he ran, he'd be there in no time.

Andy had to know more. He *needed* to know, and now. A reporter couldn't just turn off their instincts, could they? Detach their nose for news and put it in the closet with their typewriter. What would it hurt if I took a break? Andy asked himself. Isn't it my responsibility to the Papadopouloses to stay informed about what was happening at their properties? In his heart Andy knew Mr P wouldn't like him leaving work. Mrs P would fire him on the spot. But they weren't out here on this fine Monday in the spring rain, were they? How would they ever find out? He'd run over to Main and be back in two shakes of a lamb's tail.

Mr P took him for granted anyway. Always adding extra chores but never any extra pay. Andy worked day and night for a pittance. A pittance! He could hardly afford to live!

The pang of guilt passed quickly. Excitement replaced it. He burned with inquisitiveness. Forget the bosses – Andy was going. There was a major event taking place, and he wouldn't miss it. What if the strangler had struck again? Who was the victim? Were there clues?

He clamped his hand on his cap and rushed out of the yard into the alley, nothing on his mind except finding out the news. He couldn't help himself; it was a disease.

Andy Van Nortwick needed to know.

He couldn't believe what he was seeing. People in the crowd told him that a man had been killed down in the pipes, a sewer worker, and when the mayor and his entourage went down to inspect the area, they ran into the strangler. The cops nabbed him, even as he tried to choke the mayor to death! Now they were bringing the creep out of the pipes.

The variety of people in the crowd surprised Andy. The weather didn't deter them. Folks of all ages were braving the rain. He even saw a pair of young kids weaving through the throng. They seemed to be in no hurry to make it to the front but instead walked in and out near the rear.

"I wonder what he looks like?" a woman in a blue paisley headscarf said.

"He's probably pale if he lives underground. I heard he's a cannibal." The teenaged boy who mentioned people-eating climbed onto the base of a streetlamp to see over the heads of those blocking his view.

Andy asked if he minded sharing the post. The teen told him to hop on.

The metal was slippery, but Andy hooked his arm around the pole. He had a great view of the sewer entrance. The other side of street had been gouged away by shovels, machines, and Mother Nature's recent deluge. They must've started out by first removing a manhole cover, then widening the opening, scooping until they hollowed a sandy crater out of the earth. The cavity occupied most of a vacant lot between shops. Uprooted street cobblestones were dumped there in piles. They had erected a ramshackle shelter at one end of the pit. A limousine with its driver idled beside the hole, and a guard stood nearby smoking a cigar. To keep workers from sinking into the muck, they'd put down an array of plywood boards. Most of them were underwater, or soon would be, while a few already floated off like rafts. A gravel-coated ramp slanted into the bowl. Sandbags, wheelbarrows, and digging tools lay scattered. The air exuded rotten egg and dead fish fumes. Andy made out the open end of a brick-sided tube – the sewer. Judging by its size, it must've been one of the city's largest. From Andy's perch, it seemed otherworldly, a tunnel for goblins. Lightbulbs irradiated the passage, and the falling rain lent them a starry twinkle. Wisps of steam slipped out of the conduit like fleeing spirits.

A group of shadows moved in the tunnel mouth. Whoever was inside was waiting.

Newly arrived cops pushed the crowd back. Andy saw the mayor's assistant talking with a police captain.

"He'll have beady little eyes like a mole," said a man holding a disintegrating copy of the *Advertiser* over his head like an umbrella. "They're bringing him out now!"

A huddle of police wearing slickers emerged. In the center of the huddle, a handcuffed man, half walking, half being dragged, lifted his head and breathed in the surface air. Rain washed the dirt from his face. His eyes opened, and he said something to one of the cops, who reached up to the man's face and put his eyeglasses on. It was then the man saw the crowd.

He looked horrified.

"The strangler!" a voice hollered.

A cheer went up for the police. Rounds of applause followed. But mostly it was insults.

Andy watched. Here was a live monster on display, or so many of them seemed to think. Andy knew a thing or two about monsters, real and human. He knew some of them were easy to recognize, and others concealed themselves behind masks or words. The wet man being paraded around didn't look extraordinary. In fact, there was something all too familiar about him. Andy stared, then practically fell off the pole when the realization hit.

Holy moly! I know that guy! he thought. *That's Rex Murphy. I worked with him at the* Advertiser. *He's the killer?*

It made no sense. He didn't know Rex all that well. Rex had been at the paper longer than Andy had. He worked alone and hung around with the senior reporters. But, golly, he never seemed like the killing type.

During his brief newspaper career, Andy had looked up to him as a hero. If he played his cards right, he might someday be the next Rex Murphy. That's how his fantasy went, right up until the paper fired Andy. Thinking about it made his jaw muscles clench.

We went to the Amazon, and we found Maude Brion who'd been written off for dead, missing along the river... and we solved the Spider Queen mystery. We did more than see her. We had proof enough for headlines and books. And movies! Only then everything was lost.

It wasn't Maude's fault, not really. Andy didn't blame her anymore. Evil attacked them. Ursula seemed none the worse for wear, but she kept her fear under wraps like a soldier. Jake lost his leg. Maude couldn't tell dreams from life. Andy's job went kaput, most likely because their rich sponsor threatened the paper after they failed to return with the gold he desired. He killed Andy's dream. Money talked and bumped off Andy.

Now wasn't the time for thinking about himself, though. What was happening in front of him had to be another big mistake.

Rex's predicament looked worse than anything that happened to Andy– he'd only lost his job, but the flatfoots were loading Rex into a police vehicle to take him across the river to the station. Treating a reporter like a hooligan – it was unthinkable. They'd probably keep him up late into the night, questioning him under bright lights. Or maybe they'd put him in the cooler, let him stew. Andy couldn't imagine Rex doing anything at the station except peppering the cops with his own questions. Now he was going to be locked up like a gangster, and a killer at that.

They marched Rex into the back of a paddy wagon that resembled a bakery truck.

Weak-kneed, Rex staggered forward. His eyes were searching for something.

Mercy? Justice?

Half a dozen lawmen crammed inside the wagon after him and slammed the door. You'd think he was making a trip to the gallows. Andy swallowed. More like the electric chair. If a judge and jury saw fit, the system *would* send Rex out of this world riding the lightning.

Other reporters yelled out questions, as if Rex were a stranger to them. Just another story to be typed up and sold for two cents. Camera flashes burst white.

Andy had to do something. He felt helpless.

But he wasn't helpless. Andy had skills. He knew how to dig up facts. Figure things out. Put clues together. How to talk to people. He had to rescue his fellow newsman. Where was the evidence? What was going on here? He had to find out. Andy knew he was the perfect person to do it, but first he had to go back and finish his sweeping before Mrs P found out and fired him.

7

Dove Gray

Wendy Adams stopped picking pockets as soon as she saw the face of the killer the police dragged out of the sewers. She knew the man and had talked to him. She'd even helped him.

It couldn't be true. The police were arresting the wrong person. The man they had was a reporter. Rex was his name. Wendy knew he wasn't the criminal they were looking for. She knew because Rex was looking for the same creep the police wanted to find. That's what he told her when he asked for her help. Why would you want help looking for yourself?

Wendy searched for James in the crowd. He was dipping for wallets too. What other people saw when they looked at them was a couple of brown-haired children. They looked poor, but so did a lot of folks who lived in Rivertown. She and James planned to work the distracted gawkers for enough money to feed themselves. If they were lucky, they'd get a little more. Maybe they could buy food for the rest of the week. Or get a room somewhere.

She spotted James. He locked his gaze on her, and she swept a hand through her hair which was their signal that it was time to go. Wendy peered at an alley to the south. James followed her eyes. They'd take the alley to the train lines that ran along the river. There was a rusty old boxcar sitting there where they could count their loot. Then they'd make up their minds what to do next. One step at a time. That was how they lived.

Wendy was headed for the alley when she felt a hand touch her shoulder. Lightly.

"Excuse me, miss."

It was hard to tell anything about the person talking to her. They were all wrapped up with a long dove-gray wool scarf that went around their face a few times. They wore a slouch hat pulled to their eyebrows. The shadow from the hat hid everything but their eyes.

Strange eyes, Wendy thought. Later she couldn't recall their color. If asked, she would've said silver. But people don't have silver eyes. Not even animals do.

The hand on her shoulder wore a dove-gray glove the same color as the scarf. The other hand, in a matching glove, was holding up a coin purse.

"I think you dropped this," the stranger said. They shook the purse, so the coins jingled.

"Oh, thank you," Wendy said.

The stranger must've felt awful cold to bundle up like that, she thought.

Wendy was smiling and acting polite, because she needed to get away fast. The purse was one she had lifted from a woman with flowers on her umbrella standing a few feet away. The woman hadn't noticed, but she might if the stranger kept holding the purse out and shaking it like a maraca. Wendy reached out but hesitated for a second. Something didn't feel right.

"Here you go, then," the dove-gray stranger said. "If it's yours."

Shake, shake, shake.

The woman with the umbrella cocked her head, listening. She started looking around.

Wendy grasped the purse, but when she tried to take it, the stranger held on. As Wendy tugged at the purse, the stranger quickly seized her wrist. The stranger laughed then. It was a dry, cool sort of laugh. Kind of a scraping noise, wheezy-like, or the way a knife sounds as it slides on a whetstone to sharpen. It could've come from a man or a woman, a laugh like that.

Although the stranger didn't appear especially tough, the fingers inside the glove coiled like steel springs in a trap. Wendy wanted to scream. Screaming might help her or it might get her caught. She didn't want trouble with the police. She didn't want James to be alone without her, or for him to get caught because she dropped her loot. There were a lot of police around.

So, she didn't scream. Instead, she reached for her amulet she wore around her neck, because it was vibrating against her skin. She didn't think she'd ever felt it moving so much, and that scared her.

But then, just like nothing had happened, the stranger let go.

Wendy almost fell backward. She held the purse in her trembling grip. She turned to search for an open space in the crowd so she might run. There weren't any spaces. The people were packed in more snugly than before, pressing toward the sewer drama. Wendy was panicking. She had to make it to the alley.

I can drop down low, she thought. *I'll crawl through their legs if I have to.* When she looked back to see what the stranger was doing, how close they were...

The dove-gray stranger was gone.

There was no room for them to get out so quickly. It was elbow-to-elbow, with people shoving. The crowd had become a single thing that trampled the ground. She couldn't see the stranger anywhere. That made Wendy nervous. How could a person disappear like that?

Everybody pushing gave her a cramped feeling. Her face felt hot and sticky. She about jumped out of her skin when fingers intertwined with hers.

But it was only James.

"I was waiting in the alley, but you were–"

"We'll go now," she said.

And they went low between the legs, looking just ahead and no farther until they got free, not stopping until Wendy felt her amulet go still and the rusty boxcar sheltered them like home.

8
Sanatorium Dreaming

Maude opened her eyes and tried to sit up, but she couldn't. The oyster-colored hospital curtains were drawn and tied, their cords attached to little hooks set in the wall. She became aware of the sounds of rain... Her window was open. She twisted her head. Iron bars glistened blackly. Wind passed through them. They'd been repainted so many times they looked soft and chewy. Water puddled on the windowsill. It was dark outside, but the corner streetlamp glared into her room – its milky face lighting up her whole bed. A damp gust rattled the glass and gave her chills. She went to pull her blanket up only to discover her arms were immobilized. Tucking in her chin, she stared down at her body. The blanket was taut and folded over once at her waist. But it wasn't the blanket stopping her. Another gust. Her hospital gown trembled; thinned from years of washings at the industrial laundry it was almost see-through. She got goosebumps. Maude knew why she couldn't move. She was in her room at the sanatorium, but someone had put the straps back on.

Four wide brown leather belts bound her to the gurney. They must've put them on while she was asleep. She couldn't remember anything. There had to be some confusion happening here. A mistake. She tried shifting her hips and shoulders up and down. It was no use. She'd never struggle out of these. She was ready to start shouting when the door opened.

"I was about to call for you," Maude said, fighting to keep her voice down and not sound angry. Anger wouldn't do her any good. She had to remain calm, tell them what was wrong. They'd listen. Or she'd make them call Dr Fern. Either way the straps would be off soon.

"Well, are you coming in?" she asked. "I could use a hand here."

The door was to the right of her bed. Its angle offered glimpses and shadows but no direct view into the hall. Whoever was standing at the threshold didn't answer.

Maude turned her head on the pillow, waiting for the night nurse to appear. A slow feeling of foreboding began to build inside her that might switch to terror at any moment. Maybe it's just someone new, she told herself. Somebody she didn't know. As serenely as possible, she'd explain her doctor's orders. Simple as that. But in the presence of her silent visitor, words caught like fishbones in her throat.

It wasn't a nurse at the door. A familiar figure moved smoothly to the foot of the bed.

Dr Mintz had cleaned up from the last time she saw him. His cheeks were freshly shaved although the hour was late. He smelled of soap and something else… his clothes or his body emitted the sweet medicinal odor of ether. There was a bandage plastered on his neck covering one of the stab wounds she'd given him. Busy inspecting the straps, he studied the buckles until he was satisfied they were secure. Maude recognized the faded spots on his white doctor's coat. He hadn't managed to wash out all the bloodstains. He clasped her wrist to take her pulse, focusing on his watch; his fingertips were clammy suckers sticking to her skin.

When he finished, he folded his arms and met her gaze. Why was he smiling?

Nurse Heather entered and switched on the overhead light. Maude squinted under its bright attack.

"The patient is awake," Dr Mintz said. "Pulse elevated."

His face was flushed; a patch of skin flamed red above his collar where he'd scraped it too close with his razor. Sweat clung to his forehead and upper lip. His breathing made a wet clicking sound.

"Get out of here," Maude said, feeling rage boil up inside her. "You're not my doctor."

He ignored her demand. His voice was a cold gray slime pouring over her. "When Nurse Heather came to get you after your hypnotherapy session with Dr Fern, she observed you were unsteady on your feet. She also noticed the smell of alcohol – whiskey to be precise – on your breath. There were two glasses on the table in Dr Fern's office. Nurse Heather was courageous enough to retrieve those glasses. She passed them to me, and I immediately turned the evidence over to the head of my department. I am deeply concerned about Dr Fern's habit of becoming overly familiar with her patients. If it's true that she was drinking with you, then she acted unethically. Dr Fern has been put on temporary administrative leave, pending an investigation. In the meantime, all her cases have been reassigned to me. Patient Brion, you will resume your therapy at once, under my close personal supervision. That means dream enhancement, as you know."

Maude tried to digest the new information. She couldn't believe it. She'd drifted off a few hours ago, then woken up to this nightmare. Maybe this was a new category of vision, one of her extraordinarily vivid dreams. That was why she was here after all. She pinched her thigh to wake herself up. This wasn't the Dreamlands or an abandoned rubber plantation on fire along the Amazon River. Was she stuck in some horrible new loop? Sanatorium dreaming?

She hated it here. Her head pounded. Panic slithered inside her chest.

"You're not doing that to me again," she said. "I swear. You try anything tomorrow and I'll refuse. I will outright refuse." Forgetting she was belted, she tried to lift herself. The frustration was almost too much to bear.

Dr Mintz stroked the back of her hand, as if he were trying to calm her. But she knew that he knew how much it made her want to scream. "I agree," he said. "Tomorrow is much too late. You will begin your regimen tonight. There's no telling the damage Dr Fern's experiments may have done to you. I only pray there's still time to save what's left of your mind. You are a very sick woman, Maude. Delusional and violent, as I can attest."

Maude thrashed, struggling to free herself, though it was a waste of energy.

"Nurse Heather, take her to the procedure room. Administer a double dose of muscimol."

"Yes, Dr Mintz." Nurse Heather pushed her bed out the door, turning down the hall.

"I refuse! Stop wheeling me!" Maude screamed. "Wake up! I refuse! Wake up, Maude!"

But there was no waking up from this ordeal. A long night lay ahead. Dr Mintz strolled beside her gurney whistling "My Blue Heaven."

They stopped outside the elevator. Dr Mintz opened the gate, and Nurse Heather pushed Maude inside. They rode down, Mintz whistling away as they descended. The air temperature cooled. Dank smells of wet stone and mildew filled the elevator car, and Maude recognized they were now underground. It was a claustrophobic feeling, as terrifying as being entombed alive.

She felt her throat constrict, her chest tightening. It was difficult to breathe.

Sunless. Moonless. Cast down into a pit.

Swallowed up, she thought. You can't survive after you've already been eaten.

A teeth-jarring jolt signaled their arrival.

Out in the hallway, Maude looked around for someone to ask for help. Most of the lights were off for the evening, except for one glowing hideously at the end of the hall where the procedure room was. Maude had heard rumors they kept patients down here, but she'd never seen one. The vague hallways appeared deserted. *Squeak, squeak, squeak* went the spinning wheels of her gurney. Not another living soul in sight. Too late for anything good to happen.

Some nights you couldn't stop dreaming. The best you could do was scream your throat raw. Maude heard someone groaning. Then she realized that *she* was that someone.

No, there would be no escape for her, not from this place... or Dr Mintz and his needles.

There were, however, more dreams to come, more than she could take.

She gripped the gurney and waited for the onrush of terrors. Even before the first injection pricked her skin, she started screaming. The only answer was its echo in her ears.

9
The Slip

Rex was sitting alone in an interrogation room. He'd been there for a while. He wasn't sure how long because they took away his watch when the welcoming committee emptied his pockets. At least they'd removed his handcuffs. Now he could move around as much as three cockeyed chairs and a battered table covered with cigarette burns would allow. The door was locked. He'd checked it twice. He pressed his ear to the wood, but all he could hear was murmurs.

A cacophony of noise. There was no making sense of any of this. What was that pink crystal he saw in the sewer with the mayor? Did it have anything to do with the strangler murders? Earlier, the detectives who were questioning him said they had him dead to rights for three known murders and a fourth suspected slaying once Paddy O'Hara's corpse floated up.

"How many did you kill?" the fat one said. He had a thin mustache and a bad attitude.

"I didn't kill anybody."

"Let him be, Angelo. He'll tell us when he wants to," the skinny one said. He had a thick mustache, a real soup strainer that twitched as he chewed. He was eating peanuts and offered the open end of the bag to Rex. But Rex shook his head.

"No, thanks. I'm not hungry."

A uniformed man entered the room and whispered something in the fat one's chubby ear. Both detectives seemed startled by the man's presence. He wasn't a regular at the station.

Rex knew him too.

He was the chief of police. So, this episode in the pipes had the attention of the top brass.

"Well, boys, I guess I'm no small potatoes," Rex said. "How're you doing, chief?"

But the chief never looked at him. The fat one nodded. He motioned to his partner. The three policemen left the room. That was hours ago. What was going on? Did they find a clue?

Rex rubbed at his wrists where the cuffs had dug furrows in his skin. He paced, one two steps, to the other side of the cramped quarters. Might as well be a cell, he thought. I feel caged.

"This'll make a heck of a story if I don't get roughed up too bad or sent to the chair," he said. He chuckled without mirth. It was either laugh or cry. And he wasn't going to give them the satisfaction of seeing a reporter's tears. He'd make it out of this confused jumble. He had to…

I'm not saying another word to these goons. I want a lawyer. Seeing as I can't afford a lawyer, the Advertiser *will spring for one, won't they?* Rex wasn't sure how confident he felt about that. Oh, this was the jam to beat all jams. It stunk up the joint. But, if he set aside his own comfort, personal safety, and the fate of his future in the Arkham system of law and order, he'd still rather be on the inside looking out, than outside looking in. The action was right here.

Only he couldn't make head or tails of it. The mud encasing his clothes was drying and flaking off. He was leaving a dirty trail inside his interrogation room. Where were the cops?

A bolt turned in the lock, the door opened. It was Sergeant Ryan from the sewer tunnel.

Rex said, "I want a lawyer. I'm not saying another word until I get one. Call my paper."

"You're free to go, Murphy," the cop said.

Rex gawked at him.

"I know this trick," Rex said. "I take two steps out of this room, and you plug me."

"You can pick up your belongings at the front desk. Now go on," Ryan said.

"No way, pal. I know my rights. I'm staying put until I see a lawyer," Rex said. He turned and dropped into one of the chairs and put his feet up on the table – his borrowed muddy boots still dripping muck. Rex leaned back, his hands behind his head. A man without a care.

Ryan sighed. "Now the only thing you're gonna see is stars when I club you for disobeying my order. The chief says we're to release you on account of the mayor says so."

"Why would Kane let me go, huh? He's the one who wanted me here in the first place."

"I don't claim to plumb the depths of a politician's mind. But the mayor saw something down in the pipes after we left that made him change his opinion about your guilt. So, clear out."

"What did he see?"

"I haven't the foggiest."

Rex scratched his cakey beard. The sight of it made Sergeant Ryan wince and curl his lip.

"Would the mayor care to have a personal word with me?"

Ryan said, "No. He would not."

"You're sure about that?"

The cop tapped his nightstick on the table. "Closing time. Don't try my patience, Murph."

"Could you ask him for me? Pretty please? I'll wait right here, I promise."

Ryan showed him his teeth. It wasn't a smile. "The mayor has left the building."

"What about the chief?"

"Him too. It's only us lowly servants here now," Ryan said. "Cleaning up messes."

Two minutes later Rex had his things, except for his notebook, which the desk claimed they never received or checked in. He was heading for the front doors when Ryan stopped him.

"You'll go out the back door, Murphy. Front door is for guests only."

"But I was a–"

This time Ryan did smile, and Rex saw half his teeth were missing, while the other half were gold. "You don't want to exit that way. The press is waiting like a bunch of dirty seagulls, and you're a loaf of week-old stale bread. They'll eat every crumb. Have a look at yourself, son. You're not showing your Sunday best." He pointed to the doors. "They think you might be the strangler. We know better. Take advice from a fellow Irishman. Slip out the alley way. In the morning, the chief will make an official statement. Your reporter pals will flock to the next crusty tidbit."

Rex considered the offer. If he went out there, he'd be giving interviews all night. That would interfere with his other plans.

"Show me the door, Sergeant Ryan," Rex said.

"Never have I heard sweeter words," Ryan replied.

Rex almost made it to the end of the alley, and thought he was in the clear, when he heard somebody kick a trashcan and a slender figure burst out from under a pile of damp *Advertisers*.

"Rex Murphy! How did you escape?"

"Back off! I have a gun," Rex said. He dug his hand deep in his pocket.

"Don't shoot! I'm on your side."

Rex frowned at the young man with coal-blackened cheeks who was so excited to see him. He took his finger out of his pocket. "I don't have a gun. I thought you were a mugger."

"You did escape. Here I was waiting to see if the mayor might try to give the slip to the reporters staked out front and bingo! Rex Murphy shows up. Say, you need a place to hide out?"

"No, the cops released me." Rex wondered if this young fellow might be dealing without a full deck. His style gave off a staticky hum like a radio. "Say, kid, do I know you?"

The kid scrubbed his disguised face with his coat sleeve. He stuck out his hand.

"Andy Van Nortwick. Formerly of the *Advertiser*," he said. "I had a desk in the back."

Rex didn't know any Andy from the *Advertiser*. "A desk in the back... kid, it's been a long day. I'm sorry but I never heard of you."

The kid's shoulders sagged. "I used to be a reporter at the paper. Junior reporter. But they fired me. See, I went down to the Amazon chasing this story about a missing film director–"

Rex pointed at him. "The Spider Queen thing? That was you?"

"Yeah, that was me." Andy turned up his palms and gave an embarrassed shrug.

Rex shook his head. "Man, that was one crazy tale if half of what I heard tell is true."

"It's all true." Andy's voice rose with indignance. "I went down there and nailed it."

"Let's walk, kid." Rex went to throw his arm around the young reporter. The kid flinched and backed away.

Now Rex was the embarrassed one.

"Hey, I know. No offense taken. I slipped in some sludge earlier. I must smell bad."

"It's worse than bad, Mr Murphy." Andy laughed. "It's downright disgusting."

"Call me Rex. Listen, kid, I need somebody to help me out tonight. Are you available?"

"You bet. Sure thing," Andy said. The kid was trotting along beside him.

"Great." Rex wasn't sure this was his best idea, but he didn't have a lot of options.

Andy rubbed his hands together. "Where are we going? Out to the mayor's mansion?"

"No, back to the sewers," Rex said.

Any kid willing to hide under alley trash was perfect. This was the dirtiest of dirty work.

"What're we doing there?" he asked, with what sounded to Rex like a whiff of doubt.

"Hunting lamprey, kid. We're going hunting for lamprey."

10

The God-Mind

It found the utmost amusement in wreckage. Preferably the wreckage of a living thing – best of all, a human mind. It did not need food to survive, it had more subtle appetites. Pain gave it a weak nourishment; the best that pain would provide was a passing distraction. The amusement of toying with a lesser thing. To inflict, to experiment upon, to crush from existence when the impulse came – that was power. Power was life. How fragile humans were, utterly beneath contempt. The dismissible trivial specks were hardly worth the focus of a god-mind. And yet…

To watch them react. So predictably. Pathetic creatures. Bags of water walking around.

It shared nothing with them, certainly not language. The language of these very observations was not in the god-mind but a manifestation of the god-mind within the severely limited capacity of a human mind. In short, the god put these words into a dreaming human. Just to see what would happen. It could do that – penetrate the minds of lower beings. Explore. With varying degrees of success, it shot its arrows of consciousness into others.

This particular human had invited it in. That invitation was not necessary, but it made the invasion easier. No struggle. No resistance. An acquiescence – something no god would do.

The god-mind observed the sleeping human in its soft creaking bed in a darkened room of an anonymous building in its city called Arkham. How little they changed from infancy to adulthood. A squirming pink lump of needs and weaknesses. Wailing. Begging. Stumbling clumsily as it grunted and ambled along, a negligible improvement on life from the cellular level.

The god-mind induced a mild stimulation. The unconscious human twitched and whimpered without waking. This required delicacy of execution. Then it showed the human images of horror on the dreamscape, pictures to cause the human extreme distress. The human recoiled in fear. Simple creatures. Manipulatable. Pliable as clay. Entertaining to reshape.

It made this one into a killer.

Wind it up and let it go. See it indulge fantasies to hunt its own kind. Its nature warped.

Observe the ensuing chaos.

Chaos was the real purpose. The god-mind thrived on chaos. Chaos was beautiful.

Beautiful was not a god-mind word, but it was the closest thing this human had for expressing what the god-mind experienced. The god-mind created chaos. Then it watched. It tasted its own power over lesser beings. The god-mind decided that it wanted the human to name it. It already had a name in the dimensions, but the god-mind did not operate in human time. It would take its name in the past, present, and future simultaneously. The sleeping human would find the name in its dreams, see it on a parchment, later read it etched on a stone. Thinking all the while it had stumbled upon a trail of truths when in fact the "truth" was invented by a timeless, inhuman god. A difficult concept for a human to grasp. So, the god-mind obscured it in mystery.

These humans loved their mysteries. They searched for them. Craved them.

When there is no time, there is no mystery.

All is revealed, all is known. Gods put no value in mysteries.

The god-mind made the sleeping human behold its name emblazoned in blood red letters.

The mouth of the human moved. Muttering through chapped lips, "Syrx-Crugoth. Syrx-Crugoth. Syrx-Crugoth."

That was not an exact pronunciation, but it was as close as human vocal capabilities could produce. The god-mind allowed it. It was funny. Like teaching a beast to mimic sounds.

Syrx-Crugoth was *pleased* to allow it.

"Syrx-Crugoth, what shall I do to serve thee?" the dreaming human croaked hoarsely.

Syrx-Crugoth communicated on a telepathic frequency, a whispering in the ear of the human in its stinking blankets amid the drafty winds of its leaky hovel made of dead trees and hardened sand. A breath like fine black insectile hairs brushed its earlobe, pushing seed thoughts into its gelatinous brain. I am a gardener, thought the god-mind.

Fast words uttered in a ceaseless stream, whole volumes of atrocities, promises of catastrophe delineated. A battleplan. A host of false pledges and hints at untold future rewards.

When the telepathic message ended, the human laid there silently. Overstuffed. Fat with lies. Digesting information with its meager bowl of gray matter.

Thinking, dreaming…

Growing into a new kind of monster.

Syrx-Crugoth withdrew. Its light dimmed. Flickering, a sparkle. Opaqueness replaced it.

Then nothing.

The human opened its eyes to the darkness of the room. The smell of rain and wet soil filled its perceptions, then came the awareness that the god-mind had visited it while it slept. The god-mind was still there observing in the background, but the human didn't know.

"Syrx-Crugoth. I have found thee at last. I live to serve thee, and thee alone. Now thy name is known unto me. Soon I pray to see your awful face, your unforgiving crown. Grant me thy cruel blessing. Imbue my acts with the coldness of your embrace as you have before."

Rising from bed, the human switched on a light on the nightstand. Then it got up, stretched and made preparations before heading off to work. The human gathered the necessary tools. First came the bag, which it set on its bed. The elements of disguise hung in the closet, and the human put them on, humming while it dressed. It put on its mask, so to speak, that way other people wouldn't know the threat until it was too late. Hiding was important when hunting.

A gray bar of light intruded where the window shade refused to pull down all the way.

Was it day or night? the human wondered. No matter. Just more hours. The rain poured out like sand running through an hourglass; time tick-tick-ticking away.

The human had a list in its head. Syrx-Crugoth put it there. Safety lamp. *Check*. Gloves. *Check*. Knife. Sharp as ever. The god-mind withdrew from the human now, watching it sucking a bubble of its own blood from its nicked thumb. Salty and warm, the fluid tasted like pennies.

There would be a stop before hunting, before heading underground with the vermin and filth. A new receptacle for the blood was needed since the last one was too small, filling quickly.

And when slippery it proved hard to hold.

Like a lamprey caught wriggling fresh from the sea...

The human stood there at its bedside, squirming, and didn't know why.

11
Hunting Lamprey

Andy couldn't believe his luck. This morning he'd been sweeping out crummy apartment buildings. Then a few hours later, he concocted a ploy to catch the mayor leaving the police station so he could confront him about the arrest of Rex Murphy, member of the press and his former coworker at the *Advertiser*, even if the reporter didn't remember him. And now here he was working with Rex on catching the real sewer killer. The strangler! Except Rex said the two detectives didn't call the killer the "Strangler."

"They asked me if I've ever heard of the Lamprey."

"The Lamprey?" Andy said. "I take it that's not the French word for lamp?"

"It's a kind of fish. They look like eels. They've got these toothy tube-like mouths and they attach themselves onto their prey like suction cups. They chew off the scales, drilling a hole into their victims. They suck out the blood and juices. Eating flesh, organs, whatever they can."

"So they're parasites," Andy said. "Like leeches."

"That's right," Rex said as they walked. "You see the obvious parallels to the sewer killer. Whoever the murderer is, they're draining the life out of their victims. Stealing blood."

"The cops decided to name the killer the Lamprey?"

"No. The killer picked their own moniker. They sent a letter to the cops. To the police chief, in fact. It's all been kept hush-hush. A way to weed out false confessions. The detectives thought I'd admit I was the Lamprey if they showed me the letter."

"They showed you the Lamprey's letter?" Andy thrilled at access to such material. Here he was at the core of the strangler, or Lamprey, case. The inside scoop – he was hearing it from Rex Murphy himself. My bosses threw me outside, but I'm right back in, he thought.

Rex said, "I didn't have my pencil and notepad, but I can remember most of it. In the first part the killer described what a lamprey was, how they've survived in our oceans for hundreds of millions of years. Their camouflage allows them to blend into their surroundings, hiding from others, both predators and prey. They scrape along stones or swim through the murky depths, searching. Hunting. When they see their chance, they attach themselves to another fish." Rex made a sucking noise as he pretended to affix his cupped hand to Andy's shoulder. "Killing it ever so slowly." Rex pumped his hand mimicking the lamprey's ingestion of blood and flesh.

Andy must've looked distressed, because Rex let go and said, "Sorry. Got carried away."

"Not a problem," Andy said, not meaning it. "What did the rest of the letter say?"

"He went on to describe their parasitic nature. A role he admired. Then the killer said that he's a human lamprey sucking the life out of Arkham's citizens. But he's not killing for his own food. He's feeding the vital juices he takes to a superior being. It sounded as if he meant a god."

"Which god?"

Internally, Andy recoiled at the mention of strange gods. He'd been witness to a world of bizarre beliefs run amuck. He'd personally found himself offered as a sacrifice. Switching from Spider Queens to killers who'd convinced themselves they were lampreys so they could feed blood to gods didn't sound like a bargain he was ready to make. But who was he kidding? He'd do it for another shot at getting his old job back. Writing for the paper was that important to him.

"What?" Rex asked.

"What *what*?" Andy asked, shaken from his memories and concerns.

"Did you ask me what god the Lamprey was feeding?" Rex had a curious gleam in his eyes. He stopped walking and looked Andy up and down, reassessing him.

"Yes," Andy said. "Which god is he killing for?"

Rex frowned. "He didn't say." Rex glanced around the barren night streets. "Andy, you said you worked at the *Advertiser*."

"That's right."

"Then tell me the name of your editor." Rex had taken a step back. Getting ready to bolt.

"Doyle Jeffries, the same as you." Andy's answer calmed him down. He understood that Rex had had a long day. He'd been manhandled and locked up. But there was more to it. "Aren't you acting a little paranoid?" he asked.

Rex nodded. "Sure, kid. But if you knew the things I know, you'd be paranoid too."

You'd be surprised what I know, Andy thought. I've seen spiders the size of Model Ts.

But this wasn't the time or place to share horror stories.

Rex continued walking and talking. "The last part of the letter was confusing. The writing got sloppier as it went on, harder to read. The detectives snatched it away before I could finish. They were disappointed when they saw me acting more curious than guilty. They're out of their element. This killer isn't a punk with a knife or even a gangster. It creeped me out too. Ritual murder. Blood sacrifices. We're dealing with a dark and twisted mind here. Perhaps the occult."

Rex was looking at him strangely again, out of the corner of his eye.

"I'll say." Andy agreed. "The Lamprey's being bold by contacting the city's top cop the way he did. It's like he's daring him to catch him. Saying, 'Here I am. Come get me.' Do you think he lives in the sewers?" Andy couldn't help but stare at the manhole cover in the street up ahead. Normally, he'd walk right over it without thinking twice. And the storm drains – they'd passed at least three sieve-like grates since they started. There was a whole world under Arkham. A hidden network of tunnels made for transporting water but big enough to fit a person. They spread out in the darkness, connecting to every neighborhood. Like a web. Andy shuddered. *No webs, please.*

The pipes were an organized labyrinth. Built for one purpose but suitable for another: travel. A person could pop in or out anywhere, if they knew their way around the maze.

Rex said, "I can't be sure. But the sewers are involved. They're a big part of this. The key to it, if you ask me. Only the police didn't know that at the beginning. They weren't looking for a single perpetrator. The cops first thought the killings were unrelated. A series of accidents."

"What? People choked themselves, drained their own blood, and then fell in the pipes?"

Rex smiled, stroking his beard. "I know, it is hard to picture, isn't it? But the lack of imagination of our friends in blue is rivaled only by their deductive deficiencies. Oh, another thing. The missing blood? That wasn't picked up right away either. They suspected, ah, animal predation."

"Vampire rats?"

"Sewer rats, anyway. Victim One was a missing dockworker. He'd been in the pipes a while before they found him and was, shall we say, deteriorating? Now Victim Two was fresher. Another man, still unidentified. Probably not a local. Somebody passing through town who ended up passing under the town in a brick channel. Not found in the pipes but stuck in a storm drain with dead leaves and sticks. Half-exposed. Same broken neck, same type of incised neck wound, and blood loss was the cause of death. But Victim Three sealed the deal. A waitress only in the water for one day. They found her in the river. She washed out by the docks, but the belt of her green overcoat snagged on an anchor chain. Otherwise, she'd have gone to the bottom for a few days and probably gone out to sea. The curious fisherman who found her thought her bare foot was a marker buoy until he got closer. That's why we're going back to the sewers tonight."

"Why?" Andy was confused. Wouldn't that be the last place Rex wanted to revisit? Andy figured he'd want to go home and get cleaned up, a change of clothes.

"Because if I'm right, all those pipes where bodies were found will connect to the Big Drain site. To the chamber they broke into this morning, to be precise. If we follow the right tunnels, we'll find the Lamprey. Eventually. That chamber's his base. His lair, if you will."

Andy shook his head. "They've got guards posted at the Big Drain. No way we'll get in."

Rex's strides grew longer. He was picking up speed. The scent of a story will do that.

"Wrong, my boy. We can't get in that end, but we can go the other way. Start where one of the bodies was found and backtrack to the chamber. There's something in there I want to see."

"Something in the chamber? What chamber? What did they find in it?"

"They broke through a drain tunnel wall and found a kind of room. That's where they think the killer might've taken the missing worker. It's a hub of old passageways. I'm not going to tell you what they found inside, because I don't quite know myself. Say they found *something* in the chamber – call it an artifact. Or maybe a curiosity. Yes, I like that better. The curiosity was a giant crystal hanging from the ceiling, as big as a man and filled with strange colors. Mayor Kane and his entourage looked mighty curious about it. I've got a theory, Andy. I'm not ready to share it, but the parts are close to fitting. These weird killings. That business with the blood. The letter. A taunting killer giving himself an odd name. Tell me now, you ever heard of the Prism?"

Andy thought about it, then shook his head. "What's the Prism?" he asked.

"A dark legend to some. An Arkham myth, so they say. Yet I'm starting to wonder…"

After that Rex fell silent, refusing to elaborate and paused patting his pockets only to discover, and lament, the loss of his reporter's notebook. "Must've dropped it when I fell," he mumbled. "Drat! I had valuable notes on the Prism in there. Maybe we'll find it..."

Oh boy, Andy thought, Rex really knew how to flick the bait to keep a fishy following.

"So where to now?"

"To the river. We're going to begin where the last victim ended up. There's no covering over the drainpipe emptying into the Miskatonic, just an opening. We can crawl right inside."

Andy swallowed, wondering if he might've been better off sweeping out hallways.

The River Docks bustled with life during the day. Seagulls wheeled overhead. Their cries, like rubber squeaking on glass, filled the air. Bird droppings dappled every post, each shoreline rock and ship's deck. Sailors threw ropes or steered their vessels into port. Dockworkers milled about, waiting, or marched back and forth hauling goods to the warehouses. If the water sparkled just so, if the wind blew out, or if you didn't look too hard, you might've thought, *Ahh, progress.*

But Rivertown wasn't the Merchant District. And a closer inspection of the people, or the ramshackle buildings, told a different tale. The docks were narrow and never repaired. One mislaid step and you'd fall through a hole in a rotten board and go for an unplanned swim. Afterward, you'd probably spend a few days recuperating in your sickbed, or maybe even in the hospital if things got bad, your body fighting off whatever disease you caught by swallowing whichever toxins mixed with the water oozing between the Miskatonic's banks. The fortunate ones got off with a queasy stomach or an odd rash that never completely went away.

The River Docks were the epitome of decline. Luckily, Andy and Rex arrived at night. In a fog. So they couldn't see much. Rex sent Andy up to one of the ships to barter for supplies.

"How'd it go?" Rex asked when he got back. Andy showed him two candles, a box of matches, partly full, and a spool of fishing line.

"Not bad. I couldn't find any string. But I got myself a pair of boots." Andy lifted his right foot. The sole flapped daffily up and down.

"What did it cost you?" Rex asked.

"All the money I had. And my cap. Oh, and my suspenders." Andy showed him where his trousers gaped at the waist.

"Not bad," Rex said, though his expression was less confident.

"The sailor guy gave me a piece of rope."

"Oh?"

"For a belt," Andy said as he threaded it through the loops around his waist.

"Then we're ready," Rex said. He smacked his hands together.

"We are." Andy couldn't help but feel the thrill of the chase. Though what they were chasing after, he couldn't say. Maybe a killer. Maybe evidence of his elusive trail. A story? That's for sure. Redemption? Perhaps. Did he dare dream of getting his job back? It was too early to tell. But this feeling of camaraderie was better than anything he'd felt since getting fired.

The two men picked their way down the rocky shore above the pipelines. Andy tried not to think about the varieties of slime he was touching on the rocks. "When this is over, I'm going to take a nice, long, hot bath," he muttered.

"Uh huh," Rex said, distracted. He was concentrating on his next steps. When he stood directly in front of the pipeline, he paused, lighting his candle. He was careful not to drop the matchbox, stuffing it in his pocket.

"I'm going in. You wait here," he said.

"I wait?" Andy said.

"In case I don't come out. You'll have to go for help. I'll leave you this candle. Here's two matches. I'm taking the rest." Rex held the burning candle in the mouth of the first pipe. A trickle of tea-colored liquid ran out into the river. Dank air blew gently from the opening.

Andy peered over his shoulder. "How will you know which way to go?"

"I've thought about that. It's the flow, see. I'll follow the flow but going the opposite way. The body washed out here. It snagged right there." He pointed. "You can't see it now." The fog above the river – it was like staring at a gray wall. Andy saw nothing past it.

"Right out there?" He lit his candle, which proved to be utterly inadequate. The rain had stopped, but he felt colder down by the water too. He wasn't prepared for this; neither of them was.

A foghorn blew a sad note somewhere downriver toward Kingsport and the coast.

"Trust me. I saw them bringing her in. I'm going to take this candle. Now, I don't suppose I'll be able to hear you once I get going, but you might be able to hear me. Stay close. If I run into trouble, I'll shout for you. After I go deeper inside, I'll use this to signal you." Rex unwound a few feet of fishing line. He tied the end around his wrist, passing the spool to Andy.

Andy took the spool. Rex gave a couple of solid tugs to show

how he'd alert him. Giving Andy one last nod and a slap on the arm, Rex embarked.

"Here goes nothing," he said, ducking inside. His boots sloshed; the candle flickered.

Andy was so happy to learn he wasn't accompanying Rex into the sewer that he never bothered to question Rex's expedition strategy. Rex was a pro, savvy. He had experience.

It was right around the time that Rex's candlelight disappeared that the question burst into Andy's head. What was Rex going to do if he succeeded? What if he found the Lamprey?

12
Skull Moon

It was late, but Charlie was used to working after hours at City Hall. Being the mayor of Arkham was a twenty-four-hour-a-day job, he always said. He sat at his desk with his tie loosened. The only pool of light came from his desk lamp. He had a cigar burning, and a phone in his hand.

"Mandy, I'm telling you, it was the craziest thing I ever saw. The crystal had symbols etched into it. They resembled runes. I know, I thought the same thing. But we caught the Southside Strangler. He's dead." Charlie nodded. "I guess he might've carved these things down there years ago. It probably wasn't even him who did it. They looked old. I can't say exactly how I know. But I want you exploring this. You've got all those spooky old tomes at the university. Come up with anything you can about strange symbols, particularly carvings. Here in Arkham."

As he hung up, a gentle shiver ran through him. Talking about the carvings and the crystal unsettled him. There was nothing specifically threatening about them, except how he felt.

Mandy Thompson was a researcher at Miskatonic University. She was smart and had an interest in peculiarities associated with Arkham's history of occultism – things Charlie didn't, and wouldn't, talk about in public. Mandy had connections with prominent Arkham professors who knew about esoteric topics. If Charlie went to the professors directly, word would get out.

But Mandy could be discreet. He felt bad calling her after the clock had struck midnight, but he knew she often stayed up late, reading. She had trouble sleeping. Just like he did. That's how they'd met. Charlie turned insomniac for a stretch of time around the Southside Strangler slayings. He'd gone for a walk to clear his head and wound up on the Miskatonic campus. He saw a light burning and a woman sitting at a long table in one of the libraries. He knocked on the window and they both startled – Mandy when she saw his ugly mug in the glass, and Charlie when she screamed and he fell into the bushes. She'd recognized him, of course, and after she unlocked the door and helped him get untangled from the shrubbery, they struck up a conversation about sleeplessness, and unsolved murders, and how the moon looked cold and lonesome and scary at night, like a skull rolling across a black velvet cloth.

Charlie had thought about Professor William Dyer, a geologist at Miskatonic, who shared a mutual fascination about Antarctica with the mayor. The two men had met at a reception following a public lecture given by a Professor Lake from the biology department, concerning the potentially revolutionary fossil record "waiting for us" under the ice of the remote continent.

The mayor faltered in calling Dyer for the same reason he avoided contacting other faculty members. He needed matters kept private even if – especially if – they proved to be momentous.

Charlie dialed another number from his little black address book.

"Hello, this is Mayor Kane, may I speak to Oscar Hurley? Yes,

I do realize the hour. I wouldn't be calling if it wasn't important. I'm sure Mr Hurley wouldn't want to find out in the morning that he'd missed me. If you choose to decide for him, so be it. It's your hide, not mine."

Charlie waited. A minute or so later, a slurred voice came on the line.

"Charlie! To what do I owe this interruption? I was entertaining a guest in my hunting den. But a call from the mayor isn't something I turn away lightly. This had better be important, that's all I can say. You need a favor. Is that it, heh? Speak up, old boy. Before I hang up."

Charlie winced. He didn't like mixing with people like Hurley – a man who'd trample his own mother for a glint of gold. Hurley ran a mining company. Ran it over anyone who got in his way. But he was a big political donor come election time. He paid off all the candidates who had any chance of winning, so there was no way he'd lose. Then, when Hurley Mining needed help pushing through a land sale or with local permits, the phone would ring at the mayor's office. Favors worked two ways. Hurley knew this. So did Charlie.

"Oscar, I have a strange request. I need a geologist. Tomorrow morning, first thing. At the Big Drain. We discovered something in one of the tunnels we're excavating. I'd like an expert to tell me what it is, and how to proceed."

Charlie listened as Hurley slurped his drink. Something expensive. No doubt rare. He pictured Hurley clutching a crystal goblet. Richly hued liquid swirling. Maybe a vintage port. Or French brandy. Armagnac. He'd spill more on his Persian carpet than Charlie could afford.

"I have just the man. I'll send him over." Hurley cleared his throat. "You haven't struck gold, have you?" Hurley laughed. But to Charlie, it sounded like he was only half-joking.

"No, nothing you'd care about. An obstruction, really. But I don't know if the scientists will get mad at us if we blow it to smithereens. If your man thinks it's significant, why, after we dig the thing out, we'll donate it to the museum. You can put your name on the display."

"Hellfire! If it's worth any money, I'll keep it."

He wasn't kidding, Charlie knew. The man had a one-track mind. Charlie had to be careful dealing with him. Hurley appeared simple, a brute with deep pockets, but the man was shrewd, ruthless, and vindictive. If he felt Charlie was disappointing him in any way, he'd strike back.

"Thanks, Oscar. You're a true friend to me. And to the city of Arkham."

The line was dead.

Charlie went to the window, puffing on his cigar. He had the oddest sensation that he couldn't quite shake, an uncomfortable tickle inside his bones. He felt restless, fidgety.

It was foggy outside. In London they called this a peasouper. The mist had an olive-green tinge to it. Charlie was sure if he opened the window, he'd smell it too. Sulfur. As if the devil were rising and he'd called him forth. "Well, maybe I have," he thought, chuckling. Usually, fog this thick stayed down by the river. Tonight, it crept all the way to the steps of City Hall.

Up in the sky where the moon should be, he saw nothing. A gray slate. But he knew what was there – cold and lonesome, tucked in its black velvet blanket.

The skull moon. Eyes like caverns staring, unblinking, down on Arkham.

Death. That's all he could think about since Budzinski walked off in the dark with that pick in his hands and that... that frightening blankness inside of him...

Was he the strangler? Or the Lamprey, as the police chief called him. Charlie didn't know. But something was wrong with the digger, as if he were possessed. There at the end, inside the chamber, before Budzinski ran off into one of those unmarked passages, the man acted more like a creature driven by hidden impulses he couldn't understand, let alone control.

That's why Charlie called the police guard dogs off Rex Murphy. They needed to focus. Nobody was sure who was killing those people they were finding in the sewers. The cops told him they suspected an ongoing skirmish among rival bootlegging operations. Bootleggers used the sewers and storm drains to hide and transport booze. They had their own hand-dug tunnels, and there were natural caves in the area too. The Big Drain project crossed a lot of risky paths, made too many dangerous people angry. Charlie knew this. He'd had threats sent to his office. Some were told to him face to face by local "businessmen" who wanted in on the renovation, so they might steal as much as they could, cheating the citizens with inferior workmanship. Who cared if new tunnels collapsed? Who cared if the city flooded with sewage whenever it rained? Charlie did, that's who. He wanted this construction project done right. It was his legacy. A cleaner, safer, Arkham. Where people wanted to live. Where they could breathe the air and drink the water without getting sick. A healthy, vital city.

Instead, his head was filled with skulls. Unseen sinister forces menaced his thoughts. Fear sat in his gut like a heavy chunk of rock... of cloudy pink crystal... Etched with peculiar symbols that seemed so familiar and yet totally alien. Charlie shuddered. He needed to go home and climb into bed. He was tired. That was probably why he was feeling so odd. A few hours of sleep would cure him of this uneasiness. Yawning, he turned down the blinds and switched off his desk lamp. In the darkness, the orange tip of his cigar was the only sign he was still there.

The mayor stumbled out into the fog, by all observations, a man alone in his city. Streetlights floated like hazy planets in the mist. His footsteps rang on the cobbles. He walked quickly, refusing to look over his shoulder, despite his inability to shake the sensation that a cold malevolence was tracking him from the shadows all the way to his doorstep.

Awakened, and keenly aware of everything he was doing – not out of personal consideration for him or anyone living in Arkham, but rather the opposite. It cared not for people. The force of it was as impersonal as a shark, or an avalanche that crashed through a mountain village entombing houses and villagers alike under a freezing blanket of killing ice. Charlie's mind's eye flashed on such a scene, only Arkham replaced the village under the ice, and the color of its destroyer wasn't snow-white or even a scratchy gray.

It was red.

13
Molten Light

For future inclusion Entry 100.39 of the Shrouded Archive of the Thirteen Δ ≡

They came out of the tunnels into darkness. Silent. In a slow procession. In their folded hands they carried black candles to illuminate their way. The hot black wax dripped into the puddles on the tunnel floor and made a greasy hissing sound. The candleflames danced on the rock walls. The walkers wore long cloaks with deep hoods pulled forward, and the bottoms of their cloaks dragged, growing heavy with water soaked up from the drains. The hooded figures shuffled into the chamber. They gathered around the pink tooth – the Crystal Fang – and the Fang pulsed with light from within at their arrival. As if it had life (which it might have). As if it felt joy (which it certainly did not).

They took turns touching the crystal, greeting it. Candles raised, they began a jarring chant; the chant became a song, and the song was harsh. But it was not harsh to their ears. Their mouths had learned to form the unusual shapes. Their lips no longer fought the contours that made them grimace. Their jaws did not ache from speaking the words of an inhuman tongue.

Tonight was unlike any night that had come before. Because their relic had been discovered. The situation was more dangerous for them now. They needed to act at once.

So, in haste, a ritual was decided upon. New words were written, penned on a parchment with long, elegant, elaborate strokes in ink of fathomless black.

Theirs was a world of night secrets, of hiddenness glorified and cherished. Thirteen was their number. Each one was chosen. The Thirteen, also known by many names. All members equal in spirit, so it was proclaimed. Their leader was a conduit, a gateway to messages and messengers from beyond. The Crystal Fang recognized the leader's voice. All voices were heard, but the leader's voice reached a level of natural attunement making intercommunication possible. When those gathered ended their song, the Fang dimmed but remained aglow. It gave off a moist heat that filled the chamber. There was a scent to it: cold, ammoniac, alien.

The leader was the tallest member of the group. The low dome of the underground room accentuated their height as they lifted the parchment with the words of the new ceremony overhead for all to see. The leader's hood fell back. Long dark hair framed a rectangular face with upturned eyes reflecting candlelight. The cleft chin and forthright stare suggested strength.

The leader was a woman.

Her penetrating gaze swept the chamber. She had a curious black mole on her cheek that often drew the attention of others, as it did now, despite the tenebrous surroundings. Her father and grandmother had identical moles. Anyone lucky enough to have known them in life remarked upon the family resemblance across generations. For those who hadn't known them, there were surviving photos from the catastrophic fire at their ancestral home. Notoriety ensured people would seek them out. [Copies of the photos are included in the Shrouded Archive.]

She read the words of the ceremony aloud. It was the first and only time they would ever be spoken. These were not human words as we understand them. If you, or any uninitiated person, stood there in the dark recesses of the stinking world of the Arkham sewer system, you would not comprehend the meaning of anything being said. However, you might feel… a charge in the atmosphere, a change inside your body, a worming, boring deeper than your body into a part of you beyond time and bodily self. This change might be something you did not desire, but after hearing the words, you would be unable to un-hear them and would be utterly incapable of returning to being the old you. You would be the new you. A different thing than you were before. You would sense that your former self had been shed like a snakeskin on the desert floor.

It happened on the inside, your inner coil uncoiling. Stretching long. Flexing. Glistening and muscular, extending like ropes weaving hallucinatory patterns and colors. Are you better than before? Worse? That was an issue of perspective, subject to interpretation in the aftermath. This is a matter of telling what occurred that night, not analyzing the results. The telling is this.

The leader said the new words and the Fang responded.

It brightened. It revealed its chromas, displaying hues people have no names for. It pulsed. The pulsing entranced those watching from inside their cloaks. Minds opened. Soft and vulnerable, their quivering jellied sentience, cupped in pried-apart shells, cowered from the light.

The leader hesitated. The parchment wavered in her trembling hand.

She stumbled over her words. Although she was a master, she was also a student, and this lesson was difficult. Fairness was never important here. She stumbled over words she did not write herself but was appointed to recite. Another had written them with great care and precision, every quill stroke was an artist's work. She stumbled, and in stumbling, said something – not wrong, for right and wrong did not exist here – lamentable, for her at least.

But it was not a mistake. Every mistake has its unique design and designer, even the most chaotic, and it is the perfection of itself.

At the lamentable utterance a vicious bolt of molten light pierced the leader's body, passing through her so it showed on the rock wall behind her. Yet she remained upright, rigid.

Where it hit the wall, it left a burning scorch mark – a smoked star – and it changed the composition of the rock. The candleflames unraveled to strings of smoke. The Fang and its bolt were the only source of light, and their brilliance was too much to look at. Twenty-six eyes ached from seeing. But they did not close. Years later, bright lights would bother them still.

The leader did not die, though some in the room feared that had happened. They gasped, then moved toward her as one would toward a friend in trouble, but then they stopped.

For nothing could be done.

Or in this case, undone.

The leader electrified. Hairs floated up from her head like a hundred thousand feelers. She became like something from another world, or from abyssal ocean depths, sensing…

She did not drop the parchment, but her fingers curled into a tight ball, and she clutched the parchment in her fist. She was shaking all over so that if you were standing there in the dark, you would have seen her cloaked figure vibrate into a blur. You would never forget the sight.

The bolt disappeared, switched off like a light, like one of the lamps the sewer workers used. The leader dropped. Crumpled. She did not topple over but sat on her haunches, her head lolling as if she'd had her neck snapped. Like a ragdoll she folded up in a heap... for a while.

The others stood speechless, stunned.

One of the acolytes finally rushed forward to rescue the parchment before it dipped into the water. It would be preserved in their archive, a pivotal part of their history. And Arkham's.

All was not lost. Slowly they relit their tapers. The air smelled of sulfur. The leader rose to her feet. It must've been an act of sheer will to keep her composure. She replaced her hood. One by one, the Thirteen filed out of the chamber, returning to the tunnels, to their identities in the daylight world where they hid their cloaks, candles, and ritual magic in closets and drawers.

That night – the night after the daylighters discovered the relic – transformed reality. All that came before had merely set the stage, mere hints and previews, laying the groundwork, ringing in the age of the crystal, the dawn of blood.

The revolution had begun.

Here it is written by the hand of ***** Entry 10039 of the Shrouded Archive of the Thirteen △ ≡

14
The Line

Rex had been wandering in the sewer for what felt like hours. He was hopelessly lost and starting to feel the first pangs of panic. The Big Drain site was close to the river; he should've found it by now. Who knew that there were so many tunnels under Arkham? Some looked dry, most were wet. A few looked natural, carved by water, not humans. There were pipes half-filled with rubble and debris. He left those alone, worried he might get stuck. His candle was burning low. All he had remaining was a stub of wax with a guttering flame cupped in the palm of his hand.

I feel like primitive man, he thought. I've discovered fire but I've yet to put it to good use, and once it burns out, I might not be able to get it going again. He'd stumbled across bits of wood in the sewer, branches and sawn boards, but they were too damp to burn. He had a box of matches but nothing to set fire to. What would he do with a torch? Burn himself, most likely.

No, he had to head back to the river, before his light went out. He tried to push the possibility of blackout to the back of his mind.

He couldn't recall how many turns he'd made but he couldn't

have gone that far. The fishing line would have run out and he'd have felt the tug at his wrist. He tested the knotted bit secured around his shirtsleeve.

I'll just follow this back. Like Hansel and Gretel.

The line seemed awfully slack. As he gathered it in, he looped the excess around his arm.

I'm reeling myself in, he mused with a wry smile. It was surprising that he felt no tension on the line. Poor Andy was probably worried sick about him.

Rex hadn't noticed until now, but the candlelight had dimmed considerably. The pipe was mostly shadow. The light from his rapidly diminishing wick barely cast enough light to see more than a few feet ahead. Mostly it lit up his face and hands, making it hard to find the fishing line in the murky water flowing around his ankles.

Follow the flow, he reminded himself. These pipes empty at the river. Eventually, I'll get where I want to go. He bucked up his confidence to tamp down his fear. Was it a right or left coming up here? The end of the line dipped into the murk where two tunnels split. He bent over carefully, unable to discern which way his precious lifeline led. Don't drop the candle in the water, he told himself. Then you'll be in a fix. Left…

The line went left.

He felt it tightening.

Ah, must be doing something correctly. He followed the line which stood above the waterline now, like a silvery spiderweb thread, spinning out of the darkness, dripping with pearls of glistening dew. Rex was curious, looking at the line as it climbed higher into the tunnel and wrapped around an upcoming corner. A wave of cool air blew around him. He smelled ammonia.

How did the line get up so high?

He balanced the candle nub and coiled the line around his arm, but his eyes stared ahead. As he approached the curve in the pipe, he stopped.

He stood on the threshold of an intersection. The tunnel he was standing in ended in a "T." He didn't remember coming through it on his way in. Nevertheless, he must have, since the line clearly bent around the turn to the right. It was taut. So taut, he feared it might break. He twanged it with his thumb gently, watching it vibrate and shiver off droplets at eye level.

Again, he asked himself, "How'd it get up so high?" Must've snagged on a brick sticking out of the wall. Yet he hesitated before he went any farther into the junction. He raised the dwindling candleflame. The fire bent backward toward him, confirming his sense that air was blowing past him. I must be closer to the river than I thought, he guessed.

The candleflame suddenly grew much dimmer. Rex felt the heat of the wick in his palm. But he wasn't looking at the candle. He was looking ahead.

The fishing line went to the right. But to the left the tunnel glowed with a faint pink light.

It was the crystal formation he saw before! It had to be! That same unusual shade lighting the chamber with the mayor and his team. Now that pink color stained the bricks in front of Rex.

Well, he supposed even the unluckiest of people get lucky on occasion. He had his scoop. It was waiting for him right around the corner.

Any lingering feelings of panic receded as Rex walked into the place where the tunnels joined up. He looked left and saw a stronger aura of pink tinting the rough bricks and cloudy water.

It wasn't until the last possible moment that he saw the hand stretching from the right.

The gray gloved hand pinched out his candle. It was too absurd to be believed!

"See here–" Rex began to protest, until that same hand, and its twin, grasped his throat, relentlessly throttling him. He saw stars in the darkness. In his losing struggle he drifted from one darkness to another, deeper, blacker still, and more impenetrable.

15
New Mission

The phone was ringing. Even though the museum office was small, it took some time for Jake to maneuver from where he'd been standing at the bookcase over to the desk. He almost dropped his crutches but managed to save them at the last moment, all while cradling the phone handle under his jaw.

"Hello?"

"May I please speak to Ursula Downs?" A woman's voice. Firm and right to the point. Calling kind of early too. Just after six. The birds were making noise in the trees outside. The office filled with pale blue light.

"I'm sorry. Ursula Downs isn't here," he said.

"May I ask when she'll be returning?"

"Oh, six months. Give or take a month or two. She's out of the country on an expedition. In Tibet, if she's kept to her schedule. She loves to get sidetracked. You learn a lot that way, she says." Jake smiled thinking about Ursula out there having an adventure. He felt a pang of disappointment for missing out, too. This was new territory for him. He hadn't gotten used to the feeling yet. He was determined never to get too comfortable with it. Make the feeling temporary, he told himself. Let the pain become fuel. He'd been with Ursula on every one of her "official" explorations for years. But that just wasn't possible right now. He had other priorities.

"May I ask to whom I am speaking?" the woman said.

"I'm Jake. I partner with Ursula. She's going solo this time. And who are you?"

"Dr Carolyn Fern."

Jake detected an underlying tension, although the answer was straightforward. Did her formality hide something? She's being awfully cautious with me, he thought. It put his guard up.

"Are you an archaeologist, by any chance?" he asked. He scratched at his knee but couldn't get to the spot that was itching underneath the laces on the leather harness strapped to his thigh. He tried poking a pencil at it. Ahh, much better. The thing got hot and was heavier than it looked, though the ankle and foot were covered by his sock and shoe, matching his healthy leg.

"A psychologist. Did you say your name was Jake? Is this Jake Williams?"

Jake shifted his crutches off to one side and perched on the end of the desk. His curiosity was growing.

"I did, and I am. Now, why all this mystery?"

There was a pause. "I'm calling on behalf of a patient of mine. At Arkham Sanatorium. We've been unable to reach any next of kin, and it's important that we find a contact as soon as possible. She may be in grave danger, I'm afraid. Do you know a woman named Maude Brion?"

Jake felt a horrible sinking, as if he were a stone falling and falling into a deep pit.

"Yes, I know Maude. Is she hurt?"

His hands were sweaty. He felt his heart thumping. The last time he saw Maude they'd just arrived back in Arkham from Manaus, Brazil. His condition had stabilized after he'd been fighting a terrible infection on the ship home. Fever dreams. Time became a jumble for him. His confusion gave him a little insight into what Maude was going through, since her "visions" had gotten the better of her on the way back to Arkham.

They said their goodbyes in this very office. He'd been in a wheelchair, his color gray, Ursula had told him later, but the fever was gone. He just looked, and felt, wrung out. Maude was supposed to be heading back to Hollywood. Ursula tried to convince her to stay in Arkham until she felt more like herself. Andy was mad at her for ruining the film evidence they had of the Spider Queen, but even he could see she wasn't thinking right, and they'd all pleaded with her to remain in town for a while. She'd been through so much. Maude agreed to check in to a hotel and see a doctor. But the next day, when Ursula called on her at the hotel, she found Maude was gone. All three of them felt guilty then.

They'd let Maude down, abandoning her to the whole wide world, and, more dangerously, to her dreams. Her mental state was beyond fragile. She'd been traumatized like the rest of them, but her suffering might've been the worst of all; it burrowed down inside her brain.

"Sleepwalking through her days," Ursula had said.

They assumed she'd taken off for California like she'd been planning. She'd run away from Arkham, so they'd thought, but, apparently, she hadn't. She'd been here all along.

Why, he could walk to where she was staying. True, it would take him some time, but he could do it. He'd been bored lately, frankly, and Ursula's departure made his boredom more acute. He'd grown antsy, unable to sit still, unable to read a book. Life felt dull and repetitious.

Dr Fern continued, "She's undergoing treatment for sleep disturbances. But it's more complicated than that. I don't want to talk on the phone. Can we meet to discuss her case?"

"Sure, I can come to the sanatorium—" Jake started to say.

"No. Not there," Dr Fern said quickly. "What about St Mary's Hospital?"

"That's perfect. I'll be at the hospital this morning for an appointment," Jake said.

"Why is that?" Her tone sounded suspicious. Paranoia was going around these days.

"Maude and I met in the Amazon, during a tough expedition. I was injured. I lost one of my legs below the knee. I'm rehabilitating." He hadn't gotten used to talking about what had happened. When people saw him, they saw his crutches first and foremost, and although the prosthetic limb he was learning to use functioned like a leg, he hadn't mastered walking yet. His strength was coming back but balancing continued to be a challenge. He was getting better. Still, those crutches…

"I'm sorry to hear that. Maude did mention your being wounded."

"Oh, did she?" Jake wondered what Maude said about it, how much truth she revealed. Did she tell you a giant spider ate my leg? he wondered. That sort of story might get you committed.

"Let's meet at the St Mary's cafeteria. When is your appointment?" Dr Fern asked.

"Eight o'clock, sharp. I'll be finished at nine," he said. "Tell me, is Maude in danger?"

"I'd rather not say. I'll fill you in when we meet. Deal? How will I know you?"

"I'll be the guy with the crutches," he said, hating the words as they came out. The awkward self-consciousness bugged him. Then he added, "Wearing a red carnation in his lapel."

"Fine. See you at nine o'clock. I'll be sitting by the last window," she said.

They said goodbye.

Jake checked his watch. Less than two hours until his rehab appointment. What to do until then? No use worrying about Maude. He'd know the facts soon enough – though he couldn't help but feel the news wasn't going to be good. Fight the fight when it arrives, he told himself. Now clear your head.

He decided to leave early and work up a sweat before the day got rolling. Warm up the muscles by walking on cobblestones without tripping up. Down the stairs and one lap around the campus for starters. He'd been stuck inside for days because of all the rain, growing agitated in body and mind. The walk to the hospital would do him good on all fronts. Besides, he had a new mission.

He needed to buy a carnation too.

16
Intentional Mark

Andy woke with a start.

His clothes were covered with morning dew. His skin too. Wiping his hands on his pants, he shuddered at the filmy, slippery way they felt. He was disoriented, sitting there on the rocks by the river, the open sewer pipe dribbling in front of him, sounding like gravel dropping into the river below. Staring at the spool in his lap, he tried desperately to remember what was happening. Then it all caught up to him fast: he was waiting for Rex Murphy who was searching for the Lamprey inside the sewer. The thing in his lap was a spool of fishing line, and Rex had the other end tied around his wrist. They'd agreed that he'd give it a pull to signal Andy if he got in trouble. Andy looked at the spool, turning it over in his hands. It was empty. There was no line on it. He stared into the drainpipe. It was dark in there, a permanent night despite the sunrise.

I had a candle, Andy remembered. He looked for it and discovered it on one of the rocks, laying sideways in a puddle of hardened wax. At some point the flame had gone out. When I fell asleep, he realized. I was supposed to be paying attention, backing up Rex if he needed help. But it had been a long day.

The seagulls whirled. It sounded like they were laughing. Andy felt panic. He was supposed to be at work soon, and now he had let down Rex by falling asleep on him. Where was the reporter? Why hadn't he come back?

Andy unstuck the candle from the rock. He fumbled in his pockets until he found the last match he had. He struck the match and lit the candle, his mind racing. What was the last thing he could remember? He'd been sitting on the rocks. He'd found a place that felt almost comfortable, like a stone seat. And the weather was damp, a fog rolling over the boats and the docks, the water lapping at the pilings. It was quiet. The electric lights on the ships and warehouses looked fuzzy, amber haloes around them, everything softened. Up in the rigging, fog swirled, tearing itself apart on the masts; wraiths drifted among the smokestacks, playing a game of hide-and-seek, floating off or getting sucked up into the low, gray sky. Gone.

Now the fog was gone too.

Like Rex.

Andy rubbed his face to wake himself up. His skin felt rubbery like a mask.

Workers busied themselves loading and unloading cargo. Fishermen prepared their nets.

Rex. He needed to find Rex.

Andy stuck his arm into the sewer pipe. The candle flickered. Its light didn't go very far.

He took a step in and felt his boot slide forward as if a conveyor belt was pulling him along, daring him in. With his other hand he braced himself along the curved wall. The bricks were damp and cool. He took another step. The water wasn't deep right now, but that might change.

Andy looked down for any sign of the fishing line.

Nothing.

He took a few more steps.

The sounds from the dock shrunk immediately behind him, as if some unseen hand had turned a volume knob. Instead, he heard his own breathing, the trickle of the pipes, dripping.

What probably happened was that Rex got caught up in what he was doing, kept walking around and the end of the fishing spool just ran out; he'd pulled it in after him. So, what Andy had to do was find that end of the line and then trace it back to Rex. That wasn't so bad. The pipe was straight here. If he looked back, he could see daylight at the river end. He had his candle to light the way forward and the footing was good now. The old boots he'd bought off the sailor wouldn't necessarily keep his feet dry, but he had a good grip on the bottom of the tunnel.

He went ahead, venturing farther into the system. He couldn't say how long it took before he reached the first turn. Minutes felt like hours.

It was a "Y" split. Right or left?

If I always choose right, then I can find my way back out, he told himself. Right he went.

Andy tried to imagine the streets above him. Which way would lead to the Main Street tunnel entrance? The Big Drain headquarters. The chamber Rex had told him about. The hub of old passageways where the mayor and the dig team discovered the "curiosity."

Andy gazed back at the shrinking circle of light where the river was. His way out.

I'll just have to remember. Keep to the right.

He walked into the new tunnel. He told himself not to look

back, but he did. Seeing darkness and bricks was worse than he expected, bringing claustrophobia crashing down on him. As if he'd been entombed.

Just keep going. And don't think about getting lost. Ha! What a joke! It was all he could think about. Then another thought came into his head. There must be manholes above me somewhere. And ladders to climb out those manholes. Even if he got lost, he'd wander around until he found a ladder and pop out into the light of aboveground Arkham. That idea settled his nerves and kept him from retreating. That and the idea that he owed Rex an obligation. He had to back him up. Together they would nail this Lamprey story. Andy would get his old job at the *Advertiser* back in a blaze of glory.

What a comeback! Forget about the Spider Queen – even though that was a great story too! Now he had the Lamprey. One monster knocked him off the paper, and another would get him back on. That was poetic justice. He only had to find Rex first.

The tunnel widened. He could straighten up so that his shoulders didn't brush the bricks. Feeling better, he took a deep breath, filling his lungs. The smell was what you might expect, but he was getting used to that. The water wasn't too deep and he hadn't seen any rats yet. He picked up his pace, careful to dip his candle down low every few feet to search for any trace of the fishing line. Up ahead the texture of the darkness seemed to change.

He couldn't make out the details, but it was different. But when he got there, he saw it at once. Another intersection. This one was bigger.

Three pipes met at this juncture. If he continued with the pipe he was in, it curved off to the left. Two new pipes joined it from the right. The flow of water pouring out of them was faster. The water looked gray and milky and ran past his ankles. On the walls, he saw the high-water mark, elephant-gray bricks changed to brown. If it got to that level, he'd be sunk up to his chest, and the force of the water would be strong enough that he wouldn't be able to stand. He'd get carried along wherever the surge was going. Maybe it went out the pipe where he came in. Maybe, sometimes, it didn't. Could he keep his head above the water long enough to escape?

He hoped so.

"Don't scare yourself," he said out loud. "The water is shallow. Now, which way?"

If he stuck with his original plan, he'd go right. But that tunnel was narrower. And it was set higher into the wall. He'd have to step up to climb in. The top of it was lower, too. To keep going that way, he'd have to stoop over. He didn't like it. The feeling was all wrong. Rex wouldn't have gone that way. Would he?

No, Andy decided. He would've gone straight on, with the curve.

Andy was sure he'd remember his choice. But to be safe, he decided to make a mark on the wall of bricks. High enough that it wouldn't get washed away. How to make such a mark though? Rummaging in his pockets, he found a few coins. He chose the biggest one, a Buffalo nickel.

Walking up to the place where the other two pipes came in, he started scratching his initials in the cinnamon-brown bricks at eye level. It was harder than he thought to make a mark that showed up from a distance, so he decided to do just one letter. An "A" for Andy.

As he was scraping away at the crossbar in his "A," he noticed another symbol carved a bit higher. Three bricks up was a triangle. The right side of it was thicker, and there were three lines next to it. It was an intentional mark and not a random abrasion. He studied it closely.

$$\Delta \equiv$$

Had Rex drawn this? Why would he? He had the fishing line to retrace his steps.

Did sewer workers mark tunnels? Andy didn't know. But it seemed unlikely they drew this here. It seemed too crude and temporary. So, if Rex didn't do it and the workers didn't either, who did? Though there was nothing inherently frightening about the mark, he felt a chill.

Andy finished his "A" and continued along the curve.

He hadn't gone a dozen steps when he noticed a slithery mark on the surface of the water.

He lowered his candle. His fingers scooped into the cloudy gray runoff until he had hold of it.

Just a thin strand, barely noticeable unless you were looking for it. The fishing line.

Rex had gone this way!

Andy made a loop and tied it tight to his wrist, then he wrapped the line around his forearm as he gathered it up. He'd left the empty spool at the pipe mouth. He was tempted to call for Rex, but he worried who, or what else might hear him. The thought of his own voice echoing in the tunnel made him shudder. The idea that some answerer other than Rex might call back to him was unthinkable. Or rather the problem was that it was not unthinkable at all.

No, he'd keep silent and follow. The line would end at Rex. That would be a good thing.

Andy sloshed along as quick as his boots would carry him.

17
Porcupine Days

Charlie had hopes of re-entering the Big Drain site at first light. He wanted to be down in the chamber before Rivertown was awake, in order to keep things as quiet as possible. He didn't need a repeat of yesterday. The near mob scene that accompanied Rex Murphy's police escort from the premises was regrettable. Looking back, his strategy had added fuel to the flames of the rumor mill conflagration. He didn't plan on making the same mistake today. So, he showed up early with minimal accompaniment – a single burly bodyguard and Mandy Thompson. They used a sewer department vehicle and came dressed as city workers.

His bodyguard pulled up to the dig site. The police security detail was expecting them. The mayor tipped his workman's cap to the cops. They unhooked a chain blocking public access. Charlie's bodyguard drove inside, parking as close to the tunnel as possible. Exiting their vehicle, they headed straight for the tunnel mouth, stopping once they were out of sight of passing traffic. Now they were waiting for Hurley's geologist, who was ten minutes late. Charlie hated lateness. It showed a lack of respect and brought out his impatience.

"Where is that man?" he asked Mandy. "I told him daybreak. Daybreak!"

"Might he be confused about our rendezvous point?" Mandy said.

She wore baggy overalls and a slicker. Her long auburn hair was tucked up inside a floppy hat. From a distance, she resembled a digger showing up for the job. The only difference was the bulky, brown leather bag she carried, though it might've been mistaken for a tool case.

"No. I made it clear. We're headed down to the sewers. Where else would we be meeting? The middle of Independence Square?" Charlie relit his cigar and stomped in the mud.

Spying around the corner, Mandy asked, "Is this our man?"

Charlie peeked out.

A small man with owlish glasses was talking to the officers at the chain. He had unruly red muttonchops and a stout, oblong silhouette that added to his nightbird appearance. The cops weren't letting him through. The man's round cheeks grew ruddier as he became exasperated.

"It must be him," Charlie said. He called to the police, "Let him pass, boys. He's with me."

The little man waddled through the mud, attempting, but failing, to stay on the boards. He arrived at the tunnel mouth well spattered from his boots to his spectacles.

"Sorry, sorry, sorry…" he said as he neared. "I missed my trolley. I had to walk."

Charlie was prepared to dress the man down, but he appeared frazzled enough as it was. "That's fine. You're here now," the mayor said gruffly. "I hope you were worth our wait."

The man extended his hand to Charlie and then to Mandy. His

front teeth were oversized and dented his lower lip, giving the impression that his face had frozen in a perpetual grin. When he tried to shake hands with the bodyguard, the guard rebuffed him, turning away.

The small man seemed genuinely hurt by the gesture. He blinked rapidly and sighed.

"I'm Clyde Laurents," he said to Charlie and Mandy. "Chief geologist for Hurley Mining, Northern Division. Glad to make your acquaintances. What an awful first impression you must have of me. I hope to redeem myself. I'm not usually late." The geologist let out a barking laugh that echoed inside the pipe. The startled bodyguard reached for the pistol tucked in his belt.

"Bahaha… oh, it's not true. I'm always late. But I beg you. Don't judge me too harshly." The geologist noticed where the bodyguard's hand was. "For heaven's sake, don't shoot me."

Charlie raised his eyebrow at Mandy, who shrugged in reply.

What an odd fellow.

"Shall we?" Clyde asked, touching the round gold rims of his eyeglasses, wide-eyed. "I do love a mystery. I'm told you have a dandy one here, waiting to be solved." He was still breathless from his walk, or it might've been his excitement. Everything about him bristled.

Charlie passed out the safety lamps. Then he summarized their findings from yesterday. Stanley Budzinski's tale. The blockage he demolished. The hidden chamber he exposed. The mysterious crystal that sprouted from the chamber's dome.

He left out the part about Rex Murphy. He also failed to mention how Budzinski spooked him and then disappeared.

"Follow me," he said, finally. "The sooner we get this over with, the better."

The three of them headed into the open pipe. Charlie, Mandy, then Clyde. Going last, the bodyguard made sure they weren't being followed. His hand rested on the butt of his pistol. Eyes sharp, checking behind them as they advanced. The renovation had been suspended. Work halted. Diggers sent home. Charlie felt the pressure of it all mounting. His head pounded as he walked. Every day meant more money, more criticisms. More stress. He'd had a difficult enough time pushing the much-needed sewer expansion and water treatment improvements. Not everyone had been on board with his plans. He had the typical political opponents who objected to anything he proposed; add to them the interests who never wanted a single penny spent on public works. Privatization was their answer to every problem. Hands sticking out in backrooms, waiting to be filled with cash from the city coffers. Bloated contracts. No-show jobs. Overruns. Supplies that disappeared. Padded expenses. Charlie had seen his share of political corruption. He wasn't naïve. He'd taken a range of bids for the Big Drain, not all of them legit. The local crime element wanted a slice of any pie this juicy, but Charlie had insisted on playing it straight.

That made a lot of people angry.

Bad people.

People who didn't forget. Or forgive.

They exacted revenge when they didn't get their way. That was how *they* did business.

Privately, he suspected that the bodies they'd been finding in the pipes might be a not-so-subtle message that he'd picked the wrong winners for this project. He'd been wondering if that might be true especially when Paddy went missing. A shift boss on the very job in question?

Snatched at work. Likely murdered. If the act was a statement, the meaning was all too obvious.

"Nobody who works on this job will ever be safe."

Discovering the pink crystal threw Charlie for a loop. Those bizarre, engraved symbols. They were too peculiar for the brass knuckle types he was worried about, blunt men who made simple, violent statements that were hard to misinterpret. In a weird way he felt relieved. Rooting out the rotten influence of organized criminal gangs would be harder than nabbing a lone cuckoo.

"Reminds me of the gold mines," Clyde said in a chipper tone of nostalgia.

"Gold mines?" Mandy said.

Clyde nodded. "I worked up in Canada. Years ago. Porcupine Lake. Before the fire. I hunted for quartz seams. Beautiful seams up there, if you knew what you were looking for. A dark wood, though. Deep in the bush. The isolation drove men to drink. Hard days, lonely nights. I've plied my trade up in Alaska. Throughout the West. But I never had it better than Porcupine."

"Maybe because you look like a porcupine," Charlie muttered under his breath.

"What's that?" the geologist asked.

"I said, 'Maybe you'll recognize our find.'"

Mandy covered her laugh.

"Oh," said Clyde. "If it's of this earth, I'll know it. Or make a darned good guess."

Charlie paused. It hadn't even occurred to him that the crystal was an object from space. He felt suddenly nervous, which wasn't like him. This place had an ominous aura. Something more than stink hung in the air. An atmosphere of malevolence, palpable and real.

He had to push past that. Leaders must lead. They can't allow fear to torpefy them.

"Now, here's our turn. It gets narrower. But soon we'll be through to the chamber."

They entered the old drain cut in the bedrock, the place where Paddy went missing. The flow of water was lower, but Charlie knew the levels fluctuated, and today it wasn't raining.

"It's like the minotaur's labyrinth down here," Mandy said. "I was studying early maps I found researching at the library. Explorers discovered caves that were here long before any town was founded. Natural formations, mostly. They showed signs of both animal and human habitation. More caves spring up the closer we get to the river. Underground rivers drilled channels in the limestone. Arkham records indicate that when the first sewers were dug for the city, workers went missing in alarming numbers. Their bosses said the men fled the hard labor, but the workers who stayed on said that wasn't so. They just disappeared. Digging beside them one moment, gone the next. Swept away. Fallen into pits. Lost. No one could ever explain it."

"Watch your step. These slabs are loose," Charlie said. "This is it, through here."

Charlie entered the chamber first. Then he reached back to help Mandy and Clyde. He waited for his bodyguard, but the man never came up to the opening Budzinski had knocked out with his steel pick.

He poked his head back into the chiseled drain. He held out his safety lamp, swinging it around. If he couldn't spot his man, his man might see it. He stuffed himself into the hole, over the pile of broken slabs poking at his stomach.

The drain was empty. No sign of his man.

He called out, "Butch! Hey Butchie! Where you at?"

But no answer came.

Charlie leaned farther out. Seeing nothing but rock, shadows, and the trickle of dirty water.

He stepped backward into the chamber, confused and stunned.

How could a man go missing suddenly like that?

"Is there a problem?" Mandy asked.

Charlie shook his head. "No problem. My man is lagging. He probably heard something. Or had a bit of private business to attend to. All this trickling water, you know?"

Mandy made a face and swung her lamp around to take in the scope of the room they'd entered. She was entranced, just as Charlie had expected. Here was Arkham's history on display. A never-before-seen exhibition where you could get your hands dirty and gain new knowledge.

"Where's Clyde?" she asked.

"What?" Charlie said, drawing up beside her. He lifted his light to join hers.

"He was here. Then I turned to talk to you. Now he's–"

"Clyde!" Charlie shouted.

A flash of light appeared from across the domed chamber. From the other side of the pink crystal formation growing out of ceiling like an enormous malformed tooth, the light moved.

An eye.

Large. And blinking.

It slid from behind the crystal without a sound. Staring at them. Examining them. Charlie gasped. He grabbed hold of Mandy's arm and nearly knocked her over.

"I'm right here!" Clyde said. He lowered the saucer-sized magnifying lens from his face.

Mandy tapped Charlie's hand as his squeezing fingers made stars on her slicker's arm. Embarrassed, he removed his grip.

Clearing his throat, he said to Clyde, "Stay close!"

"Oh, don't worry, Mr Mayor. I won't be going anywhere. This is such a fascinating specimen. I've never encountered anything like it. Its colors alter as I move my lamp around. Almost as if..." The geologist trailed off. He raised his lamp, tracing a semicircle in the air.

"As if what? Speak up, man. That's why I've brought you here," Clyde said.

Clyde looked at them with a faintly fanatical glint behind his spectacles.

"Well, as if there's something trapped *inside* the crystal. Swimming around, or squirming. It must be an optical illusion. A trick of the light. But what a trick it is! The lights appear to pulse. Like a heartbeat. Something living." Clyde had his lens up again, inspecting the surface of the crystal. "I'm tempted to say it's quartz. Quartz is quite common. But this sample is... uncommon. As I've said, the color, or colors, are exceptional. It changes from clear to opaque and back again depending on the angle of my observance and the light. Dare I say, it dazzles? Another thing. Quartz is a hard mineral, yet I'm able to scratch into this with my fingernail." He'd donned a pair of soft gloves, but now he removed one and tested the sample again. With the same results. "That is... highly unexpected." The geologist laughed to himself in lively amusement. "Oh, I could spend all day down here. It's beautiful. How strange that it feels like we're old friends meeting for the first time. That doesn't even make sense, does it? Just... being here takes my breath away. The best thing that's happened to me since my Porcupine days."

Charlie and Mandy approached the scientist, who'd put his gloves back on before he rubbed and prodded the specimen. The man was enthralled with their find.

That must be a good sign, Charlie thought. He'll figure out what this is.

"Did you know there are carvings on it?" Clyde asked, swiveling his head around.

"Yes," Charlie said, "I did. What do you make of them? Please, tell me."

Clyde shook his head as he peered into his magnifying glass. "Not my area of expertise. But it's writing of some variety. A sort of hieroglyphics. I don't recognize it. I'm no Egyptolo… Hey, wait a minute! Look here." Clyde scooted over, duckwalking around the crystal, pointing emphatically with his finger. He jerked his chin toward the glass he was careful to hold steady.

Mandy looked first.

"It's English," she said.

Clyde nodded deeply. "That's what I thought I saw. The symbols trail off and then what appears next is a word written in English." He held up his lens for Mandy to share.

"D-I-O-N-Y-S…" she began.

"I-A-B," Charlie finished for her.

Mandy and Clyde switched their gazes to the mayor.

"I started reading it the last time I was here. But that's as far as I got," he said.

He focused on the toothlike stone rather than his companions. The formation had more color to it than he remembered from yesterday. Where a day earlier it looked a pale pink, now the swirls of pigmentation carried darker streaks, in places redder than pink. A blush of scarlet.

"It does fade a bit," Clyde admitted. He tilted his lamp to get the maximum brightness.

"There! Stop, I can read it," Mandy said. "It's... It's a name. There's a break in the line. D-I-O-N-Y-S-I-A. Dionysia. Then a new word beginning with B..." She concentrated for a second then continued, "It says, Dionysia Burroughs."

Mandy pointed past Charlie.

"Hand me my bag," she said. Feeling a bit embarrassed at her lapse of formality in these highly unusual circumstances, she added, "If you wouldn't mind, Mayor Kane."

Charlie retrieved the bag. He was surprised how heavy it was. What did she have in there? The entirety of the Orne Library's archives?

Clyde kept his lens over the writing as she searched in her bag until she located a roll of paper and a wax crayon. "Hold your light right where it is," she said to Clyde. "Mr Mayor, could you unroll this paper and press it up against the crystal. Like this."

Charlie did as he was requested. He watched as Mandy rubbed the crayon over the paper and the figures on the crystal slowly appeared as if they'd been teased out by magic. When she finished, she tore the end of the paper from the roll.

Clyde stood up and raised his lamp to illuminate the ceiling.

"You know... it looks as if the crystal has crashed right through from above. It didn't grow here. It-it... It arrived. I wonder if it's a meteorite of some unknown kind. But it's so large and pale. And soft... I don't know. Nothing makes sense to me right now, and I love it! Perhaps if isn't a meteorite, it was somehow caused by a meteorite. We must preserve it at all costs."

"Digging it out is–" Charlie began.

"Out of the question!" Clyde shouted. Then when he realized

who he was shouting at, he quickly apologized. "What I mean, Your Honor, Mr Mayor, is that you can't disrupt and possibly destroy what might be the geological find of a lifetime. This assessment will take time. I will need to contact other scientists. The top people, in my field and others, who will need to take measurements and conduct various tests. All of this must happen before there is talk of removal."

"I see," Charlie said. He did his best to sound stately. His head was pounding again. Harder than before. But he couldn't let his anxiety show.

"How long?" he asked. "Would you… estimate?"

Clyde shrugged. "Months?"

"Months! We can't delay the Big Drain for months. Impossible."

"Things of this momentous nature cannot be rushed," Clyde said, protesting gently.

While the two men talked, Mandy was busy making more wax crayon rubbings. After she finished one, she made the next, proceeding methodically around the crystal, careful not to miss any surface. She had covered about half the crystal when they all heard a sloshing from the drain.

Charlie thrust his light in the direction of the hole.

"Butchie?" he said to a figure protruding from the gap.

Sticking halfway through the hole in the wall, his bodyguard propped his upper body on his elbows. His hands were dripping wet and coated with oozy gray muck. His face betrayed no emotion, though his skin might've looked a shade or two paler than when the day began.

"I found something," he said.

"Where were you?" Charlie asked. He didn't bother to conceal his suspiciousness.

Butch jerked his head to one side. "Back there. Where the tunnels split. Thought I heard something bumping around. Might've been a rat. I didn't want to spook you. So, I went for a look-see on my own. Lucky I did. You won't believe what I found."

Mandy set her rubbings inside her bag and picked up a cloth. Her fingers were dark at the tips as if she'd dipped them in paint. Not the gray of the watery muck. No, Charlie knew what it was even before she did. Mandy's brow wrinkled as he wiped her fingers with the rag, bringing the stain over to her lamp for a closer inspection. The realization dawned on her, slowly, terribly.

The shock of it. She'd picked up a sinister clue fiddling with those carvings.

That redness smeared on the formation. It wasn't all coming from inside the rock.

Blood.

Charlie didn't want to hear what his bodyguard had to say. Because he knew. He wasn't sure exactly how he knew, but he did. He thought he knew the worst part. But he didn't.

"What is it? Another giant crystal?" Clyde said, smiling, rising from behind the tooth.

As the geologist came around the crystal from the other side, he kicked something so that it floated up from its shallow grave.

The face was ghastly. Distended. Peeling, bluish skin. Eyes bugging. Its swollen tongue protruded like a stopper. It might've been wearing a frog mask. Only it wasn't. The throat was slashed on one side, but the wound seemed minor compared to the whole bobbing horror of it.

"Oh, my goodness," Clyde said, bending away, his voice hushed. "It's a body."

Butchie grinned. It was odd to see him smile. He couldn't see what they were seeing, not from where he was, poking out of the slabs.

"Hey, how'd you know I was about to say I found a body?" he asked.

Charlie didn't know which was worse, seeing a body float up or hearing about one and having your imagination run wild. Seeing won, he decided. His imagination just wasn't that rich.

18
Sharp, Slivery

Jake felt a bead of sweat drip down his forehead. His rehabilitation therapy had been strenuous this morning. Frustrating, too. The nurses told him to be gentle with himself. Give it time, they said. He was making progress. Doing better than most at this stage of recovery. Yet that wasn't good enough for him. His muscles ached, burning from overexertion. He felt an awful cramp squeezing his leg even now, moving up inch by inch from the arch of his foot into his calf. Except the cramp he was feeling came from his missing limb. His *phantom limb*, as the nurses called it. The brain is confused, they cautioned. It's learning to adapt. Signals get crossed. Things will get better. You can't rush things along. The body needs time to heal.

But how far would it heal? Was this creeping pain going to be a part of his future? He was hoping he'd be rid of his crutches by this point. The gains were happening too slowly for him. But now wasn't the time to be distracted. He had a meeting. Jake wiped his forehead and combed his fingers through his hair before pushing through the hospital cafeteria doors. Two steps inside, he scanned the dining room, searching for Maude's psychologist. There she was.

He made a beeline for her.

"You must be Dr Fern," Jake said to the woman sitting beneath the last window of St Mary's Hospital cafeteria. She looked at him expectantly as she stirred a steaming cup of tea.

Smiling, she stood up. The psychologist was dressed in a smart, navy business suit, no white doctor's coat. Her dark hair parted down the middle, the ends tucked behind her ears. Around her neck she wore a knotted hand-painted silk scarf. The black-and-white geometric design reminded Jake of a Japanese Go board during the middlegame phase.

"And you're Jake Williams," Dr Fern said, nodding at the red carnation in his lapel.

Jake pulled out a chair with his free hand. With the other hand, he laid his crutches against the wall. "Now that we've had proper introductions, tell me what trouble Maude's in."

Dr Fern flattened her palms out on the cafeteria table. "Normally, I wouldn't discuss a patient's case with anyone but their family. However, when Maude was under my care, she either wouldn't, or couldn't, recall any living relatives. However, she did provide the names of a few friends, including yours."

The doctor smiled again.

"What do you mean Maude *was* under your care? When you called me, you said she was your patient. Is she or isn't she?" His words grew louder. The cramp gripped tighter. He felt his toes curling. Toes that weren't there. He tried not to wince. What he did was grab the edge of the table as hard as he could.

"Lower your voice," she said. "This is a delicate situation. It isn't easy for me."

Dr Fern picked up her spoon again and started stirring. Round and round… That shrill scraping set Jake's teeth on edge. Must she do that?

Typically, he wasn't bothered by trivial things. He thought of himself as calm, level-headed, and happy-go-lucky. Perhaps he was changing. Little things were getting under his skin.

"Sorry. Go on," he said.

Dr Fern said, "Maude would still be my patient if it were up to me. But the sanatorium has barred me from seeing her. I'm a psychologist. Hypnotherapy is part of the treatment plan I offer to some patients. I've had great successes in the past with patients who manifested similar symptoms to your friend. I hypnotized Maude. We had an alarming session. Although we made some valuable, but unusual, findings, it was a traumatizing experience for both of us, I'm afraid."

"Why were you barred from seeing her?" Jake asked.

The doctor sighed. She picked up her tea, raised the cup to her lips, and took a sip.

"I made a small but stupid mistake. After our session, I poured Maude a drink. Just a splash of whiskey. I didn't think it would do her any harm. I had some too. I thought it might help to calm our nerves. It certainly helped her to bond with me. I'm not making excuses. I shouldn't have done it. We were processing what had happened to us. The nurse who collected Maude to take her back to her room smelled the liquor. She reported me to another doctor, who's initiated an investigation. It's beyond my control at this point. I don't care about any discipline I might face as much as I care about what is happening to Maude. This other doctor enrolled Maude in a controversial – and in my opinion unethical – drug therapy. Far worse than any thimbleful of Canadian bootleg booze. I'm afraid that his therapy will harm

Maude's mental state, perhaps irreparably. Beyond that, I think he might just kill her with his vile experiments."

The teacup exploded in her hand.

The sound wasn't much. A percussive pop like a champagne cork. The cup disintegrated, shattering as if it had been struck with an invisible hammer, spraying them both with porcelain shards and Orange Pekoe tea.

Jake's anger evaporated as he reached for a napkin and mopped up the mess. He wasn't quite sure what had happened.

"Are you injured?" he asked Dr Fern. A few of the pieces had flown in her face.

"No, I'm fine. That was bizarre, wasn't it?" She dabbed at her scarf. "A first for me."

He couldn't have agreed more. She hadn't been crushing the cup. The handle rested in one hand, two of her fingertips pressed against the rim on the other side. How did it break?

"I apologize for being so accusatory before," he said. "My mood's been off today."

As Dr Fern stared at the glistening fragments of destroyed teacup, her brow wrinkled.

A look of horror passed over her features. She covered her twisting mouth with her hand.

Jake said, "This teacup business isn't as bad as all that, is it?"

The doctor blinked and stared.

"No, no. It's just… I thought I saw something… In fact, it almost looked like a …"

He quickly swept up the pieces into a pile.

She grabbed for his wrist as if she wanted to stop him. Then she let go and shook her head, regaining her composure. But not entirely. She'd gone ashen.

He stopped sweeping. "Like what?"

"Never mind," she said. "The broken bits made a strange pattern on the table, that's all."

"A pattern?" Jake looked at the pile. Whatever had been there, he'd effectively erased it.

"Nothing. It's not important. I've been under a great deal of pressure. The mind plays tricks on itself occasionally. Seeing things that aren't there. We humans are designed from birth to recognize patterns. To seek them out. Sometimes that leads us to think we see what we don't."

"Like faces," Jake said.

She seemed unsettled by his choice of example. Or by what she'd seen.

Jake said, "You know? Faces in the clouds. Or in the bark of a tree. The craggy surface of a rock that resembles an elephant or Abraham Lincoln's profile."

"Yes, faces," she said. Then she shrugged. "Well, it's all swept up now. There was probably a crack in the cup. Simple as that. The heat of the tea, the tap of my spoon in just the right weak spot... and boom!" She flung open her hand. "But really, I didn't think I was squeezing it that hard." She titled her head, obviously still astounded.

"You weren't squeezing," Jake said. "It flew apart. I saw it."

At the other cafeteria tables, the curious faces that had turned to watch them returned to whatever they'd been doing. Picking up their conversations, resuming their meals. Unperturbed.

"In any event, the mess is cleaned up." Jake slid the pieces off to the side.

Dr Fern kept glaring down at them with an intensity he could not dismiss. Tilting her head from side to side. Unconsciously, she reached into the pile, arranging the remnants as if she were alone and putting together a jigsaw puzzle. Her eyes grew glassy and out of focus. It was only a cup. Jake flipped the napkin over the sharp, slivery bits. She'd demolished the thing.

Covering the debris helped, and Dr Fern returned his gaze, blinking, as if she were awaking from a dream. Or coming out of a hypnotic state.

Jake realized he didn't know anything about this woman except what she'd told him. So far, he'd believed everything. He believed she was a doctor, Maude's psychologist. But who was to say she wasn't in need of her own psychologist? If what she was telling him was true, she'd been kicked off Maude's case. Yet, there was something about Dr Fern that Jake instinctively trusted. She gave off a sense of competence and honesty. In the end, wasn't that all a person could judge by?

"Dr Fern, please tell me. How can I help Maude?"

The psychologist sat back. Ignoring the teacup, she snapped back into focus.

"I've been thinking about that. Maude came to us through the courts. She was picked up by the police. They'd been called to the Miskatonic University Biology Department, the entomology laboratory to be specific, because Maude was caught releasing spider specimens from their cages, dumping them out a second-floor window onto students walking below. If she doesn't have family, then you could possibly go to court and try to obtain guardianship. But…"

"But what?" Jake said.

"That's a time-consuming process. With no guarantee that you'll be granted guardianship in the end. And by then…" Dr Fern gazed at the shattered cup wrapped in a tea-stained napkin.

"It will be too late," Jake said.

Dr Fern nodded.

"So, what options are left?"

"Well, this is off the record, you understand. But if she were my friend…"

"I'd say you are her friend." Jake smiled.

"I wonder… how do you feel about arranging an escape?"

"I love a good escape plan. Let's talk strategy for a moment, shall we–"

A commotion at the other end of the cafeteria drew their attention. Doctors and nurses began leaving their tables and rushing out, leaving their breakfasts half-eaten and coffees undrunk.

"What's going on?" Jake asked Dr Fern.

"I don't know."

Jake tried to stand but moved too quickly. He teetered. Dr Fern reached over the table to help him, putting her hand on his upper arm. He collected his crutches and rebalanced himself. "I can do it myself," he said, neither thanking nor chastising her. Simply, he *could* do it himself.

They made their way to the front of the cafeteria before it emptied out completely. Jake caught the arm of the last doctor before he could exit.

"Can you tell me what's happening?" he asked.

"Ambulances in the emergency ward." The doctor had a slice of bacon he was chewing. "The strangler struck again. Three victims in the sewers this time. But they're not all dead. Yet."

The bacon-chomping doctor shouldered his way through the door. Jake jammed one crutch in the gap before the door shut then stuck his head through.

"Did you say three victims?"

"That's right," the man called back. "Three."

19
Ole Gray

Wendy knew she shouldn't have gone back to the place where they were digging the new sewer tunnels. But she couldn't stop thinking about the gray person who grabbed her wrist and laughed at her. She decided she would just quickly walk past while James was still sleeping. Nothing would wake him until the sun came up and shone straight through a knothole in the window, slanting golden across the bedroom floor where they slept in an old, empty house not too far from the river.

Inside, the house wasn't too dirty; the doors and windows were boarded over tight, just not tight enough to keep out a couple of squirmy kids. You had to be smart to survive. And you had to keep at it day and night. The spring weather was getting warmer, but they didn't have to worry about the rain, because this house had a solid roof, and only a family of raccoons denning upstairs. The closest neighbors were far enough away that Wendy and James could sneak in and out if they did it quietly. She'd left James a note in case he woke up early, because she didn't want him getting scared. Her note said she was going out to rustle up breakfast. *Stay put, Jim!*

The last thing she needed was a frightened James running off.

She'd told James a little about the gray person. She didn't say too much. What she said was, "If you see somebody in a crowd, or anywhere, bundled up every inch in soft gray, with soft gray gloves, and a scratchy, whispery voice, run away!"

"Why?" he asked.

"Cause they're bad. Maybe they aren't even human."

"A monster?" James' eyes got big as baseballs.

"I'm not saying for certain, because I don't know. But they might be. They had a grip like a steel rattrap. They talked in a way that made you feel sort of watery inside, like your guts were melting, and they were loving every bad feeling you had. It made them feel good to scare you."

"That sure sounds like a monster," James said.

He started looking around the bedroom in the empty house, at the doorway.

"We're safe here," Wendy said. "Just remember what I told you."

Now she couldn't very well tell James she was going out looking for the person she'd told him to run away from. So instead, she said she was looking for food. He'd believe that.

What Wendy wanted to see was if she could catch sight of that peculiar, gray-clad figure who'd lurked in the crowd. Did they work here? Maybe they lived in one of the apartments? Why else were they hanging around? And why were they wrapped head-to-toe in soft gray like a ghost? Hiding in plain view. There, but not there. Every feature cloaked in shapeless disguise.

Maybe underneath the clothes, there was no person at all. Just air. Wendy shivered.

The amulet Wendy wore on her neck was able to detect danger. It recognized evil.

She let her fingers slip under her coat to touch the red stone her mother had given her. It was quiet now. Just a piece of pretty jewelry she kept hidden from strangers.

She protected it, and it protected her.

A memento. That meant an item you kept in order to remind you of someone. She didn't need reminding about her mother. She thought about her every day, living at the sanatorium until the doctors helped her get better and she felt well enough to come home and take care of Wendy. She missed her mother all the time but thinking about it only made her hurt inside and cry. She knew they'd be together again whenever her mother got out. They just had to be patient and wait.

Until then, Wendy had to manage for herself, and look after her friend, James.

Wendy saw policemen across the street guarding the sewer entrance. They had a thick chain hooked up so no one could get too close. The cops didn't even bother to look at her, a child, walking down the street. She might be on her way to school, although it was still too early for that, or she might be going to work, or to a friend's house. The cops wouldn't know or care.

Not unless they caught you breaking the law. Say, picking a wallet or coin purse. Then you'd wish you were invisible.

Wendy noticed police cars driving toward her, headed to the Big Drain site – a lot of police cars, going fast. And ambulances mixed in, too. A long line of cars.

Something was happening. Again.

The amulet started to hum, a ticklish vibration against her chest.

Wendy waited for the emergency vehicles to pass, then she crossed the street. She ducked into a narrow alley; like a cat she moved stealthily between crates and through a maze of barrels.

She darted, small and quick, finding a hole in a fence. On her hands and knees, she made it through. Then up again she popped like a jack-in-the-box, already on the move, slipping closer and closer to the edge of the construction site. She heard car doors opening, closing. Men talking in serious voices, shouting orders, but not as loud as they sometimes could be. No whistles and banging nightsticks. It was almost as if whatever they were trying to do had to be done without waking up the entire neighborhood. They sure were in a hurry. You could only keep a group of men that large quiet for so long, and the neighborhood was too alert. Windows began sliding up on the street; heads poked out, here and there. People didn't sleep lightly, or long, in Rivertown.

Wendy slinked up to the next fence that surrounded the worksite. It was too high to climb, and she couldn't see any missing or loose boards. Then she spotted a tarpaulin hanging over the fence. She grabbed it with two hands, and using it like a rope, she pulled herself overtop.

She landed on the other side in a pile of soft, damp sand.

Right out in the open!

But the cops and ambulance attendants were too busy to notice her.

She scrambled around the side of the sandpile, pressing low to the ground and peeking her head over the hill, the way stray cats watched the birds in the backyard of the old, empty house.

The cops told the ambulance drivers to pull off to the side. Other side of the yard. Now.

To the sandpile!

Wendy scooched lower. If they found her, she'd make a mad dash for the street.

But they didn't find her.

They opened the back of the ambulances and pulled out stretchers. Then they rushed the stretchers into the tunnel. They didn't even bother to shut the back doors. It must be a pretty bad accident, she thought, with lots of people hurt. Wendy was tempted to look inside the ambulances to see what was there. She'd never seen the inside of an ambulance, which was probably a good thing. But she didn't dare move from her hiding place. Too many cops.

In a few minutes, the ambulance attendants were out of the tunnel again, hustling their way over to the ambulances. This time the stretchers sagged because they had people in them.

One.

Two.

Two bodies. Both as motionless as sacks of flour. Wendy's stomach grumbled.

No, wait! Three. The ambulance attendants had a third stretcher with somebody in it.

The first stretcher looked like a huge fat man was lying on it. He was green! Whew! The smell was so bad Wendy covered her mouth and nose to keep from throwing up. The next two stretchers carried men too, judging by their shoes. She couldn't tell too much about any of them.

Except they were dripping wet and splotchy with mud.

The last one out of the tunnel was moving back and forth as if he had a stomachache.

He was bleeding from his head too. She saw a stripe of tomato red leaking from his hair.

She saw that when they pushed him inside the ambulance closest to the sandpile.

At the last second, before he vanished into the back, he turned his face and looked at her. She was about ready to scream. Into the ambulance he went without saying anything. She figured he was hurt so bad he didn't see her at all. He was young. Older than a kid but not by a whole lot.

As messy and bloody as he was, he seemed familiar to her. Nobody she knew by name.

But still...

Wendy had a good memory and a sharp eye. It was why she was such a good pickpocket. She recognized people who paid attention and which ones got distracted. She'd follow them through a crowd, maybe shopping in a store, or at a park on Sunday, or listening to a band play in the bandbox at Independence Square on a nice purple evening with the flowers in bloom. She'd wait until they let their guard down, then she'd pick 'em clean. She recalled the mean ones too, who stared razors at her and James. Suspicious types. Other dippers on the make, sometimes. Wendy used her memory as a tool for survival. And she remembered that young man on the stretcher with the bleeding, busted head. She'd seen him before. Recently. But where?

Then she remembered: it was right here at the dig site. He'd been up hanging onto the lamppost. She remembered him because she was worried that he might be spotting for somebody working the crowd. But she didn't really think so. Then she got good and spooked by Ole Gray.

She'd made up the name just now, and it fit. When she saw James again, she'd tell him, "Watch out for Ole Gray! He's bad news!"

At the same time as she was thinking about what she'd tell James, she looked across the muddy yard, past where the ambulances were parked and the cops were milling about, and she saw a figure standing near the entrance to the sewer tunnel.

It was Ole Gray!

Wendy would've howled if the cops weren't there. She almost cried out in fear anyway.

Ole Gray had a glow, but it wasn't a light making them glow. It was something else. An energy. Like her amulet's energy but somehow the opposite of it too. Nobody else was paying attention to this person, but that person stood, hands linked behind their back, rocking on their heels. Like they were waiting for a trolley or someone they knew to show up.

They were staring out from between the folds of material the color of smoke.

Staring right at Wendy.

Wendy's amulet buzzed against her skin. The warning getting stronger and stronger.

Why didn't anybody see this monster? Ole Gray rocked and people walked right past without batting an eye. Ole Gray knew it too. How invisibility worked. What a clever trickster!

A dove-gray soft-gloved hand lifted and wiggled its fingers.

Hiya there, Wendy! How's it going in Sandytown?

Wendy felt Ole Gray's voice right inside her head. She heard too. That scrapy scratchy voice like it hadn't had a glass of water to drink in couple hundred years.

I know you can hear me, Wendy. Want me to come over and build you a sandcastle?

No! You stay there!

Now don't shout at me. That's rude. Tsk-tsk-tsk.

I'm not the rude one. You are. Stick to that tunnel, or so help me, I'll yell for the cops.

And tell them what, Wendy? I haven't done a thing. Your friends in blue might remember you, though. From the time they caught you snatching wallets at the Christmas Market.

How did Ole Gray know about that? The cops let her go with a warning.

But they won't let you go next time, Wendy. That's what they said, 'member? Hmmm…

Ole Gray was reading her thoughts! Knowing he could do that repulsed her and filled her with a cold rage.

Oh, sure. It's easy. I'm in your head. It's like a picture show in here. I see everything.

Wendy couldn't take it anymore. She wanted to shake him off, but she didn't know how to get rid of the taint of Ole Gray inside her head. How could she protect herself from a thing that read her mind? Nowhere to run to. There's no hiding place if you take the seeker with you.

She saw one of the ambulance drivers step out of his vehicle and go over to the cops. He was asking them to make room so he could leave. The crowds were already gathering on the street, and the cops were pushing people back and putting sawhorses up to keep them off the chain. Wendy thought about going back the way she came, but had a better idea, one that would get her farther away, and faster. She climbed into the rear of the ambulance. She looked at the body on the stretcher. It was the kid from the lamppost with the bloody head. He was quiet now. His eyes were closed, but she heard him breathing. She made herself flat as a flapjack and slid between his stretcher and the inside wall of the ambulance. There was an extra blanket in there she pulled up over her body and head. Then she laid as still as she could. The ambulance driver climbed in – she felt the weight of him make the ambulance go down – and he checked on his patient before shutting the back doors, never noticing Wendy holding her breath under the blanket.

Then he got into the front seat and started the engine.

Going for a ride, Wendy? Are you leaving me by my lonesome? Maybe I can go too?

Nonononononooooooooo...Wendy shouted in her mind at Ole Gray.

The driver backed up the ambulance. The vehicle jounced as they drove out of the lot and onto the street. Soon they picked up speed; rolling over the cobbles made the tires thrum, and Wendy noticed that the farther the car drove down the bumpy road, the quieter her amulet got.

She felt Ole Gray pulling out of her head like a long piece of stretchy, gray taffy – taffy that if you tasted it, would be like chewing on smoke, a sour mouthful of ashes and dust. Finally, the elastic string connecting them snapped in two and Wendy was relieved to be alone with her thoughts again. She sighed quietly, as if she'd stepped out of a long, hot bath. Clean and revived.

20
Supernatural Factors

Jake and Dr Fern exited the back of the hospital, spotting the trio of mud-spattered ambulances parked outside the emergency ward. The strangler victims were a big news story. Reporters gathered under the porte-cochere outside the emergency ward's double-doorway, shoving each other and shouting questions at the police officers trying to disperse them. The cacophony was increased by the officers shouting back. Through this crush of onlookers, the medical staff were fighting their way to the ambulances.

"Looks like news of the strangler spreads fast," Jake said.

"I hear they suspect the killer may be from a far-off land," Dr Fern said.

Jake had traveled outside the country for years, and he was especially sensitive to accusations directed at suspicious foreigners. "People who live in fear look for scapegoats. Next, they'll bring up monsters and supernatural conspiracies," he said.

"You don't believe in the supernatural?" Dr Fern asked.

Should he tell her such an improbable giant devoured half his leg?

Now wasn't the time, and this wasn't the place. "Most killers have a human face."

"You didn't answer my question," the psychologist said.

Jake was carefully picking his way down the uneven hospital steps.

"Let's just say that I believe in what I've seen. And what I've seen is—"

Dr Fern tugged at his sleeve urgently. "Who's that?"

Jake paused and looked up. A commotion surrounded the ambulances as the tangle of jostling bodies moved away from the vehicles, following the stretchers as they were carried into the hospital. Blinding camera flashes went off; reporters vied to catch sight of the victims' faces.

"Did you see her?" she said.

"Where?" Jake scanned from side to side. "Who am I looking for?"

"By the open doors of the last ambulance. A girl climbed out the back and ran off."

"Did she?" Jake peered past the confusion of bodies rushing around. Pandemonium.

"I swear I saw her. She moved very fast. Short brown hair and an oversized coat."

Jake scanned. "I don't see any children."

"She went off in the direction of those evergreens." Dr Fern hurried down the steps. "I'm going to look for her. She might be injured, frightened, or in shock. I don't know how they could leave her alone. Why didn't the attendant take her into the hospital if she's arrived by ambulance?" The psychologist vented her frustration. "It's shadowy around here even in the daytime. I can only imagine how terrible a place like this seems to a child. And with this circus."

Jake looked down. He had a few more steps to negotiate. No time to fall.

"Maybe she's family? The child of a victim?" He finally reached the walkway. "You go on ahead. I'll take the path to Emergency to see if she's snuck inside."

"Good idea. I'll meet you there." The doctor rushed off, skirting the edge of the building, checking under the boughs of evergreens, spreading them apart to reveal carpets of dead pine needles and fallen cones, where the shade grew thick as paint and provided a good hiding place.

Jake figured little would come of his search. Why would a child sprint away from inside an ambulance and into the trees? Especially if she was hurt. Yet, the doctor seemed convinced about what she'd witnessed. As he approached the crowd of reporters and police, he examined the gathering for anyone who might be confused for a child. No luck. Looking back at the evergreens, he realized he'd lost sight of Dr Fern too, though the branches did appear to shake more than could be accounted for by the wind.

It's my mind playing tricks on me, he thought. I want to see Dr Fern, or a girl, so I observe hints and presences where none exist. The breeze likely swirls up against the high outer walls of St Mary's. Gusts, and birds, and squirrels – that's what's at work here. If there had been a girl, she'd gone by now anyway.

The pines shivered at him in reply.

But still, he should ask someone. It was his duty as a searcher.

"Excuse me," he said to a female reporter. "Have you noticed any children in the area?"

"What?" She appraised him sharply. "Why? Have you lost someone? Your daughter?"

"No. My friend thought she saw a girl by the ambulances. We don't want any accidents."

The reporter appeared strangely upset, but that surely couldn't be down to his simple inquiry. Wasn't she accustomed to seeing emergency vehicles and injured people? Trauma came with the newsbeat. Yet her color was pale, her aspect grim.

"Sorry, can't help you," she said. "I haven't seen any girls." She turned away.

"But you have seen something that's bothered you," Jake said. "Haven't you?"

The reporter leveled her gaze, pulled her shoulders back and took a deep breath. "Two of the victims brought in from the Big Drain site were colleagues of mine. It was a real shock to see them on stretchers. I didn't expect that. Excuse me, I'm going to sit down."

She moved away from the crowd. Jake followed her over to a pair of weathered tree stumps in the shadow of the hospital. The ground was littered with cigarettes and various footprints.

As the reporter lit a smoke, her hands were shaking. She looked up at him, wide-eyed.

"I hope you don't mind if I join you. I'm waiting for someone. I've got a leg cramp." Jake lifted his new foot. He'd laced the leather too tightly and now it was feeling pinched.

"I don't mind. Minnie Klein," she said, offering her hand. "I write for the *Advertiser*."

Jake shifted his crutches, then set the pair on the ground so he could shake hands.

"Jake Williams. Explorer." He mopped sweat from his forehead, gazing toward the pines.

She shot him a quizzical look. "I've never heard of 'The Explorer.' Is it a new tabloid? A foray into jazz journalism?" The confusion on her face must've mirrored his own. "Oh wait, you're saying *you're* an explorer." After a beat her eyes narrowed. "Your name sounds familiar. You worked with the famous Ursula Downs, didn't you? Hold it now. You must know Andy!"

It was Jake's turn to feel surprised. "Andy Van Nortwick?"

"That's him! You were with Andy in the Amazon. The Spider Queen expedition, right?"

"That's correct." He was unconsciously kneading the tingling muscles in his thigh. When he noticed her watching, he stopped and folded his hands in his lap.

She works at Andy's office. So, she knows him. Presumably she knows what happened to us. Our failed adventure. But we succeeded in finding and bringing back Hollywood's Maude Brion from the depths of the rainforest. How much did Minnie really know? How much did any stranger who wasn't there?

An internal dark cloud must've passed over Minnie Klein, because a sudden gloom froze her features. "Andy's one of the victims," she said, pointing with the hot tip of her cigarette. "Here. Right now. They just brought him in." Jake noticed her rating his reaction. Reporters did that; they read people, spying for subtle clues. He automatically put up a front and hid his shock.

"What?" Jake gazed with a new perspective at the ominous hospital looming above them. Andy was in there, injured? How terrible. He hoped it wasn't serious. But it must be. The thought of Andy lying wounded on a cot made him feel a sharp stab of sympathy and concern. Jake had been in bad shape himself on the slow voyage back up the Amazon River, then setting sail again for America, sick with fever, racked with pain. It was no picnic being laid up and helpless. He was reliving it in gaudy flashes, emotional snapshots of the trauma he'd been through. He felt a cold sweat break out, his stomach tumbling over.

"Isn't that why you're here? Trying to get in and see him. He arrived in one of those ambulances. Rex Murphy, too. The third victim had a blanket over the face. But I saw a hand dangling outside the stretcher. Blue fingers. Dead, for sure. Whoever it was, they didn't make it."

"Rex Murphy. Who is Rex Murphy?" Jake said. Why were tragedies often so complex?

Jake felt his head spinning, his mind drifting. First Maude, now Andy. He hoped Ursula was doing well. There was no specific reason to worry about her, and she hated it when he did. But it had been a part of his life for years – thinking through perils they faced together, making contingency plans. Following Ursula's lead and supporting her decisions – he did it with pride. But he worried. She was off without him, which was fine. Ursula could handle herself better than anyone else he'd ever met. Better than he could handle himself. He simply needed to get used to the idea that he might not be able to do what he'd done in the past. Forget that! He'd be the last one to settle for less just because of an injury. He'd had so many wounds before. Yet never one like this. He knew the solution. It was right there in nature, the wilderness he and Ursula so loved to explore together. Jake had to adapt. Adapt and survive. But it was easier said than done.

"Rex is another reporter from the *Advertiser*. He got nabbed by the cops in the sewers yesterday. They were saying he was the killer." She shook her head and blew out smoke, waved the fumes away. "The cops released him late last night. All he was guilty of was snooping, like any good journalist. I guess he went back to the sewers." She made a clucking sound with her tongue, although admiration shone on her face. "Rex is a real go-getter." She blocked out her next words as if they were headlines. "Dog Finds Bone. Refuses To Let Go." She flicked her ash. "Yet I wonder what Andy was doing down there. You don't think *he's* the strangler?"

"Andy? No. Not Andy. Never," Jake said, incredulously. "He arrived here in bad shape?"

Jake felt guilty for thinking about Ursula, and himself, when Andy was the one facing immediate danger. Attacked by a notorious killer! He's in the hospital! Get your priorities straight, Jake! Self-scolding provided a welcome distraction from probing the wounds in his psyche. In the past, he'd used action to avoid overthinking. He needed to keep busy. That was all.

"Gee, I'm sorry. I'm hitting you with a lot of bad news, aren't I? I talk when I get agitated. Andy was alive, I'll say that. I heard him moan. You know that the *Advertiser* fired him over the Spider Queen debacle? Not the editor's choice. Orders came from higher up in the building. The owner, Harvey Gedney. Someone got to him. Andy was cleaning out his desk when he told me he thought it was a bigshot gold mining executive pulling the strings. Exacting his revenge, Andy said. He couldn't prove anything, but boy, he was angry. I wonder what happened to him after he left the paper. One of the sports hacks said Andy got a job pushing a broom in Rivertown."

Andy was working as a janitor? Jake hadn't thought about the fallout of Andy's failure to bring back proof of the Spider Queen legend, or to locate any temple treasure, or find gold deposits for Hurley to pillage in the Brazilian jungle. Jake had been too busy healing his body to think about Andy or Maude.

Too preoccupied with Ursula taking on a new adventure without him. While he was feeling sorry for himself, Andy was getting kicked down his career ladder and Maude was losing whatever tenuous grip on sanity she had. Except for Ursula, they were a mess.

"Oscar Hurley owns the gold mining company. He bankrolled our expedition," he said.

"That's the guy! Hurley." Minnie offered Jake a cigarette, but he didn't smoke. "Your expedition didn't find any gold, did it? So, I guess that's why Hurley was sore. You don't think getting fired might've been enough to push Andy over the edge? Turn him from a nice guy…?"

"Into a maniacal killer?" Jake snorted, waving off her suggestion. "Not a chance."

"Right, right. I don't think so either. I'm only batting around ideas, just between us. I'm not printing it. Strange things happen around here. It wouldn't be the first time an Arkhamite proved to be other than what they seemed. People here keep secrets. It's what we do. Maine has blueberries, New York has money, our townsfolk entertain weird interests. We do it privately."

"Like an interest in murder?"

She shrugged. "Maybe worse than murder. Maybe murder is only the beginning."

The enigma of her suggestion hung between them. She seemed both attracted and repelled by the ramifications. Push and pull. The dark allure of the unspeakable, the unimaginable…

Jake leaned back, letting his mind wander. Murder could be the beginning of some very bad things he knew about. Like human sacrifice, for one thing. Pal, you'd better avoid that peculiar train of thought, he told himself. Don't jump to any outlandish conclusions. Maybe if you covered crime stories each day, everything started to smell like a crime. You became tainted by the waters you swam in, the sewer of human bad behavior. It twisted your mind. He was glad he had another vocation, one that didn't chase tragedy in hopes of writing a snappier headline.

"Is this how stories get written?" he asked, idly. "You accuse people of committing an evil misdeed, then see if the accusation sticks? That's a heck of way to make a living, Minnie."

"Watch it, buster. I work hard here. These legs do the necessary legwork. I verify, I'm only thinking out loud. Sometimes you can't tell how crazy an idea sounds until you speak it first."

"Like a test?"

"Sure, a test." She gave him a wry smile.

There was no doubt they were sparring. But Minnie looked tough. She liked to mix it up.

"Sorry, but Andy's my friend. I'm not standing by while you slander him," Jake said.

"Who said I'm slandering him? I'm asking, 'What if?' I like Andy. I ate pie with Andy. We were friends at the office. I'm rooting for him to make it. I'm an Andy fan."

"You've got an odd way of showing it."

"Let me explain in a way you might understand. You know what a hunch is? It's a wild idea that catches your fancy, and you can't let it go. So, you keep digging. Excavating. Grabbing up whatever fragments you find. Sifting, sifting. Until the bigger picture comes together. Maybe your hunch pans out. Maybe it's only smoke. See? It's nothing personal with Andy. It's my job."

Jake rubbed his chin. The reporter's explanation was starting to make sense.

Minnie said. "Looks like I got your wheels turning now."

"What you said sounds a bit like archaeology. It also sounds like the Andy I know."

Minnie nodded. "If he's in the hospital, he's probably a victim, not a perpetrator. The cops would shout from the rooftops, I promise you, if they thought they hooked the Lamprey."

"The Lamprey?" Now Jake was confused again. Were they suddenly talking about eels?

"It's what they're calling the killer now. This monster picked out a name, apparently. Wrote a letter to the police chief confessing to the killings. A real gem of a creep. The cops kept the letter a secret until today. The chief was briefing us at headquarters when the call came in about more victims at the Big Drain. There's press here who've come all the way from Providence and Boston. New York! The cops can't lie to us. The cover-up would be a worse scandal than the murders. It's time to come clean. People need the truth. If there's some creeper hiding under Arkham, claiming victims, what can we do about it? There'll be heck to pay if they hold back on us. The mayor was in the sewer when they found the bodies. Did you know that? It's awful fishy. Politicians don't wade in literal waste. But Charlie Kane was there, so I hear. You believe that?"

Minnie Klein wove an interesting tale; he'd credit her talents there. Jake was feeling guilty that he'd temporarily forgotten about Dr Fern. Now he had to catch up with Andy before going to help Maude. They'd been a team, they had to stick together, now more than ever.

The Survivors of the Spider Queen Club.

"How did Andy look? Was he… you know?" Jake asked, bracing for gory details.

"Bloody. But his eyes were open. Rex looked …" Minnie turned her face away. "Lifeless. I only had a quick peek. But he seemed bad..."

"I'm sorry."

"I'm sorry too. I shouldn't have blurted out the news about Andy to you. But I know he'll bounce back in no time." She glanced at Jake's crutches, caught herself staring, and looked up instead. "Well, I've got to get back to work. They locked the doors. They're not letting us inside, but they can't keep us out forever. If I hear anything and you're still around, I'll tell you."

"It was nice to meet you, Minnie."

"Same here, Jake. Read me in the papers."

"I will."

Minnie Klein stubbed out her cigarette, brushed her skirt, and headed for the crowd. She was in control again: notepad in hand, head high, red heels clicking as she went over to question a detective.

Locked doors, Jake thought. He figured he had a way around them.

"Any luck?"

It was Dr Fern. She was alone.

"Not the good kind," Jake said. "How about you?"

"Whoever that girl was, she's gone," Dr Fern said. "I think we're finally finished here."

"Not quite."

She furrowed her brow.

"We're going back into the hospital. I need a doctor," Jake said. He pushed himself upright.

"Is it your leg?"

"No, it's your credentials. I've got to check on a friend before we address Maude's situation. He'll help us, too, if he's in any condition to help." The crutch tips were digging into the grass. He yanked them out, heading for firmer ground. He hiked along, picking up speed. The thrill of danger, the prospect of forming an escape plan – better to act in the face of adversity head-on than to ponder the future with a troubled mind from a dusty office back at the museum. Problems gave Jake purpose, a project to plan. His friends needed him. He'd be there for them.

Dr Fern had to increase her pace to keep up.

21
Head Knock

"YOW! Watch it, that hurts!" Andy said.

"Now hold still. Almost finished. I've got to get this wound thoroughly cleaned out before we stitch it, or you'll be sick as a dog with a nasty infection. You were in a *sewer*."

The nurse poked at the knot on Andy's head with what felt like a red-hot blade.

Andy grimaced.

"You feel that?" she asked, surprised.

Andy said, "I feel everything. As if you're digging for pirate treasure in my skull."

The nurse stopped jabbing him, walking around the exam bed where he was sitting. She was young, with tawny brown skin and dimples in her cheeks. Dressed in white like a nun's habit. Medical uniforms of all types made Andy nervous; they had ever since he was a boy. The sterile primness of them; those occasional, small, cryptic, stains appearing in shades of bronze, rust, or vile gold; that ceremonial air of pseudo-religiosity; little odd hats like the shapeless, sock-like one worn by his nurse, a new style he'd never witnessed before. He hated going to the doctor, seeing nurses, getting shots, and most of all visiting hospitals, where in his experience people went only to die. He'd seen it in his family. Uncles, aunts, his grandparents, even the cousins – carted off to the gothic halls of a medical building, never to return. The prospect of being admitted sent tremors of dread coursing through him. He needed to get out of there now.

"Give it another minute," she said. "Do you have a headache?"

"Like I got knocked silly with a lead pipe," Andy said.

She nodded. Then wiped her hands before scribbling notes on a clipboard. "I don't think it was a lead pipe," she said. "Nothing that heavy. Your skull looks fine. The wound is superficial. Damage appears limited to the soft tissue only. There's quite a bump."

"I'm pretty sure I heard a crack when I got hit." Recalling it sickened him. "Will the doctor be here soon? I'd like to go home."

Andy's fingers involuntarily wandered to his injury, but the nurse stopped his hand.

She shook her head. "No touching. Leave it be. You'll go home when you're ready."

"I'm ready now."

She ignored him, taking his face gently in her hands and tilting his head forward to further inspect his bump. She smelled like soap that had flowers in it. Jasmine and roses.

"The object with which you were struck had an edge to it. You've got an inch-long laceration that's curved but not deep." When she pushed this time, it didn't hurt. "Dizziness?"

"I don't think so."

She let go of him and took a step back. She asked him to move each of his arms and legs independently, then together; he did as he was told.

Andy wanted out of here. When she asked him to try and stand, he jumped off the exam bed, immediately regretting it. His head whirled and his abdomen rippled. A burning sensation filled his throat. Nausea washed over him, reminding him of the chunky wastewater in the pipe.

"Oh, boy. I don't feel so hot. I think I might need to throw up."

The nurse passed him a kidney-shaped tray. "Use this."

Andy held the tray under his chin. Having it made him feel a little less queasy. He was covered with clammy sweat. The last thing he wanted to do was bring up his stomach contents in front of a nurse his own age. It was embarrassing enough getting coldcocked.

Gingerly, he climbed back onto the hospital bed. Sitting on the edge, trying not to fall over. The nurse examined his eyes. She had nice eyes: dark brown with long, thick lashes. One of her eyebrows suddenly arched.

"What?" Andy asked, pulling back. "Did you see something? Something bad?"

"Hmm. You might have a concussion. Your speech sounds fine. No slurring."

"I'd hate to lose control of my words. I'm a reporter. Words are my stock in trade."

Andy looked at the window. The sunlight felt too bright. He squinted, shading his eyes.

The nurse was adding to her notes. Then she opened and closed drawers until she found a few clinking instruments he tried not to look at and a stack of gauze. A roll of bandages.

"It must be exciting. Chasing a big story. Having people read what you write," she said.

"Oh, it's glamorous. You get to slop around in sewers with killers. Travel to faraway lands where strangers feed you drugs.

Monsters try and eat you. Your boss hounds you. Everyone else hates you. It's a great profession for fools."

"Why do people hate you?" she asked curiously. Her face screwed up as if he were a fool. "I like reading the newspapers. Keeps me informed about my city and the world."

She opened a bottle that gave off a sharp astringent odor and added it to her collection.

"It's not everyone. Some people have a hard time hearing the truth. They prefer to keep things hiding in darkness while we drag them into the light. Instead, they want to kill the messenger." She scratched something on her clipboard. "You're not quoting me, are you?"

"Did you say something you shouldn't have?" She gave him a mischievous look.

He couldn't be in too bad of shape if she was teasing him, he thought. Or maybe she was trying to keep him calm because he was injured seriously. Andy couldn't decide.

Now he understood why people got suspicious when you talked to them and then wrote down what they said. "Say, do you think I'm likely to make it?" he asked, smiling.

"Probably." Her expression remained deadpan.

Andy couldn't tell if she was joking. With his pounding head, he was having trouble with subtleties. His worries about hospitals didn't help. "Is there a chance I might not… live?"

She laughed at him then. Finally, he felt better. Nobody would laugh at a dying man.

"My prediction is that you'll fully recover," she said. "You need a few stitches. And you might have a concussion. Tell me what happened again. How you got this knock on the head."

"I was searching for a friend of mine in the sewer. Somebody walloped me. Then I woke up in the dark. Groggy. While I was sitting there figuring out what to do next, I saw a light coming around the corner, shining right at me. So bright I couldn't look at it. A mountain of a guy, too. He asked me what I was doing there. I couldn't really talk yet. The light hurt my eyes. I guess I passed out. Later, the ambulance drivers carted me out. Now I'm here talking to you."

"Why did you think your friend would be in the sewers?" She wrinkled her nose and Andy was suddenly aware that he was coated with sewer slime. He was probably ripe as a hog, but he didn't even notice it anymore. Begrimed. Bloody. Ambushed. Quite the package.

"He was investigating a story. Like I said, I'm a reporter. Was a reporter... still am one... my friend and I are both reporters. We were working on something together."

"Are you feeling confused?"

"No more than I was before. Well, maybe a bit more. The head knock has nothing to do with that. What I'm trying to say is that I'm confused because the situation is confusing. Not because I got my bell rung. If that makes any sense." He sighed. "My thinking's the same as it ever was. A little fuzzy, lost in obscurity..." He wiggled his fingers. "You know, nebulous."

"Nebulous?"

He nodded. "Yeah, nebulous."

She considered what he said, then wrote more notes.

"Is that doc ever going to get here?"

"Sooner than you think." She rested her hands on her hips.

He knew he was acting impatiently, but the place gave him the willies. And there was the matter of Rex. "I hope he gets here fast. I have work to do. My friend might be in deep trouble."

"We're busy here in the emergency ward. Two patients were brought in with you. From the same sewer tunnels. Both are in much worse shape than you. Consider yourself lucky."

Andy grew more alert. His brain was clearing up. Slowly. He sat upright. Pain stabbed behind his eyes. "A pal was in the sewers with me. Is he here? Was he hurt badly?"

"I can't say."

"Why not?" Fear was creeping up on him. Rex dead, floating in the muck, bloodless. Drained by the Lamprey. Another victim. Andy had let him down, going and falling asleep on him like a no-good loafer. Sure, he'd been tired. But the search for the truth was more important.

"Because I don't know." She walked back behind Andy. "Let's get you stitched."

"Won't the doc do that?"

Andy was more worried about Rex than he was about himself. He'd be fine if he could get out of this hospital. He needed to get fixed quickly and see if Rex was one of the other patients in the ward. But it had to be Rex. How many people went traipsing in the sewers?

"What's this fishing line tied to your wrist?" the nurse asked, waving a pale strand.

Andy had forgotten about that. He looked down at his forearm and saw the line had been cut off. "I was tied to my friend. We were using it to keep track of one another in the sewer maze." He guessed this sounded quite odd. Men tying themselves up. It even sounded odd to him, and he'd done it. "It's complicated." The nurse was working on his head wound again, pull and tug, but he couldn't feel anything, only a vague sense of something squirming on top of his head, like a fat toad. "Did any of the other patients that came in have fishing line tied to their wrists?"

"One of them did."

"That's my friend!" Andy felt relief that turned to distress. "Is he alive?"

"Hold still." The nurse was picking up and dropping metal instruments into a metal pan.

Andy started to turn around and noticed a pile of bloody gauze and dirty red cotton balls.

Oh boy, he thought. That's a lot of blood. My blood. Coldness sloshed over him. His mouth tasted dry, as if he'd been chewing hay.

He sat still, refusing to let his gaze wander. He raised the curved tray under his chin again. Think about something else, he told himself. Black blobs invaded his vision. He coughed.

"Hold still," she said. "Almost finished."

"Finished?" He sounded far away to himself. Where was the doctor?

The nurse said nothing. She was probably tired of his questions, he thought. He couldn't blame her. Patients probably asked her questions constantly. She must deal with it all day long.

He coughed again. "Sorry," he said.

"You feeling sick?"

"A bit. I might've swallowed some of that sewer water while I was laying in it."

She walked around the exam table and stood in front of him. Assessing. Diagnosing. He stared at her until he realized his mistake. It cleared up for him like fog blowing away.

"You're the doc, aren't you?" He felt silly asking. It was obvious now. The clues had been there. He was aching all over, not from the beating he took but from embarrassment.

"Dr Lena Singleton. I'm visiting on an exchange program with a hospital in Chicago."

Andy sagged. He hadn't wanted to make a fool of himself. Yet he'd done it perfectly.

"Hi, Dr Singleton. I'm Andy. The worst patient you've ever had," he said.

"You'd be surprised, Andy." She started wrapping a long bandage around his head.

"All my past doctors have looked like old grandfatherly types. I hated every one of them. They gave me the creeps. I guess I expected to meet someone like that. I was wrong. Obviously."

She pinned the bandage in place. "All set. Not too tight, is it?"

He shook his head. "Snug as a bug."

"I'm writing you two prescriptions. One is for pain, the other will combat infection."

Andy watched her, wishing he'd been smarter. He'd never been college material. He certainly couldn't have done what she'd done. Medical school. All those books... and the blood.

"Do you have anything for stupidity?"

"There is no pill for that." She was teasing him, but she didn't seem to be angry about his mistake as she finished writing her notes for the druggist.

Andy was about to ask her about Chicago, a city he wanted to visit someday – now there was a town bursting at the seams with crime stories! – when the hanging curtain dividing his bed from the other exam areas was pulled aside, and a face popped in. A face he recognized.

"Jake Williams! What're you doing here?"

"I was going to ask you the same thing," Jake said. "This is my friend, Dr Carolyn Fern."

Andy nodded.

"Pleased to meet you. This is Dr Singleton. Best doc in the world. She sewed me up."

"Hello," Dr Singleton said.

The two doctors nodded, acknowledging each other.

Andy said, "I was down in the sewers working on a story about the Lamprey. You might know him as the sewer strangler from the papers. He's got a few other names, too. Wait till I tell you the scoop. But I think the Lamprey sneaked up on me and put my lights out. I went down there with a colleague of mine. Name of Rex Murphy. He's here too. I guess we both got waylaid like a couple of amateurs. Huh. Danger has my number. Calls me on a regular basis. Did you happen to see Rex? Thin guy with a small beard. Round eyeglasses. He had fishing line tied to his wrist like me. It's a long story…

"Hey, what's up with you two? Rex made it out, didn't he?"

Dr Fern exchanged glances with Dr Singleton. Something passed between them unsaid.

Dr Singleton handed Andy his prescriptions. "Take your pills. Keep the stitches dry. Come see me in one week." She excused herself. The curtain swayed behind her.

"Andy," Jake said solemnly, "we need to talk."

22
Modus Operandi

The Lamprey sat coiled in an uncomfortable hospital chair. Waiting. Watching. Gray on gray. An unremarkable figure. Forgettable. Forgotten until it was too late. Then the Lamprey would latch onto its chosen victim. Sometimes it did it on a quiet street corner, with all the shops closed, or along a strip of cavernous warehouses. Seizing victims who were alone. Pressing itself flat against a wall – swimming in shadows – the Lamprey stalked, edging ever closer. Then...

Strike!

Dragging its prey into an open manhole, a pried-away storm grate... down, down, down. Going underground was sweet relief. In the sewers it could do the necessary work.

It needed to find the girl. Wendy. Where was Wendy?

The little pickpocket from the crowd. She'd been there at the sewer tunnel today. Hiding outside the Big Drain. Like a scout. An enemy spy. Lurkers hate other lurkers, recoiling, repelled at the sight, which feels more like a touch, of another's eyes. Wherefore art thou, Wendy?

What is the reason for you? The Lamprey wanted to know why she was watching.

What did the girl know? And how did she receive this special knowledge?

Who was Wendy?

They had forged a link, the two of them, the Lamprey and Wendy. They could talk with their minds. The Lamprey didn't share this connection with many people. Perhaps the closest comparisons were the blood donors – that's how the Lamprey thought of its victims. In their last moments, a kind of peacefulness drifted down, as cold as snow falling on a winter's night. Their skin always grew colder at the end. Nothing dramatic. Just a gentle shift from life to death that the Lamprey detected. The Lamprey never acted out of malice. This wasn't for the Lamprey – no, no, no – the donors served a greater purpose. The magic inside them that had to come out.

So, the police had three new victims. Evidence to trample, clues to ignore.

That should keep them busy for a while.

It gave the Lamprey time to think. To breathe.

The chair sat at an intersection of two hallways, just off the center, against a dingy wall.

Perfect.

The Lamprey closed its eyes and listened. It soaked up information.

Doctors have strong voices, usually. You can snatch them from the air. Cops are loud too, using their blunt words to shove people around, to intimidate, and to assert their dominance.

The Lamprey was quiet. Not a peep. Turn the lip lock and toss away the key. Or if it talked, it made sure not to alarm, never to scare. Don't want to draw any unneeded attention.

One victim was dead. The Lamprey knew that. Now everyone else did too. Hoo-rah.

That first reporter, the one the Lamprey ran into so unexpectedly – Rex Murphy – was here too, with the busy, busy doctors. The Lamprey gasped when it first sighted him exploring in the pipes with his candle flame doubled in his eyeglasses, then it thought, *This is a gift, a new donor delivered to me by Syrx-Crugoth who must be gaining strength enough to send me help.* The Lamprey caught Rex by the throat and throttled him. In the dark. Bringing him to his knees. No time to think, then he went slack as a worm on the pavement. The Lamprey was getting set to drain him, to take his donation for Syrx-Crugoth, to free the god from its prison. But there was that oddity – the fishing line tied to Rex's wrist. Oh, the Lamprey didn't like that one tiny bit.

It kept a pair of handcuffs in its bag of tricks in case a donor might wake up during the donation. It never needed to use them before. But Rex was different. It handcuffed him to a small steampipe running along the top of the tunnel and left him hanging there while it followed the fishing line through the tubular maze. Turns and turns. At the pipe mouth, where a former donor had been flushed into the river, the Lamprey saw someone sitting on the rocks. A man. A young man. Ahh. He was asleep. Mouth agape, snoring.

Could the Lamprey take two donors tonight?

Was this the bounty of Syrx-Crugoth?

A foghorn blew from one of the ships heading into port.

The young man stirred. Licking his lips. Slouching farther down in the crabby, craggy, wet seat strewn with seaweed, snails, and gull droppings. He curled on himself like a wharf cat.

I can take him.

I will take him.

Then there were new voices from above, outside the pipe. Two sailors, talking gruffly.

They'd noticed the same youth passed out on the Miskatonic's shores and took him for one who had indulged too much in bootleg liquor and sought the cool relief of the slimy rocks.

They laughed. Misrecognized him as a kindred spirit, devotee of the spirits. One of us, they said. Big voices, from likely big men. Men used to a raw, rough life earned on the water.

The Lamprey retreated into the pipe deeper, seeking the shadows. Direct confrontations were not the Lamprey's method. Surprise. Ambush. Quick immobilization. A slow emptying of blood, life, energy – these were the modi operandi that had proved to be so successful in the past.

Going toe-to-toe with ruffians was a bad proposition.

And so it was that the Lamprey decided not to get greedy. It left the young man where he was. Dumbly snuggled against the riverbank. Dreaming. It followed back the way it had come.

Or so it thought.

When the Lamprey searched the pipe bottom for that gossamer string used to harvest creatures from the water – the fishing line – it came up empty. Despite all the time spent executing duties in this network of crumbly bricks and limestone, the pipes were still confusing.

The Lamprey was lost.

So, up, up, up a rusty iron ladder driven into the limestone, the Lamprey grunted and shoved aside a manhole cover, hearing the skirling, scraping rasp of steel on cobbles, for a peek.

It was still dark. But dawn was breaking. A gray milky light ran down the city walls. Filling crevices. Pooling. Soon the daylight would descend. And daylight was never preferred. There! What were those? A pair of eyes spotted the uncovered manhole. Not human. Dog? Cat?

Neither.

A possum with its white cone face and beady black dollish eyes. Eating at a trashcan.

The Lamprey laughed, muffling its mouth with a glove. We are scavengers, you and me.

Two scavengers inhabiting the dusky blue fringe of the coming day. Seeking our nibbles.

The Lamprey, staring higher, failed to recognize the buildings on this block. But it could read the street signs in the morning twilight. Lich Street and Powder Mill! So far from the stomping grounds! No wonder things had looked unfamiliar down below. There was a panic now settling on the Lamprey's heart, weighing down each thump with a crooked tilt, a squirt of fear.

Must find my way home. So desperate was the feeling that the Lamprey considered walking above the streets until it could find a good place to venture down again. The dawning light burned like a fuse that grew brighter and brighter – then BOOM! All the plans, all the work for naught! The god would be angry, very angry. Righteously so. *I live to serve. But I am failing.*

Then a reset. Like the tide drawing off a beach leaving it raked smooth, clean, untrodden.

The Lamprey concentrated and deduced its way back to Rex Murphy, newspaperman. Unhooking him from the pipe, the Lamprey noted that he had not yet regained consciousness. If he were dead already it would be difficult to extract his contribution. But no, he had a heartbeat. Faint, but unmistakable. Tick-tock. Lifting its ear off his chest, the Lamprey hauled him through the slop closer to the violated chamber where the crystal waited, aglow.

Where Syrx-Crugoth waited.

"My watch? What about my watch? Why do you ask?" the Lamprey said to no one there.

Listening to the murmurings of Syrx-Crugoth.

"What do you mean there is no time?"

But gods are never, ever wrong.

"I won't argue. I'd never argue with thee, mighty one. O ye without mercy. I am thine."

The Lamprey did as it was told. Thumping Rex's noggin for good measure. No time for drowning. No time to steal his energy. Then, remembering about the fishing line as it tangled its wrists – frustration! – the Lamprey made a trap for the young man from the rocks. A sound of sloshing footsteps told the truth – that Syrx-Crugoth was correct. Time was short. Here came the wakened youth. The Lamprey thumped him too. Tried to crack his skull apart. Then slipping out, out of the pipes before discovery. This was not the time for revelations. Hide! Run! Run! RUN!

Alas, sitting here in the hospital chair, analyzing obstacles, the Lamprey made a mental list.

Rex was alive. No donation received.

The young man – Andy was his name, if the voices behind the curtain were to be trusted – was alive and conscious. Talking. Hardly the worse for wear! But did he see me? Could he make an identification? No. No worries. No donation received.

The last donor discovered. Donation successful. But police interest intensifying.

Where is the girl? Who is the girl? Why is the girl?

Then came the most amazing thing. The Lamprey did not have to seek the girl because...

I've found you, Wen. Long time, no see. Miss me?

She was hiding in an empty examination stall. The Lamprey spotted her little muddy shoes. And she stiffened. What was she doing in here? Such a strange child. Gifted, no doubt.

In public she was safer than she might've guessed. The Lamprey was a shy monster.

I'm not going to hurt you. Not here. I want to talk. I want you to know we can be friends.

Leave me alone, she said telepathically. Stop following me.

But you're the one following me, I think, Wendy dear. Do you know my name?

No. I don't want to know it.

I'm called the Lamprey. I have other names, but that's my favorite. If you'd only peek outside the curtain, you'd see me sitting in a chair up the hallway. I promise to stay in my seat. I am visiting the hospital to check on a couple of old friends from the drainpipe. If you'd only give me a chance, I'd show you that I can be friendly, especially when I'm curious about someone...

But she didn't listen. She broke from her hiding place like a rabbit and burst into the adjacent examination area, where two people were talking to Andy, who'd fouled up this day.

The Lamprey rose and left. No one bothered to notice. Soft steps, a gray blur. Ghostly.

It looked for the door to the lower levels. The basement and sub-basement. The drains.

Why won't she believe me when I say I'm curious? That was the honest truth. The Lamprey didn't harm people for no reason, or simply because it wanted to. The donors had magic in them.

Powerful, special magic. It had to find the magic and make the magic come out.

Syrx-Crugoth said so.

And gods never lie because they never have to.

Wendy should have known that. She had the most special magic the Lamprey ever saw.

23
Fear Itself

"Talk about what?" Andy asked. "You mean Rex? Does he look bad? You can tell me."

Dr Fern tugged the curtain closed. The chaos of the emergency ward faded into the background. A stifled moan, a shriek down a far corridor. The doctor turned; her look was grave.

"Rex is in a coma," she said. "He hasn't regained consciousness since he arrived. His prognosis is unknown. I could only get a snapshot of his condition from his attending physician, but it's worrisome. I saw him briefly while I was talking to his team. They are doing their best."

"The Lamprey got him?" Andy asked, choking on his words. "I knew it. He got us both."

Dr Fern went on. "It looks like Rex was strangled. So, I'd say yes, the Lamprey is the likely suspect. There's evidence of bruising around Rex's throat. His eyes are bloodshot. He's also been handcuffed for some time. He has contusions around his wrists, a possible fracture, and a dislocated shoulder, as if he were dragged or suspended by his arms. The police think he was held captive for a while. The mayor's out there in the ward somewhere. We heard he was down in the sewer when they found you, inspecting this anomalous object they discovered."

"Mayor Kane was in the sewer and neither of us got to interview him," Andy said, shaking his head wryly. "What a story that might've been. Geez, if Rex knew, it would kill him." Andy realized what he'd said. His shoulders slumped in shame. "I should keep my trap shut."

The horror was sinking in. They'd been on the right track. The Lamprey did return to the sewers. They'd been close. Too close. Now they were paying the price for tempting danger.

"There is some good news," Jake said.

Andy lifted his head, brightening. Jake always tried to find the silver lining in a thundercloud.

"What good news?"

"Your colleague was choked, but not slashed. It looks like you might've interrupted the Lamprey before they completed their attack. Rex is lucky to have his blood. You saved him."

Andy swallowed. It was nothing to feel proud of. "I should've been there sooner."

Any relief he was experiencing battled with the guilt and disappointment he felt in himself. *I'm trying to win back my job, but instead I almost end up dead, and I nearly get another journalist killed.* Hardly a stellar comeback. But Jake was right about one thing: Rex was a lucky guy – but only if he eventually woke up from his oblivion.

Andy touched his throat. The Lamprey had knocked him out too, and he might've been strangled and drained like the other victims. It could've easily been poor Rex *and* poor Andy. A couple of dead reporters down the drain, floating in the river.

"Don't be too hard on yourself," Dr Fern said, offering her psychological counsel.

"You're right. It's water under the bridge, or down the sewer pipe. The point is to stop the murders and get the story. Did they find any clues about the Lamprey?" Andy asked.

"There was the third body," Jake said. "That's a bit of gruesome evidence to dissect."

"Body? So, that's one dead this round. Dr Singleton said three people were brought in from the Big Drain site." An obvious question came to mind. "Do we know who it is?"

Jake shrugged and said, "I spoke to your friend from the paper, Minnie Klein. She didn't have a positive I.D."

"Minnie Klein." Andy hadn't thought of Minnie in a while. He tried not to dwell on the office, what people were doing, the kind of hot stories they might be chasing; it made him sad. The idea that life continued in his absence made him feel like a ghost. Minnie was a good reporter. Fun too. They used to get pie and coffee and talk about their careers.

"Paddy O'Hara," Dr Fern said.

"Who?" Jake asked.

"I think that might be the name of the person whose body they found. He was the missing shift boss from the Big Drain." She glanced up at them to see if her information had any effect.

"How do you know that?" Andy asked, surprised.

She swiveled from where she'd been standing by the slit of the curtain. In her hand was a water-logged notepad. "I read it in here. In this notebook." The pages were rippled and swollen.

"Where did you get that?" Jake said.

"I took it from the trash in the exam area where your friend is.

He had the book sticking out of his pocket. The nurses tossed it with his dirty clothes. I thought, maybe this is important?"

"The cops didn't try and stop you? They just let you take it?" Andy asked.

"They didn't see me. I don't think they know about it. That's good though, right?"

Andy gasped. "Yes! That's great. You've got a reporter's instincts. May I see it, please?" Dr Fern passed the wrinkled, stained pages to Andy. His lips pursed in disappointment. "The ink is smeared. Several of the pages are stuck together. But I think parts are salvageable." He wiped the cardboard covers gently with a hospital sheet, handling the crinkly pages as if they were the remnants of an ancient scroll.

Then he said, "Rex told me he lost this in the sewer back when he was arrested. He must've found it again in the wee hours when he went back for another look." The damp paper was coming apart in his fingers, dissolving into bite-size mushy pieces. Inky words transformed into black watercolor blooms. "Gosh, what a mess. Most of the pages are destroyed."

Jake said, "Not so fast there, Andy. May I?"

With two hands Andy handed off the soggy notebook to Jake. "It's hopeless."

Jake said, "I've saved maps lost overboard in frigid mountain lakes and raging rivers during a monsoon. I've resurrected tomes that had more in common with decaying plants than any written record. Once I even recovered a sea chart from the belly of a deceased tiger shark. Never say never. We must dry it. Then try again. I promise you that the situation is far from hopeless."

Just then there was a flurry of activity from the edge of the curtain beside Andy's bed. The curtain lifted, and a young girl rushed into the examination area. She appeared terrified.

"That's her," Dr Fern said. "The girl I saw climbing from the ambulance!"

Everyone froze in place. The girl was trying to catch her breath. She watched their eyes.

"Are you feeling all right?" Jake asked the new arrival.

She appeared to be searching for something or someone. A relative? A public authority figure? Perhaps it was only a friendly face she was looking for. A person who looked like a helper. Hospitals are living gothic horror tales, Andy thought. Full of blood and guts. Instruments of torture. Locked rooms. Death stalked these halls with its scythe poised to harvest. It *was* scary.

"We're not going to hurt you," he said. "Everyone here is kind. You're safe."

"No, I'm not safe," the girl said.

Dr Fern stepped toward her, then crouched down to her level so they'd see eye-to-eye.

"My name is Dr Fern. I work here. I promise you that we will keep you safe. What's your name?" She smiled and held out her hand in case the girl wanted to hold it.

The girl didn't move. She was ready to bolt again at the slightest provocation. More than nervous, she was electrified with trepidation. She turned her head slowly from side to side, scanning, evidently listening, not to them, or only to them, but for another sound.

"They aren't here anymore," she said.

"Who isn't here?" the psychologist asked. "The person who wants to harm you?"

"It isn't a person."

"What is it?" Andy asked.

The girl seemed unsure if she should trust them. Looking from face to face, she made up her mind. She took the doctor's hand and squeezed her fingers.

"It's a monster. I called it Ole Gray. That's a name I made up. It told me its real name."

"What name?" Dr Fern asked softly. "You can tell us."

"The Lamprey," she said. "Don't let it get me. My name is Wendy. Wendy Adams."

"I've got you, Wendy," Dr Fern said.

Jake and Andy were speechless. The two of them looked around as a sudden chill entered the private, screened-off space. Both men stared dumbly at the floor. The girl and the psychologist were looking too. Andy didn't see the thing beneath them as much as he sensed it. The air smelled of ammonia, of fear itself.

Of a dark presence.

Down there.

Unseen, but felt. Andy experienced this entity in a way difficult to describe – yet he perceived it as physically as he perceived what any of his senses told him. Something was there.

Vague. Enormous.

His stomach dropped as if he were falling. He watched his breath turn foggy white. All their breaths steaming out of them like spirits…

Back and forth the thing changed in the darkness, perhaps unaware of its own conspicuous power, or more likely shameless, uncaring, as it oozed energy that penetrated the ground, basements, and floors. Emanating from below. Like a huge ancient chunk of ice radiating cold, cold, so cold…

How Andy knew this he could not articulate, but he knew its truth nonetheless.

"It uses the sewer tunnels," Wendy said. "It's under St Mary's now. Right beneath us."

Andy didn't doubt her. From the looks on their faces the rest of them didn't either.

24
Black Cherry

"Witchcraft?"

Charlie turned his gaze from the windows of his office. His blue eyes bulged.

"Yes, I'm afraid so," said Mandy. She was seated directly across from the politician.

Charlie sighed. After yesterday's drama, he'd hoped for a calmer day today. It wasn't going to happen; he could see that now. He'd called for this early morning meeting late last night, telling everyone to go home and get some sleep, though he hadn't gotten much himself, sitting up in his library sipping warm milk, nibbling on molasses cookies his butler brought him.

He had sat up most of the night beside a small table with a candlestick telephone. How he loathed the thing, but without it his job would've been impossible. This way he kept in contact with his advisors. He made calls to his appointees, to the papers, and his political allies. He ran the city more and more through wires than he did in person. A sad state of affairs.

So, he told the members of his newly minted Lamprey Task

Force to rest up and be at his office at 6:30AM sharp to give him good counsel on how to tackle this problem with murders and unidentifiable artifacts getting in the way of the Big Drain. "We need to save the city," he said.

Now he gazed down the long table, thinking the city might be doomed. The end was near.

"Before you tell me more, Miss Thompson, I'd like to clarify what I've heard thus far." The mayor cleared his throat. He screwed and unscrewed the cap of his fountain pen. "Chief," Charlie nodded to the only person in uniform in the room, "you said it's your belief despite these threatening letters you've received, that the bodies we've been finding are most likely, partially or in total, the result of ongoing city gang wars stemming from bootlegging networks that operate quite literally underground. Is this correct?"

The craggy-faced, bleary-eyed police chief looked half-awake, but he nodded. "That's right." The chief gave out words like he approved days off for his subordinates, very sparingly.

Charlie pointed the end of his pen at him. "Don't the gangs usually shoot their victims?"

"Well…" the chief hesitated, "not always. They're clever boys. Violent in a variety of ways. Machine guns. Pistols. Switchblade knives. Bombings are part of their despicable arsenal."

"Uh-huh. But have they, in the past, strangled then drained people of blood? It doesn't seem very efficient to me. I've always found men of violence tend to be focused on the quick and dirty way of doing things. They don't have the time or inclination to be… experimental."

"You'd be surprised," the chief said unconvincingly. "Especially at the young ones."

Charlie's face was stony. "Have your detectives uncovered a single shred of evidence connecting any of the victims to our colorful local criminal organizations?" the mayor said.

The chief spoke into his fingers, tented before his lips, as if in prayer. "No, sir."

Charlie cupped his ear. "I'm sorry, I couldn't hear you. Will you please speak up?"

The chief shifted in his chair. The leather squeaked as if he were squishing a mouse. "No, sir. We have not." His hands spread flat on the table, fingers drumming softly.

"You have not. And no bullets. No known gang connections. Not a drop of booze or a single broken bottle in any of the spots where bodies were discovered." Charlie shuffled the papers in front of him for a minute as the chief grew increasingly impatient. Eventually he said curtly, "Thank you, chief."

The chief massaged his jaw as if he'd been punched.

He might rather have been, Charlie thought. At least then he'd know how to respond.

Charlie looked at the trio of representatives from the Big Drain renovation team. They might have been three brothers from the same inane family of excuse-makers.

"You musketeers have nothing new to offer? You don't even have a decent set of reliable maps for the waterworks honeycombing the foundation of our fair New England town. You've failed to secure the main construction site. And yet all you can tell me, in excruciating detail I might add, is the cost of this enterprise which increases it seems by the hour, perhaps by the minute. I'm sorry for the loss of your man, Paddy O'Hara. I'm deeply concerned for many reasons about the whereabouts of your missing digger, Stanley Budzinski. Anything I left out?"

The three silently shook their heads.

"Very well, then." Charlie shifted his focus to the window. Clouds racing, trees bending. A windy day on the rise. The leafy greenery thrashed at the lower panes of glass.

"Our geological expert, Mr Clyde Laurents, has failed to make our little gather–"

With that introduction, the door flew open, and the ruddy, sweaty, mutton-chopped man entered. He paused as if he were expecting the office to be unoccupied; his mouth hung open.

"Oh, dear," he said. "This is awkward."

"Mr Laurents!" Charlie exclaimed. "So, you've decided to grace us with your presence."

"Why, yes, Mr Mayor. It was never in doubt. I mean my attending. It's only my cuckoo clock is broken – or there may be a chance I neglected to wind it before going to bed – but either way, I did not wake to the usual bongs as I typically do most mornings. I apologize profusely."

The geologist whipped off his old-fashioned derby hat and placed it on the table, revealing a nest of unruly ginger curls in dire need of a pair of scissors and a good, stiff brush.

Charlie couldn't help but chuckle. How could he remain angry at this odd fellow?

"You are just in time to give us your report," he said to Clyde, who had dropped his umbrella while simultaneously unlatching and kicking over his battered leather satchel, spilling forth the tools of his trade – rock hammer, magnifying lens, and a pair of scratched goggles – onto the polished marble floor. The geologist fell to his knees to contain the accident.

He scooped the contents back into his bag and smiled around the group.

"My report?" he asked. "Which report is that?"

"On the crystal," Charlie said. "Its nature and possible origin. Preliminary assessment?"

"Of course!" Clyde smiled a toothy grin. He found his seat and smoothed his untamable cowlicks. "I rechecked my test results and measurements. Poring over my reference books until my fingertips bled." He showed Mandy his fingers. "We keep a sample collection over at Hurley Mining. Well, I pulled so many drawers out I thought my shoulder might come loose. I think I'll need a new magnifying lens because the one in my bag is plum worn out." Clyde laughed at his touch of humor. "I have reached a conclusion. Which I will stand by."

Those gathered at the long table waited. Charlie leaned forward, close enough he might've snatched the geologist by the collar. "Yes, Clyde. Well, don't keep us in suspense. What is it? What is the crystal?"

"Oh." Clyde nodded once dramatically. "It is… unprecedented." When no one reacted, the scientist made another attempt. "The specimen is simply fantastic. Without parallel in the geological record. One-of-a-kind. At least on this planet. My suspicions are that it crashed here – not looking the way we see it now, but encapsulated in an outer shell, likely made of iron, that was blasted away on impact. Leaving the inner crystal cluster intact. Think of a passenger arriving in a breakaway carriage. I'd like to conduct an in-depth study of the surrounding rock layers inside the chamber at once."

The chief commenced with a phlegmy cough that verged on an outright burst of laughter. His face turned full magenta. "So, you're saying it's from outer space? Like moon cheese?"

Clyde chuffed at that.

"It comes to us from farther away than the moon. I'm no expert on meteoroids and planetoids, by any means. Although that'd be an excellent place to start. It's not from around here. The positioning of the crystal tells me it formed at another location. Who knows where?" Clyde pointed to the ceiling of the mayor's office and grinned.

"How did it get into the sewer? The chamber was here first. It broke through the chamber dome. We could see that. Wouldn't such an impact have been noticed and written down?" Charlie said. "Wouldn't the area of destruction have been vast and catastrophic?"

"I've been thinking about that," Clyde said, stroking his throat. "Know what I think?"

"That would be impossible," Charlie muttered.

"I think the crystal was here first, and whoever built that hub of drainage tunnels did it around the formation. Part of the crystal shows obvious signs of a previous repair. A split that's been filled in with cement. Crudely achieved, without question the work of human hands. In my opinion an act of conservation. I think that the waters of Arkham flowed around this crystal for centuries. I think the diggers discovered it and left it there. Because they sensed it was special."

"Special?"

"One-of-a-kind, as I said, Mr Mayor."

Charlie sat with his eyes closed, but he was clearly breathing. The sound of his sonorous breaths was the only noise in the room, until he opened his eyes, looking directly at Mandy, and said, "Miss Thompson, as you can see, I am at a loss for words. And for solutions. Will you please enlighten us as to the results of your research into the copious Arkham archives, if any?"

"As I was saying earlier, I believe the crystal is directly linked to Arkham's long and storied history of witchcraft. I have documents that support my theory. And a tale to share."

Clyde Laurents gasped and grabbed his derby hat as if he were about to flee. Charlie reached across the tabletop and clamped onto Clyde's freckled wrist.

"It's fine, Clyde. The witches are long dead by now. Sit tight. Show some respect."

Clyde grumbled and shook his head, releasing his hat as he settled back in his chair.

"Continue, please," Charlie said to Mandy.

Where he had either been bored or perplexed with the previous briefings, Mandy's statement garnered his full attention. The others seemed riveted as well.

"I analyzed my crayon rubbings of the symbols and the names in the message chiseled into the crystal," Mandy began. "The symbols matched one collection in the Orne Library. The pertinent documents come from the 1693 trial of an Arkhamite woman who faced charges of witchcraft and murder. We have letters and a few personal accounts of the legal proceedings. Testimony against the woman claimed that she was the leader of a coven of witches known as the Prism. Scant proof of the Prism's existence survives anywhere in the archives. But there are a small number of references, from many years later, that mention rumors about a nefarious coven practicing in Arkham that closely resembles descriptions in the 1693 testimony and some contemporaneous diary fragments. The woman from the trial had her name etched in the crystal."

"Dionysia Burroughs?" Charlie said. "She was the woman charged with murder?"

Mandy nodded. "Dionysia Burroughs and her husband were farmers. He was deceased at the time of the trial. They came to Arkham from Salem. I can't tell you when or under what circumstances. Their farm was prosperous until Mr Burroughs' death. Dionysia sold the property for a tidy sum, with the agreement she would be allowed to remain as sole tenant of a house there, rent-free. In the years following, she was renowned for the size of her chickens' eggs and her sewing skills. Townspeople sought her advice. One diary remarked upon her unusual height."

"What happened to her?" the chief wanted to know.

"She was convicted. The judge sentenced her to be hanged," Mandy said.

The chief slapped his palm loudly against the table. "Good! Justice served!"

Clyde jumped, nearly tipping over backward in his seat.

Mandy frowned and went on. "However, before her sentence could be carried out, she disappeared from the jail, never to be seen again. Suspicions were that she fled back to Salem but no trace of her was reported there. Others said they saw her living wild in the woods. Her followers were rounded up, arrested. Questioned under duress. Several were hanged. The most recent rumor was that she took her favorite coven members with her and moved underground."

Clyde sucked air in through his teeth. "That is quite a tale, to be sure!"

"Answer me this, Miss Thompson," Charlie said. "Is it conceivable that the Prism did flee into the caves and tunnels under this city, and that their offspring, either literal or spiritual or a mixture of both, have persisted in our town? Might they still exist in Arkham to this day? To me, I confess, it is conceivable. Do you believe that members of the Prism might be responsible for the carvings discovered on the crystal? I'm asking only if it is possible – not certain, only possible."

"The odds are long on your hypotheses. But yes, it's a possibility, I suppose. Yes."

"Chief? I want you to marshal your best officers. Use every resource. This is the top priority. If the Prism survives in my city, I demand all followers of this cult be weeded out, brought in for questioning, and held in custody until we can determine their involvement in these murders. Evil dwells in our midst. Find them. Catch them. Bring them down. Am I understood?"

"Yes, sir. But just so you know, I never heard a whisper of these witchy hooligans."

"Nevertheless. Exhaust your men looking for them. Beat the bushes. Search!"

Charlie turned to the trio from the Big Drain project. "Gentlemen, rip that crystal out from under this city. I don't care what it takes. Use jackhammers and dynamite if need be."

Clyde was on his feet now. "You can't do that! It's priceless. These men aren't qualified. They'll ruin a treasure that belongs to all of us. To the world. To posterity. Not to mention the scientific repercussions. You cannot destroy that which you fail to comprehend. It's immoral!"

Charlie rose from his chair. He was not an unreasonable man. He believed in fairness.

"Clyde, I hear you. Loud and clear. I'm giving you twenty-four hours to talk to your expert friends. If they can tell me a more compelling story than Mandy Thompson, then I may – *may* – reconsider how we remove the crystal. But it will be removed.

For the Big Drain to be dug, and to the benefit of the citizens of Arkham to whom I am but a loyal and humble servant."

"Thank you, Mr Mayor." Clyde clutched Charlie's hand fiercely. "You won't regret it."

Mandy looked skeptical at best. She'd done good work on a wretched timetable, but to Charlie it seemed that she was wondering if he were overreacting. But she was a studious person while he believed that bold moves made swiftly were the hallmark of exceptional leadership.

He had to do something. He didn't have the luxury of more research. He had to act.

The others filed out of the room. The wind howled. Trees shook their green wigs.

Charlie felt better. He opened his humidor, struck a match, and puff puffed.

Today was already a positive day. He hoped the feeling would last longer than his cigar.

25

The Bucket

Andy was back at work sweeping the hallway of a Rivertown apartment house. His head was killing him. Yesterday had been a crazy day. He almost died; he'd reunited with Jake Williams; he met Dr Fern and learned about Maude's horrible situation at the sanatorium. Despite it all, he had slept like the dead. He always hated that saying, and he wished it hadn't come to his mind now. But you can't help things that pop into your head. They just do.

The hallway was an ungodly mess. Somebody had broken another window. There was scattered glass on the floor, glass down the stairs, glass everywhere from when the brick came crashing through. He made little piles of the broken pieces with his broom. That was simple enough. It kept him from falling apart himself. I'll make order out of chaos, he told himself. One hallway at a time. Holding the world together.

"Wendy," Andy called down the stairs. "Could you bring the bucket up here?"

"Sure thing," Wendy said.

He heard the rhythmic squeak-squeak of the bucket handle

as she climbed the stairs. He heard her voice chattering away. She wasn't talking to him or herself but to the other kid she ran with, James. James was down there with her, being his other assistant.

After their bizarre ordeal at the hospital, Jake invited them all back to his office at the museum. Wendy had told them her story – well, part of it, the how-I-got-to-here part – then she said she needed to return to her house and look in on James. She was in a panic about him. When they all got there and saw where she and James were living, it made everybody feel like a change was due. Dr Fern offered to take them to her place, but Wendy surprised them by asking if they might stay with Andy. Andy couldn't refuse two poor kids down on their luck. He figured that Wendy had trouble trusting adults, and since he was the closest to her age, she'd picked him. He was embarrassed by the condition of his digs, but Wendy and James acted as if they'd been booked into a suite at the Silver Gate Hotel, carrying on while he cooked them their dinner.

"You live here?" James asked, skeptically. "By yourself? Nobody bossing you around?"

It was only three ill-lit, stuffy rooms added to the back of small New England cottage.

"Nobody but my bosses at my job. And my landlady when the rent's past due."

"You got it made," James said. "I wish I lived here."

"It's awful nice," Wendy agreed. "I always wanted to live in Easttown."

Andy was dubious. "You did?" He thought Easttown appeared so old, decrepit, and creaky it might one day collapse in the dust. A raggedy neighborhood full of worn-out laborers. His modest house was painted a drab oyster that was peeling away. A widow lived in the front rooms. Andy's three were a kitchen, where he spent most of his time, a bedroom where he slept, and a storage closet with nothing in it but some two-by-fours and a stack of red bricks. He kept the door to the closet shut and never went in there. Now the kids were using it. In the yard was a vine-covered privy with a moon-shape cut in the door. He warned them to watch out for spiders. They had a water pump. The water was cold and tasted like iron, but it quenched your thirst.

"The houses are so far away from each other. You've got room to play," James observed.

Did the boy think he still played outside?

On second thought perhaps I do, Andy thought.

"It's so quiet here," Wendy said. "Peaceful. I'll bet you hear frogs croaking at night."

Andy hadn't previously seen the value in that. The woods were nearby, but he never wandered. There were too many homemade stills and amateur bootleggers with rifles to worry about. He finished heating the soup, added salt and pepper. They had stale bread for dipping.

"Dinner is served," he said.

Nobody talked for a while, just spoons rattling and hums of satisfaction at the hot meal.

Andy filled their cups with water pumped into an old milk bottle he used as a pitcher.

"This is delicious," James said, his mouth half full of potato cubes and carrot wheels.

"Oh, thank you. It's the specialty of the house," Andy said, scooping more into the bowls. He didn't tell them that he got his vegetables from the stock Davy Schoffner at the General Store thought wasn't up to standard to sell because it was mushy or had sat on the shelves for too long. It was fit for consumption. You just had to trim the bad parts. Not knowing made it taste better.

"Compliments to the chef!" Wendy said.

Andy wondered where she'd heard that before. Seeing the kids so happy made him feel good, but it also made him think about how tough they must've had it. That made him sad again.

Between slurps of vegetable soup, Wendy had a couple of surprises to share with her host.

"I saw you that day," she said.

"Which day is that, madam?" Andy was having fun with his guests, the first he'd had since he'd moved after losing his job at the paper. It felt strange talking to people here. He was always silent and alone in this place, kicking around memories and bemoaning his hard luck.

"The day they arrested Rex Murphy at the Big Drain."

Andy swallowed his soup wrong and started coughing. What did she say? How did she know Rex? What was she doing there? He remembered her now: she and James were the two kids hanging back in the crowd.

"Did that go down the wrong pipe?" James asked, thumping him on the back.

Andy lifted his arm to block more of the helpful blows. "Easy there. I don't need a busted spine to go with my head." He looked at them with new eyes. Who were these kids?

James had gone back to his place, his head down into his soup. A thin smile lingered on his lips.

Andy broke off a heel of bread to sop up the liquid in his bowl. He was waiting for the best opportunity to continue. Turned out, he didn't have to wait long. Wendy gave it to him.

"Aren't you going to ask me how I know Rex?" she said.

Her eyes were crinkling. She had an impish streak; both kids did. He wondered if their attitude helped them to survive, that sly knowingness, the pride of being cleverer than most.

"How do you know Rex, Wendy?" Andy didn't mind playing along. He was foxy too.

"I met him when he was looking for Ole Gray – I mean, the Lamprey. Rex talked to me one day on the street. I told him about the manholes in Rivertown." She said the last part while going for a drink of water and the words came out hollow and echoey as if she were in a pipe.

Andy chewed his wet bread. "What manholes?"

He was thinking back to the alley when Rex first told him about the Lamprey. Andy had considered the maze of passages, how the network spread out like roads hidden under the city.

"The manholes that were left open sometimes. I saw somebody pulling them up with a metal hook late one night. The covers are too heavy to lift without a hook. You can't get your fingers under the edge. This somebody I saw was lifting the manholes a little bit and sliding wedges under the edge to keep them up. Not so much that most people would even notice. But I noticed after I saw them doing it. The covers tilted up so that if you knew about it, you could get your fingers in, grab hold, and slide the covers off. Without using a tool."

Andy sat back, thinking. She was a clever girl. The Lamprey was deviously clever too.

"Why would he wedge them up if he already had the hook tool?" he said.

Wendy shrugged. "The tool is long. Maybe he didn't want to carry it around."

Andy nodded. That could be a very good reason. People would notice such a thing.

"You told this to Rex?"

"Yep. He paid me to show him which manholes were wedged up. I'd memorized them."

"Could you show me?" Andy asked.

Wendy held out her empty palm. James pointed his finger into the center and giggled.

"Pay up," James said.

They had learned to hustle for what they needed to survive. Andy couldn't blame them.

"I don't have Rex Murphy money," Andy said. "Maybe I could trade you something."

"I don't want to trade." Wendy wiped her chin and tipped her chair back on two legs.

Andy felt offended. Here he was helping her and her friend, and she refused to cooperate. He didn't have a problem with negotiating. Stonewalling was another matter. "Why not?"

"Because I'm not going to help you."

Andy's frustration was shifting into annoyance. He was putting them up in his home.

"Why won't you help me?"

Wendy stopped looking at him and concentrated on the table. James was licking his bowl, oblivious to the change in mood that had taken over the tiny tumbledown Easttown kitchen.

Finally, she said, "I don't want the Lamprey to get you, that's why. You're too nice."

Andy felt like he might cry. She was worried about him. This kid, who had no house, whose parents couldn't take care of her right now. Her mom was locked away in a sanatorium like Maude. Her father – Andy didn't know anything about her father except that he wasn't around now. She and James were out on a little raft adrift in the big, scary river of life. Anything might tip them over and drown them in sorrows and calamity. Yet she was looking out for Andy.

"Look what happened to Rex," she said. "He wanted a story and now he can't wake up."

"I'll be careful," Andy promised. "I used to be a reporter. I can handle myself."

"Rex is a reporter. He was careful, you said," she said. Wendy had an answer for everything. Andy liked that about her. She wouldn't give in when somebody pushed back. She made you earn it. It reminded Andy of Ursula Downs. And of Maude, when she was healthy. Maybe Wendy would grow up to be like them. Fighters. Resilient. She was already on her way.

"I'll need to be more careful than Rex, won't I? Plus, you're forgetting. I've got Jake to help me. He's a pro who's been in more scrapes than a barber's razor. It'll be sweet sailing."

"What about Dr Fern? Do you like her?" Wendy seemed keenly interested in his answer, although he couldn't imagine why. Her curiosity made Andy think harder about the question.

"Sure, I like Dr Fern," he said, watching for her reaction. But the kid had a poker face. "I don't know her, really. What I do know is that somebody like Dr Fern isn't going to want to go trudging around the slimy Arkham sewers, is she? She's a doctor. Her battlefield is the mind – not the streets, or what's under them. Would you want to go hunting for a killer in the sewers?"

"Yeah, probably," Wendy admitted. "I'd do it. If anybody'd ask me."

"You would?" James gasped.

Andy was taken aback by her response too. He figured she'd had her fill of monster encounters. Why, the dark presence they all experienced at the hospital was enough to frighten off the average citizen of any age. If he were Wendy, he'd hightail it for the hills. Get out now.

Wendy said, "I know the streets. I've got a way of sensing danger that helps me. Besides, if I don't do something to stop the Lamprey, it's only a matter of time before the Lamprey comes hunting for me. I feel it. Better to be the hunter than the hunted."

Andy had to admit she had a point.

Wendy combed her hair out of her eyes. They were sharp, bright. Her cheeks flushed, and she seemed ready to go out there right now with a lamp and a half-baked plan. She might look like an ordinary child, but she had grit. Maybe more than any reporter he knew. More than Andy.

More than Rex.

"Hey, I've got an idea," she said. "How about I help you and Jake find the Lamprey? Then you'll get your old job back."

"Why do you care if I get my job back?" Andy wondered where she was going with this.

"So you can help me."

"Help you how?"

"Help me find my father," Wendy said.

Her voice was soft, but Andy heard the faintest hope in it.

He had no comeback. Other than to accept her offer.

They shook on it.

James didn't seem sure he knew what was happening, but he shook with them too.

This conversation went back through Andy's head as he saw

the kids reach the top of the stairs. "Set the bucket right over here," he said. "Jimmy Boy, you got that dustpan I gave you?"

James whipped the dustpan from behind his back as if he'd performed a magic trick.

"You hold that pan down next to the bucket. Let me sweep this glass into it," Andy said.

James squatted low as a baseball catcher. The tip of his tongue poking out of the corner of his mouth, concentrating.

Whisk, whisk, whisk – Andy slid the glass into the shovel.

"Perfect-o. Now dump it," he said.

James lifted the dustpan and its sparkling spoils. He tipped the shovel into the bucket, not spilling a single shard. Then he stepped back, proudly.

Andy propped a hand on his shoulder.

"I'll teach you all I know, my young protégé in the janitorial arts. Let's eradicate the piles on the stairs and dump the whole kit and kaboodle out in the alley." Andy bent over the bucket and grabbed the squeaky handle. His gaze drifted over the scintillating, jagged debris…

And then he was still standing there, poised over the glassy wreckage, but his body had frozen while his mind had broken loose, floating out of him along the hallway ceiling, past the dusty light fixture full of dead bugs, until it reached a corner where a spiderweb hung flaccidly.

He felt the sticky threads clinging to him. That queasy sensation thrust him backward in time to the rainforest and the perils he faced from an arachnid the size of a Ford Model T.

Where am I?

Andy tried to talk, but no words came out of his lips. Time didn't seem to be moving for any of them, because when he gazed down at Wendy and James, they looked like a pair of mannequins in a store window. What was more disturbing was that for a moment he thought no more of them than he would have a pair of store dummies. He had to force himself to see them as human beings, then make himself care about humans. It wasn't the way his mind worked. An overpowering influence infected his thinking. Clouding his worldview.

What the heck is going on?

Andy felt a ticklish vibration along his back. It buzzed. He turned his attention to the edge of the web where a pin-sized hole went into the wood molding. He saw hairy legs. Eight of them. Blooming out of the hole like a gray flower. He felt the eyes on him. So many eyes.

This isn't happening, he thought. I'm down there working. Sweeping hallways.

I must be dreaming.

Then he felt the coldness blowing over him like a snowman's breath. It was the same coldness they all sensed yesterday lurking beneath them in the sewers under the hospital. A dark presence. It wasn't in the spider. The spider was just a spider, terrible as it was.

This darkness was something… else… He sensed it was trying to attach, to join with him.

Then, quite unconsciously, Andy was back in his body, seeing out of the eyes in his head, not a mind vision. He was looking into the bucket full of glass.

The shards were moving around, rearranging themselves like pieces of a puzzle toyed with by an invisible hand. Only they didn't reform as the shattered windowpane they had once been. No. They made the semblance of a face. A serrated, uneven visage – spikes, points, and knifelike edges glistening, the most stinging surfaces jutted toward him. Twinkling with menace.

Where the eyes should be were two glimmering holes. Blank in the middle. There was no nose, just a flatness. But the mouth was the worst part. Clear teeth. Some tapered thin as needles, others created triangular thorns. The mouth was overpacked with translucent teeth. They started moving as if with intelligence. He intuited a desire to communicate. Instead of words, the sounds produced were a crunching, grinding collision of broken fragments rubbing against one another. The harsh mashing bristled in Andy's ears. He clenched his jaw until it throbbed with his pulse.

Then the face started talking.

That thing in the bucket spoke to him. Glittering dust flaked from its lips. A fine powdery, pearly mist floated up toward Andy's eyes. He tried to shut them to keep it out.

Glass. Ground glass in my eyes.

The tiniest splinters spinning up at me about to shred my eyeballs.

"The witches," the voice said.

"What? I don't know what you want from me," Andy said. "Leave me alone."

"The Pahpah*pah*… the Prism," the voice said. "The witches. The Prism."

Andy squinted at the glassy mist suspended in the air, and at the face made of shards below it in the bucket. Was this the Prism attempting to contact him? Were witches attacking him from afar? The face folded in on itself. A brittle toppling. Disintegration. The sloshing collection of bright scraps and slivers, chips and glinting specks, particles jingling like a bucketful of coins or seashells scavenged off a beach – it swirled in the bucket like ice.

The eyes, mouth, face – vanished. But the words it said stuck with him.

"The witches. The Prism," Andy said. Where had he heard of the Prism before? It was Rex. He'd mentioned it in the alley that first night they'd met. What did it refer to? Was the Prism something the witches had, or something they wanted? He couldn't answer that question.

He'd never forget that horridly sharp face spitting words at him, a nightmare that sliced into the depths of his being, that had the power to knock him out of his body, to chill his feelings.

"What did you say?" James wanted to know. He was acting like it was a joke, a game they were playing together. Andy didn't feel like he was fully himself yet. He was still blunted.

But Wendy knew this was no game. She touched the front of her shirt, the center of her chest. "We're in danger," she said to James.

James shrunk back against the wall and looked up and down the empty hallway as Wendy said to Andy, "Are you feeling dizzy? Is it your head wound?"

Perhaps it was the result of the blow he'd taken to his skull, a delayed symptom of damage. He tried moving his head to test it, to get his wits back and dispel the numbness. It was like waking up from a nap, not remembering how exactly you'd fallen asleep. The disorientation.

Could these surreal images be the result of a concussion? He didn't know.

"I think it's going away," he said, staggering.

Andy sat on the top step and waited for the fogginess to clear, to emerge from this daze.

Then after a while. "It's gone now. The danger is gone."

"Yes," Wendy said. "I think so too. You saw something, didn't you? What did you see?"

"I'm not certain. A face. Maybe. That's how it wanted me to see it. But it was a mask."

Wendy was struggling to understand him. She went to where he'd been standing.

"In the bucket? In the glass, you saw a mask?" she asked, as if she hadn't heard him. Andy nodded. "We need to leave. We should go find Jake," she said.

"I can't do this alone. I thought I could keep us safe, but now I'm not sure," he said.

Wendy said, "Jake was going to Arkham Sanatorium to see about helping your friend. That's what he told Dr Fern last night." She went to James, put her arm around his trembling shoulders.

James was sucking his thumb. He didn't know what to make of what was happening, so he retreated into himself, into an inner place where he might shelter. Andy knew the feeling well.

"Jake was going to try and talk to Maude," Andy said.

"I don't like sanatoriums," Wendy said. "I hate them even more than regular hospitals."

Andy recognized her anxiety. James was scared but unable to put his fear into words.

"You two don't have to go. You and James can stay with Dr Fern. She gave me her home address. We'll stop by. She isn't working today, but she said Jake would be better off without her when he went to visit the sanatorium. I'll meet up with Jake. Everything will work out, you'll see."

Andy didn't know who he was trying to convince, Wendy or himself.

"Where's my broom? I need that. And the dustpan. James, will you help me there?"

James came unstuck from his inward retreat and took the dustpan. Wendy had hold of Andy's broom. They went down the stairs together, as if they were joined in a huddle, even though three on a step was two too many. Bracing himself before stepping out into the wind swirling around the building, Andy carried the bucket to the alley, dumping it without looking in the trash. The can's lid nearly flew from his hand as the air currents tugged at it. He slammed it down. The kids held onto the fence to keep upright. Andy decided they were leaving this housecleaning unfinished. If he lost this job, so be it. Without his job, he'd lose his rented rooms. But they had more important tasks to attend to. Their lives were at stake. Maybe other lives too.

The wind was blowing, fierce as a scream circling all the way around the whole planet. Trees and lampposts shuddered as if they might uproot. He and the children ran through the streets, covering their ears, pretending they didn't hear it, the howling hiding within the wind.

26
Things Growing

Maude woke to witches. Witches swimming, afloat before her eyes. Witch voices stopping up her ears with cloggy, guttural language, the letters spilling out of order, sounds harsh and chaotic, out of tune with this world, dissonant, more like the hoots, howls, and growls of forest animals; perhaps they had their own music. Earth music, mystical strains. She felt afraid of them.

At first.

Maude had been fighting the terror all night, and possibly all through the next day as well. She tried to tell what time it was by looking at the window. Midmorning? Afternoon?

Clouds raced over the rooftops across from the sanatorium. High winds. Gray on gray.

Time was broken. Fragments, fragments. The shards of a mirror reflected in her eyes.

Her mind was shattered. She feared it had cracked beyond repair. Yet she wouldn't give up. She sought order but found a hopeless jumble of images, emotions, and psychic confusion.

This much she could tell. She was still in the hospital. The sanatorium. Arkham.

She might not be able to locate herself in time, but she recognized her place.

She was not in the Dreamlands.

Dr Mintz had tried to force her to go there. "Visit the place that compels you the most," he'd said. "Treat yourself... Lose yourself."

She hadn't. She'd fooled him and his "dream enhancer." Upon waking, her mouth tasted strange, like a type of fruit she could not name. Overripe, a musty sweetness. Probably a side effect of the drug.

She awoke not in the Amazon jungle. But this place, this city of Arkham, was the most terrifying locale of all. Because it contained everything that haunted every other place. Here was the source. The fount of doom. Portal of portals. The wellspring of horror existed right here.

Concentrate, she told herself. If your tethers are close to severing, you will drift eternally.

Don't let chaos win, she told herself. Patch together what's left of your world. Hold on.

Spinning, spinning, as if she were stranded on a raft, approaching rapids. The thundery danger, a sense she was gaining speed. No oars on the raft. No way to steer. No anchor to throw over the side. Faster, faster. The rough cosmic currents carried her toward inevitable disaster. A feeling of nausea wrapped her like a hot blanket. Her stomach dropped as the raft dipped and spun. The unmooring led to a realization of loneliness. *I am lost.*

No. I am in my hospital bed. Bound. In my room. Alone.

I am Maude Brion.

The room smells like burning hair. I am weak, thirsty. I am not dead.

I am Maude Brion. I survived horrors in the jungle. I have crossed dimensions.

The hallucination, if that was what it was, became impossible to ignore. She addressed it.

I see witches dancing before me. Here and not here at the same time. I see their circle. I hear them chanting. I smell their candles and the burning hair – my hair – what is this, then?

Maude turned herself into a camera in order to protect herself – a mental game, a technique she learned when filming her documentaries. See the way the camera sees. The lens eye. Nothing outside it exists. This is all that is real. What do you see?

I see witches. Worshiping. Conducting their esoteric rituals. Their figures hover several inches in the air above my grimy, warped hospital floor. It is like a film reel playing in three dimensions before me. I see the witches, and I see *through* the witches. Like a double exposure.

Through the witches she saw the window to her room open. I will escape!

The urge to break out was overpowering.

But no. She felt the wind blowing freely into her room but through bars, steel bars. I am a prisoner, she remembered. I can't tell what is dreaming and what is real, so they locked me up.

One of the witches looked at Maude.

"Woman? Who are you? Why do you intrude on our rites?"

The witch talked to her without moving their lips.

"I am Maude Brion. I am a film director. An actress before that. I have seen the Spider Queen. I have visited the Dreamlands. The doctors say I am not thinking correctly. I need help."

Her answers felt inadequate. Is that who I am? Is that what I am?

All the witches were looking at her now. She didn't see whole faces. She saw rough cloaks and candles and noses, cheekbones, mouths, and chins. In the center of the witches was a glittering encrustation of crystals lit from within. It cast a pink-rose-purple light that wavered.

"Do you need help?" the tallest witch, who had been communicating with her, asked.

"I do."

"How may we help you, Maude?"

Maude tried to sit up, but the straps held her fast.

"Loosen my straps, please." There's a good place to start. Get me off this bed. Free me.

The witches bowed, humming like a hive of bees. Their hum filled the room with a gooey, honey sound. Warm fuzziness buzzed inside of her. Energy. Something was happening.

A tugging – movement under the blanket. Is this real? Would she know if it were?

Then the straps slithered unbuckled off her arms, her torso, and her legs.

"You did it!" she said, rubbing at her wrists. Maude leaped from the bed before the straps might cinch around her again. Her ankles were sore. She touched the grooves in her skin where the belts had been fastened to her. She twirled in her hospital gown. Free! Light as a feather!

Maude stopped. Muffled voices, not the witches, these came through the door. Nurses?

Where were her clothes?

In the closet?

She grabbed the cold, tarnished knob to the wardrobe door and pulled. There they were.

She hadn't worn them since they brought her here. Her jungle apparel – pants and a shirt.

Going exploring, she dressed and slipped on her boots. She sat on the floor, tying the laces. The witches were fading. She could only make out their silhouettes. They were ignoring her. Returning to the business of their gathering. They swayed. The tall one held a stout knife.

"Wait! Wait!" Maude shouted. Then she shot a glance at the door to her room. Would the nurses hear? Would that monster Dr Mintz come barging in to take her for more "enhancement"?

Had she heard a hand being placed gently on the door, the edge of a shoe squeaking…?

The tall witch shifted her attitude, annoyed at the interruption. She posed a question.

"What is it?"

"The bars in my window," Maude asked. "Can you get rid of them for me?"

It took longer this time. The entire room shook for a few seconds. Maude wondered if she were imagining this. It's like an earthquake, she thought. Hospital alarm bells were ringing. Plaster dust sifted down from the cracks in the ceiling. A loud snapping as she watched the bars tip outward, bending toward the street. But they stuck firm. The witches couldn't do it, she sighed. Well, they at least they tried.

Maude went to the window and touched the thick black bars.

Hot!

They dropped out of the window frame onto a roof below. The nurses had to hear that! The window was open now. She couldn't believe it. If this were a dream, she wanted to keep dreaming. The cruelty of waking would be too great to bear. She glanced back at her door before quickly crawling onto the windowsill. One last look inside her room. The door was opening. A glimpse of a nurse's whites, the deep undertones of a man's voice in tense conversation with the nurse. Maude teetered… and jumped!

This was no dream.

Maude tasted the wind, smelling things growing, and the tang of smoky fires.

I am free! Maude Brion is a prisoner no more. Goodbye, sanatorium. The witches freed me.

She fell a few feet onto a short, slanted roof. Voices shouted from above. Beside her were the still-warm bars. She kicked them over the side, listening as they landed heavily on the lawn. She was sitting atop a toolshed where the groundskeepers stored rakes and shears. Scooting on her bottom, she slipped over the edge.

"I must go. I must run." Maude felt like a wild thing, a creature of the woods, born outside, meant to live outside – a literal outsider. Misunderstood. Powerful. "I have magic in me," she said, not knowing what she meant but liking saying the words aloud. "I am magic."

The trees in front of her appeared like green supplicants reaching for the sky. She saw the life flowing in them. There was a low, spiked iron fence surrounding the grounds. Boundaries. Grids and divisions. Someone always trying to pen in that which they can never control. Maude ran between the trees, feeling their lifeforce. She vaulted the fence easily. Alarm bells rang out. She was outside, alone. She became highly aware of springtime. Buds and greenness everywhere the eye looked. Growth. Succulent renewal. Rebirth.

I'll go wherever I please. Whenever I want. Now and forever. No one ties me down.

I am powerful. I thought I was weak, but I am strong.

Act quickly, she thought. Where should I go?

The winds tossed her hair around. It whipped at her shirt. It was pushing her to go.

Where?

It didn't matter. What mattered was to go *now*. Go fast and far and don't look back.

Maude ran.

27
Fresh Air

Jake stood dumbfounded inside Maude's hospital room. It wasn't her room anymore, apparently. The nurse leaning out the window had stopped calling for Maude. She'd seen her running, darting between houses. Escaping the sanatorium. Jake hadn't had time to launch his plan to get Maude out.

Maude had done it herself.

The nurse was saying something to him about secured straps and iron bars. Flustered, she pushed past him. Orderlies and nurses began rushing around. Doctors too. One doctor made a beeline for Maude's room. He seemed by equal measures prim and infuriated. He wagged his finger in Jake's face.

"You are responsible for the flight of a seriously unstable woman!"

"You'd better get your hand away from me if you want to keep it," Jake said.

The doctor lowered his hand and took a step back, holding up his clipboard as a shield. Jake noticed lines of strange symbols written on the paper attached to the clipboard. The writing looked almost runic, but Jake couldn't read the marks clearly.

They might've been the doodles of a bored clinician who'd rather be spending his time conducting research. The doctor thrust his chin out defiantly. "How did you get in here? Did you demolish the bars with a sledgehammer?"

He was close enough that if Jake wanted to, he could've batted him sideways with his crutch. The nurse came back into the room and, seeing the hostilities, stood between the men.

"Dr Mintz, this man was with me," she said. "He did not aid in the patient's absconding from the premises. I assure you that he was as surprised as I was that she wasn't here."

"Who is he?" Dr Mintz asked, regaining confidence in his status as an authority.

"Jake Williams," Jake said. "I'm a friend of Maude's. If what I hear is true, you've been conducting rather unorthodox treatments on patients committed under the care of the courts. I think a judge might want to know what you're doing. And about your lax security measures."

Dr Mintz blinked. A line of perspiration formed on his upper lip, which quivered slightly.

"Nurse Heather, please escort Mr Williams out of the sanatorium."

Jake executed a right angle turn and took two steps toward the hallway. Then he shot a look over his shoulder at the doctor. "I'll see myself out. Oh, and by the way, when news of this hits the *Advertiser*, I think their readers are going to be very interested in how you conduct your practice. Experimenting on people. It's scandalous."

"Get out," Dr Mintz said.

"I'm going. See you in the papers, doc. I know a reporter or two who are going to love this."

Jake quickened his step, vaulting himself down the sanatorium's main corridor. Startled orderlies pressed themselves against the walls to avoid being bowled over. He was going so fast he nearly ran down Andy heading the opposite way, passing through the front archway; their eyes locking in the moment before the collision. Andy braced the door open with one arm. Jake pulled up short, practically skidding on his bootheels. He paused long enough to catch Andy up on the details of Maude's escape.

"Do you think we can find her?" Andy had to raise his voice above the blowing gale.

They filled each other in on their separate eventful mornings as they walked together, the sanatorium's spires shrinking behind them the farther they went. Andy didn't share the part about the broken glass face in the bucket; he'd tell Jake about that later. Instead, he said he had a feeling that he should help Jake with Maude, that two friends were better than one.

"She isn't an escaped feline from the zoo, Andy. She's our friend, Maude, remember?"

Jake ambulated down the sidewalk, glancing between the buildings they passed.

"Sorry, I know that. What I mean is, which way did she go? How do we catch up to her?"

Andy was struggling to match Jake's athletic pace on his shorter legs.

Jake said, "I'm not sure exactly. The nurse was looking in this direction. Up the block."

All those years spotting lions, tigers, and jaguars weren't for nothing, and he used his visual acuity to peer into distances far and wide, seeking a sign of anything out of the ordinary, a lingering disturbance that spoke of Maude's recent hasty retreat.

But, as he'd told Andy, Maude was someone other than a cat. She didn't operate purely on instinct. She had a mind of her own.

Andy stretched his neck, looking. He sighed, clutching at his bandages under his old newsboy cap. His face contorted in discomfort. Gusts of wind were setting the world in wild motion. The overstimulation appeared to pain him. Jake couldn't keep pushing him at this pace. He stopped so that Andy might have time to recover. The former reporter propped against an Italianate Victorian mansion's terra cotta planter filled with hyperactive Boston ferns.

"Let's think." Jake rested on his crutches. "Where would Maude go?"

"She likes movies. Maybe she went to a movie house."

Jake considered that. "It's kind of early in the day. But maybe. Where else?"

Andy scratched his chin.

"If she's looking for a place to hide out, she might try checking into a hotel."

Jake shook his head. "She's low on dough… if she has any money in her pocket at all."

"I'm low on dough. You'd think that would give me better ideas."

"What about a restaurant?" Jake said. "There must be a diner or something around."

"Restaurants cost dough too. I haven't eaten in one since I got fired."

"She could duck in and find a seat at the counter. Order a cup of coffee," Jake said.

"I don't know," Andy said. "If I was cooped up in a locked ward for days on end, I wouldn't skip right inside again first chance I got. I'd roam. Enjoy a taste of the fresh air."

The fresh air felt like it was pummeling them now. Maybe a storm was brewing. But the threatening skies had stayed dry so far. If it weren't for the winds, it might be a pleasant spring lunch hour–

Jake knocked the tip of crutch against the sidewalk. "Andy, you're a genius. Follow me."

"Where're we going?"

"Someplace where a person might linger outside without drawing too much attention."

Andy snapped his fingers. "A park!"

"Independence Square," Jake said. "I'll bet she's there right now."

They hurried off.

28
Hyacinth Blooms

Charlie had hoped to stop Mandy from leaving the building after their meeting. He wanted to talk about her research in more detail, away from the others, in case she had evidence she wasn't comfortable sharing in front of them. He called down to the lobby, but the main desk said there was no one meeting that description lingering about. He was ready to call the Orne Library and see if she had returned, or to leave a message for her once she arrived back, when his secretary rang his line and said, "Mandy Thompson is here, Your Honor. She wonders if she might have a word with you."

"By all means," Charlie said, glad he didn't need to hunt her down. "Send her in."

"She isn't alone, sir."

"Not alone? Who's with her?"

"Another woman."

"Someone with an appointment?" Charlie was confused. Mandy had been the only woman in the meeting.

"No, sir. She was waiting for you when Miss Thompson came out after you adjourned."

"Send the other woman away. Tell her to make an appointment."

There was a pause. He listened to dampened voices murmuring. It made his skin itch. His secretary came back on the line.

"Miss Thompson said they both need to see you together. It's important."

Charlie gave up. "Send them both in."

He dumped his ashtray in the trashcan under his desk and cracked his knuckles.

The enormous oak double doors to his office swung open. His secretary ushered in the pair of women, then pulled the doors shut. Charlie felt suddenly sealed in.

How silly, he thought. It's my office.

Mandy appeared perhaps a bit less composed than when she'd left the meeting. She didn't usually show her cards, so any slight alteration had the potential to signal major changes beneath the surface. She hung back a half step, which was highly uncharacteristic.

The other woman was formidable from a physical standpoint.

Charlie rose to greet the newcomer. He smiled his customary political smile and extended his well-used hand of friendship. The woman was more than a head taller than Charlie. He had to tilt up to meet her stare. Her approach was cool, unsmiling. She gripped his hand and released it in an instant, clearly treating the touching hands as a mere formality to be served.

"My name is Hyacinth Burroughs. I've been waiting to see you. You have something of mine," she said.

"City Hall has only just opened."

"I was waiting outside. I'd hoped to meet you when you arrived. The matter is urgent."

"I enter by a side door." Charlie felt as though he were making excuses. For what? He could not tell. Did she say Burroughs? She did, didn't she? He wasn't sure what to do with that.

"I see. Very well. We are meeting now."

She allowed an abbreviated smile.

"Please, make yourself comfortable." Charlie risked a glance at Mandy.

She offered him nothing to go on, a blank slate. He was perplexed and intrigued.

After they all sat down, Mandy spoke up, finally. "Hyacinth Burroughs has come to us today from Providence. She's a dealer in antiques. She told me some history which may shed light on our recent events."

"My family is originally from Salem," Hyacinth interjected. "Old stock. We were founders. Until we transplanted–"

"Founders of what?" Charlie said. He looked from Hyacinth to Mandy and back.

"This country," Hyacinth said.

"Ah, of course. Please go on."

"As I was saying, my ancestors transplanted from Salem to Arkham, years ago."

"Many years?"

"In the 1680s. I think you have heard of one of my relatives. Dionysia Burroughs?"

This is what it feels like to be buried under an avalanche, he thought.

He knew what Mandy was feeling, because he was feeling it himself right now.

Shock.

In the next half hour Charlie absorbed a tremendous amount of information about the woman sitting before him. Later he would learn more from detectives he sent to gather additional intelligence.

In short, she was a young, successful businesswoman with deep roots. But that did not tell the tale that Charlie needed to know. Mandy filled in the blank spots. Well, most of them.

Hyacinth Burroughs, the woman seated across his desk, appeared much older than someone in her mid-twenties. Perhaps more accurately, she seemed of no easily determined age. She might've been anywhere from a mature late teen to a youthfully robust person nearing forty. Therefore, her demeanor became the clue by which her age was judged. Serious, solemn, and formal was her mode of speaking. She carried herself with confident resolve, as one who has endured – and plans to continue enduring for a great while longer – all the travails and trivialities life mustered to sling at her. A strong, prominent chin led the way, as well as eyes of a piercing aqueous blue that were notable for being difficult to combat in their intensity. Reports said that Hyacinth Burroughs was hard to please and impossible to ignore. People were known to either admire and follow her or to avoid her altogether if they could. She made enemies, cared not a whit that she did, and to her few close friends she remained loyal, devoted, and a champion.

There came a point during the meeting when she produced a drawing and passed it to Charlie. Although it was the other way up, with its thicker base on the ground, he recognized it immediately as the formation they'd found in the sewer.

"That's the Fang," Hyacinth said. "A rare colored crystal discovered in my ancestors' field while they were plowing one morning. My people brought it with them from Salem to Arkham in the back of a covered wagon. They traveled at night to avoid detection. Theft was always a worry. While they lived here, they hid the Fang in the back of their barn, behind a false wall. After the death of the eldest male in the family – well, you know about his wife Dionysia's trial, the harassment and harmful accusations. She had the Fang moved, fearing correctly that it would be destroyed or stolen by a seething Arkham mob. Around the time she disappeared, so did the Fang. It belongs to our family. You've located it. I would like it back. Take care you don't damage it, or I will have no choice but to take legal action against the city. It's priceless."

"I see." Charlie stroked the bridge of his nose. He admired her competence, but he also saw its potential danger if she turned out to be a foe. "How did you hear about our discovery?"

"The newspapers were vague. Still, I was curious when I read about a strange oddity found during the search for a missing man working underground on the Big Drain. There were persistent family rumors the Fang had been buried, either by friends of Dionysia or thieves who betrayed her. After that, the trail grows cold. Previous attempts to unearth the Fang failed."

"Hmm, yet you are convinced that your heirloom resides in our sewer," Charlie said.

Hyacinth said, "Mandy Thompson confirmed it."

Charlie looked at Mandy. The corner of his mouth twitched. "Oh, did she?"

"I might have," Mandy admitted, blushing.

"She did," Hyacinth said.

"Miss Thompson may have spoken prematurely. We have yet to determine anything."

Hyacinth hesitated, peering into a corner as she weighed her next words carefully. "I've had a letter with a detailed description of your find. There was an inscription on the crystal, no? With my family member's name on it. I think that's all the proof I need. Don't you?"

Charlie didn't answer. He had one searing question. "Who wrote this letter?"

"It was anonymous. But the description is, pardon the pun, crystal clear," she said.

They stared at each other. Charlie's gears were turning. The antiques dealer presented a strong case. Perhaps Charlie might make this work to his advantage, but for now he didn't see how. He wanted to ask her if she knew what the symbols on the crystal meant. But if he admitted knowledge of the inscription, then he would be confirming they had the Fang. He wasn't ready to go that far. Who was leaking information to this woman? Who knew details both about the crystal in the sewer and the Burroughs' family history? Why hadn't that person told Charlie about this possible lead in a murder investigation? Most of all he wanted to ask about the Prism.

"You've given me a lot to think about," Charlie said. "I admire your passion."

"I'm glad you do. Know that flattery will not delay my cause. I deduce by the fact that you've listened to my long story that you must indeed have our Fang. You cannot declare ignorance."

"I wouldn't dream of it," he said, smiling in the same way he did during public debates.

"Wouldn't you? Most people cannot control their dreams. Do you enjoy the ability?" Her query, like the entirety of this very odd meeting, left Charlie stunned and bewildered.

"It was only a metaphorical statement," he said. Was she teasing him?

"Very well. I am a literal woman. I say what I mean. I never had a talent for affectation."

Charlie ignored her slight. Politicians were immune to such barbs; he'd grown thick crocodile skin after his years of verbal jousting. "May I keep this drawing?"

"No." She snatched it back.

"You've caught me at an awkward time. This new knowledge is hard to digest, Miss–"

Charlie hadn't finished his reply, but already Hyacinth Burroughs was standing up to leave.

She said, "I'm sure you have advisors to consult. I'm staying at the Silver Gate Hotel. Send a message when you are prepared to discuss the transfer of the Fang. Thank you, Mayor."

Having said her piece, she was gone.

Mandy threw a bemused glance at him before following the woman out.

"How about that?" Charlie said to himself. "The day has only begun, and I'm exhausted."

29
Three Times

Holy smokes, Andy thought. There she is.

Maude was seated under the band pavilion in Independence Square as if she were waiting for a musical act to take the stage. She appeared oblivious to the winds raking everything that was not nailed down, clawing the park grounds free of loose, unwanted things. The gray birches were dancers wigging out to a jazz combo, lost in the beat, not a care in the world about who was watching. Only no band played. The skies began to darken like a bad bruise. Andy saw a flash of lightning spear a cloud. Thunder followed; a low, grumbling protestation muttered from a distant room. It was midday. The Square was empty. Here and there, pedestrians hurried through, holding onto their hats or silk headscarves, carrying precautionary umbrellas under their arms as they rushed to destinations unknown before the weather changed. Nobody was sitting down.

Nobody except Maude Brion. Actress. Filmmaker. Arkham Sanatorium's newest escapee.

"Hey, Jake," Andy whispered. "What's our approach here? Direct or indirect?"

Jake had stopped, positioning them behind Founder's Rock

in the center of the Square. He kept a constant eye on Maude, peeking around a rugged edge of the tall, oblong stone.

"Keep back, Andy. I don't want her to see us yet."

Andy glanced up at the bronze plaque listing the names of the colonists who laid claim to establishing this bizarre melancholic burg. When he was a boy, Andy's mother told him a local legend. "Rub the Founder's Rock three times. You will attain guidance in any matter you seek."

He thought about testing it right now. Weren't he and Jake in need of special guidance? Who better than Arkham's forefathers and mothers to ask? Maybe the Founders knew what to do. Andy wiggled his fingers as if the stone might bite him. Why was he afraid of a superstition?

"Looks like she's just sitting there. Happy as a clam," Jake said.

Andy tipped his head out for a quick peek.

"I said stay out of sight," Jake said.

"She doesn't look so happy to me."

"It's just an old expression."

"Like, 'rub the Founder's Rock three times. You will attain guidance in any matter you seek?'" Andy had his fingers extended again. He tapped his fingernails lightly on the gray stone.

"What did you say?" Jake sounded exasperated.

"Oh, nothing."

"Stop fooling around," Jake said. "This is serious. We could come at her from two sides at once. Then if she bolts, we'll tackle her on the lawn."

Andy scoffed. He was feeling tired, and the wind was like a bully whispering in his ear.

"Who's the one acting like she's a wildcat, now? Hint. It isn't me."

Jake shot him a dirty look.

Andy had scored a point on Jake, and he saw that Jake knew it. Andy *was* taking this seriously. Seriously enough to consider tapping into the ancient wisdom of the relic set up like a monolith on the village green. Then it dawned on Andy that Founder's Rock wasn't so different from the crystal curiosity Rex said he saw hanging from the ceiling of the underground chamber.

What was it with people and big, spooky rocks?

Andy's head throbbed from walking. He kept seeing that clear face of busted glass, grinding words at him. He'd tried pushing the image out of his mind, as if it were only a nightmare, but he'd seen the glass simulation talking to him in broad daylight. He hadn't been asleep; he'd been working.

The witches. The Prism.

Rex knew about the Prism. He wrote about it in his notebook, but he didn't get a chance to fill Andy in. They had Rex's notebook now, but they couldn't read it. Every time Andy got a little closer to understanding something about this story, he ended up more confused.

But Maude didn't confuse him.

She was on the other side of this stone. Wouldn't she be thrilled to see them? Especially if she was on the run?

"Why can't we go up to her and say, 'Hiya there, Maude, remember us? Your old spider chasing pals?' What's she going to do, let out a banshee scream and attack us? I don't figure on her doing that. She was a cool customer, even when she was off destroying our evidence of the Spider Queen and my career along with it. She did her business discreetly. Real quiet-like. She was dreamy, smooth as syrup. That's how she looks to me now. Like a sleepwalker but sitting."

"Maude might be delusional," Jake said. "She was committed to a sanatorium."

"And we were going break her out. Dr Fern didn't say she was delusional. She said Maude needed our help. So, which is it?"

"Which is what?" Jake was acting more and more annoyed, as if he wanted Andy gone.

"I say let's help her," Andy said. "The best way to help her is to talk to her."

Andy's temples were banging. Maybe the howling wind was making it worse. He thought he felt raindrops. Great, now they'd get drenched. His bandages would get soggy. His clothes...

"I feel rain," Andy said mournfully. Jake didn't reply. He was too busy conducting reconnaissance.

"What's that noise? What're you doing, Andy?"

"Nothing. I was just rubbing on this rock. It had something on it. Hey, do you think this giant bronze plaque might attract lightning? Because I saw some flashes in the clouds. I mean, if the rock gets struck, we're sitting ducks. We'll light up like a pair of Edison lightbulbs."

Jake shushed him.

Andy barely heard him. He made his request. The Rock had looked like it needed rubbing, so he asked it if he should do that. He wanted to touch it anyway. He felt compelled.

To Andy's surprise, the Rock answered him.

It said, "Go already. Get this over with, Andy. Sheesh."

Or at least it might've been the rock. Andy's head was killing him. He was tired, dizzy, and out of patience. Instead of waiting for Jake to tell him what to do, he decided to listen to the Founders... or their Rock. Maybe it was his own voice in his head, or maybe it was that creepy, brittle voice he felt when that glass face in the bucket talked to him. But he couldn't sit here anymore. He circled the other way around Founder's Rock. When Jake figured out what he was doing it was too late and he was already strolling straight up to the pavilion, arms swinging.

Maude could've looked right at him, if she wanted to. But she was fixated on this other person cutting diagonally through the Square in front of her.

A tall man... no, wait – it was a woman. Dressed all in gray, her back very straight, her face forward like the prow of a ship. The wind didn't seem to faze her, while Andy felt like the wind was shoving him backward. He had to lean into it when it gusted, clamping down on his cap and bandages. He was up under the pavilion shelter before Maude seemed to notice him. He sat down next to her like they met here every afternoon to swap stories and eat lunch.

"Hey, Maude. What's new with you? Anything interesting?"

She didn't try to run off. In fact, what she did was cover his hand with hers. Her skin was hot and dry, like she had a fever. She kept watching the tall lady crossing the lawn in front of them. The tall gray lady didn't care one whit about them or what they were doing. She glided along, like how an Olympic swimmer knifed through the water, pristinely.

"Do you see her, Andy?"

"The tall gray lady?" Andy said.

"You do see her, don't you?"

"Sure, I see her. She's right there. Why, is she a friend of yours?"

"She might be. She reminds me of a friend. I think she's a friend. She helped me get away from that hospital. From that wicked doctor with his procedures... Who is she, I wonder?"

Andy was really confused. This lady helped Maude to escape.

"Why don't you call her over then?" Andy asked. "I'd like to meet her."

"I'm not certain I can call to her. She comes to me. If summoned, she will not respond."

What the heck did that mean? Andy was about ready to shout to the tall lady himself. Except Jake was there now with them, out of breath, red-faced and frustrated with Andy. Andy didn't care. This whole day had been too weird for him. His head hurt, too.

"Hello, Maude," Jake said.

Maude turned and looked at each of them in turn. She smiled and looked glad to see her friends. She didn't seem like someone who was going to run. There was a calmness to her, a tranquility. In that moment under the pavilion, Andy forgave her for undermining his biggest story ever, for effectively killing his career – unless he managed to resurrect it from the dead. He let it go, all of it. Just so he might get a taste of the peaceful acceptance Maude had mastered.

"Do you see her, Jake?" she asked.

"See who?"

"The tall gray lady," Andy said. "Walking through the Square. She's right over–"

Independence Square was empty except for the three of them. The lady was gone. Andy stood and twisted around, but she wasn't there. She should have been still in the plaza, even if she took off at a mad dash. Maude was looking too, although she was laughing more than looking. She clenched her fists and pounded them on her khaki-covered thighs, laughing...

A purple-white flash exploded with blinding brightness. Crack! A bolt of lightning struck a birch. The tree split, started to burn. A huge branch broke free in the wind, blowing away, in flames... Thunder boomed as another bolt hit the plaza. Then a third. The ground shook.

The heavens opened the floodgates. Rain began to pour down in sheets the colors of ash and lead.

30
Grating Voice

James never liked thunderstorms, but Wendy did. The bigger the better, if they weren't caught sleeping outside. They were inside now, with Dr Fern in her tidy Cape Cod cottage which looked much nicer than Andy's plain, undecorated rooms. Dr Fern's place was simple and comfy. Her furniture showed taste, but not like you weren't supposed to touch things; the bright wall paints had a warm, homey feeling. She owned lots of books and pretty, multicolored lamps; small glass animal figurines sat on the shelves. A rocking chair angled to one side of the sofa with a wicker basket of knitting needles and yarns beside it. On the floor lay a rectangular emerald rug the size of a garden plot, framed with swirling patterns of silvery vines. Pillows dotted the room in forest shades of every shape and texture, sporting buttons and fringey braided tassels. Paradise, Wendy thought. A home.

"That's quite a storm," Dr Fern said. She was standing in the shadows behind Wendy.

"I like storms."

James was tucked away in the kitchen, listening to the cathedral radio Dr Fern had, drinking ice-cold lemonade and eating a tomato and butter sandwich on white bread with fruit cocktail on the side.

Wendy sat in a window seat with gold velvet cushions, staring into the front yard. There was a knitted blanket, if you felt chilled, and more pillows were piled against the windowsill. Dr Fern's black cat – who was shy but blinked her eyes slowly at Wendy when she talked to her – purred, perching atop a high red bookcase beside the door and a hook full of heavy-looking keys.

"What's your cat's name?" Wendy asked.

"Hecate," Dr Fern said. "You're sitting in her other favorite spot. She likes to look out."

"Looking out is better than looking in."

The psychologist tilted her head after Wendy said that, as if she wanted to ask a question. But she didn't ask it.

They sat together on the gold cushions watching the storm wash the street. Hecate purred behind them. The sound of James's radio was too garbled and far away to understand, like someone mumbling underwater, Wendy thought. Then she wondered, who talks underwater?

"Oh, look," Dr Fern said suddenly, pointing out through the glass.

From out of the storm, hazy shapes were closing in on them, nearing the house, the door. Wendy started to panic. But her amulet was quiet, and she trusted it to warn her.

"It's Andy and Jake," she said at last, recognizing them. Her heart leaped.

"They have Maude. I can't believe it." Dr Fern's mouth stayed open as she watched.

Wendy thought the doctor sounded glad and nervous mixed together. Dr Fern went to let them in. When she opened the door, the cat turned her head, stopped purring, and observed the rain sloshing inside, wetting the floor, and the three people rushing in. All wet, dripping. Talking.

Jake was telling Dr Fern all that happened when he went to the sanatorium. Maude filled in the parts that Jake didn't know, and Andy was strangely quiet, except for apologizing for making a mess of Dr Fern's entryway.

"Let's get you dried off," Dr Fern said to them, passing out towels from the bathroom.

She put on a kettle to make tea. James stayed at the radio, which was good because Wendy thought he'd get upset if he heard the conversation they were having in the parlor. They were talking about witches. Hecate jumped from the bookcase to the window seat, but she wasn't looking out at the rain-filled street, the gurgling gutters, and the drippy leaves on the trees. She was watching them, as if she were listening closely.

But that's silly, Wendy thought.

Maude finished telling them all how she escaped. The witch vision she had, the iron bars. Then Andy said what happened to him in the hallway while they were sweeping. How he floated away from himself, met a spider, and saw the glass make faces and talk.

Dr Fern didn't say a word. She was like Hecate, good at listening. Soaking things in.

Wendy was good at that too. Witchy talk was scary. But if her amulet remained quiet, she figured they were safe. Jake seemed to be having a hard time believing what everyone was saying. His leg was bothering him. Though he never complained, Wendy could tell, because he was kneading his thigh with both hands and squinting his eyes tightly as he did it.

"The witches helped me," Maude said.

"That face in the bucket wasn't helping anyone. I hated it,"

Andy said. "If that face was one of the witches, I want no part of them. They got inside my head. Something made me float."

"But you didn't float," Jake said. "Right, Wendy? Nothing happened to you and James."

"I didn't see him float," she said.

"You imagined it, Andy. You got whacked on the head. You had a spell," Jake said.

"A witch's spell?" Andy asked sarcastically. "I know what I saw. It was real."

"I don't buy it," Jake said. "Maude, I believe you think you saw witches. Or people wearing cloaks who you think were witches. But you admit Dr Mintz drugged you. That creep was toying with your brain, tinkering with it like a watchmaker. He wanted to induce dreams."

"I saw something too," Dr Fern said. "I think it must be connected to what Andy saw."

Surprised, they turned in unison toward her. She sat, perching on the end of the couch, balancing her cup and saucer on her knees. The cup rattled until she lifted it and took a sip.

"Jake, remember the St Mary's cafeteria? When my cup shattered suddenly?" Jake said he did. "In the remnants of that shattered cup I saw a face. The porcelain fragments rearranged the same way Andy says the glass did in his bucket. The shards became an edgy, jagged visage."

"See? The psychologist says I'm not making this up. It wasn't in my head. It was real. And it had to do with the Prism. It was some sort of witchcraft, and I, for one, didn't like it."

Dr Fern said, "Andy, what we saw in those pieces might not have been intended for anyone but us. That's why we were the only ones who saw it. The communiqué was targeted."

"Then that's why I didn't see a face, although I was sitting right there too," Jake said.

"Exactly. You were like Wendy and James. Witness to the visionary experience. Not participants. But Andy and I, for some unknown reason, visual and audio manifestations from an intelligent source – let's call it an entity – that spoke to us directly. The shards were merely a device. Like a chalkboard only we could see. The entity put words on our chalkboards."

"What did yours say?" Andy asked.

"It said, 'Find her. She's here. Help me. Find the girl.'"

Wendy recoiled at the sound of those words. Her amulet was vibrating. It was a soft vibration, like Hecate's purr. Danger. Danger is close. That's what the buzzing said to her.

"I'm the girl," Wendy said before she could stop herself. Saying it out loud made it more real. The amulet thrummed more vigorously against her breastbone.

"Why didn't you tell me?" Jake asked Dr Fern.

Dr Fern sighed as she set aside her cup. "I'd only just met you. I wasn't certain what I'd seen, or whether it was real. I've never hallucinated before. But, in the past, I have shared dream visions with my patients. This had a similar… I don't how to describe it. A similar flavor."

"Like what happened with me during the hypnosis session," Maude said.

"Precisely."

"Why is this starting now?" Andy said. "Why would people who've never had visions suddenly start having them? What's happening to us?" His bandages were sliding out from under his cap. He had dark rings around his eyes. His skin was pasty, and he needed a shave.

"I don't know, Andy. If it were one person, there might be a host of possibilities, physical and psychological. But for three of us to begin seeing and hearing strange things..."

"Four of us," Wendy said. "I hear the Lamprey in my head. I see him when no one else seems to notice he's around. That never happened before I met the Lamprey for the first time."

"Which was when?" Dr Fern asked.

"The day Rex was arrested at the Big Drain. The Lamprey was in the crowd."

"I'm the only one not experiencing this peculiar phenomenon," Jake said. "Why?" He was practically shouting at them. He dug his fingers into his leg as if he wanted to rip into the muscles. His knuckles turned white. He gritted his teeth and let out a snarl like a dog.

"Maybe it doesn't like you," Wendy said.

Dr Fern laid a gentle hand on Jake's shoulder.

"Or maybe you experience it in a different form. As physical pain. Nerve stimulation."

The front door to Dr Fern's cottage flung itself open. Wind, rain and sticks blew inside. The animal figurines vibrated on the shelves. Hecate ran for the bedroom. The door slammed again.

James's radio suddenly roared very, very loud. A harsh clashing like smashed glass rolling back and forth in a washtub. But inside the cacophony something was speaking sibilantly.

"The Prism. The Witches. I am Syrx-Crugoth. Syrx-Crugoth. SyrxCrugothSyrxCru..."

They all ran into the other room. Wendy clamped her hands over her ears. The voice blared deafeningly loud. The plates and glasses in the cupboards were shaking. Chair legs rattled.

The voice hissed like a sack of vipers. Wendy felt the sound crawling on her skin.

James sat at the kitchen table. A spoonful of fruit cocktail frozen halfway to his mouth. He was staring at the thunderous radio, transfixed. Fruit nectar dripped from his spoon. As if he were in a trance, asleep with his eyes open, he stared and stared. He didn't blink or move.

Wendy twisted the radio knob, killing the power and cutting off the grating voice. The silence was a kind of shock too. They felt it. The storm had passed. Beyond this kitchen, farther than the boundaries of this house, all of Arkham had quieted. A hush.

Hush.

Wendy ran to James and hugged him. The boy was scared but otherwise unharmed. Andy inspected the radio, then pulled the plug from the wall. Jake stood in the doorway in awe.

"Whatever this entity is, I think we have its attention," Dr Fern said, soberly.

Wendy held onto James, wishing she had the ability to turn them both invisible.

31
Dark Cell

The storm had passed. Charlie was hungry and didn't plan to stay cooped up in his office any longer. The room felt smaller since Hyacinth Burroughs' visit. He needed to get out and walk around, to clear his head. He'd go for a stroll. He heard they'd opened a new steak restaurant over on the corner of Whatley Street and Noyes. He had a taste for a bloody ribeye and a crisphead wedge salad with Thousand Island dressing and a scattering of those cute baby shrimps.

He grabbed his hat and told his secretary he was heading out to eat.

"Dining alone?" she inquired as she lifted the receiver of her telephone but kept the switch hook depressed with her finger. "Want me to call your driver?"

"Afraid so. And no driver. I have thinking to do. A little food, and stretching my legs usually helps." He offered to bring her back something from the restaurant. She declined.

Earlier Charlie had called Mandy Thompson at the Orne, hoping to persuade her to join him for a meal and to talk over Hyacinth's offer. Mandy declined politely, saying she was entombing herself in the local lore, digging up whatever she might find about the Burroughs clan, the Prism, and the cursed crystal stuck in the entrails of Arkham. Hyacinth's appearance had opened avenues for investigation. Charlie admitted that for now he couldn't determine if Hyacinth was friend or foe. Mandy likewise reserved her judgment until she gathered more facts.

So, Charlie was left to wrestle with his own musings regarding Hyacinth. Let her have the Fang! *I don't want it,* he thought. *But I need to know who you are before I surrender it. How does strangeness only lead to more strangeness? Why am I besieged with anomalous conundrums?* This onslaught of uncanniness was hardly the usual business of a small-time city's mayor. Witches, occult murders, the hum of panic in the streets – pure mayhem.

He yearned for the normal logjam of bare-knuckled political brawls, sycophantic favor-seekers, and petty corruption to gum up his day and trouble his sleep. Charlie doubted whether his counterparts in Kingsport and Salem dealt with such daily madness. But he would never tell them anything.

This was a private affair, Arkham family turmoil. They'd keep it in-house as much as possible. Remove the Fang. Catch the killer, or killers. Push the Big Drain project back into high gear. Enlarge those sewer and drainage tunnels so that everything flowed as smoothly under the city as it did above ground. What a joke.

Charlie slipped out the side door of City Hall. Humid. No raindrops. He headed east. Storms typically left the air cooler. But Charlie felt stuffier than he had indoors. He loosened his necktie.

Few citizens were out. Good. He didn't feel like stopping for conversation. The streets were chocolatey brown. They smelled of disturbed earth. It reminded him of when he was a boy, digging for nightcrawlers in his backyard, dropping them in a sawdust-filled coffee tin, so he could go fishing on the banks of the Miskatonic. Not far from here, he'd hooked some big ones. Nowadays, he wouldn't dare to eat anything that came out of the river. The foulness staining the air and water leached into the flesh. It wasn't the kind of thing you wanted to consume, to get inside you.

Storekeepers who recognized him tipped their caps as he passed, waving and smiling.

Do they like me? Or is it the power they respect? Envy? Fear?

A car was motoring slowly along the curb to his left. Why won't they pass? he thought, irritated. Are they gawking? Am I such a celebrity?

He waved them on without bothering to turn. Probably someone who wanted something. All day long I talk of money, he thought. They come to me with their hands out. Complainers and threat-makers. A decent man feels his soul being beaten to a pulp. I must bring myself back from the dead each day. Ah, politics.

Charlie picked up his pace. At the next corner he turned.

The car followed.

"Good grief, leave me alone."

Charlie knew they couldn't hear him, whoever it was creeping in the car.

A black car. He spied out of the corner of his eye.

Shiny from the rain. Like a long black mirror following me. Maybe it's a hearse.

He laughed.

It must be the press, he concluded. Only reporters had such gall. Rudeness personified. They knew no boundaries. Invasion of privacy was their stock in trade. Hacks. Fabulists.

He experienced a twinge of guilt just then. Because of Rex Murphy. He'd done the man wrong by having him arrested when he knew he wasn't the Lamprey. He was unfair to Rex, playing hardball. Now the poor guy was fighting for his life at St Mary's.

The car sped up suddenly and passed him, screeching ahead around the next corner.

Good riddance. They'd finally given up.

Charlie envisioned the steak he'd be served. The glistening meat charred black, crispy leaves of fresh lettuce and the herbal dressing. He wished he could order a glass of wine.

He was remembering what a good glass of red tasted like when he reached the intersection. A car door opened to his right. A figure rushed at him. He turned to meet them head-on, his fists raised in pugilistic defense. If they thought he'd back off, they were wrong. He'd clobber them even if they were journalists. You don't ambush a man like this.

Especially the mayor.

He didn't see a face. Only a twirl of material roughly the size and shape of a handkerchief, like a magician's flourish spinning in his assailant's hand. Ta-dah!

The scarf-like cloth spiraled in his face.

That's when he felt the double punch to his kidney. Brutal, efficient. Executed from a second assailant who knew how to deliver a blow. Charlie felt as if he'd been gored from behind by a bull. He never saw that one coming. His knees buckled. The pain was acute, breathtaking.

That's when Charlie found out what the material was for.

It was a blindfold. After his assailant distracted him, he maneuvered to cut off his sight.

The kidney puncher grabbed his wrist and expertly snapped a

handcuff to it. Then he wrenched Charlie's other arm nearly out of the socket. Applied the second cuff. Snap!

The blindfold was cinched around his head.

Charlie had no strength. No fight left in him. Only pain. All his space was full of pain.

The one who blindfolded him kicked him in the nether regions.

Charlie lost his hat. He dry-heaved.

The pair of kidnappers dragged him like a sack of potatoes, shoving him into their waiting vehicle. The shiny black car, Charlie knew. They hadn't gone away, just gone ahead of him. Parking around the corner. Out of sight. Where they waited for him.

He walked right into their trap.

They must've been strong, because Charlie was no lightweight, and they handled him easily. They threw him on the floor of the backseat, kept him pinned down with their legs.

The nearest one seized the back of his neck. Squeezing so firmly that Charlie saw stars.

"You're a dead man, Charlie," the kidnapper said.

"And you're a fool for thinking you can abduct the mayor and get away with it," he panted.

The hand clamped like a vise. Pushed down, forcing his nose into the car floor. He felt grit under his cheek. A stale, moldy smell like stagnant water and mud filled his nostrils.

And something much worse.

Disgusted, he tried to pull back, gagging.

The hand forced him down harder.

Sewage.

A definite whiff of sewage.

"Who are you?" Charlie asked.

His heart was pumping. Real fear sizzled in his stomach. He tried struggling but it was no use. They had his hands behind him. He was immobilized, weighed down under two behemoths.

"Why, don't you know?" The voice hissed. "I'm the Lamprey. You're going to die."

Then one of them – he never knew which one – delivered a blow to the back of his head.

A dark cell opened in the car floor and swallowed him.

He went into nothingness. Utter, instant, inescapable.

Complete.

Nothingness.

32
Rope Teams

Glass lamps glowed in the parlor. The sun was setting. They hadn't experienced any more visitations since the radio growled its gargling, glassy voice at them in the kitchen. The plug was still out of the wall, though. Nobody wanted to hear that otherworldly tongue again. Dr Fern sat in her rocker, swaying back and forth with her black cat curled asleep on her lap. Jake and Maude sat together on the couch, while Wendy and Andy chose pillows and the floor. The conversation had gone round and round, but Andy knew he was losing the argument.

They were planning to follow in Rex's footsteps. He thought that was a terrible idea. They were making the same mistake Rex did, rushing in, not knowing what lay ahead. Andy was the only one who wanted to wait and see if they could decipher the notes in Rex's water-damaged notebook. They needed more information. He was all for adventure. Heck, he was the reason they went to the Amazon on their search for Maude and the mysterious Spider Queen. This time was different, he insisted. He ticked the differences off on his fingers.

"*One*. We know there's a killer on the loose. A very successful killer who almost retired Rex and me the last time we went into the tunnels.

"*Two*. We know the killer is likely still in the tunnels. He hasn't left town because, why would he? He likes it here and he's getting what he wants. Victims. So, he either lives a subterrestrial life, or he uses the passageways as a means of traveling, secretly moving through the metropolis. Maybe he spies on his prey before he takes them into the pipes to kill them. I suppose it's possible he just does his ugly deeds down there, like a dirty workshop. Out of sight. In the dark. He likes the privacy the sewer gives him. But I'm betting he hangs out in the drains even when he's not killing. It's his lair. In the past, the only people he's had to worry about bothering him are sanitation workers inspecting the pipes, doing repairs. Then the Big Drain renovation comes along. There's a boatload of noisy diggers dropped into his space. The murders begin. Coincidence? Who knows? The timing is interesting, though. Lately, the sewage system has turned into a regular Grand Central Station: diggers, cops, reporters, even the mayor is tromping through his territory. So, he withdraws, sinking deeper into the drainpipes. We know there are old tunnels. Very, very old tunnels. Nobody has a map. It's where he feels comfortable, and where we are at a distinct disadvantage.

"Where was I? Oh, yes. *Number three*. This killer possesses some sort of weird occult powers. He's able to get into our minds. Who knows how much he can see there? What if he's reading our thoughts? Listening to our conversations? What if he knows we're coming? We're heading into a deathtrap. Maybe that's why he's given us these visions in the first place. They're bait. Luring us underground."

Andy had done his best. But his arguments weren't enough to convince the others. When they took a vote, he lost.

Jake wanted to visit the tunnels. To stake them out. "Action is better than inaction. If we move now, we keep the Lamprey off balance. We're going in as a team. Four against one."

Dr Fern had no desire to enter the sewers, just as Andy had guessed. She was planning to remain at her house with James. They couldn't leave James alone. He was absolutely petrified by the idea of crawling into the tunnels. Dr Fern was Andy's closest ally for taking a step back, delaying any expedition until they had more data. She advised Maude that she was in no shape to face another trauma. She pointed out that Jake hadn't had a chance to heal either. He'd underestimated the mental rehabilitation that went hand in hand with his physical comeback.

The girl had been the deciding factor in their taking on this journey to hunt for a killer.

"We must protect Wendy at all costs," Dr Fern had said. "The Lamprey seems to be particularly drawn to her. He can psychically link to her, at will it seems, although Wendy has successfully broken the link by physically distancing herself from him. We don't know if the face which appeared to Andy and me in broken shards of glass and porcelain is the Lamprey. But these manifestations appear to be long-distance. I'm afraid the occurrences are too coincidental to be random. My fear is that the Lamprey will attain the ability to contact Wendy without having to be near her. This prospect is most alarming. It's also not something we can go to the police about. They'd laugh us out of the stationhouse. Or have us visiting the Arkham Sanatorium."

"You don't want that," Maude interjected.

Dr Fern seemed pained by what Maude said, although she did not try to refute her.

"By pursuing the Lamprey, you might force him to react, putting him on his heels. Get him to run or hole up. Then the upper hand will be ours. He'll be too busy to haunt Wendy."

"I agree wholeheartedly. Make him play defense," Jake said.

Maude had stood up and begun to pace in Dr Fern's parlor. "When Andy briefed us about Rex Murphy and the Lamprey story, he mentioned a 'crystal curiosity' that Rex saw in the sewer chamber. The witches who helped me to escape were in a chamber. I saw a crystal. They were conducting a ritual, worshiping it, I think. That chamber must be the same one Rex found. I can't explain this, but I feel that there's an energy emitting from this crystal that the witches know about. Andy, you and Rex were discovered near this crystal. The digger whose body they found was inside that chamber. It must all be part of the same story, somehow. My witches. Your Lamprey. The pink crystal in the chamber room. The answers are there. Calling to us."

Wendy said, "I'm ready to go after the Lamprey. If I'm with all of you, I feel safe."

Andy resisted frightening the girl, but he wasn't sure that he felt too safe himself.

The witches. The Prism.

I am Syrx-Crugoth.

What did that last part even mean? Was it a name? Or was it a type of creature?

Sear-Rick's-crew-goth.

Andy didn't like how it made his mouth feel when he said it. Or what it stirred in him: cold panic. An undercurrent accompanying the icy dread was even more disturbing, a disregard for those around him; it wasn't just that he didn't care about other people – he wanted to hurt them, to throw their lives into danger and watch them suffer. The feeling was fleeting. He pushed it down, and then away. But he was afraid of more than Syrx-Crugoth. He feared himself and how quickly his internal mood had shifted. He felt the risk of his own unpredictability.

Jake supplied them with lanterns and ropes from his gear closet at the Miskatonic Museum. "We'll tie ourselves together, in teams of two. Like you did with Rex, Andy. That was solid thinking. Using the buddy system. Like mountaineering, we'll have rope teams. Pairing up is a basic safety principle, harder to get lost. Though it might slow us down, speed isn't a priority."

"I'll go with Andy," Wendy said.

Jake nodded. "Wendy, I want to make certain you're prepared. How do you feel?"

"I'd prefer not crawling in the sewer. But if there's no other way..." she said, shrugging.

Jake nodded and smiled then looked to Andy. "Teaming with Wendy is acceptable?"

"Fine with me." Andy looped the coil of rope over his head and shoulder. "Don't get your hopes up too high. I don't plan on venturing all that far. Any sign of danger, we're pulling out."

Wendy checked her lantern.

"We'll have candles for backup, in case the lanterns run out of fuel," Jake said.

"Is it dangerous to carry an open flame?" Maude asked. "What about gases?"

"It's certainly a risk," Jake said. "I don't have the proper lamps for mines. Sewers are less hazardous. I've used these lanterns in caves before without any problem. If you're worried, we–"

"I'm not worried," Maude said. "Let's go."

"One last thing." Jake rummaged around in the closet which was too small to fit more than one person. He stood inside the narrow storage area which gave off an aroma of mildew and old campfire smoke that had soaked into the canvas bags, tents, and sleeping rolls.

He hauled out a large camera.

"If we see anyone down there in the tunnels, or anything of interest like an odd passageway or items of interest, anything at all, I'd like to get a photo for evidence that we can study later."

Maude reached for the camera, blocking Andy who'd started toward the closet with his arms outstretched, ready to take possession of the boxy, black and metal Speed Graphic.

"I'll take that," she said.

Andy harrumphed. Oh, perfect. Let's have Maude be responsible for photo evidence. She only unspooled the reels from the Spider Queen's temple, casting the finds of their last excursion into doubt and spoiling Andy's chance at a book deal.

It's only fame, he told himself, biting his tongue. I'm letting the past go. If I don't, I'll never move forward. This story is what counts now. Finding the Lamprey. T hat would get him back on the *Advertiser* staff. They couldn't deny him.

"Sure thing, you take it," he said to Maude, failing to hide the tightness in his words.

"I am a professional with a camera," she said. "I know how to get the shot I need under less-than-optimal conditions. I've done it before." She looked over the camera, hanging the strap around her neck. She attached the flash, put her eye to the viewfinder, and dialed the lens.

"Be my guest," Andy said.

"Film?" she asked Jake.

"Already loaded. There's extra in this bag." He passed her an olive-colored backpack.

Jake twisted himself out of the closet. His crutches banged the doorframe. He bumped the door closed with his backside and traversed the overcrowded office.

Andy saw him watching Wendy, who looked pensive.

"You sure you're ready?" Jake asked her.

"The four of us can do this," she said. Andy thought he heard her voice quavering.

"Well, I'm scared enough for both of us," Andy said.

"I'm a little scared," Wendy admitted.

"We all are," said Maude.

Jake said, "You'd be a fool not to be." He opened a desk drawer and pulled out a pistol, which he tucked into his belt. "Just in case. I hope I don't have to use it in such close quarters."

"What weapon do we get?" Andy asked, nodding toward his partner.

"Our wits," Wendy said.

"Splendid."

Andy would've felt better knowing he had more firepower in his arsenal than that.

Nonetheless, he'd make do.

33
Nocturnal Animals

They divided up. Andy and Wendy returned to the drainpipe by the River Docks, on the banks of the Miskatonic River. Andy stated that was the only place he wanted to enter the tunnels.

"I'm confident I can retrace my steps. 'Keep right' was my policy. Avoid making any lefts. If nothing else, I'll find where I was attacked. I even etched my initial on the wall. We'll look for that," he said, matter-of-factly. Once he'd lost the debate about reentering the sewers, he'd become committed to doing his best. Wendy had brought out his big brotherly instincts.

Jake wanted to climb down at the Big Drain site. That was going to be impossible. They'd start there and drop down as close as possible, without being obvious. Dr Fern drove them by the location to check on the security measures. Maude ducked as they passed the quartet of policemen guarding the construction entrance. The cops turned toward them in unison, like spotlighted deer in a cornfield. Moony, bored faces in need of a shave. Wary "keep away" glares.

"I'm a wanted woman." Maude threw up a blocking hand, filtering her glimpses of them.

"They have bigger fish to fry than you," Jake said, smiling at her slumping in her seat.

"Ah, yes – fried lamprey. A restaurant delicacy."

"Exactly," he said.

Maude might've been suffering from nightmares and visions, but her humor had survived, probably because it was an effective defense mechanism. Jake prized her for it.

"I counted eight coppers," James said. He was kneeling on the backseat, spying out the rear window. "Four at the street. Four more at the tunnel."

Dr Fern drove a moonstone blue Chrysler Imperial with a leather top. Jake was surprised she owned a speedster. When James had first seen the car, he'd wanted the doc to open her up on the road and go racing, but they had business to attend to. They drove past the closed dig site, took the first right turn, and started looking for a manhole to pop into. It was deserted enough that a quick exit wouldn't be an issue.

"There's one," James said. "You drove over it."

Dr Fern braked, then backed up slowly. "James, keep a lookout for trouble."

"Will do." The boy was enjoying himself. His earlier fears had settled wherever the youngster packed them away. He must have an atticful by now, Jake thought. Living on high alert, dodging threats real and imaginary; he lacked constancy, other than his bond with Wendy.

The streetlamps poured golden syrup over everything in the neighborhood. Above, the moon watched like a moldy face in the tar-black sky, peeping over the icy peaks of a cloudbank.

Jake retrieved the mountain climbing ice axe he brought from the gear closet.

Dr Fern idled the Chrysler while Jake and Maude slid out. Jake scraped around the edge of the manhole until he hooked the tip of the ice axe into the groove. He levered up the heavy iron lid.

"Got it," he said as he cranked it up out of the street like a nail from a board.

Maude grabbed the cover to prevent it from slamming down if the axe slipped. She flipped it over. It shimmed on the street like a giant's coin. The noise was loud, but this street was shops, everything shut down for the night. Faceless mannequins watched in the dressmaker's window. A barber's sign displayed a razor, a pair of open scissors; his empty red chair faced the street.

"Gentlemen first," Maude said.

The hole looked like it belonged in a piece of machinery. It didn't seem fit for humans. More akin to a reservoir for oil. The rusty top rung of a ladder resembled a thin cured sausage.

Jake tied a rope to his crutches and lowered them down into the darkness. Maude helped him sit on the street, then he inserted himself into the opening. He found his footing and gripped the ladder. Slowly, step by step, he shimmed down, using both his artificial leg and his uninjured foot to find the next rung. He wasn't winning any speed records, but he made it to the bottom. He picked up his crutches. Maude passed him the lanterns and the ice axe. Then she descended. She paused to drag the manhole cover back over the gap.

She was grunting with frustration.

"Something wrong?" he called up.

"It's upside-down. I can't flip it over," she said.

"It doesn't need to be perfect. We're not coming out this way. As long as it covers the access, we're good. We can always come back and fix it in the morning."

The lid capped the opening with a satisfying thud. A moment later, Maude joined him. Jake was tying a bandana over his nose and mouth, but still his eyes watered.

Maude said, "I don't think that's going to help."

"It'll make me feel better," he said. "The stink is worse than I imagined."

"I think today's rain made it worse."

They were up to their ankles in runny gray muck. The flow was steady. Maude raised a lantern. "Which way?"

"The Big Drain entrance is behind us. I see a cross pipe going to the left. We'll take it."

"Sounds as good as anything," Maude said. She started off.

Jake's first attempts to place his crutch tips firmly in the slippery, swirling opaque waters were not pretty. He almost fell twice. But as soon as he started wedging the tips higher up the walls, he discovered a pair of shallow ledges running near the surface of the water. The level footing gave him more stability. He hung his lantern from the horizontal bar of his right crutch. It swung wildly with each step he took, making the sewer look more like a tilting funhouse attraction. Maude ambled ahead. He fought to catch up. After he reached her, they made a turn that seemed to go off in the right direction and kept plunging ahead, hoping to spot evidence of excavation or new construction, anything signaling they were on the right track.

Instead, it was more and more of the same.

The slime grew thicker on the walls. He suspected the mossy green gelatinous layer might be fungus. The smell was vegetal, earthy, like mushrooms. It reminded Jake of navigating rotting jungle paths and gooey Southern swamps. Humidity hung in the air. Thin, hair-like root fibers dangled from between the bricks at the apex of the tunnel like pale, frilly trimmings. The intrusive tendrils were long enough that they brushed his head as he passed underneath, giving an unpleasant tickle. These blind searchers broke into the pipes seeking nutrients and moisture. Life has a way of showing up where you least expect it.

"A bit farther, I think," he said. "We're close."

They tromped on.

It was Maude who conceded, eventually, what they both knew to be true.

"We're lost," she said. "This can't be right. We've walked and walked. I've counted more than three hundred steps since we turned into this pipe. We should've found the new diggings by now." She propped her back against the wall, examining her boots for leakage.

Jake was happy to have a chance to catch his breath. Ambulation in the tunnel was more debilitating than he'd expected. His shirt was drenched with sweat. He'd torn off his bandana and retied it on his head to keep the salty perspiration from stinging his irritated eyes.

"I concur," he said.

"So, what now, Mr Professional Explorer?"

"I don't recall you being shy about trekking into the unknown. Do you remember where we met? Not Times Square if memory serves me."

Jake shined his light back behind them, not that he could see very far. Rounded walls striped with high water marks. The lardy porridge of filth collected at the bottom of the channel. How long had it been like this in Arkham's unlighted underworld? It looked very old.

There wasn't much choice involved in what he and Maude had done thus far. They'd taken the one turn and hadn't encountered another intersection after that. The lack of variety in the telescoping landscape began to give Jake vague claustrophobic surges. I might wander here for ages, he thought. Was it that very stagnancy that appealed to the Lamprey? The timelessness. No sunrises or sunsets. A suspended world. Not outside of Arkham but underpinning it – a base.

"Backtrack," he said. "That's all we can do."

"All right, let me squeeze around you. I like to be in front." She slithered under his arm.

"I do feel like a bit of a one-man band back here. Clink and clank," he said.

Maude reached for his shirtfront, grabbing up a handful to balance herself as she maneuvered past him. He detected the slightest whiff of sweat, hair, breath – human body smells.

"What's that?" she said in a whisper. She snapped her head toward their original destination, the way they'd rejected.

"Where? I don't see…" Jake strained to make out anything. The water was a band of shiny gray rubber they'd stepped onto, stretched out, wavering.

Maude pressed a finger to his lips. Then she turned down the wick of his lantern and lowered her flame to a soft orange tongue that flicked at the glass globe. She crouched low.

"I saw something ahead of us. A light."

Jake peered into the darkness.

"If you saw their light, they probably saw ours," he said.

"I know." Maude slipped around him again, back where she'd been when they began. She held her lantern barely above the water slurping at their legs. "I'm going for a look. Stay here."

"What? Why?"

"You're too noisy," she said. "Too slow…"

Jake was ready to object, but Maude had already gone. It reminded him of being with Ursula. He was always playing catch-up. If he called to Maude now, it would put them both in danger. If he followed, he might do the same. He was slower than she was under these circumstances, so his only choice was to wait. He hated waiting. It made him feel useless, although he knew intellectually that there was nothing useless about providing backup support. He hated inertness. "All drama, no excitement" – that was how he'd described it to Ursula one time scaling the cliffs above Peru's Sacred Valley.

"I feel the emotional strain, but I can't do anything to alleviate it," he'd said.

"Poor you," Ursula had replied. Then she climbed higher.

Jake imagined Maude would give him much the same response.

Where was she? She'd left him in the dark. The tiny bud of his flame lingered near extinction. He couldn't see a trace of her light. Or any other light, farther on. He knew the darkness played tricks on you; it made you start to see what wasn't there. Things you hoped to see and things you feared. It was like a screen you projected your inner thoughts onto. He hated himself for thinking it, but hadn't Maude been hospitalized for virtually the same thing: being unable to distinguish between what was real and what she dreamed? Had he let her go off on her own, guided by a damaged psyche?

Suddenly he felt a strong tug at his waist. The ropes! They were attached to one another.

He felt two more tugs in quick succession. Then a pause. Then three pulls.

She was signaling him to come ahead. At least that was how he interpreted it. *Follow me.*

He hung his lantern back on his crutch and tried walking as quietly as possible. The rope remained taut, so he guessed Maude was gathering the slack as he got closer to her.

He was essentially stumbling in the dark, barking his knuckles on the wall. He tried going faster and slipped, catching himself before he tumbled forward. The glow from his lamp illuminated little more than his body and a foot or two immediately in front of him.

The rest was a blank chalkboard.

Flashes pulsed in his sight. He knew they were the effects of blood pounding behind his eyes as he exerted all his strength, all his agility, and his willpower to keep going.

She was pulling faster now, almost too fast.

Something hidden underneath the water tripped him – a sunken stick, or a piece of pipe. Perhaps a broken tool. He wanted to cry out. "Curses, Maude! I have a new leg I'm learning to use here! Slow it down, please!"

Then another thought burst into his brain.

What if it wasn't Maude dragging him in? What if she were incapacitated? Silenced.

He had his ice axe clipped to his belt. In a pinch, it would make a formidable weapon. Jake prepared himself to meet his enemy. His mind showed him spider eyes and jaws.

"Here!" she whispered.

It was Maude. Her face emerged from the tunnel's darkness into his lantern's shine. Jake's heart was pounding. His forward momentum nearly caused him to topple over her.

"Down, down…" She caught him and kept them both from going over.

"I can't crouch," he said.

She nodded, thin-lipped, determined. She situated herself at the junction of two tunnels, theirs and another. This intersection wasn't a "T" but the new tunnel cut hard left around her left shoulder. He saw the open end of a second pipe to their right. It formed an "X" rather than a "T," he realized. Maude leaned into the section of cross-tunnel he was too far away to gaze into.

"I hear voices," she said to him. She pointed her thumb around the corner.

Jake tried to listen. His pulse filled his ears like ocean waves. The trill of the water in the pipes flowing. A drip, drip, drip from the walls, and a steady leak from somewhere above.

Too much water. It drowned out other sounds.

He strained, craning his neck forward, cupping his hands behind his ears.

I'm a bat, he thought. I hear in the darkness. I see with my ears. Listen, listen...

There!

He heard them too. Voices.

A kind of murmuring interspersed with grunts. It almost sounded beastly, like hogs in a pen feeding on their slop. Then Jake realized that the men – their voices sounded deep and low, gruff – were moving around in the sewer sludge, kicking up gobs of wet gunk, splashing, and the tunnel distorted their words and the noises they were making while at their task.

One of the men suddenly barked with laughter.

Another shouted. It was difficult to tell whether they were comrades or enemies.

Jake planted his crutch squarely in the crossroads and tilted forward. He had to see. Maude curled closer to the brick corner to give him more room. She was looking too. Jake bent over a bit more.

Bright lights. Lanterns. Some hanging from sticks jammed across the top of the tunnel. So, that must've been what he tripped over a while ago, one of these lantern-hanging sticks the men were using. They'd dropped it in the tunnel and didn't bother picking it up. Men. At least he thought they were men. They dressed the way workmen do. Shades of drab. But these men wore hoods over their heads. The hoods looked like pillowcases or maybe burlap sacks with eyeholes slashed in the fabric. Some of them were carrying barrels. Two to a cask. Those that weren't lugging cargo had machine guns in their hands. This was a delivery run with armed guards.

More shouting from deeper inside the tunnel. Definitely unfriendly words.

"Who're you?"

"Come out 'fore we blast you. Get your hands up!"

Are they talking to me? Jake thought.

But the men were all facing away from him and Maude. They hadn't even seen them.

Before Jake had a chance to react, the tunnel around the corner erupted with gunfire.

Bullets flew down the passage, chipping away at the brickwork, sending a shower of bright sparks and deafening racket that pounded in his ears. He lurched back and would've fallen if Maude hadn't grabbed him by the belt. They started back into their long straight tunnel – the way they'd come in – when the roar of a shotgun sounded and buckshot tore a chunk of bricks loose from the tunnel ceiling, almost blinding them. Their attacker aimed too high. Maude hurried into the only pipe that didn't have men in it or a direct line of fire from the shotgun. Jake clambered after her.

Directly behind them, the machine gunners were exchanging fire with their adversaries, and none of them took notice of Maude and Jake entering their tunnel. But the shotgun-wielding shooter was sloshing up to the junction right behind them in pursuit. He'd make the corner soon.

An ice axe is no match for a shotgun, Jake thought. I'll be cut down before I get close enough to hit back. They staggered ahead. It was like a nightmare. No matter how fast Jake tried to go, his boots and crutches kept getting stuck in the thick goo. He was certain that at any second, he'd feel the scorching blast of scattergun pellets peppering his back. Bullets from the firefight whizzed past them, pinging the sides of the tunnel, ricocheting into the water, sending bits of brick like shrapnel buzzing around the sewer pipe.

Maude was suddenly not in front of Jake anymore. He wondered absurdly if she'd plunged into an unseen crater concealed in the pipe.

She hadn't.

A hard jerk sent him careening off-balance, sideways. He braced, expecting to crash into a wall of bricks. But he entered a shaft, not made of bricks, but of rough, eroded limestone. He bashed into Maude, heard her muffled groan, but she was strong enough to hold them both up.

The shotgun boomed. The eruption joined the chatter of machine guns and the screams and hollers of men at violent war with one another. They threw jeers and insults while they reloaded their weapons. The shotgun erupted again, but farther away this time. Their pursuer had turned to join the gun battle. Jake's ears were ringing so loudly he wondered if the men could hear each other at all, or if their whoops were more for themselves than for the foes they wished to kill. Regardless, it seemed that he and Maude were out of the melee, at least for now.

Jake twisted toward her to ask if she'd been hit.

"Look!" she said.

She was dragging him down the narrow vent of rock.

Suddenly, she stopped and raised her lantern.

There, propped up on a ledge, was a man. He was dressed like the others they'd seen in the tunnel, hood and all. Only this man was dead. He was wet all over, dripping still from the tips of his boot laces and the underside of his exposed double chin. Jake reached in and pulled the man's mask up to his brow. He was no one Jake recognized. A hoodlum with a talent for rough violence and illicit activities. But this dead man had no bullet wounds, no buckshot holes in his shirt. He'd been strangled. His neck was a mass of finger-shaped bruises, and his fat tongue lolled. Above his shirt collar was the telltale incision where the Lamprey had drained off his blood. He gaped at them in a frozen leer. Maude pulled his mask back down, shuddering.

"Why would someone do that?" she asked.

Neither of them had an answer. There was no answer that made any sense.

Maude lifted the Speed Graphic slung around her neck and snapped a photograph.

The flash blinded Jake. Afterimages hovered ghostly before his field of vision.

"Let's go," Jake said, worrying that the flash might've given away their hiding place.

They left the corpse sitting there. Shadows blanketed him as their lanterns passed.

Jake felt cool air blowing in their faces. He smelled woodsmoke.

Ahead of him, Maude was framed by a halo of yellow and orange. The water was drying up, and it dawned on Jake that they were walking up an incline. The shaft widened abruptly into a vaulted grotto. Instead of muck under his heels, he sensed the crunch and slide of gritty sand.

They emerged into a cave.

He wobbled up behind Maude. From the near distance came the cough of a truck motor starting, tires throwing pebbles, and the squeak of a vehicle hitting potholes, cracking tree limbs.

She was taking in the scene before them. A firepit. A steel pole for stirring the embers stuck in the sand. Canteens and cigarette butts were littered about the fire. To their right, rows of whiskey barrels – same as the ones he'd seen in the pipes – were stacked against the cave wall.

Whiskey stills stood to their left, perched atop stone foundations. Their copper skins shining in the firelight. Tubes and collecting pots, like a mad scientist's experiment, branched off in every direction. However, this was not the work of scientists but of bootleggers.

Only there were no bootleggers here.

Not now.

They must've been disturbed in the middle of their operation. Signs of hasty retreat abounded. Jake knew that could change in an instant. The men who'd been working these pots must've fled. For just on the other side a cave opened like a spreading mouth, revealing a leafy patch of lush, surrounding woods.

The Black Cave, Jake realized. That's where we are. Haven of smugglers and the like.

The sewer and drainage systems must connect to it. Overlapping networks linked.

He knew the rumors about illegal whiskey coming in and going out along the Miskatonic River by night. He'd even heard mention of the Black Cave itself. He'd never been here before.

Few had.

Because it was the haunt of gangsters and other sinister forces. Or so the stories said.

"We need to leave here now," he told Maude.

"What is this? A backwoods distillery?"

"Gangsterland. We stepped into a turf war between rivals. Not a good place to be."

"Is that what killed that man with the purple neck back there?" she asked.

"I don't think so."

"Me neither."

Outside the raggedy mouth of the cave, they saw leaves flapping, the shapes of trees, and fleeing footprints scattered in the sand. They went forward cautiously. Tire tracks. A dirt road.

He pointed toward the blue-black night on the other side of the lane.

"The river is out there. We're in Rivertown. We missed our mark. Ended up at the water's edge. Whoever got chased away by the sounds of that gun battle, they'll be back soon."

"What do we do?" Maude gazed up at the moonlight filtering through the treetops.

"Take the road. If we see headlights or hear an engine, we'll dive into the trees."

Only later, after they made it back to the relative security of the city's glow, did they dare to discuss the eyes they saw watching them as they walked out. Eyes twinkling in the moonlight. What about the steps they listened to as the others traveled beside them, in parallel, partially hidden behind a thin screen of scrubby evergreens, pacing them out of the woods, making sure that they left? Jake and Maude had no good explanation. At first, they assumed the eyes and the footsteps belonged to nocturnal animals. But animals don't walk on two legs or wear long robes.

Apparently, they weren't the only ones flushed from the caves that night by the bootleggers' war. One of the others revealed themselves accidentally as they dashed across their trail before disappearing. Not a gangster, but a woman – judging by her legs and footwear, visible as she lifted the edge of her robe to step over the ruts in the road.

34
Ruby Red

Wendy pinched her nose. "It stinks like dead fish." She sounded like she had a bad cold.

"That's the river," Andy said. "This wind is blowing in tonight. You might not believe me, but it's a better smell than usual. This is my second time in the pipes, you know?"

Wendy tried breathing through her mouth. It didn't make that much of a difference. She was tasting and smelling hot, flyspecked sardines baking on rocks in the sun. She pictured their round seedlike eyes dried up and hard; plump worms squirmed through their guts. In her imagination, the dingiest of seagulls turned up their beaks at the putrid stench and flew away. It was like being locked in a tomb at the cemetery. She and James had tried hiding in a mausoleum once, when they couldn't find anywhere else to sleep. Who would bother them at a burial ground? But it was too creepy. The quietness exuded a kind of pressure, like it wanted to shout at you. She had trouble breathing in the vaults. Before sunset, she and James hightailed it out of the cemetery. Better to sleep in the park, or the edge of the woods, or in a fort made of empty crates, hidden in an alley behind the fish warehouses. They might meet a friendly stray cat to cuddle.

In the cemetery there were no people, but you didn't feel alone either.

It was the same way she was feeling now in the sewer.

Something knew they were here. As if they were inside a living thing, and it *felt them*.

They'd made a couple of turns. Andy was talking the whole time, which made Wendy feel better because it was harder to think if you had to pay attention and listen. She didn't want to think. Not about the awful smell, which was getting worse. Or about the tight tunnels which felt cramped to Wendy even though she wasn't very big. Or most of all, she didn't want to think about the Lamprey. Because the idea of thinking about him made her worry that he might become aware of her. Like ripples spreading in a pond, one might touch him. He might get a quiver up his back, a tingle in his slick, nasty Lamprey mind. Then he'd start talking to her.

That was the worst – having him jump out at you from inside your own skull.

"I might've mentioned that I scratched my initial on the wall last time I was here," Andy said. "But did I tell you there was already an ancient symbol written in the same spot?"

"How do you know it was an ancient symbol?" Wendy asked.

Her neck hairs prickled.

She wanted to keep Andy talking, but she also knew about ancient designs. Her mother had chalked them all over their house. That was after her father was lost at sea, before her mother went to the hospital. Sigils. That's what they were called. Her mother drew them for protection.

Andy tilted his head, evidently considering her question. "It looked like a word sign that might've come from the time before alphabets. Ever hear of the Sumerians? They're older than the Egyptians. They pressed symbols into clay. I saw a triangle with three lines next to it. Probably black magic. The Miskatonic Museum has a few examples of clay symbols displayed on exhibit. I covered them for a story I wrote a while back."

Wendy had been to the Miskatonic Museum. It was easy to sneak in there if you were a kid and you acted polite. It was a good place to kill time on a slow morning, especially if the weather was acting up. She hadn't seen anything like what Andy was talking about. She didn't find any sigils. Maybe she was going to the wrong exhibits, or Andy was confused.

She said, "Maybe a tree branch got caught in the rushing water during a storm and twirled against the crumbly brick, scratching out a mark that only seemed like a person made it."

Andy shook his head and laughed. Then he shrugged. "Maybe... If I see it again, I'll take a closer look. You're a tough audience, kid."

"It might've been anything. Graffiti. A bored sewer worker's scribble," she said. "Some people draw symbols called sigils to help stay safe from harm. A sigil might be a good thing."

Andy stopped marching and gazed back at her. He didn't seem angry, just curious.

"What?" she asked him. She was only making conversation. Wasn't that the kind of thing older people did?

"Nothing," he said. His face screwed up like he had more to say. He gestured with his chin toward the coils of extra rope around her waist. "How're you doing? Hanging in there?"

Wendy held up one of her hands. It was covered in sticky

gunk. She'd slipped and automatically put her hand against the wall, landing – splat! – in a mushy spot. Now, she didn't know what to do about it. She couldn't wipe it on her clothes. She certainly didn't want to dip her hand in the soupy, disgusting liquid surrounding her boots and swish it around. She wasn't even looking downward at this point, not after what she'd seen floating by.

"My hand," she said, "is ruined." She wanted to cry, or at least take a hot bath. But she wasn't going to tell Andy and risk feeling embarrassed. It was bad enough that she showed him.

Andy smiled. He dug out a handkerchief from his pocket and gave it to her.

"Keep it," he said. "I have more at home."

"Oh, thanks," she said, wiping her fingers clean and letting go of the cloth in the stream. Andy didn't notice.

"Hey, see here! It's my mark." He scrambled ahead, kicking up chunky waves. He pointed proudly to a faint letter "A" scratched on a brick at eye level. He started sidestepping.

"And the ancient symbol should be right about…" He trailed off.

He shined his lantern around, high and low, but couldn't find it. Stopping at one place where the bricks look scrubbed, he studied the lighter smudge, tapping his finger on the wall.

"Somebody erased it," he said.

"Too bad," Wendy said. She would've liked to see it, to find out if matched any sigils.

Then he smiled wide. "It must've been a clue! We must be getting close now. Let's keep moving. I smell a hot story in our future." He went crashing ahead into the foul tubular gloom.

That's not a story you're smelling, Wendy thought.

She wasn't scared of where they were heading. She felt safe with Andy. Her amulet was quiet, and she resisted handling it, but the necklace with its crooked eye-in-star pendant bumped against her as she lifted her knees high to tread through the scummy sludge. She wasn't afraid of where they might be heading, but she was increasingly uncomfortable with the qualities of where they were. It was too snug. Her breathing had become shallow and fast. She didn't say anything to Andy, but she felt like every few steps somebody was throwing a wet blanket over her head, weighing her down. She couldn't suck in air through the layers. It wasn't the bad smells that bothered her. She was getting used to them. Wendy had an awful, terrible feeling that she and her partner were spiraling deep inside the earth, so deep they'd never find their way out again. They'd be trapped. The air would run out, or water would burst in. They'd be lost in the dark.

The walls closing in…

Squeezing smaller and smaller until the end of the drainpipe would funnel to nothing.

Watery muck would rise and get in their mouths. They'd have to swallow it.

The thought made her gag.

"Hey, Wendy," Andy said. He put his lantern up by her face.

She shut her eyes against the brightness. Her body was swaying on two rubbery legs.

"Yeah?" she said, in a husky whisper. She had no breath to waste on talking.

"You don't look too good."

She felt the warmth of the lamplight leave the side of her face. When she slitted her eyes open, Andy looked different. He wasn't scary. She blinked away the blurs. But he didn't change.

He was pink – or, at least, half of him was. From the tunnel off to his left, a pink light shone on him.

Wendy's amulet was doing something it never had done before. It was pulling her in two directions. Forward and back. It tapped lightly against her chest. The pendant knocking gently like a small but insistent fist on a door.

"Over there, Andy," she said. "I see pretty lights floating against the ceiling. They look like candy, don't they?"

Andy opened his mouth as if he was going to object, but his head swiveled, and he saw what she was seeing. He was speechless. Candy-colored lights. Like something from a storybook or a dream. Not only pink but purple and orangey-red. They kept changing, getting stronger, bolder, and more vibrant. The light was painting the walls with alternating colors. Swaths of coral, rose red, apple red...

Deep, deep blood red.

Andy was walking into the multicolored tunnel made of flaming blocks.

The flames were made of light, only light. Fire-licked. But this wasn't from a fire.

Wendy felt a coolness. The sewer smell became more mineral, like well water. Damp stones, like rust and pennies. Tasting salt, she stayed behind Andy. Her feet were moving without her having to think. She set her lantern down in the opaque gray water and didn't even care when it snuffed out. The current carried it away. The coolness felt good. Fresh on her skin.

She wasn't afraid.

But she should've been.

At the end of the tunnel was a room. A red room with tunnels all around, like spokes on a wheel, and a risen dome in the middle. At the center of the room a giant crystal hung down like the tooth of a dragon piercing through the earth. The crystal was sharp in some places, worn in others. Red lights were shooting out of it. They hit the walls and changed angles. It was like being inside a twirling red kaleidoscope. Wendy was too amazed to be frightened.

Andy stopped at the edge of the room. They were bathed in the rich shower of scarlet radiance.

They weren't alone.

Someone was standing behind the crystal. The figure wore a long robe with a hood pulled up over their head like a monk in a church painting. Or like Little Red Riding Hood. But Wendy knew that whoever was inside that hood wasn't a little girl. It was a wolf.

Or, rather, a Lamprey.

Something about the crystal made her amulet work differently. Wendy expected to feel it vibrating because she was in danger. But it was as if the amulet had no energy, all its power was drained off. Instead, the crystal was pulsing, like a heart. It was beating in time with *her heart*, she realized. Her boots were glued to the floor. That's how they felt. Stuck.

Wendy's hair was standing up like when she brushed it out on a dry winter day.

Andy was rubbing his forearm. He had goosebumps.

The Lamprey was pouring red paint on the crystal. Splashing it. Rubbing it in. Flicking out the last few drips from a container and making the hue turn a darker red. It wasn't paint he was splattering. Wendy knew that. But she wouldn't let herself think, like when she refused to look at the filthy water. She turned her face away and sighed like a person giving something up. Yet she couldn't ignore what was happening. Ignoring things didn't make them go away.

When she looked back again, the cloaked figured startled.

The Lamprey hadn't known that she was behind him. The power of the crystal's energy was too strong. It interfered with signals. The atmosphere crackled. Air fizzed in Wendy's nose. She breathed it in. She had a strange feeling in her feet. Floaty. Like her body was a clear bubble. A bubble filling up with red light. She was a red balloon on a red string drifting high into a red sky.

The hooded figure dropped its jar streaked with congealing blood.

"Wendy?" the Lamprey said, sounding genuinely surprised.

It wasn't his voice in her head this time, but a real human voice, except the crystal was doing something to the sound of it, making it fuzz and snap like bacon frying, like a radio stuck between stations. The crystal glowed cherry red ruby red darkdarkdarkredredredredbloodred...

Andy grabbed Wendy. He picked her up. He kept her from floating away from herself.

He ran with her down the tunnel away from the Lamprey and the crystal, crashing through the water. She bounced on his shoulder, looking backward into the ruddy chamber.

The Lamprey moved quickly to the mouth of the tunnel. He didn't walk but rather glided. When he lifted his arms, his robe sleeves spread into a pair of red velvety wings.

The Lamprey called out, "Where are you going? Don't you understand? There's nowhere you can hide. Nowhere I can't follow. I have the power of Syrx-Crugoth. I am his servant. I am the stars, the moon, and the water flowing under Arkham. I am in the blood. I am the city! Me!"

Then Wendy saw other figures wearing similar cloaks gathering behind the Lamprey.

She could see through them as if they were made of glass. They put their hands on the back of the Lamprey. Farther to the rear loomed a deformed giant, crouching, its back bent against the roof of the dome. The giant's crooked body was composed of glistening points, sharp edges – a cluster of chipped, splintery knives, broken shards, daggers, hooked sickles, and shivs.

"The crystal is moving," Wendy said. "It's coming after us. They're all coming."

"Don't look." Andy huffed as he ran. Searching to retrace their way out.

He twisted around to see if they were being followed.

The crowd in the chamber pressed into the tunnel. Were they going to chase them?

Wendy's amulet slipped from under her shirt and floated up in front of her eyes, blocking the reddened scene from view.

Andy found an empty passage. Turned into it. Ran. Another tunnel, another turn.

Running, running…

35
Costly Mistakes

Charlie woke to wetness dribbling down the sides of his face. Leaking through his collar, rivulets ran cold fingernails along his back and chest. He snapped into instant alertness as the pouring liquid soaked his blindfold and he was choking, coughing, spitting out the rancid taste and grit.

"Look who's up."

Men's laughter. Their snickers echoed.

Charlie tried to stand, found he was tied to a chair, his arms and ankles bound. Cords encircled his torso. His blindfold had slipped from the force of the water they'd slopped over him from a bucket. He saw a man with the bucket in his grip, backing away. Charlie blinked, trying to clear his vision. The man wore a pinstriped suit, his pantlegs tucked into high rubber boots.

He had a mask on. It was a cloth sack like a scarecrow. Crazy eyes inside the eyeholes.

Charlie peeked over the edge of his blindfold, taking in details as quickly as he could.

There was another figure leaning in a concrete archway, observing Charlie's dousing.

"Fix his blindfold," the second one said. He was another well-dressed scarecrow. His suit fit better. Silk tie; a tasteful collar pin. He wore a pocket watch chain. A gold ring on his finger, set with diamonds and a large green rectangular emerald, was a particularly ostentatious touch.

The bucket man adjusted Charlie's blindfold, cinching it tightly behind his head.

Darkness again. Though Charlie kept seeing those bugged-out blue eyes jittering at him.

"What do you want?" Charlie asked.

"I told you. You're going to die. I'm the Lamprey," Bucket Man said.

"Then get it over with and kill me."

"Not so fast. We're just getting started. You've been out cold most of the time."

"Do it, coward," Charlie said. "Kill the mayor. Pull the switch on your electric chair."

"Looks to me like you're the one strapped to a chair. And you're not scaring anyone."

"Untie me then. We'll see who's afraid and who's not, big fella," Charlie said.

Bucket Man punched him. Charlie's head whipped to the side. He tasted blood, felt his lip swelling. He'd taken harder blows on the playground. "That's all you've got?" Charlie said.

Bucket Man pressed something cold, hard, and round against the bone of his forehead.

"Know what this is?" Bucket Man screwed the gun barrel around. Cocked the hammer.

"That's enough." It was the other man talking now. Archway. He was a leader, the one Charlie needed to negotiate with. He had the authority to decide whether the trigger got pulled.

Charlie's life was in his hands. Bucket Man was a weapon under Archway's control.

"What are you going to do with me?" Charlie asked. It was clear which man he was speaking to in this concrete bunker. Charlie knew they were underground; he recognized the odors by now. He surmised that they must be in an Arkham sub-basement near an access point to the city's drainage system. In the water-works.

Archway said, "We're going to sacrifice you."

"Why?"

"For the betterment of the city. You make bad decisions. Costly mistakes."

"Every politician makes mistakes. I do my best. Are you hoping to get a ransom for me?"

"Ransom?" Archway's boots squeaked, suggesting he'd moved forward. "Nobody pays for the dead."

"Is that what I am? A dead man?"

"Haven't you been paying attention? You're a gift. We're offering you as an example."

"Are you the Prism?" If Charlie was going to die, he wanted to know the identity of his killers. *Then I can get my revenge in the next world,* he thought. *I'll haunt your dreams, buckos.*

There was no reply.

"I'm the Lamprey," Bucket Man said again.

He's trying hard to convince me, Charlie thought. *Why's that important if I'm a goner?*

"But are you the Prism?" Charlie said. "Do you belong to them? Where's Hyacinth? Let me talk to her. Is it the Fang you're concerned about? What's the power of the crystal? Tell me."

He waited again for a response to his queries.

The two men were whispering to each other. Hissing like a pair of gossipy vipers.

"Enough talking," Archway said, finally. Then he spoke to Bucket Man. "Keep an eye on him. I need to prepare things. If he won't shut up, gag him. We'll be ready soon. I want him alive, understand? If he isn't alive, it won't work. I'll leave your bones here for the rats to gnaw."

"Don't worry, boss," Bucket Man said.

Charlie listened to Archway's squeaky boots walking away. Archway climbed a set of banging metal stairs, went out a door at the top that closed with a steely clunk. Then it was quiet.

"I think we're alone now," Bucket Man said menacingly. "Just you and the Lamprey."

The Lamprey, yes. That's who you want me to think you are.

I don't doubt you're a murderer, but are you the one responsible for these killings?

The mayor had nothing to say to this odious man. He stayed quiet, not desiring the gag.

Besides, he needed to think.

And these two kidnapping hooligans had given him more than his fair share to ponder.

36
Hyacinth's Meeting

"Quiet, please. Quiet." The leader hammered the gavel. Thirteen cloaked figures gathered around the oblong table ceased their various conversations. All heads turned to the tallest figure seated at the head.

Hyacinth Burroughs removed her hood. Candlelight illuminated her, a jaundiced glare.

The others followed, as was their custom. Men and women, members of the Arkham community, they would not have drawn any undue attention if not for their heavy formal robes. In truth, they each made a point of being inconspicuous, because throughout history people like them – witches – had been hunted, tortured, and murdered for a host of reasons. Across the globe they existed under constant threat. Precautions became a necessary part of life, as did secrecy, and methods of defense, natural and supernatural. They met at odd hours in obscure places, away from prying, judgmental eyes. Such was the case here. Witches survived on the periphery, on the threshold of worlds. They were the ultimate outsiders. Truly, Arkham was different from any other location on the map, but even in this city their kind had to be discreet. History proved that.

Concealment was the key.

"Thank you," she said. "I call to order this gathering of the Prism to convey to the coven the results of my meeting with Mayor Kane. As you all know, the mayor has become a problem, which I hope we are in the process of solving. More importantly, the public's discovery of the sacred Fang has put our mission in grave jeopardy. Times have never been more dire. I pled our case to have the Fang handed over to us. To me. But I do not entertain any fantasy that an answer will come soon enough to make a difference. Syrx-Crugoth grows more powerful every day."

Calls of spontaneous affirmation erupted around the table. Fists pounded loudly. Heads nodded in universal agreement. The black candelabras trembled on the table which had been cut from a single lightning-struck tree dating to the first Prismatic coven founded in the New World.

Hyacinth lifted a long-fingered hand.

Silence returned.

"We have a responsibility to deliver the God of Chaos and Cruelty to its rightful destination. As you know, our ritual from the other evening was a complete failure. I blame myself. I stumbled upon my recitation of the new ceremony. I am lucky to have survived."

"It was my fault, I fear. I wrote the language too ornately," a voice confessed from Hyacinth's left side. The brother witch shook his head, disappointment evident on his face.

"Nonsense," Hyacinth said. "We all heard my mistake. We'll have no more chances if we make another."

"What shall we do?" a third member of the coven, a raven-haired woman, asked.

Hyacinth said, "My ancestor, Dionysia Burroughs, has linked her arms to the Cruelest One for centuries. Syrx-Crugoth required no less of her. But she grows weaker even as the god's strength grows. The Fang is their past. They have endured together inside the crystal, sealed outside of time in a marriage, of sorts. The age of their mutual containment is ending. Freedom is coming. We must be the instruments of a double birthing. Birth and death coexist, side by side."

"Do we have time?" a voice from the end of the table asked. A younger woman with warm, brandy-colored, darting eyes. She wore spectacles that mirrored the wavy candleflames.

"The mayor is seeking further opinions on the nature of the Fang," the writer said.

Chuckles all about.

Hyacinth smiled.

"They will never know its true purpose unless they hear it from one of us. I believe that my visit at best caused a temporary delay. But they will remove the Fang soon," she said.

The impact of her statement sunk like a dagger into the hearts of the gathering.

The brother witch who wrote the last ceremony said, "We must act as soon as possible. I have rewritten the ritual. All that remains is to perform it again."

"Rewritten?" Hyacinth was shocked to learn of this development. "You said nothing to me."

"Dear leader, you have been busy out in the world of unbelievers. I have simplified the wording. I'm convinced it will work now. We must remain optimistic. Bold strategies, when called for, have never been an issue before. The Thirteen are nimble, flexible, and swift to act."

Around the table the members acknowledged their prior swift interventions, and successes.

"What about the murders?" the spectacled witch inquired. Offerings were her specialty. It was never as simple as outsiders thought. You didn't just drop toads and bats into a cauldron.

"What about them?" Hyacinth straightened in her chair. Her spine clicked audibly.

"They continue…?"

"Yes," Hyacinth said. The subject of the murders had divided, and nearly destroyed, the coven. "It is settled. Very well then. We are prepared to try again to unlock the cage?"

Thirteen nods.

She continued, "I will make contact when all the preparations have been made. We will need to secure the Fang's chamber. I'll enact a spell to confuse the tunnels for the authorities."

The brother witch offered his help but Hyacinth declined, saying, "This I can do on my own."

The brother witch nodded, then he addressed the coven, with his quill poised. "The Thirteen are in agreement? One and all?" Each member stated their assent for the record. He made a note in their archives, since he was both the scribe of rituals and recordkeeper.

The coven adjourned, dispersing into the morning twilight. They left by separate exits from the large, though unpopular, rooming house where they rented a windowless upper room. One by one they rejoined the residents of Arkham, and like them, went about their daily lives.

Alone again, Hyacinth shuddered. She despised herself for lying to her brothers and sisters in the coven. Shedding her cloak, she packed it away in her suitcase, preparing to return to the Silver Gate hotel. She divided her time between Providence, Salem,

Kingsport, Dunwich, and Arkham. For her living she dealt in antiques, but her passion belonged with the Prism, and now she would betray them. That is what she felt in her soul – treachery and deception. But how could she tell them the truth about what really happened during the last attempt to perform the ritual?

She had not simply failed to release the imprisoned from the Fang. Something else went wrong. She was no longer Hyacinth Burroughs. It sounded too absurd to even think about. But still it was the truth. Her ancestor Dionysia had somehow projected herself into Hyacinth. Now Hyacinth was Hyacinth-Dionysia. She felt the old woman crouching inside of her. Waiting. If any of the Prism had asked her previously if she would've welcomed her ancestor's spirit into her body, Hyacinth would've said, "Gladly. She is my blood, and I am her legacy. We are kin."

That was before it actually happened. Since Dionysia had come into her, she had felt sick, invaded by disease, and at war with her own identity. Dionysia was not a good guest. She was an infection, a stain, a pollution set loose in her soul. The woman spoke to her at night while she lay awake in bed. She did not tell tales of bygone covens, ancient ceremonies, and gods immortal.

No.

Her words were death. Death and destruction. She told Hyacinth that she meant to annihilate her. *I shall cast you into the void. I shall make you suffer as I have. I shall banish you.*

"Why would you do this to me?" Hyacinth asked her as she lay under her blankets shivering.

I need a body, Dionysia said.

"We can't share?" Hyacinth asked.

Share? the old woman laughed at her. *I don't share. I break apart and I take.*

Hyacinth fought to push the old woman deep inside herself, but Dionysia's withered arms were strong as clinging vines. She refused to go. The best Hyacinth could manage was to confuse the woman, sending her on journeys inside herself where the colonial witch would tire and sleep. Dionysia was stronger at night. At night Hyacinth no longer slept. She fought a witch war inside herself. She'd torn apart her hotel room, peeling wallpaper from the walls, smashing furniture, breaking every glass that room service delivered. Dionysia liked to play with the broken glass.

It distracted her. The sparkles and the sharpness – she made a puzzling game of them.

Hyacinth was afraid the Silver Gate might throw her out. She'd told the manager she suffered from headaches, and from nightmares where she walked in her sleep. She paid for the damage to the room. And still she wasn't sure they would allow her to stay much longer. They moved her to an unoccupied wing of the hotel. For the sake of our other guests, they said.

Hyacinth apologized for her illness. She promised no more outbursts of destruction.

That morning, before the coven meeting, Dionysia had visited Hyacinth.

In a bathroom mirror. Hyacinth drove her fist into her reflection. Not of her own volition. Dionysia forced her to do it. The mirror cracked in an interesting pattern. That was when the old witch showed up. Over her shoulder, emerging out of a mirror crack, like a spindly spider.

Syrx-Crugoth, Dionysia said, nodding. She flicked her gnarled fingers and mirror shards fell into the bathroom sink. Hyacinth knew all about Syrx-Crugoth. The coven talked of nothing but the god. Syrx-Crugoth had become their obsession. They learned the lore, the prayers and prophecies. The god manifested in sharp and fragmented objects. Hyacinth had no doubt who Dionysia served. The Fang had become a school where Syrx-Crugoth gave lessons.

Syrx-Crugoth will fill the gutters of Arkham with blood, Dionysia told her.

Hyacinth stood transfixed by her own reflection, by the web of cracks in the bathroom mirror, by Dionysia's wizened face speaking to her – and by the hard-edged shadow in the back.

Lurking behind them all, as angular and terrifying to behold as an angel or a demon.

If Hyacinth turned, would Syrx-Crugoth be standing in the claw-footed bathtub in the Silver Gate bathroom? Perhaps yes, perhaps no. But in the mirror, the god was present. Clearly.

The god cut into her psyche as sharply as a razor ripping through a sheet of silk.

We will destroy all, Dionysia continued. *First Arkham, then New England. Lastly, the world. I will start by having you as my morsel, sweet-smelling Hyacinth. I will eat you whole.*

Dionysia laughed, a wet and terrible noise.

Hyacinth pried the mirror loose from the wall and put it in the closet.

She threw a blanket over it and slammed the door.

Then she went to her morning meeting where she assured her group she was in control.

37
Morning Papers

The Lamprey loved to read the morning papers, to read about himself and his misdeeds. On his way to breakfast, he picked one up from a newsboy hawking them downtown. Chaos was ordinary now. Every fabric of society unraveled once you got things going in the right direction. The unthinkable became thinkable. Yesterday's impossibility was today's new reality. It was such a grand show. He felt like clapping as it all fell into ruins. Today was no disappointment.

One item was particularly interesting: Mayor Charlie Kane had been kidnapped off the streets in the middle of the day.

Witnesses from an insurance office watched as the city's top official was brutally assaulted… dragged into the back of a car that sped off. Kidnappers have yet to make contact…

Or so the police said. Who could trust them, between their incompetence and corruption?

Another tantalizing editorial tidbit:

Gangland violence undermines this city as rival bootlegging operations fight a blazing turf war… Gun battle in the sewers of Arkham… Crime is thriving. Three bullet-riddled corpses…

The Lamprey eagerly read on as he ordered his eggs and dry toast. The waitress departed.

Seizure of massive supplies of whiskey from the Black Cave. Oh my!

Murder in the sewers was the Lamprey's favorite topic in the news. He sped ahead, eyes gliding along the page, following the narrow print column so packed with juicy details. Police raided the Black Cave, axing liquor barrels and dismantling six copper stills. No bootleggers were arrested. But another body was discovered deeper in the cave. Here we go…

He licked his lips. He could hardly stand it. The good parts. A review of his handiwork.

The deceased bootlegger apparently drowned.

Drowned! Untrue! Lies! The papers were lying again!

No! No! No! Wrong!

He crumpled the edge of the paper. This story was unworthy. He turned the page.

Detectives fear the mayor may have fallen victim to accelerating hostilities… vying for top dog in the illegal liquor market… his disappearance cannot be merely coincidental…

Hmm…

The Lamprey set down his paper and looked around the diner.

No one knows me, he thought.

Or what I am.

Or to whom I belong.

They aren't expecting it. The thing that was coming was going to be… so eventful.

Everyone I see here will be dead, the Lamprey thought, sipping his coffee.

Good coffee. When his eggs and toast came, he devoured them. So tasty.

Too bad it would all be gone in a matter of what? Days? Hours?

Chaos will reign. Order will be overturned. The living will die, and the dead will live again. He just felt wonderful, absolutely wonderful. He left a good tip for his waitress, held the door for a handsome elderly couple out for their breakfast. Their last breakfast? he wondered.

Oh, he had a certain jolly spring in his step today. He couldn't stop grinning.

Because if everything went as he planned it to go, today would be the end of all this.

38
The Receivers

The Amazon River has turned to blood. Maude's raft has no oars. She's spinning in an eddy. She hears the rapids before she sees them. Pink mist hangs in the air above the water. It tastes like salt. She wipes her damp face. Her hands are covered with sticky blood. On the riverbanks, the boxy shapes of buildings rise like flat-topped mountains. The trees don't look right. Maples?

This is not Brazil.

Unaccountably, there is a signpost staked along the river's edge. WELCOME TO ARKHAM

Vultures sit atop the sign. They are eating... unrecognizable meat... Crows have joined them in the grass. Maude lifts her head higher. Was that a ribcage sticking up from the weeds?

The bloody river is both thick and swift, like lava flowing down a hillside.

She sees people ahead, swimming in the river. Hordes of them. Not swimming, drowning. Their panicked faces turn toward her as her raft passes. They don't try to climb aboard. Instead, they watch. As she drifts through them, she hears hollow bumps thudding against her hull. She peers over the side. Dead

Lair of the Crystal Fang

bodies outnumber the living. They are meat logs floating in the river. Some of them are trying to swim. Skeleton arms, skulls with raggedy patches of hair slicked with gore from the clotting tributary. They have no lungs so they can't drown, no hearts to stop beating. The struggling cadavers paw at the stream as if they can't remember how or why they are swimming. Shellfish cling to their russet seaweed wigs.

The beefy ones are more buoyant. Birds are hitchhiking and feeding at the same time.

Suddenly, Maude spots a sinuous swirling in the river behind her runaway barge.

It appears to be an enormous tube of mottled brown eel-like fish flesh. It ripples as it propels itself forward at an alarming rate. With a great splash, it leaps from the river and plants its sucking mouthparts on the raft, nearly capsizing her. Much bigger than an anaconda, or any riverine creature she's ever seen, she stares into its blank black goggle eyes. The row of holes behind the eyes must be the gills. The creature's snout pumps, attempting to latch onto her raft.

A lamprey, she thinks.

I am he. Who are thee? How do you like what we've done with the place? Isn't it cozy?

He's speaking to me, Maude realizes. I'm listening to a fish.

The Lamprey's voice is strange in every way, a mix of diction and tone that unnerves her.

As she looks into his metallic eyes, the raft passes into a tunnel shaped like a mouth. It even has teeth sticking down. They're made of broken bottles stuffed into gaps between bricks.

The last thing she sees are the Lamprey's shiny jellied eyes peering at her inquisitively.

She considers jumping overboard, but the prospect of being afloat in the channel is hardly appealing. Her lower half feels cool and tight, increasingly restricted. She looks down. Sees the Lamprey has her clamped in its raspy jaws. She screams. Her cries boom in the enclosed space.

"Maude! Maude, wake up!"

Maude opened her eyes. She was lying on a couch. Dr Fern stopped shaking her when she saw Maude was awake. Maude's heart pounded. She was stiff, fists clenched at her sides.

"You were dreaming," Dr Fern said.

Across the parlor, Jake assessed them from a chair. He looked dazed. His hair was mussed. He'd been sleeping too. She hoped his slumber had been more restful than her own. An undisturbed Andy lay curled on the floor under a quilt, his newsy cap tugged over his face. Dr Fern had already dressed for the day. An earlier riser, Maude thought. Despite the semidarkness in the room, Maude saw cracks of gray daylight seeping in from around the curtains. A wedge of milky blue light fell diagonally from the kitchen. Hecate the cat slinked along the baseboard, inspecting her territory and the newcomers who'd slept there for hours.

Maude didn't see the children, Wendy and James, anywhere.

"A nightmare," Maude mumbled to her psychologist. "I'll be fine."

"The Dreamlands or the jungle?"

"Neither. A new place. Just as horrible. Do you have anything to drink? I'm thirsty."

Maude recalled how her thirst got them both in trouble at the sanatorium. She winced.

"I was just putting a kettle on the stove for tea."

Maude sat up, kicked off the blanket wrapped around her

thighs. There's the Lamprey, she thought. But she wasn't feeling very humorous this morning. They had almost died last night, all four of them in the sewers. Dr Fern's house was their rendezvous point. After she and Jake walked uphill into Rivertown from the Black Cave, they stole a ride to Dr Fern's neighborhood in the back of an ice truck out making deliveries to the fish warehouses. Andy and Wendy arrived at the house later, on foot, looking haggard. They all went to sleep. They'd talk things over in the morning, they said. No one was eager for a chat. They'd spent their energies on staying alive.

But it was a victory that they were alive, at least for now.

"Let me help you with the tea," Maude said. "Where are the kids?"

"In the extra bedroom. I think Wendy might be stirring. She was calling out in her sleep."

The Lamprey is visiting everyone's dreams, Maude thought. Busy swimming in the deep, looking for prey to hook into, life to drain, energy to steal. He's a vampire in seafood clothing.

The two women entered the kitchen. Dr Fern had been baking muffins, and the smell was heavenly. She'd put out butter and berry jam.

Maude sat at the table, head in her hands.

"Are you feeling all right?"

"No." Maude rubbed her arms to get the blood moving. "Nothing new there." She yawned.

"You know, I've been thinking," Dr Fern said as she took out plates and set the table.

"About what?"

The doctor sat down while the water boiled. "About that," she said, pointing at the radio.

"What about it? It hasn't been talking in that splintery, godawful voice again, has it?"

Dr Fern shook her head. "It's still unplugged."

Maude gave her a look that said, "Go on, continue." She was too exhausted for conversation. Her neck ached and her back had a serious kink.

The doctor's notepad was covered with jottings and inky diagrams. She'd been hard at work while they were plumbing the depths, dodging bullets and monsters in Arkham's cloaca.

"Syrx-Crugoth, whatever that is, talked to us through that radio when it wanted to make contact. It appeared in Andy's bucket and my shattered mug. You've been having new visions unrelated to the Dreamlands or your rainforest nightmares. You interacted with the things you saw. The Lamprey sends messages into Wendy's mind, if he can get close to her. Jake's phantom physical pains attack him suddenly out of nowhere. They switch on… like the radio here."

Maude turned up two empty palms on the tabletop. She was lost.

"What does it mean, doc?"

"It's like we've all become receivers. We're like living radios. And something outside of us is broadcasting over Arkham. We're picking up on these signals. They're not all coming from the same channels, so to speak, but they're being sent from the same place, a central location."

"In the sewers," Maude said. She was starting to follow the doctor's line of reasoning.

Dr Fern nodded. "Whatever is out there, it needs us to show up in the world. It can't get here without us. We're the way in. The Fang is made of crystals, right? Crystals store energy."

The tea kettle started whistling. Both women jumped.

Dr Fern filled their cups and shared a box of teabags. Jake had joined them. He was propped in the doorway on his crutches, scratching himself. "I'll have a cup if there's any left."

Dr Fern told him where the mugs were in the cupboard. He fetched one, filled it.

"We're all receivers," Maude said.

"I feel like I received a beating with baseball bats," Jake said, "during the night."

He'd left his artificial leg in the other room. Maude couldn't help but flash back on the horrific state of his injuries when they'd sailed with him on the river back to Manaus, and then again to New York. She'd been in quite a state herself. Not speaking, suspended between worlds.

But she'd paid enough attention to know the severe trauma he'd endured.

They each had their own damages to overcome, wounds to heal, visible and invisible.

"How do you propose we stop these transmissions?" Maude asked Dr Fern.

"Destroy the crystal," she said.

From the other room, Wendy shrieked.

By the time they made it into her room, Andy was already there. He and James were standing next to Wendy's bed. Wendy was awake, sitting up. She had the amulet pressed to her chest. Sunlight through the curtains made the room appear as if it were underwater. A calm, blue-tinted mermaid's kingdom of peace and tranquility. There were starfish and seashells on the walls. A ceramic octopus, whose tendrils formed a pair of bookends on a shelf, scrutinized them.

"This can't keep happening," Andy said. "We saw him in the chamber. The Lamprey."

"He won't leave me alone," Wendy said angrily.

Maude sat down on the end of the girl's bed. She's tough, Maude thought. There was no point in trying to shield her from the reality of their situation. She was living in it right now.

"Dr Fern thinks we need to destroy the Fang. It's a transmitter that allows supernatural forces to contact us, to insert themselves in our dreams and visions, physically and mentally."

"I'm all for that," Andy said. "But how? A sledgehammer?"

"What about dynamite?" Jake said.

They all looked at Jake.

"Do you have any dynamite?" Dr Fern said.

Jake ducked his head sheepishly. "Yes?"

39
Adventurers' Club

They'd spent almost two days preparing for their expedition. No matter how they went about it, the risks were going to be extreme. The Lamprey, Syrx-Crugoth, gangsters, and who knew what else awaited them in the subterranean realm under the town. Luckily, things had gone quiet as far as otherworldly contact was concerned. It almost made Jake start to doubt Dr Fern's theory about the Fang sending out transmissions citywide, pinging signals from alternate dimensions the way a bully shoots spitballs from the back of a classroom, hitting heads, and causing general havoc.

They weren't taking any chances by splitting up this time. They'd go in together, roped as a team of four at nightfall – not that daylight existed underground. Andy said he knew the way in by now. Jake took a pistol. Andy borrowed his ice axe. Maude carried the dynamite that Jake uncrated from a box at the back of his office closet at the museum. He handed it to her carefully.

"Do your bosses know you have this?" she asked.

"What do you think?" he said. Then he followed merrily with, "What bosses?"

He checked their ropes.

"What weapon do I get?" Wendy asked.

Jake thought a minute, then he let her have the Speed Graphic camera that Maude had used the other night to photograph the Lamprey's latest victim in the Black Cave. It was bulky for a child to carry, but she'd proven herself to be more tenacious than the average person her age. Or any age. Besides, the camera would give her something to focus on, literally. A photo of the Lamprey, who always seemed to find a path to her, might prove to be the best evidence in his eventual apprehension by the law. At least it improved her mood, uplifting her dampened spirits.

"How do I work this?" she asked.

Maude stepped in, showing her how to load the film and take a picture.

"The flash attaches here." Maude slid the piece in place. "There. Now you're set."

Wendy was excited to have responsibility for an important item of equipment. Jake was glad it wasn't a weapon. No matter how resilient the girl had grown living on the streets, weapons were best left to older people, with maturity. Case in point was Andy. Jake looked at him taking practice swings with the ice axe in the corner. If he wasn't careful, he was likely to–

Cher-chunk.

"Oh," Andy said. "Sorry. I'm really, really sorry. It got away from me."

He tried to extract the point of the ice axe out of their office globe. It wasn't coming out. He put his foot against the side of the spheroid… and caved in the entirety of North America.

"Andy," Jake said.

"That broke very easily. Was it old?"

"Very. An antique. Ursula received it as a gift from the Worldwide Adventurers' Club."

Jake had made the name up. The globe was from a junk sale.

"They must have others," Andy said. "I'm sure if you said there's been an accident."

Andy peered into the hollow Earth. What was he expecting to discover, exactly? A civilization of dinosaurs and alien species? He had a gift for mixing naivete with nosiness.

"Just leave it, Andy. But you can be the one to inform Ursula when she gets back."

That put the fear into him. He backed away from the planet's destruction, hanging the axe through a loop on his pants. Wendy pretended to shoot a photo of him. Maude covered her laugh.

Jake had one more thing he wanted to discuss before they returned to the sewer tunnels.

"I happened to grab a copy of the newspaper from the museum lobby." He slapped the periodical on the desk. "Not only has the Black Cave been raided and the latest Lamprey victim been discovered, now the mayor is missing. Kidnapped. All hell is breaking loose in the city."

Wendy had no reaction as she fiddled with the camera. Maude raised an eyebrow.

Andy snatched the paper from the desk and began reading with his jaw dropping open.

"I can't believe Kane got nabbed," Andy said. "This is the biggest story in the city."

"Precisely," Jake said. "That's bad news for the mayor, but good news for us."

"How's that?" Maude asked. Now her interest was piqued.

"If the cops are busy looking for the mayor, then they won't be spending as much time investigating the sewer. We can slip in and do our job without worrying about the gun-toting men in blue showing up unexpectedly and mistaking us for a pack of whiskey smugglers."

"Unless…" Andy said.

"Unless what?" Jake said. He'd seen no downside to the distraction.

"Unless the kidnappers took the mayor into the sewers. And that's where he's stashed."

40
Up, Up

Charlie was numb. He couldn't feel his hands or his feet. He tried wiggling his toes. Nothing. His hands were like two frozen porkchops stuck to the ends of his arms. Even if they untied him now, he didn't think he could walk without falling. He hoped the lack of circulation wasn't killing him, piece by piece. He considered asking Bucket Man to loosen his bonds, but from the sound of the snores he was hearing, the guy was out cold, having a siesta. Archway wouldn't be happy if he found him. Part of Charlie was hoping the boss man would show up and catch his bodyguard shirking his duties. Hearing him take a good lashing would be a vicarious pleasure.

Bucket Man must've been reading his thoughts because he coughed and woke up. Then, for good measure, he came over and kicked Charlie in the shins.

The fool. Charlie hardly felt a thing.

"Your time's almost up, Mayor. The city's going to get a new fat cat in charge. One who's smart. Somebody who knows where his bread is buttered. It's too bad you won't see it."

The heavy door clunked open. Squeaky boots slamming down

on steely stairs. Archway was back. And from the sound of it, he'd brought more henchmen with him.

"It's time," Archway said. "Cut him loose. Get him up on his feet. Leave the blindfold."

The boys did as the boss told them.

Charlie wasn't brash enough to think he could fight off what he counted as four men.

As he expected, he had trouble standing. His legs tingled painfully, like a hundred bites.

"Stop playing!" Bucket Man shouted in his ear.

"He's not playing," Archway said. "You tied him too tight. He can't feel his legs."

Charlie felt himself teetering.

"Take his arms. Drag him if you have to. Follow me."

Rough hands took hold of his arms. The two newcomers pulled him forward. He tried to step along but couldn't keep up with them. They were walking in shallow water.

"Boss, you know which way it is? I don't like tunnels," Bucket Man said. He was in front with Archway. Their voices sounded hollow. We're in a tunnel of some kind, Charlie realized.

"Shut up and hold that light steady. You're making me dizzy," Archway said.

They walked in silence for a long time after that. Charlie felt them turn him seven times. He tried to memorize the directions in case he'd need to backtrack. But in his struggle to regain his footing, he lost track of the sequence of turns, how many rights and lefts. The good news was that he had feeling in his hands and feet. They felt swollen but no longer numbed.

"Stop. This is it." It was Archway talking. "Can you stand now, old man?" he asked Charlie.

"I think so."

"Let go of him a minute," Archway said.

As soon as they released Charlie, he was hit in the chest, and he went over backward into a slurry of filth. His blindfold slipped. The hoodlums were cackling, Bucket Man especially.

Archway was the one who'd pushed him down.

Charlie reached up and tore off his blindfold.

Bucket Man moved to strike him. But Archway blocked him with his hand.

"It doesn't matter now," he said.

"Are you going to kill me?" Charlie asked. "And then leave me in the sewer?"

He expected the answer to be a bullet. If the shot was to his head, he'd never hear it.

Bucket Man had his gun out. This is it, Charlie thought. He scooped up a handful of muck and flung it into Bucket Man's eyeholes. Then he kicked him, good and hard, in the knee.

The self-professed Lamprey went down whimpering like a baby. He raised his gat, pointed it at the mayor of Arkham. Archway twisted the weapon from his hand.

"You dunce," he said, kicking his other knee. To the other pair he said, "Up, up."

He pointed the gun barrel at Charlie as the men helped him to his feet.

"Another move like that and I will plug you personally," Archway said.

Then the bossman checked his pocket watch. Charlie took in his surroundings: there was no doubt they were somewhere in the sewer system. Directly behind Archway was a corroded ladder leading to the surface. Archway held a safety lamp. There was another one underwater between Bucket Man's splayed legs. He was coated in vile slime.

As am I, Charlie saw as he examined himself.

"What's next?" Charlie said.

"You climb up the ladder," Archway said. Charlie could see it, but he heard the sneer.

"What's up there?"

"Go and find out."

Charlie hesitated.

"Get going! Or I'll plug you. Up, up."

Charlie staggered forward. Archway stepped aside to let him pass. Charlie took hold of the rungs. They were cold, rough. He lifted his foot onto the lowest bar, staring up into darkness.

"There's no way out."

"Yes, there is," Archway said. "When you get to the top, push."

Charlie climbed. He couldn't hear any noises. He didn't see any light. As he reached the top rung, he used one hand to feel above him. Flat. He pushed. Heavy. A manhole cover.

"Brace your legs and use two hands to push. Then climb out. I'm counting to three, then I'm firing this gat. If you're still here, you won't like the feeling." Archway poked the gun into his backside. "Now get going. Move. Or else." More hard pokes.

Charlie gritted his teeth and pushed the manhole cover with both hands. It was stuck.

"One."

He pushed harder.

"Two."

Charlie grunted as he used all his strength to shove the manhole cover aside. As the lid tipped over, he felt fresh air on his cheeks... and four hands boosting him hard from below.

They propelled him out of the opening.

He was on the street. On his hands and knees. It was dark but he detected streetlamps.

Greenery.

"Over there! There!"

"It's the mayor! It's Mayor Kane! He's alive!"

A crowd was racing toward him. Charlie was confused. He turned his head and saw the familiar steps of City Hall. He looked back at the green under the lamps of Independence Square.

Then the flashes started going off, as the press photographers snapped their photos.

He sat back on his wet haunches, relieved to be alive as slime squished out of his shoes.

They snapped and snapped.

41
The Deeper

"Third time's the charm," Andy said as he reentered the pipe at the River Docks. What he was thinking but didn't say was: Is it a good charm or bad charm? Because it felt like the deeper they followed this story, the less they knew for certain. He wanted more than blind luck on his side.

They walked in – Andy, Wendy, Maude – and Jake guarded their backs. He'd given up the crutches, which he said were too cumbersome in the pipes, trading them in for a walking stick he'd modified himself. It telescoped down. He could use it either as a cane or a crutch, whatever the situation called for. "I was hoping to try this out in therapy. But nothing beats the real world." The ropes swayed between the members of the team. "Our futures are tied together," he said, coaching them into feeling positive and not utterly terrified of whatever waited below.

"We should share what we fear most," Jake continued. "Get it out in the open so we can support each other better. I'll go first. I'm afraid that I'll slow you all down. I haven't mastered my new leg, and this terrain is among the most challenging I've faced. There, I said it."

"I don't like the squeezed feeling I get in the pipes. It makes it difficult to breathe," Wendy said. Adding quickly, "And the dark. I hate the dark. The dark plus the narrowness…" She shivered.

"Andy?" Jake queried. "What about you?"

"I don't want us to fail," Andy said.

"None of us want that," Jake said. "What are your individual fears?"

"I don't know. That I won't get my job back. That I'll die an unknown."

"Fame isn't all it's cracked up to be," Maude said.

"I'm willing to see and find out."

Andy stuck to his routine, taking only "right" turns. They were making good progress.

Maude said, "I'm afraid that I'll lose my sense of reality completely, once and for all. Then my mind, soul, spirit, or what have you, will drift endlessly. I'll lose who I am, my self."

Goodness! Andy thought. That was an awful fear to have. He hadn't considered anything so… philosophical. Besides, he didn't care about his self if his self couldn't be a reporter. If no one paid attention to anything he wrote, he'd simply disappear. Like dust, he'd be swept away.

"We're not too far. There's my letter 'A,'" he said, pointing to the marked brick.

"Is it just me, or does this feel too easy?" Maude asked.

"We're getting used to it. That's all. Every climb's new, but our confidence grows."

Jake sloshed at the back of their line. His new walking stick appeared to help him move with a higher degree of flexibility. Three points stabilized him in the tube. His free hand swung out for added balance. So far, he wasn't slowing anyone down. His fears seemed unfounded.

Andy turned back around to face front again. If Wendy takes a photo of the Fang before we blow it up, then that'll be the last photo ever taken. I can use that. Readers will pay to see it.

"Almost there," Andy said.

The hours passed. None of them could say how long, because no one had brought a watch. They kept taking righthand turns. They weren't circling. The sewers weren't laid out in circles. Every length of tunnel they passed through appeared to be new territory. Yet it was all identical to the sections they had trudged through previously. Andy began marking the walls with the ice axe. Scratching Roman numerals at intervals of every hundred, then fifty, then twenty-five paces. They never passed one of their own marks, never saw a ladder up to an access point in the street.

In retrospect, it was peculiar how no one spoke. They seemed to have fallen into a trance.

It was Wendy who stopped them.

"My amulet," she said.

Maude had nearly walked into her. Andy felt the tug at the rope around his waist but, at first, he only pulled harder to go forward, as if he were dragging a weight through the water, instead of his teammates and friends.

"Andy, stop," Jake called out.

"Why should I do that?" he wondered out loud.

He turned around slowly. The other people were blurs. The brick walls grew fuzzy, indistinct. I need to walk, he thought. He didn't say that but just started to untie himself, to get free.

Jake fired his pistol behind them into the long empty tunnel. The blast shook Andy from his reverie. He was blinking, and deaf.

As the ringing in his ears quieted, he heard Maude talking to him. "Get a grip on yourself," she said.

Andy rubbed his face. It felt rubbery, thick. Wendy reached up and pinched his cheek.

"Hey! Ow!"

"My amulet is vibrating," she said. "Something's wrong. We've been walking too long."

"We're almost there," Andy said. Hadn't he just told them that?

"Which way should we go, Wendy?" Maude asked. "Use the amulet to guide us."

It didn't work right the last time we got close to the Fang, Andy thought. Why should it work now? Andy shined his lantern around the sewer tunnel. They all looked awful, as if they'd been sick for a long time and hadn't seen the sun. How long have we been doing this? Exploring?

"I think we turn right, just up ahead," Wendy said.

Andy moved his light. It was a solid wall of bricks as far as the eye could see.

"It's the same. There is no turn," he said.

But Wendy had crammed past him, feeling along the wall, searching for an opening.

Then she was gone.

"Wendy!"

Andy rushed forward. The rope that connected them – it passed into the wall. Maude and Jake bunched up behind him.

"How is that possible?" Andy asked.

With a grim look of determination, Maude walked straight into the wall...

And she went through.

Andy stuck his hand out. It disappeared at the wrist. He caught his breath. There was no pain. It was as if he'd put his hand into water. Jake linked arms with him. They both took a step.

Into another tunnel! Wendy was right. There was a turn.

Wendy and Maude were standing there, inside the new passageway. Bathed in pink light. Making sure they weren't tangled in their ropes, the group proceeded together.

A short distance ahead the pink lights were noticeably brighter. They danced on the walls. Andy didn't know what faerie lights were, but he imagined them to be like what he was observing – a bright radiance that lured him onward despite his instinct for self-preservation.

Andy knew what he'd seen walking around in those colored lights the last time.

He'd seen killers, witches, and a monster.

Yet still they inched closer, unable to look away or resist. Andy saw Wendy's necklace pulled taut around her neck, the pendant floating in midair, as if an invisible hand gripped it.

At the threshold, they stopped.

Witches.

A circle of witches wearing long cloaks ringed the crystal formation. It pulsed like a heartbeat. Andy felt his chest. It was the same rhythm. He'd synced up to the rock. The witches were making noise, humming in unison, arms outspread. Don't they see us? Andy thought.

As soon as he thought it, one of the witches looked at him. He saw her face. It was a woman he didn't know with round spectacles. Her mouth dropped open in shock.

"Look!" she said. "Intruders."

The other twelve witches turned simultaneously to stare at them. The humming ceased.

The tallest witch stepped from around the Crystal Fang and pulled back her hood.

"Who are you?" she said.

Maude shed her ropes and entered the pinkened chamber. "I know you," she said.

The tall witch looked deeply into her. Then she nodded. "The woman from the sanatorium."

"Why did you help me?" Maude asked.

"Because you needed us," the witch said. "You asked for our assistance."

"I did."

"Why do you come here? This is a dangerous place. You don't belong," the witch said.

"We came to destroy that crystal," Andy said. "Now get out of my way."

"Stop right there," the witch said. "Approach no farther. I am warning you."

Andy stepped free from the coils of his ropes. He had the ice axe in his hand, raised over his head. He gritted his teeth and ran at the crystal.

The witch lifted her long fingers.

The burning…

It began inside of him. As if she'd filled his stomach with a shovelful of fiery embers.

"I'm dying," he said, gasping. He sank to his knees, clutching his stomach. "Dying…"

42
Betrayer's Name

"Don't be silly. You aren't dying. I've only prevented you from doing a very foolish thing. Did you suppose that I would allow you to attack me, or to damage the Crystal Fang?" Hyacinth said to the young man who was touching his chest as if he expected to find a hint of fire there.

He picked himself up.

"You're evil," the young man said to her. "All of you. Pure evil. We're here to stop you." His language was strong, but it lacked the confidence he'd shown before she immobilized him.

"If you're here to stop us, then you don't understand what evil is," Hyacinth said.

"Oh, I don't, don't I?"

What the youth lacked in knowledge he made up for with gusto. He didn't pose any real danger to the Prism, Hyacinth surmised. She wasn't too certain about his friends, although curiously one was a child. What was a child doing wandering in the disease-ridden waters of this waste hole? Were they crazy bringing her here? Even if they didn't have a clue what the Fang meant, this was a hazardous environment, full of risks for a small one. Hyacinth said, "My fellow members of the Prism, spread out. Make room for the newcomers to approach."

"Not so fast," the youth said.

"What is your name?" Hyacinth asked as the witches moved away from the crystal.

"I'm Andy Van Nortwick. Former reporter for the *Advertiser*. I work independently."

"I'll bet you do," she said.

"It's temporary," he said.

"Of course. Most things are."

"We're not falling for your witchy tricks. You're the one that made us get lost for hours in the pipes, aren't you?" He thrust his chin up, begging her to argue, or to lie. She did neither.

"You weren't lost for hours. It was a time illusion as well as a spatial one. Yes, I cast that spell. But not for you. I did it to keep the police away from our activities." Hyacinth kept her attention on the other male. He had a gun. She didn't like the way he was studying the room while appearing not to. He was planning an escape route. But was he going to try anything unwise before he needed to escape? The witches continued to fan out; the armed man tensed.

The woman from the sanatorium was her best ally here, so she directed her next words to her.

"The Prism is not in the business of hurting people. We helped you, did we not? We have always helped people. It's what we are designed and trained to do. For centuries we've intervened behind the scenes to keep good people safe. This chapter of the Prism has had its fair share of work. We are the guardians of Arkham, Salem, Kingsport, and Providence, mainly. I am the leader. My name is Hyacinth Burroughs. Please tell me your names so we may be civilized."

"I'm Maude Brion. He's Jake Williams. The girl is Wendy Adams," Maude said. "You know Andy." Maude stepped beside the coven leader, waving Jake and Wendy to come nearer.

Jake went to them.

Wendy hesitated. "My amulet," she said, lingering toward the back of the chamber.

"Such protective objects have a tendency to malfunction in proximity to the Fang," Hyacinth said. She understood the child's reluctance. "Remain where you are if you wish." She sensed strong survival skills in the girl, as well as a protective shield. And something else, harder to identify…

"Who is Syrx-Crugoth?" Andy wanted to know. He hadn't lost any steam or skepticism.

Hyacinth was astounded to hear him utter the Cruelest One's name. It was unsafe to do so this close to the Fang. Hyacinth had to be careful what she said next. They'd been interrupted in the middle of the most important ritual ceremony in the history of the Prism. Vulnerabilities lay exposed, like a bare throat under a wolf's slavering jaws. One wrong move and they'd be awash in blood and guts. Don't want to start a feeding frenzy. Not now. Control wasn't guaranteed.

"That god you named is a chaotic god who would like nothing better than to tip over Arkham and stomp out all the human ants speeding about. The Prism imprisoned… S-C along with my ancestor Dionysia in 1693." Hyacinth turned to the crystal and gestured. "Inside the Fang. Dionysia lured him. Unfortunately, she did not slip away before the crystal was sealed. Attempts were made to free her without releasing S-C. Some were as crude as a hammer and chisel. When even the most sophisticated method failed, it was decided to leave them there, interlinked, sentenced to an eternity of torment. Only recently have we been forced to revisit the problem."

"Why?" Jake asked.

She looked back toward him. "Because Dionysia deteriorated over these last two hundred years. Her psyche is being worked upon by the Evil One who embraces her. He is feeding off her considerable powers. And he is feeding elsewhere, beyond the confines of the crystal. His powers are extending. We can no longer contain him. If the Fang is disturbed, he will escape. If the Fang is undisturbed, he may still escape. We have been at work, night and day, searching for a solution. To save Arkham."

"Tell them about our most recent attempt," said her raven-haired sister witch.

Hyacinth had hoped to avoid this. Inside her, Dionysia was boiling with rage. To speak the truth about her might drive her deeper into the recesses of Hyacinth's soulscape, or it might bring her forth. Hyacinth could not keep this up alone. She needed the coven to know the truth.

"We tried to free Dionysia with a new ritual. I stumbled in my recitation of the sacred texts, and a bolt of pure energy emanating from the Crystal Fang struck me. What I have not confessed to my fellow witches is that the ritual was in many ways a success. Dionysia lives within me now." Hyacinth stumbled backward as she uttered these true words.

She touched the crystal.

The coven members gasped, and several of them gathered around their stricken leader. Jake and Maude even got closer to her. Andy was already standing within a few steps.

"Stay back! I am tainted with her now, and she's not the woman whom we admired. No. The foul stench of the Cruelest One has corrupted her brave, beautiful spirit. She rots me. She torments and shreds my soul to ribbons, filling my ears with trickles of poison. If I did not know better, I would swear she was S-C himself." Hyacinth produced a stout ceremonial blade from under her cloak. "Come any closer, I will bleed myself out of this miserable state."

"Leader," said the spectacled witch. "Let us help you."

"If you get blood on the crystal, the color will turn red. I've seen it," Andy said to them.

"What? When?"

"The other night. One of you was pouring blood from a sacrificial victim on the Fang. This whole chamber was swirling with reds. I saw you all here, but your bodies were clear."

"We send our spiritual bodies to guard the crystal," Hyacinth said. "If you saw them, they were trying to stop the blood abomination from taking place. We've had nothing to do with those heinous murders. We suspect the killings are responsible for S-C's rising strength. Someone has been feeding him. Nurturing him. Aiding his cause across dimensions to annihilate this world."

Hyacinth leaned her back against the crystal. She sheathed her blade. The crystal pulled at her spine as if it were sucking at the nubs of her backbone through her robe.

It's draining me, she thought. The two of them inside, Syrx-Crugoth and Dionysia.

How can I withstand their attack? Who am I but one person? They are two.

The spectacled witch spoke to Andy. "You say you saw one of

us pouring blood on the crystal. Which one? Point to the witch. We will deal with our own as only we can."

Andy looked into their faces. "I can't tell. Though it was a man, not a woman. He talks to Wendy. He calls himself the Lamprey. He's the killer and the one you're looking for."

"A man?" Hyacinth said. "We have only two men in our number now. One stands right here in front of me. He is the oldest member of our coven, and I do not doubt his good faith."

The man lowered his hood. He was bald, owlish, and his eyes were filled with tears.

"Who's the other?" Maude asked.

"Wendy can help you find him," Andy said. "Wendy, show them the Lamprey."

When they looked for Wendy, she was nowhere to be found. Her ropes were in a pile at the tunnel entrance where they had come in. In all the confusion, she had slipped off somewhere.

Hyacinth knew now. She knew the betrayer's name. It was never her fault. He'd written the ritual with the intention of making her stumble. He'd been the one the whole time.

"He is our secretary. I'm afraid he has taken the child," she said.

Andy was calling for the girl. But their secretary knew these tunnels the best of all. He knew the crystal too. It seemed clear to Hyacinth now. Her mind opened and filled with light.

"It's Clyde. He's stolen the girl," she said. "Clyde Laurents."

43
God Fever

Clyde had Wendy firmly by the wrist, dragging her down the tunnel. He wasn't sure how long it would take them to realize he'd run off with the girl, clamping one hand over her mouth as he pulled her away from the chamber. He knew the sewers best of all, and he was used to hiding.

"If you scream, I will leave you here. Alone in the dark with the rats. I can call them. Would you like that? To see the rats scurrying for a scrumptious little meal?"

He took his hand away.

"No," she said.

"Very well." Clyde had no way of summoning rats. But the girl didn't know that.

He did have a knife.

"It is nice to meet you without disguises, Wendy. I wish the circumstances were better."

He hustled the girl along, climbing up into a narrow tube, much smaller than the main tunnels. He barely fit. I'm getting fat in my old age, he thought. I was slim as a weasel when I was learning my craft up at Porcupine Lake. Dabbling in magic for the first time. Calling out to forest gods. To ancient alien beings that lived under the hard rock, the icy glacial lakes. Blind spectral creatures that dwelled in darkness but saw so much more of the universe than humans ever had. He'd seen glimpses of them in the goldmines when he was taking samples. He told no one. They would have called his sanity into question. Cabin fever, they would've said.

If he had any fever, it was god fever. He was burning up with occultist yearning, an unquenchable thirst for forbidden knowledge. He'd begged these creatures to teach him as he knelt in the mines. *We're hungry*, they said. *Feed us.* "What do you eat?" he asked. They told him. "I can get those for you. If I do, will you share your wisdom with me?" *We will.*

After that his fellow miners started disappearing. Clyde was better at this new work than he expected. He learned so much! Perhaps he went overboard in his insatiable appetite for enlightenment. In any case, it ended poorly. He'd had to set the wilderness on fire to avoid being arrested. They'd discovered him feeding the creatures, leaving them a cartload of fresh offerings in the goldmine.

Wendy whimpered.

"What's wrong with you?" he asked. "Why are you breathing like that?"

"I don't like the tiny spaces," she said. "Or the darkness."

Clyde turned up the flame on the safety lamp he always carried under his cloak.

"Is that better?" he asked.

She nodded.

"It's not much farther in this snug conduit. It connects two tunnels. The other, where we're heading, is much wider. To be honest, I don't like the tightness much either. But I've learned to get used to it. I've spent years underground. Half my life, if I added it up. We'll stop for a moment until you catch your breath. Don't get any ideas." He showed her the blade, then put it back. It was no use adding stress to the girl. He could see she was having a tough time of it.

"You're the Lamprey?" she said. But it wasn't really a question, more a confirmation.

Clyde bowed his head in the small, bricked cylinder. "I was worried you'd point me out back there. Before we could get away. But Syrx-Crugoth protected me."

He flicked his fingernail at the pendant. "This is your protection, isn't it? I sense its power. Too weak a match for my god in any case." He hit the amulet again, harder this time.

"Stop that," she said.

"Those things don't work right around the Fang. It's similar to how magnetic deposits interfere with compasses. Do you like science?" Clyde knew she was clever. In his experience, clever people were drawn to science, like moths to a flame.

"I guess I like science," Wendy said.

Clyde nodded. "Well, science isn't everything. What's beyond science is where things get really intriguing. Out on the fringes ..." He wiggled his fingers.

"Why are you doing all this?" the girl asked.

What intrepidity she had!

"Why? I'll tell you why. Because you and your friends ruined a perfectly good plan that took me years to execute. It was finally happening! Then you got in the way."

"In the way? How?" She was curious, which Clyde couldn't fault her for. He'd been curious his whole life.

"Those witches back there aren't what they seem. Oh no. They say they guard this city. Tell me, Wendy, do you feel guarded? Living on the streets. Are they looking out for you? No! You're looking out for yourself. Picking pockets, lifting purses. I'm not judging you. They are, or they would. I admire you. You're a private operator, like me. We go it alone."

"I have James. I have my friends. And my parents would help me if they–"

Clyde felt his anger rising volcanically.

"Friends? Fiends is more like it. James is a burden to you. I watched you through our psychic connection. I wasn't always talking when I was inside your head. Sometimes, I kept my mouth shut and just surveyed your activities. A little bit of spying. No one got hurt. And I saw that you do almost everything on your own." He could see the child looking at him now, horrified. "Anyway, those witches. My coven. They imprisoned the greatest teacher I have ever met. Would you imprison a teacher, Wendy?" He didn't give her a chance to answer. "Syrx-Crugoth knows so much, yet Hyacinth's ancestor tricked him into a cage. She was so clumsy, she locked herself in too. But the prison is crumbling, child. I've been chipping away at the walls on my side. Syrx-Crugoth digs on his side. And when we meet..." Clyde clapped his hand. The child startled.

She began to take deep, raggedy breaths again. Her skin was sweaty and pale.

"There, there. Calm yourself," he told her. "You're getting worked up for no reason. You can't stop any of it. It's foreordained. That's a complicated concept. Let's say, it's unstoppable."

The girl's color was returning. So, apparently, was her inquisitiveness.

"Why do you kill people?" she asked.

She would make an excellent student if it weren't for the fact that he had to…

"They aren't going to just hand over their blood now, are they?" Clyde said.

"No, I guess not."

"Well, now you see my dilemma. Blood is vital in my mission to release Syrx-Crugoth. I am a devotee to the god. I serve *voluntarily*. He isn't forcing me. I act on his behalf of my own free will. I am one blood donation away from breaking the god free. Hyacinth was going to be my final donor. You see, I convinced her that Dionysia, her ancestor, is possessing her. She's not. It's Syrx-Crugoth. He's donned a Dionysia mask. Anyway, Hyacinth was about to offer herself to the Crystal Fang. She was going to spill her own blood on it during the ritual I painstakingly wrote for her. And then you had to… What was that? Did you hear something?"

Clyde seized her wrist again and yanked, towing her through the murky muck.

When he reached the larger tunnel, he crawled out before he helped her down.

He shined his lamp. This was an ancient drain, carved by a blind river through the limestone over millions of years, with no one knowing, no human involvement. The greatest planetary achievement didn't have anything to do with humans. People were a blight, a scourge living on a rock, a sprinkling of insignificant lifeforms scuttling about, thinking they were gods.

The fools.

He was going to take pleasure in their eradication.

Without humans, the earth would be unhindered, the potential was limitless.

Syrx-Crugoth had told him so.

He knew he wouldn't live to see it. Syrx-Crugoth made that plain too. But he would behold the chaotic last moments, the upheaval and panic, the smoking crater, so to speak.

That was sufficient.

44
Soft Sticks

Wendy paused at the lip of the narrow tunnel. It was the worst pipe she'd been in. And to feel herself stuffed into a nasty burrow with the Lamprey... The two of them had been slopping along in debris of soft sticks and moldering black leaves, the stink of decay like a rotting log...

She knew what she had to do. What she had to *try* to do to get away from him, because sooner or later he was going to be bad. He looked harmless. A red-faced portly man with funny whiskers and a sheen of oily sweat; his smell reminded her of goats. Wendy knew what the Lamprey did to people eventually.

He'd said so himself.

They aren't going to just hand over their blood now, are they?

Wendy bit her lip and sat in the watery trickle leaking out of the stick-filled drainpipe.

The Lamprey put his hands on her waist to help her down.

"Wait," she said.

"Why? What's wrong?" he sounded impatient and verging on angry.

"My pants are snagged on a branch. I don't want them to tear."

The Lamprey sighed.

"Can't you unsnag them?"

Wendy twisted and put her hands behind her back as if she were trying to loosen herself.

"I can't see it. Will you lift your lamp, please?"

The Lamprey squinted at her, and for a moment she wondered if he suspected her of trickery, but then he lifted the safety lamp and shined it into her tunnel.

With all her strength Wendy kicked the lantern. The light went spinning off to the side.

For good measure she kicked out again. One foot swished through the air, but the other connected with the side of the Lamprey's turned face. She felt her boot mash into his jaw, and she heard his teeth clack together as he fell heavily backward into the bigger tunnel.

It was pure darkness now.

She hadn't heard his lamp shatter, but it was out.

The tunnel ahead and the tunnel behind were nothing but black. A ghostly flickering in the darkness was only her eyes adjusting to the sudden blackout.

"I must go now," she told herself. "Go, Wendy!"

On her hands and knees, she began to crawl. The remains of plants and leaves washed underground in storms squished between her fingers. It felt like a carpet of bug carcasses and living things wiggling in the silty ooze, worming through her fingers over the backs of her hands.

I can't keep going, she thought with a horrible realization. I can't do it.

Can't.

It was so dark.

She arched her back and whacked the top of her head into the bricks above. She felt a lump rising on the crown of her head, in her hair, which was dripping with muddy, rank slime.

I'm stuck here. The air will run out and I will suffocate.

I'll choke, she thought.

When she breathed, it was like sipping at a straw. Cool little nips of air, but not enough, never enough to fill her up and make her relax enough to crawl, crawl, crawl. He'd taken her so far – how would she ever make it back to the witches, the crystal, and her friends back in the pink rays of light? Maybe she'd knocked the Lamprey back and he'd hit his head really hard on the bricks. Maybe he wouldn't wake up and find his lamp and relight it. Maybe…

Behind her, the Lamprey groaned.

Then he howled her name.

"Wennndyyyyyy!"

She started moving. Hand over hand, she scrambled onward. Scraping her knees, digging her raw fingertips into the flow of lush litter. Not thinking. Just going. Move, keep moving.

Getting away from him no matter what lay ahead.

Into the pipe, as dark as dark gets, Wendy crawled.

45
Black Arts

Andy wasn't ready to accept these so-called witches at their word. But he simply had no choice but to suspend his questioning of their leader until they rescued Wendy. Wasn't this Clyde Laurents one of them? How could they have let Wendy be taken by the monster who had been stalking her for days? He was angry enough to spit.

The witches suggested that they split up to look for Wendy. They knew the tunnels well. Andy was reluctant to divide himself from his teammates and go off into some dark hole with a practitioner of the black arts, and he said as much to the spectacled witch who was now his new colleague, an ally of circumstance as far as he was concerned.

"But we don't perform black arts," she said, sounding defensive. "Not all of us. I can't speak for Clyde. He always was a bit of a cold fish, telling odd stories about his time in the goldmines in Canada and elsewhere. He was more at home with rocks and minerals than with people. Not that there's anything inherently wrong with that," she said. "Kindred feeling with the earth is a blessing. A lifelong friendship."

She had joined hands with Andy. Her grip was warm. With his other hand, he managed to keep the beam of his lantern shining ahead.

"My name is Andrea. Andrea and Andy," she said.

"What does that mean?"

Andrea shrugged. "Nothing. They sound alike."

She had a familiarity with the intricate pipes and led him into a juncture that presented an array of more tunnel mouths from which to choose. From a central point, one might proceed in different directions; the choices angled out before them. The compartment in which they stood was half the size of the chamber with the crystal in it, although it was but built along the same plan, a half-hub in a semicircle. Andrea and Andy stopped.

"Which way, I wonder," she said.

"If you don't practice black arts, then what were you doing back there? It looked like sorcery to me. I met an occultist who tried to feed me to a spider. Would you do that?"

Andrea laughed. "Never. Look, it's pretty simple. Evil people use magic for evil. Good people use it for good. Sorcerers. Occultists. Witches. You can't put us all in the same basket."

From a pipe to their left, situated higher up on the wall, came the bellowing roar of a man in anguish. Or hot fury.

"Is that Clyde? That's him, isn't it?" Andy asked. He rushed to the drainpipe. There were smooth steps carved into the wall underneath it. He mounted the steps and inserted his lantern, peering in. The tunnel was choked with detritus, a mat of vegetation in various stages of decomposition. He shined his light on the floor at the foot of the steps. A pile of the same debris lay there, as if it had recently been kicked out. He looked in again. It was difficult to tell, but...

"I see footprints," Andrea said over his shoulder. She clambered past him.

"What are you doing?" he demanded.

"I'll go in a bit and see what I can see. Sounds are tricky down here. They might still be in another pipe, only we're hearing the sound bouncing around this opening."

Andy passed her the lantern, knowing that if she took it and left him, he'd be alone in the dark. That prospect sent a freezing chill into him, but he saw no better alternative.

"Here. See if you can find Wendy," he said. "I'll wait here in case they come out from one of those other tunnels."

"You're sure?" Andrea said.

"Yes?" Andy said with a shrug.

Before he could change his mind, Andrea snatched the lantern and wriggled into the pipe to the accompaniment of slithery, squelching noises. Andy watched her until the glow was no more than a dot. Then he squatted down, being careful not to tumble in the darkness, and he leaned back into the wall. The bricks behind him shifted; a few wobbled and spilled away – a miniature landslide. Andy found himself sitting in a narrow niche, uninjured, the seat of his pants in dampness. Sheltered from three sides, he felt a bit less vulnerable, yet his thoughts soon wandered to what categories of vermin might've been living behind those loose bricks. Still, he didn't dare leave now. Instead, he sat and waited.

Soon there came a heavy thud from somewhere in the dark, inside the half-hub. He froze.

Whatever had dropped was now walking around. He peered in the blackness and watched as a dim light ballooned into the warm glow of a lantern, and someone much bigger than Wendy hurried past, hunched and whispering to themself, as they slogged into another of the channels.

It might've been a searcher looking for Wendy, Andy thought. He hoisted himself up and crept down the steps slowly to investigate, trying to be as quiet as possible. He moved by feel in the total darkness, sticking his arms out to guide himself.

Oh, how he wished he had a light of his own.

It must've been one of the witches, or even Maude or Jake, he told himself. The electric tingle in his spine suggested otherwise. Had the Lamprey doubled back? If Andy dared to stick his head into the channel where the cloaked whisperer had vanished, would the Lamprey lunge out and throttle him?

Andy was working up the courage to explore further when the space around him brightened from black to a muted general gloom. He saw curved bricked walls, and limestone too, tendrils of roots hanging down; slabs striped with water marks shaded grayer the higher they climbed. Looking into the depths of shadows disoriented him, making him feel dizzy and unbalanced. His boots crunched gravel under the gray water as he restabilized his footing.

"Andy?"

The emerging light was throwing wild, swinging shadows inside the half-hub room.

He turned to see Andrea's head and shoulders popping out of the smallest drainpipe.

She was smiling. "Look who found me," she said.

Wendy poked her face into view. Her smile beamed, stronger than any lantern ever could.

Andy, Wendy, and Andrea called out to the others. They regrouped at the half-hub. Andy wasn't worried about attracting the Lamprey – he was on the run. Wendy told them Clyde's plan – the parts he shared with her after he took her away. Hyacinth staggered visibly at hearing the news.

"I have been blaming Dionysia when it was S-C all along. Clyde has been playing me for a dupe, conning me into acting out his nefarious designs. A puppet. A pawn. That's what I have become instead of a leader to my coven. My lack of insight jeopardizes this city, and beyond."

"You take too much of the blame," the raven-haired witch said. "He fooled us all."

"There is good news," Andy said. He'd roped himself to Wendy again, and she had tight hold of his sleeve. Jake and Maude were connected to each other as well.

"Share it, Andy," Jake said.

"We foiled his plans. Without a victim to drain, he can't release Syrx-Crugoth. We've got him on the run. He's probably popped up on the streets and heading out of town as we speak."

Andy hooked his thumbs in his suspenders. He had his story now. He knew the identity of the Lamprey. He wasn't sure how the Prism felt about publicity, but the Fang mystery was solved too. Heck, even if he left them in the background, he had a hair-raising tale no editor could possibly refuse. The cops would track down Clyde Laurents once word got out.

Where would he hide? Without his anonymity he was just another delusional creeper. His picture would be hanging in every police station and post office from Maine to Mississippi.

The murders. The city's nightmare. Wendy's disguised stalker. It was over.

46
Final Donation

A dejected Clyde swore under his breath when he came upon the man standing in the pipe with the steel pick in his hands. The man looked the way Clyde expected the dead might after they'd risen from their graves, something he'd see if he ever broke Syrx-Crugoth out of witch-jail. This stranger was a ghastly pale thing, stubbly on the chin, sporting a mop of shocking hair, and a pound or so of caked-on grit.

"Hello there?" Clyde said.

Despite his undernourished look and vacant stare, the man was too large to ignore. As was the steel pick in his oversized hands.

The man offered no reply or any acknowledgment that he noticed Clyde standing not ten yards from him down a dark and lonely section of muddy city drainpipe. He was gaunt, his chapped lips peeled. Dark rings wreathed his bloodshot eyes. And yet... he seemed familiar.

Clyde stepped closer, concealing his short, sharpened blade behind his back. He held his cracked safety lamp out in front of him, wondering if he could blind the man with his lamp in order to grab hold of that nasty steel pick.

What had happened to this unlucky fellow? He reminded Clyde of the Canadian miners after he stunned them but before they collapsed, not understanding that they were already well on their way to dying. Clyde often snuck up on them, sliding a shiv into a kidney or up inside the ribs with a wiggle-waggle. Ashen skin, cloudy eyes.

The man was so still that Clyde considered the possibility that the fellow had somehow died on his feet and remained standing, statue-like, a monument to diggers who had perished in the sewers.

Was he a ghost? A spectral visitor who'd come to punish Clyde for his crimes?

Clyde crept closer. Rocking his light back and forth to distract the man. Then, in a fit of impulsivity, he revealed his blade hand. Flicking the metallic weapon before the man's nose. *Swish-swish.*

Nothing.

"Well, well, aren't you a human oddity?" Clyde said, relaxing.

"I am a gift," the man said.

Clyde leaped backward as if he'd been stung, brandishing his knife. He wasn't a fighter. He wanted no part in a brawl even if his opponent appeared catatonic and half-starved.

"What did you say?"

"I am a gift. Syrx-Crugoth sends me with his regards."

Clyde remembered the man now. He was the bulky digger who'd knocked down the wall and broken into the Fang's chamber. He'd watched the man from the shadows, after Clyde had choked the shift boss, dragging his unconscious body into a vacant pipe for later exsanguination.

Clyde thought about what the man had just said.

"I'm sorry," Clyde said. "Would you please repeat that?"

Instead of repeating himself, the man dropped the steel pick in the water. He shuffled up to Clyde and tipped his head all the way back, offering his bristly blond, whiskery throat to him.

"Delightful," Clyde said.

He had no proper jar, but he did have a canteen on his belt. Murder was thirsty work.

It would have to suffice. He unscrewed the cap and drank, then poured out the excess.

"Hold steady for me," he said as he swept in. The man never moved, not even to blink.

Clyde collected his final donation.

47
Turbulent Red

The chamber turned a crimson red and the ground shook. Maude was walking with Hyacinth at the front of the line of witches and explorers when she noticed the water changing colors, going from gray to scarlet. She crouched, dipping her fingers, then did the unthinkable. She tasted it.

"Blood," she said.

"This is an earthquake," Jake said. "We'd better get ourselves above ground, and fast."

"No," Hyacinth said. She strode forward into the chamber which contained the Fang. Maude went with her.

Clyde was tapping out the last drops of a canteen onto the crystal and chanting in a low, sonorous voice. He swayed and grabbed the formation as the ground jolted more violently.

"What's wrong with his eyes?" Wendy asked, standing next to Andy. To see Clyde again after she'd escaped from him must've been a huge shock, but she didn't run. She crossed the chamber and picked up the Speed Graphic camera from where she'd dropped it when Clyde had abducted her. She looped the strap over her head.

Clyde lifted his grinning face to them in triumph. His eyes were indistinguishable from the crystal. They protruded in angular points, clear, without irises or pupils, like cubes of bloodshot ice embedded in his eye sockets. Still, he saw them – if not with his visual organs, then in his mind.

"I've done it. It is complete. Syrx-Crugoth rises, unleashed. Chaos is a tyrant god."

The Crystal Fang cracked, then split into two halves. From between the pieces, a cloud the color of liver billowed up, quickly filling the chamber. Bricks fell from the tunnel walls. The wastewater turned deep red, sloshing as if it were a stormy sea, an unstaunched wound, gushing forth from the ceiling. The stained waters were rising, flooding the chamber. They gurgled and bubbled as gallons more spewed forth from the base of the crystal. Andrea dashed through the vermilion fog enveloping the chamber toward Wendy.

Maude had tasted this salty mist in her dream, and she realized now that the dream had not been a memory or a door to another dimension – it was a window to the future, a prophetic vision of Arkham drowning in blood. Maude knew what would happen next: the dead would rise; the living would suffer horrors incomprehensible; to herald Syrx-Crugoth's arrival, Clyde would change into a monstrous form. Through the thickening mist, she saw it happening already. Clyde thrashing on the floor, gouging the crystals from his eyes, ripping off his clothes, transforming into a grotesque combination of eel and man.

Maude put her hands on Wendy and Andy. They startled, breaking their entrancement. She jerked her chin toward Andrea, who was approaching. "Go with her. Get out. There's nothing for you here. Protect each other. Go. GO!"

The witch nodded to Maude. No words were necessary. Time was not a luxury they could afford. Maude thought of Clyde, how he must pay for what he had done to them, to the world. She'd seen enough of men mad with ego and power setting fire to the world – be it an Amazonian rainforest or a New England town, undone by flames or a conflagration of blood. Was there no limit to their arrogance? She wanted to end him. To have him know she was the one who did it. She lunged. And the rope encircling her waist jerked her back. To Jake.

"Slack. Give me slack. Cut it if you have to," she yelled furiously.

Jake threw off his coils, and with the loosening around her middle, she stepped free.

The vapors in the room did not choke her as she advanced toward Clyde. It was worse than that. They slid easily down her throat into her lungs. The poison of Syrx-Crugoth. It was inside her. Inside everyone now.

Clyde the Lamprey wallowed in the blood, coughing and sputtering. His teeth were not human teeth anymore. Maude grabbed his arm, and the arm was not attached to anything. She cast the dismembered limb away. She watched as his human legs retracted into a writhing snakelike body. Smooth features replaced his former face. Gill holes opened. He was an aberration born of his own fantastical ravings, a creature never meant to exist, an insult to nature.

"Help me," he said to her.

The mouth that spoke those words was not human, lending the words a strange repulsiveness. Maude looked down, sickened at the sight of the monster Clyde had become. Who was he to ask for her help? This was his show. He'd devised and created it. He killed innocents to make it come true.

And yet, even if he wasn't human anymore, she was. And her humanity would not allow her to leave any creature to suffer so profoundly.

"Let's get him up," Maude said to Jake.

Together they strained to bring Clyde upright. He was slippery, as if he'd been skinned, and it took all their strength to keep him out of the bloody waters.

From inside the Crystal Fang, the hissing mist ceased with a final sigh, as if an enormous pressure had been discharged. Then silence. Witches ran for the surface, but not Hyacinth.

Hyacinth was looking for Dionysia.

She stared down into the cloven crystal, uttering words not of a human tongue. Hyacinth's eyes opened wide, and her features contorted with horror. Maude knew what was happening to her. She was seeing the unseeable. Her mind was overwhelmed. Maude wanted to help Hyacinth, as she had aided Maude.

"Please," Clyde gasped at them. "No more."

Maude made a decision that she swore she'd never regret.

"Push him back," she told Jake.

"What?" Jake said.

"Thrust him backward onto it! Quickly!"

Clyde seemed to understand what was coming. His sightless eyes blinked. He moaned one last great sad bellow before his twitching sucker mouth fell slack and formed a silent O.

Maude and Jake put their shoulders into the Lamprey-man and shoved, just as the head of Syrx-Crugoth emerged. The god's glassy horns pierced through his acolyte. It lifted him, high, higher, until the tubular gray body that had been Clyde Laurents smashed against the brick dome.

Dead.

Syrx-Crugoth shook his horns. The Lamprey's corpse spiraled off, landing with a splash.

Maude seized Hyacinth and pulled her away from the flow of sharp objects coming up from the crystal innards. They unfolded and multiplied. An encrustation of jointed, razor-like appendages spilled forth. They made a light glassy clinking as they extended out of the cell; each of them was connected to a central core – the massive, and still growing, body of Syrx-Crugoth.

Maude, Jake, Hyacinth – they were mesmerized.

The blood-water levels were rising. The shattered serrated extremities whipped the air.

No vision, not even in the Dreamlands, had prepared Maude for something like this. It was too much, an upheaval of edges, a reverse avalanche of cutting, knife-like points, of needles, spikes, barbs and prongs – all clear as crystal, deadly, honed to inflict pain and injury, cruelty.

Hyacinth had regained her composure and she said urgently, "I know the way. Run with me."

The liquid in the chamber swirled around their lower bodies, hindering Jake more than the two women. Maude tried to assist him, but he pushed her away. He yanked up on the top end of his walking stick, extending it to its full length to reach into the deeper water.

"I've got this," he said. "Now we need to–"

Before Jake could finish, an explosion of blood-water lifted them all off their feet, and the force of the liquid propelled them into the tunnels.

Hyacinth and Maude shot into a tunnel on the right.

Maude looked back. Her last glimpse of Jake: he was fighting to follow them, holding his lantern on his chest as he paddled through the river of blood with his walking stick. The power of the flood was too much. It carried him into another pipe. The women were washed down their own tunnel. A crashing screech, as if the earth had ripped open. Chips of shattered brick rained on them and on the unstoppable flow of turbulent red.

48
Briar Patch

Ursula is going to be so angry with me, Jake thought. She'll be disappointed that I died in a sewer instead of on a mountaintop or some other rugged terrain.

He wasn't even out searching to obtain a rare artifact or striving for an archaeological discovery that would change the shape of history. No, he was going to drown in a pipe full of supernaturally produced body fluids.

That is, if he was lucky.

If he was unlucky, the jagged fusion of sharp objects that was the horror of Syrx-Crugoth would mince him into chunks.

He didn't like his options.

It sounded like a parade of clashing knives and broken bottles was coming his way.

He didn't want to see it. He'd seen enough. Curse Clyde, and his slithery dead self. Curse him across dimensions, through gates and portals, into the eternal space beyond the beyond.

Jake braced his walking stick into a notch where a brick had come loose, leaving a sizable gap. He jabbed the end of the stick into the gap and boosted himself onto a ledge formed in the earthquake. The initial quake had finished. He wasn't sure if what he was feeling now were aftershocks or if the big one was on its way. What difference did it make? Probably none.

He shimmied along the ledge, carrying his lantern and using his stick to clear debris. Better to fight until the bitter end. Keep going.

Maude and Hyacinth must've made it to the surface by now, joining Andy and Wendy. He'd miss his friends. He'd miss Ursula. Having adventures was secondary to the people. The people were the reasons that adventures meant anything. You had your stories together, to trade around the fire when you grew old and stiff and disinclined to leave the hearth.

He hoped he'd given his friends good stories to remember him by.

"There you are."

He raised his lantern in surprise at hearing a voice. So close, a few feet down the ledge.

"Maude?"

She was carefully inching along a crumbling lip of deteriorated concrete. She lifted her chin and smiled at him. She had something in her hand. A stick? More like a baton with a stem.

"I made it out. But realized I'd forgotten about this," she said, waving it at him.

The dynamite.

"You've come back to blow me up?"

"Not you, silly. Mr Crugoth. Have you seen him lately?"

"No, but I hear him." Jake pointed down in the direction of the chamber.

The clashing was so loud Maude must've heard it too. A Niagara Falls of razors.

"Things are interesting up top. Wait until you see," she said. "I think I spotted a cadaver in a top hat, strolling to the docks. Things have really changed since we've been gone."

Jake could only joke so much, given the darkness and the lives at stake.

"Andy and Wendy?" he asked.

"They're with Andrea and Hyacinth. Everyone is out. Well, not Clyde."

"Not us," he said.

"I was wondering something as I was crawling down here looking for you," she said.

"Yes?"

"Do you have any matches? Because I don't."

Jake patted his shirt pockets. He felt a tin box, took it out, shook it. "They're dry too."

"Then it's settled. We find the monster. Light the dynamite stick. And find our way back out before it all goes kerflooey. It should be a snap." She'd made it to him. The blood had leveled off. The scraping of the Cruelest One was getting louder. Jake shined his light around the tunnel. "I think it's not too deep. Still navigable. He's making enough noise we'll find him."

"Then let's do it," she said.

They linked their arms and jumped into the blood-water together. Half-swimming, half-walking, they pushed against the current. Jake used his stick to hook a corner and hauled them forward. Maude grabbed on, twisting herself to peek around the bend. "There he is," she said.

"Let me see."

Syrx-Crugoth filled the sewer pipe. A behemoth of fragmentary shards, interconnected into a jumble that flowed and broke apart and reabsorbed itself in a constant motion of cutting, grinding hideousness, an atrocity and an eyesore that in its grotesqueness never broached beauty.

"I hate it," he said.

"Agreed."

"Let's see what we can do to ruin it," he said.

They had no plan other than brute force. Using each other for support, they found a rhythm and waded through the subterranean river. Jake provided light, Maude took point.

When they were close enough, she held the dynamite over her shoulder and said, "Fire."

Jake hung the lantern from his lower jaw and struck a match. Put the flame to the fuse. It spit sparks.

"Here goes my best pitch," she said. She tossed the dynamite, aiming high. The explosive stuck in a snarl of needling barbs resembling a briar patch. The god ignored them. Syrx-Crugoth had no fear of insignificant humans, apparently. Grinding a path to the surface was the god's single goal.

"Now hold on," Jake said to Maude. "Ready for another ride?"

She wrapped her arms around his neck. He picked his feet up off the sewer floor, letting the flow slide under him. Leaning back, they rode the current sluicing through the tunnel. He steered with his stick as if they were in a kayak. They weren't going quietly. Maude whooped, and Jake hollered. They took whichever channel had the strongest flow. Once or twice, they were almost forced apart, but neither of them was going to let that happen. Even though they were waiting for the blast at their backs, when it finally came, they were still surprised by it. If they both screamed, the world would never know. That was going to be their secret. There must've been a build-up of combustible gases, because the whole sewer system started to come apart at the seams. Bricks and slabs of stone. Debris from trees and chunks of concrete. Maude had been holding the lantern, but a wave doused the wick, snuffing the nub of light.

"Don't let go," Jake said.

"Don't you let me," Maude said back.

"I won't."

In the darkness, they rode on and on. It felt so long. The blood-water kept flowing. They hadn't been buried alive in the tunnels. They didn't drown. And they didn't stop – not until the sewer pipe spewed them out into the Miskatonic River.

49
Gas Leak

"Gas leak," Mayor Kane said to the audience of reporters.

"All due respect, Mr Mayor, but the magnitude of the explosion was much greater than what could be reasonably be expected from a–"

Charlie held up his hand and repeated his words slowly. "It was a gas leak."

The interrupted reporter threw up his hands in disbelief.

A hand went up.

"Minnie, what is your question?" Charlie said.

"*Advertiser* readers want to know about the dead people they saw walking around the city. Did a gas leak bring Arkham's dead back to life?"

Chuckles and titters of laughter.

"I don't think your intelligent readers really believe they saw dead people… walking. We had an earthquake of unusual strength. Unprecedented in this county, as I understand it. The quake had unfortunate consequences, one of which was the disinterment of several dozen graves from the Christchurch

Cemetery. The effect of the shaking may have caused some folks to think they saw expired citizens walking." Charlie waved his hand as if he were sniffing a pot of soup.

"Walking all the way to the docks?" Minnie asked.

"It's all downhill."

"Mr Mayor, I have a question."

"Mr Murphy. It's good to see you up and around again. I've missed your sunny presence at these meetings."

"Thank you, sir. Glad to be back." Rex tapped his pencil against his notepad, smiling.

"Yes, Mr Murphy. Your question."

"What about the blood red sky reported by hundreds of citizens. Surely that wasn't–"

"A gas leak," Charlie said. "Gases in the sky making weird colors. With that I am sorry to bring this press briefing to a close."

"What about the fallout from the Big Drain debacle? And your own kidnapping and the inability of the police department under your regime to solve these crimes?" Rex said.

Charlie went back to the podium. "We solved the Lamprey case. Clyde Laurents is dead. The streets are safe."

"Safe for you?"

The question came not from a reporter, but from Charlie's new opponent, seeking to depose him from office and take the mayor's seat, Donnie Donegan. Reputedly tied to the gangs. Owner of a construction company. He'd bid on the Big Drain and had offered Charlie a bribe. Now he wanted Charlie's job, so he didn't have to offer bribes. He'd just keep all the money for himself.

"Mr Donegan, I feel safe in Arkham."

Donegan cut through the crowd. People naturally got out of his way. Except for Charlie.

"You didn't look too safe covered in grime, popping out of that sewer. I saw the photos."

Donegan turned to the reporters. After all, they were who he was talking to. "For a more respectable photo of a more responsible mayor, please look this way, gentlemen." He grinned and waved to the cameras.

Flash bulbs burst.

As Donegan raised his hand, the emerald set into a gold ring on his finger sent a winking spark into Charlie's eye. Out here, in the daylight, it shone more brightly than it had done down in the sewer when Donnie Donegan had been standing in the gloom of an archway.

"Oh, I've got you, boyo," Charlie thought. "It's only a matter of when."

But he had other affairs to attend to first.

50
Crystal Fang

Wendy watched as the witches gathered around the Crystal Fang. They were the Thirteen again, since Maude had joined the coven, replacing Clyde. His body never turned up, although fishermen claimed to have spotted the corpse of a distended aquatic creature floating downriver toward the ocean. But then, fishermen are always seeing things and telling tall tales.

The chamber was drained, and even swept. Safety lamps hung on poles, and everyone had their own light, just in case. The smell was still bad. But the mayor promised that the new renovations would make the waterworks safe for the city. Major sections of the drainage systems had been destroyed in the blast. Maude and Jake had made it out – Andy and Wendy had too, but then Andy's luck had taken a plummet, quite literally.

She glanced around the chamber hoping to see him with the others, knowing he wouldn't be there. He'd been in the wrong place at the wrong time. Sitting on a curb, streetside, waiting to hear if Maude and Jake got out. Staring up at the red sky, thinking his story just got a whole lot bigger. Then the dynamite in Syrx-Crugoth's spiky clutches exploded. Andy happened to be sitting right above it. The curb buckled, a rift appeared, and Andy fell into it.

Gone.

The ceremony began, and Wendy tried to drag herself out of her thoughts, to pay attention, or at least pretend to.

Hyacinth said a blessing. She read a list of words from a scroll that Wendy couldn't understand. The sounds were like music in parts, and like a kind of fast chant in others.

They were bringing Dionysia home. Her spirit had been inside the Crystal Fang for centuries. But she'd done her job, keeping the Cruelest God from breaking out, until Clyde came along and decided he was better off siding with evil than with his friends. Wendy never would get that. Some people were bad people, plain and simple, she guessed. They grew to their nature.

When the witches raised their arms together a sparkle of green light lit the chamber.

Then it winked out.

Wendy guessed that was Dionysia. Going home.

The mayor stood next to the wreckage of the Fang. He shook hands with all the witches.

Wendy overheard him asking Hyacinth, "Might you do a favor for your mayor? I need a spell cast, you see. On someone I know who intends me harm. Is that something you can do?" The two of them walked away, deep in conversation.

Wendy moved to stand closer to the Crystal Fang; it didn't look scary now. The crystals were duller than she remembered. All that had been left of Syrx-Crugoth was a few shards. The Prism put them in a lead box and sealed the box with a curse. Hyacinth told Wendy not to worry: the box was leaving Arkham, going far away where it would never be found by any person.

Back out in the daylight, Dr Fern and James were waiting for her. Dr Fern had said it was a private ceremony, and they didn't belong with the others so she wouldn't be going down. James wouldn't understand all they were doing. Besides, it was secret. Shared by the team of explorers who'd been witness to it, and the witches who helped them. The mayor had so many cops on guard, you'd think the sewers were full of gold.

Wendy walked with Dr Fern and James. James had a candied apple, and they'd gotten one for her too, but she wasn't hungry. So, James finished his and started in on hers. Dr Fern told her Ursula Downs was arriving back in town next week. Jake was already talking about their next expedition. Maude was seeing Dr Fern, not at the sanatorium, but at her house, for long talks.

They were walking to St Mary's Hospital now, and the route made Wendy think about the first time she was here, when she met them all.

Having good memories makes you happy and sad, she'd learned.

Inside the hospital, Dr Fern and James were headed to the cafeteria for some lemonade and cake when Wendy stopped and said, "I'll catch up with you later."

"Got some pressing business?" Dr Fern asked, raising an eyebrow.

"I've got to see a man about a thing."

"Well, if it's the man I think it is, don't be too long with him – he needs his rest."

Wendy walked up the stairs and down the long hallways until she found the right room. She heard voices talking, but she pushed the door open anyway.

Andy sat up in bed and smiled at her.

"How'd it go?" he asked.

He didn't say, *How'd the ceremony go? Or, how were the witches?*

That was because Dr Singleton was there. She was still taking care of Andy, because when he fell in the rift, he mangled himself up pretty thoroughly. The good news was he'd recover; the bad news was it would take a while. Dr Singleton finished checking him and left them alone.

Wendy pulled up a chair but she didn't sit right away. She went into Andy's drawer and got out a present. She'd put it there the other day when she came for a visit, and he was sleeping. He slept a lot, although he still looked like a raccoon with dark patches around his eyes, and the bruises plumped him up some.

"This is for you," she said. "Open it. Dr Fern helped me pick it out."

Andy untied the ribbon. He made a little tear in the giftwrap and peeled it slowly.

"It's a notepad," Wendy said. "And there's a pencil, too."

"Why, yes there is. Thank you very much, Wendy."

He was getting ready to set the pad and pencil aside when she said, "I sharpened the pencil. We get started today. Well, not if you don't feel good. But if you do…"

"Get started on what?" he asked. Wendy felt downhearted all of a sudden. Did he forget? How could he forget?

"Our deal," she said, trying not to sound too sour. "We had a deal, remember?"

"Oh," he said. And she could tell he wasn't sure what the deal was.

"I help you find the Lamprey and get your job back, then you help me find my father." Andy nodded slowly but remained silent, staring at his notebook. Now she felt thoroughly discouraged. "Aren't you going to help me like you said?"

"Sure I am." He scratched his chin with the end of his pencil.

"Only, I'm thinking we're going to need two notepads and two pencils. That way we can compare notes."

Wendy went back to the drawer and opened it again, taking out the other package she'd put there. "You aren't going to believe this," she said.

But he did, and he smiled.

ABOUT THE AUTHOR

S A SIDOR is the author of four dark crime thrillers and more recently two splendid supernatural-pulp adventures, *Fury From the Tomb* and *The Beast of Nightfall Lodge*. He lives near Chicago with his family.

sasidor.com
twitter.com/SA_Sidor

UNFATHOMABLE

The steamship *Atlantica* makes way to Boston, but dark shadows trail the ship, staying just out of sight beneath the waves. The ship's passengers seem unnaturally fixated, staring out to sea with a silent, desperate longing. The investigators' dreams are plagued by eerie underwater nightmares. And now, a passenger has been murdered.

Suspicion, hidden loyalties, and devious strategy rule the day! *Unfathomable* puts the players in command of a steamship, but not every player can be trusted. While monstrous Deep Ones stream forth from the crushing ocean depths, any player could secretly be a nefarious cultist or a horrifying hybrid Deep One. The investigators must take care not to turn their backs on anyone—it will take all their cunning to save their ship from a watery grave. Battle swarming Deep Ones, uncover the traitors, and steer the *Atlantica* safely home in *Unfathomable*!

ARKHAM HORROR™

The Red Coterie has been unveiled…

A secret organization ruthlessly seeks
power over supernatural terrors
in this globe-trotting anthology of
arcane mystery & adventure.